ANCIENT HIGHWAY

**Center Point
Large Print**

**This Large Print Book carries the
Seal of Approval of N.A.V.H.**

ANCIENT HIGHWAY

BRET LOTT

CENTER POINT PUBLISHING
THORNDIKE, MAINE

This Center Point Large Print edition
is published in the year 2008 by arrangement with
The Random House Publishing Group,
a division of Random House, Inc.

The text of this Large Print edition is unabridged. In other
aspects, this book may vary from the original edition.
Printed in the United States of America.
Set in 16-point Times New Roman type.

ISBN: 978-1-60285-233-4

Library of Congress Cataloging-in-Publication Data

Lott, Bret.
    Ancient highway / Bret Lott.--Center Point large print ed.
      p. cm.
    ISBN: 978-1-60285-233-4 (lib. bdg. : alk. paper)
    1. Family--United States--Fiction. 2. Large type books. I. Title.

PS3562.O784A84 2008b
813'.54--dc22

2008008976

for my father,
WILMAN SEQUOIA LOTT

Anyone who has looked Hope in the face will never forget it. He will search for it everywhere he goes, among all kinds of men. And he will dream of finding it again someday, somewhere, perhaps among those closest to him. In every man there is the possibility of his being—or, to be more exact, of his becoming—another man.

—Octavio Paz, *The Labyrinth of Solitude*

Earl

1

He'd heard it already, the cold and steady promise way off, building and building but still way off, not yet even to the trestle over Rogers Creek. But coming.

He pulled closed the door off the kitchen quiet as he could, his hand on the knob and twisting it so as to ease the latch with no noise at all, and it seemed a kind of good luck sign to him, that no-sound to help him on his way.

He had his good clothes in the pillowcase, the white shirt and stiff denim dungarees and the yellow tie he'd taken from Frank's things the day after he passed, and though he'd never worn the tie, only kept it like a secret fact out of Frank's life that no one else would ever know, he was sure he'd look good in it when he went for his first screen test.

That's what they called them, he'd seen in the magazines he'd read. A screen test, and his blood quickened at the thought of that, a test to see if you could be on the screen. A test he was certain he would pass, *knew* he would pass.

He had a few copies of the magazines in the pillowcase, too—two *Photoplays,* one *Motion Picture*—he'd somehow managed to keep as secret as Frank's tie, and there were sandwiches in there, wrapped in wax paper and made not but a minute ago. He'd tiptoed his way to the kitchen in the dark, sliced off thick hanks of bread on the butcher block, then found in the icebox a couple leftover slices of ham, slathered the bread with butter from the crock inside the icebox too, then got the wax paper from the drawer beside the stove. And he had two dollars in his pocket, maybe enough for whatever other food he'd need for the three or four days he figured it would take to get to California.

He was ready.

He was *going*.

He heard the promise out there build, knew the train was just past the creek now, but before he ran he stepped off the porch, looked at the house like it might say good-bye itself, like it might ask for his autograph before anything ever began. But it was only a house, he saw, one he had already left with this closing of a kitchen door.

And then he looked up at the stars out here, and how sharp they were, how eager and close and true they were, and he thought of how many nights he'd sat in his bed and looked out at them all, waiting for this night when they'd accompany him on his way, and he thought too of that word itself, *stars,* and about Hollywood, USA, and why it was the perfect word to call those folks out there, because of how they shone against the wall in the dark of the Rose.

But here was the rumble of the train coming and coming, and he turned and ran through the yard, cut across the Robineauxs' lot behind their house, and behind the Crosslands', afraid someone might see him on the street though no lights were on in any of the houses, and now he was out past the Crosslands' and angled to the right and out onto the street, no more houses on Blackbourn until his daddy's at the dead end, less than a quarter mile away now, and he ran harder, faster, because here was the train coming up from behind him, here was the train, and he could see in his mind's eye the train running past Pacific Street now, and now about to cross Beaulah, the sound of that train growing closer though it'd slowed down some like every time for rumbling right through the middle of town just that minute.

He could feel cool night air in his hair as he ran, and felt too the sweat coming up on him for this running, and for this charge through him of the steady and hulking and joyful promise the sound of a train passing through town truly is, and now he was almost to his daddy's shack at the dead end of Blackbourn, the Texas & Pacific line right out his back door.

He cut into the heavy grass near to knee high between Blackbourn and the railbed, the train coming and coming, and now he saw the headlight of the train casting out into the darkness in front of him, the railbed a good thirty yards or so away, his daddy's white shack off to his right and dark, no one in the world out here save for an engineer and a brakeman and whatever hoboes he knew would help him up and in when they saw him running alongside this train slowed for the nothing town of Hawkins, Texas, a train ready to pick up speed to take him all the way west, all the way to Hollywood, USA, and as he ran he could feel the wet through his dungarees of this grass out here, he could feel it at his shins and at his knees, proof enough he was really here and doing this, and here, here was the train itself passing him now not ten yards to his left, an awesome and huge and black and hurtling thing with its black wheels and piston rods shoving and shoving and he could see the little cab and the engineer sitting inside lit with the smallest light in the world, an old man with his eyes to the rails, looking west and west and west because maybe he knew what Hollywood and California were like and why it was important to get there even on a night like this one with its stars out and shining down hard.

Now he broke out of the grass and onto the gravel and there was the coal car passing him, and the first and second and third boxcar, all of them sealed shut, and he tried to swallow and couldn't, because it seemed for just this moment, just this moment here, that the promise had been taken away, the door shut, his life over at age fourteen, Earl Holmes returned to a momma wouldn't trade the crap out of a goose for him, and a daddy she'd kicked out for no good reason he knew.

That was the life he'd be returned to now, right here, and to all those sisters and brothers, and to the black hole of Frank gone these eight years, and here was yet another boxcar shut tight, and another, and still he ran, a burning down deep in his lungs now that gave his legs to know there wasn't much more of this he could do, and still he ran, and it seemed even that the train and that engineer had maybe already given it the gun, started the speed-up that made the cold and steady promise of the sound of a train change pitch on its way out of town.

It seemed the train was moving faster now, and faster, and that his life was gone.

But then, then, here was another boxcar, and the gaping black promise of a door open wide, and he saw too a hand, and another, saw them right here, right here, and he ran harder now and harder, and the burn in his lungs and legs melted to pure joy and power and meaning, and he reached, reached and reached, and here, here was his hand in someone's hand, and another hand on his wrist, calloused hands that pulled at him of a sudden, and he slapped the pillowcase up and into that black promise of an open boxcar door and these angels of mercy inside to help him, and his legs left the ground, him heaved up and onto rough planks and into the hard and welcome jostle and boom of this boxcar banging down the track.

"Welcome aboard, sonny," he heard out of the dark, the angels and their calloused hands already gone, settled back against the walls in this black before him, a black beyond black, the only light here the light in from stars outside, and he nodded, said too loud, "Thank you for the hand up, gentlemen," because he knew this was just like a flicker show, just like a flicker, and that he'd better get ready now to act in one every chance he got, whether he was standing on a street corner in downtown Hollywood or in a boxcar headed west.

He heard laughter from both his left and right, laughter thick and hollow at once. But it was laughter, and he stood up straight now, did a bow for them, and heard somebody out in the dark say, "Little Lost John, just sit the hell down 'fore you fall out the door," and he nodded, took a step and another straight ahead of him, a hand out in front of him until he touched a rough wood wall he couldn't see, and then he turned, eased his back down the wall until he was sitting, before him now the open boxcar door.

He could see the tree line out there, maybe a hundred yards off, and above it those stars.

Here it was: the world out there, waiting for him, this boxcar a theater, the open door a screen, these rough wood planks red velvet chairs, and the bang and scrape of boxcar to boxcar, wheels to rails, an old woman at a piano and making love to the story of stars and forest and night out there.

Hurrah, he whispered and felt the warm wet of tears sudden upon him, and he closed his eyes, blinked at these tears to rid himself of them because he didn't want to be seen crying in this car full of tramps, but also because crying seemed not the way at all to begin the story, this flicker show of his life.

Then he smiled, because here it came to him, perfect and unbidden and true all at once, the way his story would genuinely begin, the way—of course!—it *had* to begin!

He saw the intertitle that would begin this all, saw the brilliant white letters curlicued and strong up on the silver screen, saw the words that would introduce the audience to this story of a boy with a momma couldn't give a damn about him, a daddy gone to live in a shack, a dead brother who loved him, and a million brothers and sisters who couldn't remember his name, and how this boy ran away one night, jumped onboard a train outside his little hometown and rode the rails west to find fortune and fame in the flickers.

He looked at the open boxcar door, this silver screen that revealed the opening shot of the flicker of his life, and saw stars shimmer above the trees.

He closed his eyes, let roll the words:

Our story begins . . .

2

S ix days later he watched one man kill another.

Here had been the tired man huddled across the campfire from him, his eyes to the burning scraps of wood the dozen or so of them were gathered round, all of them waiting for the next freight train to start up out of Albuquerque, and the next ride they could grab to wherever that ride might take them.

And though the man's eyes weren't crossed, he wore a donkey-tail mustache just the same, and Earl let himself imagine the man was that slapstick Ben Turpin. Here was Ben Turpin, right out of *Hogan's*

Alley or *Steel Preferred,* same bushy mustache, same skinny face, sitting at a campfire outside Albuquerque, waiting for a train.

Six days gone, when all he'd planned was three or four for the ride out to Hollywood. But he'd taken off on the wrong line out of Dallas, ended up sleeping two nights in Tulsa before hitching on a line back into Texas. Only now he was headed the right way. The only way mattered: west.

He'd been looking in the fire himself, thinking on food, of course. The sandwiches had only lasted two days, and the two dollars was mostly gone for food in Tulsa and yet again in Dallas. He'd lost the pillowcase with his clothes and Frank's yellow tie when he'd jumped on the train south out of Tulsa. And of course the magazines and their pictures of the studios were in there, and now he'd have no idea what to look for when he arrived.

But it was losing the tie that was the worst of it— he'd kept the fact he even had it a secret from every- body in the house for the last eight years, had taken it from Frank's drawer even before they'd laid him out and dressed him for the burial.

He looked from the fire to Ben Turpin huddled across from him. He saw the man's shoes, the sole pulled away from the toe on one of them, the leather sole itself separated into two flaps all the world like tongues one on top of the other. Almost like Charlie Chaplin's shoes. The man's battered hat sat nearly flush on his head, knees drawn up to his chest, his skinny arms held tight around his bony legs, same again as Ben Turpin, and Earl smiled.

Then the flicker show continued on: here came up from the dark just behind Ben Turpin a man who looked all the world like Montagu Love himself, straight out of *The Ancient Highway:* the shaggy sideburns and greasy skin of the villainous logger Hurd all sweaty and heavy there in the cabin and eyeing Billie Dove, the dark-eyed Canadian beauty whose land Hurd wants to steal away.

Then here, now, Montagu Love lifted high above Ben Turpin's head a bottle Earl hadn't seen him holding, and for a moment it seemed he were watching all this on a screen, himself settled deep into a red velvet chair in a field of red velvet chairs, all of it lived out to the music the old woman played on the piano down beneath the screen, her eyes sometimes to the sheet music before her, but more often looking up to the story above her, to what Earl and everyone else in the house had to know was the pageantry, the mystery, the suspense of a life bigger and better and just beyond their own small lives.

Some nights, after he'd come home from sneaking out to the flickers, he dreamt he was with Little Mary, and he could feel her ringlets brush against his chest; or sometimes it was Vilma Bánky, the silver of her hair, the silk of her nightclothes as he clutched her in his arms same as Ronald Colman in *The Night of Love,* her frightened of him but wanting him all the same, and here would be Vilma's or Mary's or any of a dozen star-

15

lets' smile in his dreams, her fingertips to his chin, her lips and cheeks too close, too close, the thin tendrils of her hair down her cheeks just touching him, and then he'd wake with a shot to find himself in the dark of the house on Blackbourn. Still in Hawkins, Texas, in a room with four of his six brothers, in the next room four of his five sisters, the all of them littered about their rooms like the Foreign Legion in *Beau Geste,* himself Colman again, this time to the desert rabble around him.

Here he would wake: Hawkins, Texas. As far from Hollywood as he could possibly be.

On those nights he looked out the window of the room, and watched the night sky out there, the stars lined up same as ever, the same line of trees off in the distance on the slow march away for the logging he knew soon enough he'd call his own life. He could see in the gray and black out there a scattering of houses, all dark as his own, all peopled with lives as empty and pointless as his own, fields either growing thick with cotton or stubbled over, waiting for the next year, and the next, while everywhere else in Texas, it seemed, people were getting rich off the oil, even in cities close as Tyler.

But it wasn't the rich of oil he wanted. Not even that. He was fourteen, and on these nights, he saw the possibility of his life, of the road it might take were he brave enough to walk it, same as the hero of *The Ancient Highway,* the rugged and handsome Jack Holt, who battled Montagu Love fist to fist in that cabin up in Canada, all to save Billie Dove.

He saw himself on the screen, while beneath him music played.

And now, at a campfire outside Albuquerque, Montagu Love brought down hard the bottle on the battered hat Ben Turpin wore, and here was the flicker show: Ben Turpin's eyes opened wide with the explosion of glass, those eyes crossed deeper than Earl'd ever seen Ben Turpin's crossed, while out the corner of his mouth popped the tip of his tongue. His arms let go his legs, and he seemed to spill out of himself of a sudden, a balled-up rag doll shaken out loose in vaudeville abandon.

Earl laughed, let out a hard shock of sound to the silence of the other men around him, and he glanced at them an instant, both to left and to right.

They were already up, each man at the campfire with his eyes to Montagu Love, all of them tensed, he could see, ready for whatever might come next, though Earl had no clear idea.

Ben Turpin's hat slipped from his head, fell to his lap, Montagu Love still above him, hair down in his eyes for the force of the swing. He held the jagged end of the bottle in his hand, him half-turned from them all for the swing down and through. His eyes were to Ben Turpin's head, and Earl let himself look, finally, at the center of everything around this campfire.

The tired man's scalp lay open from just above his left eye straight back to beyond what Earl could see, the skull revealed beneath it smashed flat and in shards.

Then a runnel of blood, black against the white of the man's forehead, trailed down and into the man's left eye, still open, still crossed like the other, as though he were focused on a fly perched at the bridge of his nose.

That was when his tongue lolled all the way out, and the man slumped full to the ground, slowly, as though he meant to play it that way.

Earl stood, his eyes carried by the purposeful feel of the way the man fell to the ground, the move more liquid than bone and flesh, to see what it looked like: Ben Turpin coldcocked with a bottle by Montagu Love.

He looked, saw in the light from the fire that Ben Turpin's arms lay at his sides now, his legs out long and thin as they would ever be, but still. He couldn't see the man's scalp from this angle, or the way the skull had pushed flat into him. But here was that one eye filled with blood, both of them still open and crossed, his tongue out even farther and touching now the ground beside his face, and here now too, in the dirt above Turpin's head, was pooling black blood, no longer a line of it running down into his face, but flowing free out the top.

Ben Turpin shivered head to toe, one quick and quiet bolt of lightning through him so that he seemed almost to lift from the ground.

But soon as it came upon him the shiver stopped, and Earl heard a deep and full and dark trembling of breath from the man, a kind of ancient escape of sound, as though the sound itself were seeable, a cloud out of him, or a tumble free of stone, and the man was dead.

Earl knew it, and only then. He'd heard this sound before, knew it in the instant it settled in his ears for the truth of what it was.

But there was another sound now, colder and darker, low and growing, as though the breath the dead man had given out were taken in by the ground itself, soaked into its heart same as the blood was soaking down and in to stain this piece of earth with the death of a man.

He looked up at the killer. He wasn't Montagu Love now, but a man with a broken bottle, at his feet a man he'd killed.

He was looking at Earl, and slowly lifted the bottle up, pointed it at him.

Here was the dark sound, and Earl thought it his blood running through him same as he heard in his ears of a night, staring up at stars out his window while everyone else in the house breathed in sleep.

But this blood in him was black, he knew, for the low pitch of sound it made in him. Black, thick as oil: a dead man's blood.

The killer took a breath, his arm out straight now and lined up like a gun, his eyes, the drunken wet shine of them in the firelight, lined up with the broken edge of glass like a sight on a barrel.

"You!" the man shouted over the low and growing tremble, and Earl felt through him a piece of the lightning that'd shot through the dead man, felt his skin prickle over with just that single word.

He felt his feet move beneath him, take one step back, and another.

But the killer moved with him step for step, the bottle still out and at him. "You!" he shouted again. "You were with him!" his words slow and thick, strands of his hair still down into his eyes, the fire beside him now. "You stole it!" he shouted.

Earl took in a breath of his own, opened his mouth to speak a denial—he'd never seen the man before, hadn't stolen anything—but nothing came, and now he felt a hard pull at his shoulder, and he turned, saw the face of an old man close beside him, the old man's eyes open wide, a crushed hat same as the dead man's on his head. His shoulders were hunched up, his mouth moving with words in and through and around this low tremble of black blood in Earl, the old man's face too close to Earl's, and he saw in the firelight a glimpse of crumbled teeth, saw wrinkles deep-set beside the man's eyes, the gristle of a beard that was no beard, but an old man gone unshaven too long.

The old man was saying something, Earl knew, though he could not hear him for the slow thunder that seemed to swallow them all with its dark and depth, and Earl finally turned his head full, saw behind them both the railbed, saw dimly in the light off the fire the freight train they were all waiting for, a dull monster unbidden and welcome at once, lumbering and swift and full of itself for the way, like always, it moved past them all with no care for what lay here.

A train, westbound. Here was the sound, that black blood through him.

The old man pulled even harder at Earl now, his eyes shooting to the fire and back to Earl, to the fire and back again.

"Boy," he shouted full out, the whisper gone, "you want to hobo this train, you got to go now!"

He let his eyes go once more to behind them and the fire, and Earl looked back too, saw there beside the fire the killer on the ground, passed out, his arm out straight and still with the bottle in it, stretched out on the ground.

And just beyond him the dead man.

Earl turned, the old man already five yards ahead of him and running, a hitch in his leg, his arms up like chicken wings. Beyond him moved the train, and Earl saw men scrambling up the gravel bed, running alongside the train, still slow enough to climb on for its being out of the station only a mile or so back, the all of them reaching up to black squares of open doors, pale hands reaching out to hoist them aboard like every time he'd climbed on so far.

Earl was running too, passed already the old man, who'd taken off his hat and held it in his hand, and here was the cinder and gravel, the hulk of the boxcar beside him, and the pale angel hands come once more from the dark inside to reach for his own held out to them, and he took one, felt the pull of someone he did not know up and onto the hard wooden floor of the boxcar.

Still on his stomach, he turned, reached out to the old man right there, right there, slowing down now, it seemed, in one hand still that hat, the other hand up now, and Earl and another man grabbed hold hard of the old man's arms, one arm each, and hauled him into the boxcar and beside them, the all of them letting out of a sudden huge breaths and drawing them back in just as hard, and there came from within the depths of the boxcar a kind of laughter, deep and quiet and more like the tumble free of stones the tired man's last breath out had sounded like than Earl wanted to hear.

Laughter, yet again, this time at the three of them there on their backs on the rough wood floor of a boxcar.

He was on a train once more, but inside him now a death—a murder—more inside him than any tilt of the head a forsaken woman at a piano might make, and more inside him than any dream of blond ringlets or soft full lips.

He'd seen it.

Here was laughter, quiet as death, solid as death.

He'd watched his older brother Frank die, there in the bedroom in Hawkins he'd watched stars from. He'd died of the influenza when Earl was only six and a child inside a room he wasn't allowed in. But Frank had been his protector, the oldest brother, older than Earl by eleven years. Between them were Wilda and

Curtis and Buster, Barney and Raymond and Chilton and Mildred and Connie May; three more came after Earl: Pearl and Thelma and Helen, three girl babies that cawed and mewled and messed such that Earl might not even be alive for the word or touch he got from Momma and Daddy.

It was Frank who'd taken to him, Frank the one to fork up a pork chop to lay on Earl's plate at dinner when the mob of children began the war for food, Frank the one to lift him up and into the wagon when they rode into Gladewater or Mineola in the fight for who would sit where every trip ever was.

For those small gifts—for, finally, the attention he was given in a family too full of family—Earl had climbed in the window to their room from outside, a gray morning cool and wet with rain as he slipped from the front room and the cluster of family there, aunts and uncles and brothers and sisters all knotted and fretting, his momma chief among them, though his daddy was there too, in from the woods.

There had stood his momma at the center of everything with her apron in her hands and wringing it, wringing it, as though she might expel from it the sickness in her oldest son like water from a wet rag. He'd seen her grow old, he believed, in just the five days Frank had been down with the 'flu: her brown hair, though wound in the same tight bun at the nape of her neck, had gone grayer than he'd ever noticed, her green eyes, it seemed to Earl, grown just as gray behind her spectacles, wrinkles beside them suddenly upon her, and across her brow, and beside her mouth. Even her hands as she wrung the apron were the hands of an older lady, he believed. Someone else's hands.

Hovering behind and beside her was his daddy, his hair white for as long as Earl remembered, but him even more quiet than he always was, a cigarette tense at his lips drawn thin, no words at all out of him while kin touched his shoulder, whispered to him, fretted and fretted.

Earl would not be missed, he knew. If he ever had been, or ever would be. And so he'd gone out to the porch and down the front steps, carefully made his way alongside the house, rain down on him, until he stood beneath the open window, felt with his fingertips for the windowsill, and jumped once, twice, three times before he was high enough to hook his arm over the sill. He struggled up, his shoes searching for purchase on the white clapboard siding and then finding it, and he rolled into the room, and sat up.

Frank lay in his bed, quilt pulled tight to his chin, his black hair matted with fever, his thin mustache even thinner, it seemed, for the pale of his face.

His eyes were open wide, Earl could see, at the surprise of a little brother suddenly with him.

But more than surprise, Earl saw too. There was more to the startled shine of his eyes than that, and Earl had known even then, in that instant of his brother's eyes on his own, it was fear he saw.

Earl still sat on the floor, legs out in front of him, and he wondered what there was for him to do, now

24

that he had stolen inside a sickroom, outside the door beside Frank's bed his momma, and her two sisters over from Gladewater, and most of the children. And his daddy. The whole world out there, and here only Earl and Frank.

And so Earl leaned forward between his knees, tucked his head down and rolled forward on himself, did a somersault on the bedroom floor, in himself now that fearful surprise he'd seen on his brother's face, but in him too his desire for something else from Frank, something he might be able to give Earl before he died.

Because Earl knew he would die. His momma'd spoken it in broken tones last night once the boys were sent to bed on the sleeping porch, Frank left alone in their room. She'd cried it to Daddy, the two of them in their own room, their window not but a few feet from where Earl lay in a sheet, the midsummer air too thick to let in sleep for any of them. He lay there in the heat and thick, and imagined his momma and daddy the way they always were at night: Momma's hair down in twin braids, her spectacles off and tucked into a handkerchief and set on the dresser, his father in his nightshirt and smoking his last cigarette of the day.

But then she said it: "He's going to die," she let out, and Daddy'd answered, "God wills his own way."

Earl heard the fact of no comfort in the words, same as his momma must have heard, for this was when she cried deepest, surest, her voice broken glass and blood all at once, and he knew that every one of his brothers heard the all of it too, from Curtis, who lay on his back at the far end of the sleeping porch and who'd already lit up a cigarette, him fifteen and already more grown and gone than Frank or any of them, right down to Chilton right here beside Earl, him a year older than Earl, his breaths in and out shallow and quick for the words he'd heard, Earl knew.

Frank would die.

Curtis drew in on his cigarette, the ember in the dark bright and distant and restless in the way it flared and fell, flared and fell. Chilton breathed in and out, in and out, each sound a sharp edge. And Raymond and Barney and Buster, Earl could feel on the quiet around him, on the thick air everywhere, lay awake too.

Six brothers, each in his own envelope of quiet, his own stretched silence and wonder and fear.

Earl rolled out from the somersault, ended up a couple-three feet closer to the bed, and to Frank, whose fever-wet hair made him look as though it might have been him out in the rain, him to climb in a window to see his favorite brother.

Here was still the startled shine in his eyes, eyes brimmed and full, as though Earl had made him want to cry for surprising him, for a somersault in a sick-room on a rainy day in June.

But then there crept on his brother's face a smile, slow and bewildered, uncertain of itself. But a smile, and here with Earl was the brother lifting him to the wagon, the brother holding him in his lap and teaching him to tie his shoes, the brother poking a fork at

Curtis's hand when he grabbed for that pork chop already on Earl's own plate.

Frank.

Earl put his arms out to either side and held them high, whispered hard just for Frank, all for Frank, "Hurrah!"

Frank smiled even better, even truer, and reached a hand out from beneath the quilt, a hand all the world like a sign to Earl of how his brother wouldn't die, not now, not here, with this smile upon him. Their momma was wrong, he knew, and Earl got to his feet, stepped close to the bed, Frank's eyes on him still full and wet, but with a smile now, one that Earl had brought to him, and one that was a gift right back to Earl.

Frank touched Earl's head, his hand too warm, Earl could feel as his brother's fingers moved along his scalp slow and thoughtful.

Frank said, "Be a good boy," his voice clouded and thick, as though he'd said it from far away, said it through morning mist on an empty field. "Be a good boy," he said again, the words even slower, even farther away and hidden, though Frank was right here, his warm hand in Earl's wet hair.

Frank closed his eyes, withdrew his hand slow as could be from Earl's head, brought it back beneath the quilt. He seemed to draw himself into himself, seemed to move somewhere else: his eyes clenched closed, his shoulders beneath the quilt inched up, his head sank deeper into the pillow. His chin trembled a moment, the sparse hairs on his upper lip quivering for it, and he took in a breath, quick and important, everything in him focused clear and certain on that measure of air he drew in.

He held it, held it, and held it still, the tremble in his chin gone, his mouth closed tight, and Earl saw a tear leave his closed eye, slip down from the corner of his eyelid shut tight and trail into his thin sideburn, and disappear.

"Frank," Earl whispered and put his hands together at his chest, pressed hard against himself.

Then Frank let out the breath he'd taken in, the all of it out of him a dark and full tremble of breath, an ancient escape of sound. A tumble free of stone.

Frank lay still, his eyes suddenly held closed not by will but by something else, something even and calm, as though his closed eyes were held closed by nothing more than the gentlest touch to his lids.

The door burst open, their momma through it and suddenly beside Earl, one hand still holding the apron, the other already to Frank's forehead and cheek and chest and forehead again, in her quick moves hope in hope in hope for some sign he wasn't, as Earl already knew, dead. There, just behind her in the doorway, stood his daddy, mouth open, eyes creased nearly closed for the smoke up off that cigarette still tense at his lips.

Earl was six years old, and knew already the sound of death.

But Frank had smiled. Frank had smiled.

He looked at Frank, his eyes closed forever, he knew.

"Hurrah," Earl whispered quiet as he could, one last time just for Frank, one last time all for Frank, the word out of him only and already a memory of his brother's smile, brand-new and as ancient as the sound he'd heard.

That was when his momma wheeled to him beside her, but still with a hand to Frank's forehead. She let go the apron, raised her hand to him, and he could see in her eyes behind her spectacles, saw even before she brought down hard her open palm across his cheek, that she did not know him. *Who is this boy?* he could see in the glaze of her eyes, in the gray and green of them, and the knot of her eyebrows, the set of her teeth as she bared them at him, set for the slap that came to him.

He saw his daddy behind her, his eyes on Earl too, still creased close, smoke up off the tip of the cigarette.

Earl's eyes shot closed with the force of her hand, white shimmers of light filled him, his own breath left him, all in this instant.

"Hurrah, you say," she seethed in a whisper.

He'd felt himself falling into that white shimmer, a white that became for an instant warm morning mist on an empty field, himself in a somersault as he fell, Frank smiling at him.

Frank had smiled.

His momma let out a cry, keen and simple and empty, all at once.

Hurrah! Earl spoke without speaking, and fell.

3

Twelve days after Frank had died, his littlest sister, baby Helen, would die of the influenza as well. Oldest and youngest gone in less than two weeks.

In two months, his daddy would move into the shack a half mile down Blackbourn, backed right up to the Texas & Pacific line. Asked to leave by his momma.

In three years Curtis would be dead, too, a tree down on him in the woods a mile and a half in from Road 23, the sawyer forgetting this once to call out the fall.

And one afternoon when he was eleven and the family was in Tyler for no reason he can now recall, he put down a nickel at the booth out front of the Rose.

The painted woman behind the glass smiled at him, her mouth moving for chewing gum, her hair, black as India ink, bobbed just beneath her ears in the way his momma said was sin. "Baby doll," she said, "you sure you're man enough to watch a flicker like this one?" and blew a bubble, popped it.

Earl shrugged, felt himself blush. He looked behind him a moment, scanned the storefronts and sidewalk for any of his family.

This was sin, too, he knew: going to a flicker show. A sin seventy times seven that of chewing gum, even worse than bobbing your hair. This was a strange place, an alien place, a place he'd only heard comment on from his oldest sister, Wilda, too many times at supper, his momma's call to quiet over whether or not she could go see "a flicker" always loud and final, no matter the pout and sighs and tears his sister gave.

But they wouldn't miss him. Not today or any day, unless one or another of his sisters or brothers saw him going in. Then there'd be trouble, the joyful kind only a brother or sister could know for turning in one of their own.

The street was empty, save for the parked automobiles, more of them on this stretch of street than there were in the entire town of Hawkins.

He turned to her, shrugged again, said, "I am."

"Then you are, sug," she said, and smiled down at him, slipped beneath the glass a red ticket printed with the words *The Rose.* He moved past the booth and to the twin glass doors into the place, and stepped into a room with polished green stone for a floor, the walls hung with red velvet drapes, on the walls too framed signs for flickers, colorful pictures of men and women and jungles and castles and automobiles, and he turned to his left, saw against that wall, back from the door so that he hadn't seen it from outside, a glass counter, behind it another woman, this one with the same bob as the woman in the booth but her hair the red of a rooster's comb.

She stood with her hands to the counter, smiling at him, chewing gum herself, and Earl saw beneath the glass counter trays full of penny candies as bright and glorious as jewels. On the counter stood a popcorn machine like he'd seen on the street here in Tyler and sometimes in Mineola, but this one set right on the counter and not in a wheeled cart. There were white cups made out of paper sitting on the counter too, in them brown water, it looked like, rows of them waiting for whoever would drink the stuff, and he wondered if this were liquor itself, the flickers such a sinful place they sold it right out in the open no matter the law.

"Son?" he heard from behind him, and he turned, saw a man in a white shirt and red vest and black bow tie nod at him, a hand out to Earl. "Your ticket," the man said, and Earl heard behind him a pop of gum, a small laugh, and the man's eyes went quickly behind Earl and to the woman, Earl knew. The man gave a small smile at her, a small shake of his head, and motioned with his hand for Earl to come to him.

Earl thought, of course, that he was in trouble now, that in fact he wasn't man enough to go to a flicker show, or perhaps somehow Wilda or Barney, or Chilton or maybe even Pearl had seen him, had run for Momma, and now he'd have to give the ticket back.

Earl moved toward him slowly, the ticket in both hands, fingers holding tight to either end, and now the man gestured again, waved Earl toward him. Behind the man was a doorway in, parted red velvet curtains waiting to give Earl the mystery of this place: the flicker show. And now he might never know.

Earl let go the ticket with one hand, held it out to the man, who took it, quickly tore it in half, and Earl felt the blood rush to his neck, and into his face. Here was humiliation genuine and full: his ticket, torn in half in front of him, and he looked down.

The man held half the ticket out to Earl, and Earl reached for it, took it, his medicine given and taken, and turned to the door, to the world out there already brighter, already harsher for how his eyes had adjusted to here, and to these dark red drapes, these women with sinful hair, these jewels beneath glass.

"Son?" he heard again, on the word boredom, he could hear, and a kind of laughter too, and Earl turned, saw the man in the doorway to the theater itself, there between the parted curtains. "We going to start in near a minute," he said. "Let's get you a seat now," he said, and it came to him that there was a system to this all, a ritual, he guessed, that involved the man tearing your ticket in two and taking you in.

The man had a half smile, his eyes moving quick from Earl to the red-haired woman, who gave out a sharp laugh, said, "Your first time, honey?"

Earl looked at her. She was smiling too, had her hands on her hips, the white blouse she had on finer than any of his sisters or even his momma owned, though it was only a blouse, buttons and a collar. But it was made of a material that seemed to shine and seemed to let you see through it all at once, and he thought he might be able to see through the material thin white straps at her shoulder: her underclothing.

"Yes ma'am," he said, and looked down, saw his shoes, the worn-out of them, the toes muddy and scuffed on this polished green stone.

"We still need to get a seat," the man said, exasperated now, and Earl looked up, saw the man held an arm out into the doorway, and Earl glanced at the woman, said, "Thank you, ma'am," for no reason at all. The woman said, "You just enjoy it, honey," and gave out the same sharp laugh, and Earl turned, plunged into the unknown past the parted red curtains, the man with the other end of his ticket already inside.

The room was huge and near-dark, an aisle down the center and along both walls, at the front of the room a stage, behind it a wall hung with more red velvet drapes top to bottom, the walls all around hung with that same red velvet, long curtains of it all around.

Here he was, and he knew even then that the frightened pleasure he felt at this all—there was a piano up front, too, there in front of the stage, down level with the seats in here, the seats a field of red velvet rows scattered with people already waiting for the flicker to begin, and there were electric lights on the wall but the light so low it looked all the world like candlelight—he knew even then that this pleasure and guilt at that pleasure was because of his momma, and that call to quiet Wilda got every time.

He was where he shouldn't be. He was man enough to do this, to be here.

This was sin.

They moved down the center aisle, and suddenly the man stopped, turned to Earl, and put out his hand again, this time pointing down a row of seats to Earl's left. The man in the vest smiled at him, nodded down the row, and Earl stepped in, moved down three seats, and sat in a chair softer than any chair he'd ever known.

Earl took in a deep breath, closed his eyes a moment at the softness, at the comfort, but then opened them again, quick turned to see if the man was still there, if there was some further step in this system of being seated he might have missed.

But the man was already back up the aisle to that open doorway, and Earl took in the fact there were others around him, though not many, and for this he was thankful. The fewer people here, the smaller the chance he would be discovered.

He turned to the stage, and thought about the penny candies, and about the popcorn. He thought about those cups of brown water, and how much any of that all might cost.

He thought about those straps at the woman's shoulder.

Then a woman stepped from behind the stage up front. She was older, he could tell from here, and had on what looked like a black dress with a white collar. Her hair was down, long and gray, it looked. No bun, no braids. He'd never seen such a thing before: a woman that age with her hair down.

Then she sat down, and played. She said nothing, made no announcements at all, though he did not know why he might have thought such a thing would happen. He wondered, too, at what this was about.

Wasn't this a flicker? Why was a woman playing a piano, and was this what he'd paid a nickel for? Was this why they all seemed to be laughing at him up front, from the woman in the booth who'd asked if he were man enough to the man and his half smile?

The music was good, he knew, and the woman gave in to it, moved with it and under it, music not at all like the Sunday music he'd heard his whole life, but with a kind of sadness to it, and a kind of shine, too, he didn't hear in the tunes from the Psalter.

There was a story to the music, he could hear. This was a story already, he knew, and slowly, slowly, the lights went down and then out altogether, while in the same few seconds the drapes behind the stage opened up, all of it a seamless few seconds: the lowering of light, the parting of curtains.

And the flicker began.

He hadn't even seen out front what he was paying for, so afraid he'd been as he'd made his way to the booth, the nickel hot in his hand. And suddenly there were upon the wall—a huge wall, bigger than any wall in any building he'd even been in, even the barns he knew—words, white on a black background, the words *Folly of Vanity,* and then here were people, beautiful people, and words between them, and a story of a young woman just married, and the way she spent money and spent it. The story rolled and pitched, and words came on the wall, and people around him laughed, a sound he'd not heard before, people gathered in a large room and laughing together.

But there was trouble in the story too, as the young woman—a beautiful woman, a woman who wore dresses that showed more skin of a woman than he'd ever seen in his life, even with five sisters; she was a woman with a kind of smile he'd never seen before, a smile that bewildered him, and tempted him, and gave him calm all at once; a woman with skin so fair and white it became the color of the wall she was moving upon—this woman spent her husband's money too quickly, too carelessly.

Now there was a man who was after her, a rich man who had a yacht and who took the woman and her husband out on it for a party, the rich man now after the young woman, and a woman with bobbed hair and lips too painted was after the young husband, and this was tearing at Earl as he watched, this betrayal of love and yet the temptation too of all that money, and the rich man gave the young woman a necklace of pearls to replace the false ones her husband had bought her. They were beautiful, these pearls, as the rich man placed them on her bare neck, the rich man behind her and looking at her with eyes too evil, too full of desire, Earl and everyone here knew, though the young woman could not see him behind her as he gave her the necklace.

But then.

Then.

Then, as though this all weren't dream enough, weren't adventure enough—the dresses this woman wore! Her bare shoulders! The wealth Earl bore witness to there on the yacht, with its gleaming wooden walls and vast beds and portholes of brass!—then the woman jumped overboard, chased by the rich man, and Earl felt himself grab hold of the chair arms and sit up straight, as though he meant without thinking to dive in after her, so real was this all.

But then magic moved in him fully, for as she fell the flicker followed her down and down, and suddenly, magically, the flicker changed from black and white and gray to green and to blue in there too, and now he himself was underwater with her, and here was Neptune himself! And here were more women—mermaids! these were mermaids!—with seashells just covering their breasts, and he felt himself turn from the wall at what he knew he should not see, these barest of women, and then let himself look, let himself see the wonder of a world beneath the sea, of women beautiful and near naked, Neptune's beard long and white, his trident sharp and long, and now they were all celebrating this woman's being there with them, men and women dancing and lavishing her with gifts from the sea and a throne upon which to sit, and the woman loved it all, the attention, the gifts, the men around her and the beautiful mermaids and Neptune himself—she loved it all.

Then a witch appeared in the midst of all this happiness, this celebration, her hair black and swirled high on her head, her clothes a swirl of black as well, her eyes painted thick and dark, and she reached for the pearl necklace, the gift from the rich man still round the woman's neck, and tore it off to reveal at the base of the woman's neck a ring of black marks where the luster of pearls—true beauty—had left the mark of vanity. She'd been shown, finally, to be the vainglorious girl she had been all along, spending her husband's money, accepting gifts from evil men for the fact of the gifts themselves.

And then she awoke, the all of this a dream, a fantastic and wonderful and terrifying dream, and Earl smiled at the surprise of this all, found himself easing back in his seat, his hands letting go the arms for what felt the first time since she'd jumped overboard. The woman awoke, and found herself in bed aboard the yacht, her husband with her, and the two pledged again their love as they had when they so recently wed. They kissed—a man and a woman kissing!—to seal their love, her vanity forgiven, the folly finished.

The lights came up, the woman at the piano finally stopping, and he realized only then that she'd played all the way through, all without stopping, telling a story with that piano to match the story on the screen, sounds he hadn't heard but heard nonetheless, and now folks around him were clapping for the story, for the people on the wall, and for the music.

The older woman bowed, her hair falling off her shoulders while the curtains drew closed as smooth and slow as they had drawn open.

It was over.

He swallowed, stood, saw people filing out up the aisle and for the doorway with the parted curtains.

They were smiling, talking to each other, and he felt himself smiling too as he moved to the aisle, started up.

There was light up there, beyond the curtains and over the shoulders of those people moving in front of him. Light from the world outside this place, where magic came to him in pictures that moved, and pictures that changed to blues and greens too, and he thought of the beauty of the woman this whole story was about, the woman who learned the folly of vanity, and whose bared shoulders seemed to him even more a delight, more a sin, than the nearly naked mermaids had been.

He moved into the lobby, back onto that green stone floor, and looked at the framed signs on the wall to his left, there against the red velvet curtains.

There was the sign for the flicker, and he went to it, looked at the picture there of the young woman, smiling over her shoulder in one of those bare-shouldered dresses as she climbed into the back of a sedan—That was in the flicker! He'd seen that in the flicker!—above the picture the title, *Folly of Vanity,* in big letters.

Beneath it, in letters slightly smaller, was her name. *Billie Dove.*

He said the name out loud, savored it a moment. A perfect name. A strange name, and he said it again.

"Unless you got another nickel, son," he heard behind him, "then you'll need to head on back to the farm."

He turned, saw the man in the vest looking down at him, arms crossed, and Earl smiled, said, "Don't have one now, but I'll be back." He nodded at the man, then looked past him to the red-haired woman still behind the counter. "Ma'am!" he called to her, him still smiling, and nodded to her, touched an imaginary hat just like the husband did in the flicker when he'd taken Billie Dove's hand and helped her into the sedan.

The girl smiled back at him, shook her head, crossed her arms. "Aw, scram, you," she said and nodded hard at the door.

But she was still smiling, maybe even bigger now, and Earl turned, squinted for the light in on him from outside, late afternoon light still strong and certain. His family would still be in town, most likely still tied up at the hardware like they always were when they spent the day here. But if they weren't, if they'd already headed home, he didn't care. He could hitch a ride with someone. He wouldn't be missed.

He put his hands to the glass door, felt the heat off it. He looked one way and the other out there, scanning for a brother or sister.

He thought of Neptune, those colors, and the music, and the lips of that woman, Billie Dove, and the clothes they all wore, the automobiles they drove, the yacht they sailed.

He thought of the applause he'd heard from around him, and of the way he'd had to hold himself in the seat, and the way he'd sat back once it was all done.

All of it behind him, in this theater, in a room with a white wall revealed when curtains were drawn.

"Hurrah," he whispered, and pushed open the door, stepped out into that light.

"Let's go now," he heard, and felt himself pushed hard. "Lost John, you got to go now, you got to get!" he heard, and felt himself pushed hard again, and he opened his eyes to the boxcar, light bursting into his eyes for it, and he quick put up a hand, blocked it out.

The men were all up now, he could see, the open door letting in light too bright, too sharp, and he squinted shut his eyes, turned his head from it.

"It's the bulls," he heard the old man's voice, right there next to him, and the old man pushed him hard yet again. "They're coming to get you, boy, for a witness to a murder!"

Earl opened his eyes, put his hands to the wooden floor. His shoulders ached for the way he'd slept sitting up, but it didn't matter now, for the men in the car were suddenly all calling to him, and he saw them at the open door, waving to him, calling to him, squatting low like they had last night at the fire just after Earl had let out his laugh.

Earl looked at the old man, his face open and fearful, nodding at Earl, helping him stand, helping him toward the door.

His eyes still weren't set for the light from outside, so that the open door was only white, brighter than any white he could recall save for the odd look at the sun now and again. And still he was being called, the men waving to him as the old man moved him along, moved him along.

His feet were cold, he knew that much, and he was tired, and he was hungry. But then he took in the words from the old man: *the bulls, a witness, murder.*

"Boy, it's now or never," the old man said, and they were at the open door, the men crowding around him, touching his shoulder, patting his back, words out of them strange and confusing: *Take care,* he heard, and *Keep your mouth shut,* and *Give my best to Sparky.*

"Lost John," the old man said, "you got to jump before they catch you," and now Earl felt his blood moving quick, felt course through him last night, and the killer's pointing to him and naming him as the thief, and he thought of the police finding the killer and naming Earl in this all, an accomplice somehow.

He was at the edge of the door now, saw outside rock and white sun and low mountains, but rows of something, quick lines of green flat on the ground stretching away from the railbed and toward those low rock mountains. Where was he? What was this green in rows?

But he'd seen a murder. He'd been named.

His feet were cold, colder than he'd felt them before any morning he'd awakened to this far, and he looked down, saw his feet on the threshold of the open door.

His shoes were gone, and his socks.

Someone pushed him then, and in an instant he hit the ground at a roll, down along rock and sand and gravel, the sun stuttering above him as he rolled over and over, and already he could hear the laughter peeling away and ahead of him.

He stopped, finally, felt pain at his elbow and in both knees, hard pain he thought might mean blood, and he sat up, saw both knees of his dungarees were torn clean through, saw the skin inside the rips already welling with blood.

Far ahead, the old man leaned out the open door, held up a hand, and Earl could see even from here, even through the dust his own body had kicked up, even through the loud and dark tremble of the freight train passing beside him not fifteen feet away, his shoes, tied together and hanging by the laces from his first finger.

"Looks like these is about my size, Lost John!" he called out, and laughed, the sound a hard cackle that cut clean through the rumble of the train, and he disappeared back inside.

Earl blinked the dust out of his eyes, tried to stand and found he could. He had cuts in the palm of his right hand, but his elbow wasn't bleeding, the sleeve not torn. He looked down at his knees, saw the blood wasn't too bad.

But he had no shoes.

He turned from the railbed, looked behind him to this farmland, to the rows of green knobs stretching far as he could see.

Lettuce. This was lettuce, here in the middle of the desert.

He looked one last time at the train, past him altogether now, the caboose a quarter mile or so away.

He'd seen Tom Mix do this before, jump from a train. Lucky for him he'd seen that, and knew how to roll.

He looked around one more time, at the rows of lettuce—there was more of it on the other side of the tracks—and at those low mountains miles away, and at a sky bluer than blue, sky crisp for how blue it was. There had to be a farmhouse somewhere near here, he knew. Someone to help get him back on the road west.

He looked at his bloodied palm, picked dirt and gravel from it, and started barefoot down the row closest to him, and away.

Joan

4

She steps out into brilliant light. This is nothing new to her, the way she has to squint to get her eyes used to the sunlight out front of Grauman's Chinese: she's been to the movies a hundred times, a thousand, though she's still not even ten. She's not even a *decade* old, a word she wants to use to tell people how old she is, but can't for another five months and twelve days.

Then she'll be a *decade* old, just before summer starts and school will be out, and maybe because she will be a *decade* old her momma and daddy will listen to her, finally, and let her go live in Texas, where she knows her real home is. Where her cousins Betty Jo and Fern live, and where the world looks exactly the same as the movie they've just seen.

Song of the South is the most perfect movie there has ever been, she's already decided, though the movie is just over, the three of them—she stands between her momma and daddy, holding their hands—out on the sidewalk in front of the theater, behind them the giant red *pagoda,* which in China is a kind of church, she read in one of her books from school. But this *pagoda* is a theater, the best one in the United States, her daddy has told her a hundred times. Now it's even better of a theater, because this is where she saw *Song of the South* just now, the best movie there has ever been.

There were people in this one and Walt Disney cartoons both, all of them in the same movie, and though she's seen color movies before—she even saw *Gone With the Wind* three years ago, back when she was still in second grade—there was something to the colors in this movie that made her believe what she saw more than she believed any movie she's ever been to see.

And the music. The music!

Zip-a-dee-doo-dah, zip-a-dee-ay! she wants to sing out loud right now, right now, and *Plenty of sunshine headin' my way* she wants to sing too for this beautiful sky above them, just like in the movie.

And for her momma and daddy together with her

right now, just like Johnny got in the end of the movie. His momma and daddy, back together again, and in love with each other again.

There was music all the way through, the music never stopping but for the quiet when Johnny was in bed back in the *plantation* after that bull got him, and then it was quiet for only a minute, until Uncle Remus came in to tell Johnny he was going to be okay.

But she'd cried at this movie, too, there inside the theater with its high high ceiling and that chandelier above them all, a huge star hanging up there in some kind of magic way, and around it up there at the ceiling those Chinese dragons chasing each other, something she loved to look at every time they went inside. She loved the Chinese lanterns on the walls, too, and all the red velvet drapes and red velvet seats that yawned open when you sat down on them. She loved it in there, the way everything was meant to get her and everyone else set and ready for the movie they were all about to see, like a beautiful lady all dressed up to sing a song, the song the real reason you were listening, but the beauty of the lady singing it making that song all the more beautiful.

She loved it in there, even if you cried. Even if the reason you cried wasn't a reason you wanted to think about.

They all three stop once they are almost to the curb, the street bustling as it always is, the sidewalk cluttered with people just out of the theater like themselves, cluttered too with the people who are out here every day they ever come here.

This is when her daddy starts looking, like he always does.

This is part of her daddy being an *actor,* he's told her a hundred times, this looking at everything when they come out of the movies at Grauman's Chinese.

She looks out at the street too. Here are the same old soldiers, and here are sailors too, though the war has been over for a year and a half. But most of the men out here wear hats and suits, and some, like her daddy, wear short-sleeve shirts.

They will stand here like this for a while, her daddy looking and looking, Joan knows, because they always do. Then they will take the Yellow Car streetcar home, like they always do, and though her momma and daddy don't know it, Joan has the way home by heart so that in case she ever has to she can get home from here. It's a song she made up, the directions, but not really made up by her all the way, because the tune is "American Patrol," the song she had to listen to a thousand times when she was practicing for her tap dance *recital* last year. That was before Daddy got home, when she was living in her real home in Texas and Granny Holmes was paying for everything, tap dance included, and here comes the song without her even thinking of it: *Oh, you must take Hollywood, you must pass Highland, you must pass Vine and North Western, then change at Sunset right there at Hillhurst, Alvarado is your home. Oh, you must take Hollywood . . .*

Her Granny Holmes is rich. She paid to have a picture taken of Joan in her costume, and pictures of Fern and Betty Jo, all three of them lined up in a row and stepping up to an X made of tape on the floor there in the studio in Mineola. Joan was dressed like a soldier in *khaki,* but with a skirt on instead of pants and with sequins sewed in the edges of everything, from her sleeves to around the top of her hat to the hem of the skirt.

She had black patent-leather tap dance shoes Granny paid for too, and Joan and Betty Jo and Fern liked to walk around in them in Granny's house on Blackbourn Street just to hear the crackly sounds they made. In the picture she's saluting, and she is smiling, though she wanted to wear a sailor suit because of her daddy, even if he was a *Merchant Marine* and not in the Navy.

Like every time they are here at Grauman's Chinese there are pretty women everywhere, some in dresses so tight it makes them walk with too many steps, and some women who wear pants too, though you would never wear that in Texas, Joan knows.

I swan! her aunts would say if they ever saw a thing like that, a woman wearing pants, and though she'd heard *I swan!* a thousand times when she lived in Texas, *I swan!* still makes no sense to her. *I swan what?* she has always wanted to know, and all she can ever picture are the swans she sometimes sees in the lake at Echo Park, only three blocks from where they live.

Other women out here wear regular dresses, like her momma, and she sees women who wear their hair up off their necks and with small hats her momma calls *pillboxes,* though she's never seen a box of pills that big, and though when the war was going on and they were in Texas she would sometimes hear on Granny Holmes's radio the word *pillbox* when they were talking about guns and the fighting.

"Earl?" her momma says beside her, and Joan glances up to her. She wears her blond hair in a snood on her neck, and has on the same dress she always wears when they go to the movies: a navy blue dotted-swiss dress with the thinnest white belt at her waist, and with a white sailor collar, and the white high-heeled shoes. "Earl, will you just sack it?" her momma says. "Can we just go home?"

Though her momma's wearing the sunglasses the eye doctor makes her wear every time she goes outside, Joan can see behind the round green lenses her momma's eyes squinted like they always are, her mouth open for how hard she squints, her teeth together.

"Please, Earl," her momma says. "Let's just go on home. My head," she says.

"You never know," her daddy says, and she squints up at him, sees him give a half smile, give his head the smallest shake. He holds her left hand, and she sees him above her against the blue afternoon sky, against this *plenty of sunshine,* and she sees he is looking and looking, like he always does every time they ever come out of Grauman's Chinese.

"You just never know," he says again, and then, almost in a whisper to himself, like he's telling himself a secret out here on the street, "You never know who you'll see, or who'll see you."

He's handsome, she knows. He has a mustache thin as a pipe cleaner on his upper lip, just like that man Clark Gable, and he wears his black hair slick and combed straight back over the top of his head, same as that man did in the movie too. Her daddy doesn't wear a hat, and though almost every man she ever sees wears one, her daddy won't because, he's told her a hundred times, they can't see you if you wear a hat.

"You and your street corner screen tests," her momma says and lets out a breath big and deep. She lets go Joan's hand, opens her purse, the white one that matches her belt and shoes, and pulls out a pack of Lucky Strikes, fishes again for her lighter.

But Joan is looking at her daddy, and his mustache, that hair. She's looking at his gray silky shirt, a shirt Joan has heard her daddy tell her momma makes his eyes stand out, though she doesn't know what that means.

My daddy is in the movies, she thinks, and she tries to smile, though she isn't certain it is a real smile or a squint like her momma makes, the sun out here is so bright. She even has the name she does because, her daddy's told her a thousand times, the day she was born he had a screen test with Joan Crawford, and because she is such a wonderful actress he decided to name his daughter after her, though Joan has seen her

51

in only one movie, *Mildred Pierce,* a movie that was scary and complicated and had a bad daughter and Joan Crawford as her momma, all of them crazy about getting money and about owning restaurants.

And it's because her daddy is an *actor* that they have to live here and not in Texas, her momma's told her, though she hasn't seen her daddy in a single movie yet.

When he was gone, things were wonderful. Not because he was gone, but because they got to go live in Texas all that time, where the trees were all as green as the ones in *Song of the South,* and where there were other children she could play with like in the movie too. Her cousins were there, and family all around everywhere.

Texas was her home, she'd figured out when they'd lived there, while her daddy was in the war. That was where her real home was.

When they lived here in California before, back when she was nearly a baby, the apartment they had was on the third floor of a building that had no screens in the windows so that bugs flew in at night and especially if you had the lights on and the curtains opened. She doesn't remember where that place was, but there was only one bed they all three slept in, and a small table and two chairs. That's all she can remember. And the view out the window, onto a small street that led to a big one, where streetcars were running when she went to sleep and when she woke up.

He's been home for over a year, and every morning Joan is still trying to get used to him being in this different apartment they live in now. She has to be extra quiet when she and Momma get up to get Joan ready for the walk to Alvarado Street School, and to get Momma ready for her job at Transparent Shade Company.

But mornings in Texas, before Daddy came home and they had to move back here, Joan went into her momma's bedroom—Joan slept on the *sleeping porch* off the back of Granny Holmes's house, her momma in the same room her daddy slept in when he was a boy, Granny told her a hundred times—and climbed into her bed, where Joan was always careful to speak quietly because of her momma's headaches. Every morning back then Joan touched at her momma's forehead to wake her up, trying to push away gently as she could the wrinkles her momma had up there, even when she was asleep all the way.

Then Daddy came home, and they moved back here without Daddy ever even coming to Texas to get them. Now he sleeps in the bed with Momma—Joan sleeps on the divan in the other room, where they have three chairs for the small table, a red plaid beanbag ashtray in the center of it, and a narrow counter with a hot plate and little sink; they have to go down the hall to the bathroom that the four apartments on this floor have to share—and he's always asleep all the way every time she gets up. Momma tells her it's because he worked so hard in the *Merchant Marines* and now with his job at Albert Sheets Restaurant that he needs all the sleep he can get. But he also goes to the movies three and sometimes four nights a week, after they have eaten dinner and after Joan is in the bedroom pretending to be asleep. Sometimes they all go, or just Daddy and Joan together, but mostly it's her daddy going to the movies alone, and him getting home so late that *of course* he has to sleep.

In the afternoon, while Joan is doing her homework, her daddy comes home, and he tells her who he has seen at the restaurant, names she never recognizes but that she smiles and nods at all the same. And late at night, after she has gone to sleep in her momma and daddy's bed and if her daddy hasn't gone to the movies, she lies awake and listens to them talk, or at least to her daddy talk, about *screen tests* and *glossies* and *shoots.*

He was in the *Merchant Marines,* she thinks, which is like being in the Navy but different. Like the difference between the people at a restaurant who do the cooking and the people who bring the food to be cooked. Her daddy, her momma's told her, was one of the people who brought things the soldiers needed so the soldiers could fight, and win the war.

Sometimes they will yell at each other, and Joan has heard her daddy leave even later, heard the door slam and his steps on the wooden stairs outside as he goes. Sometimes she hears her momma cry, or yell at him even louder than he can yell until sometimes, sometimes, neighbors yell at them to be quiet.

Sometimes her momma opens the door just a bit and looks in at her after they have yelled like this, and always Joan pretends she is asleep all the way.

Sometimes, sometimes, her momma will sit down on the bed beside her, even though Joan is pretending to be asleep all the way, and her momma will sing to her in the quietest way, sing to her songs about blue skies and about sitting under apple trees and a song about a mood indigo, though she doesn't know what that means.

But her favorite song is the one with the words "I get so lonely thinking of you," about how her momma is always thinking of Joan, always, even though she's lonely.

Her momma's voice is perfect, even though she sings only loud enough for Joan to hear in her sleep, Joan can tell. Her momma doesn't want to wake her up, she can tell with how quiet she sings, but her voice is always clear and beautiful and full of the blue skies and apple trees and thinking of Joan.

The thing about her momma singing, though, is that Joan wants to pretend to wake up so that she can tell her momma how happy it makes her to hear it, and to tell her too not to be lonely. But she is afraid her momma will stop if she wakes up, because the only time her momma sings to her is when she believes Joan is asleep all the way.

So she pretends to sleep, and she listens.

Though she tries with everything she has to stay awake and listen to it all, to the sound of her momma's voice on those nights she sings to her, or to listen for her daddy to come back or for her momma to stop crying or maybe just for her momma to call out her name when she opens the door just a bit, still she falls asleep every time, and wakes up on the divan the next morning.

She's not allowed in to wake up her momma anymore, because he's in there asleep all the way. Her momma wakes herself up now, and quiet as they can they get ready for what they still have to do every day: Joan and school, her momma and her work.

And her momma's forehead is always wrinkled up in the morning, Joan sees every day, no one to wake her up carefully and push the wrinkles away.

She'd cried at *Song of the South,* she finally lets herself think, because though she does not want to think about it, she has nothing else to do while they wait for her daddy to finish what he always does, this looking and looking. But it wasn't the kind of crying she was used to, the kind of crying she did at the movies whenever the story got sad, like when Snow White bit that apple, and when Dumbo got lost from the circus, and especially when Bambi's momma got killed—she'd cried right out loud in the theater, and heard other children crying, all around her.

She knew, too, that you were *supposed* to cry in the movies, that that was what you were meant to do there. Her daddy'd told her this on their way out from *Bambi* when she asked him why he hadn't cried when Bambi's momma got killed.

It was nighttime when they saw that one, and back

before he went to the war. She was just a little girl, and she can't remember why her momma wasn't with them—maybe she was in bed after work, and having one of her headaches. Joan was almost a baby back when she saw *Bambi,* back when every time they ever came to Grauman's Chinese she went straight to the cement handprints and footprints and got down on her hands and knees and tried out the different sizes.

Back then, when she was just a little girl, she wondered when her hands and feet would fit the concrete ones, and back then too her daddy'd stand beside her while she tried to make her hands fit, and he'd tell her the names of the people whose hands these were.

Now she can read, and she knows now what this is all about, these handprints in wet cement: they are movie stars, and sometimes when they have a *premiere* the owners of the theater make them put their hands and feet in it, and the movie stars have to write their names and something funny.

But the night they came out of *Bambi,* she'd asked her daddy why he didn't cry in there, because there seemed something extra sad to her about the fact her daddy didn't cry. On top of the sound of the other children crying in there, she'd thought she could hear some mommas and daddies crying too, and she'd glanced up from where she'd held her hands to her face right after Bambi's daddy tells him his momma's not coming back to see her own daddy, his eyes open same as ever, his head tilted a little to one side, just watching. Not crying.

"Why didn't you cry?" she'd asked as they walked out the big glass doors and into the night outside, though the lights everywhere made it light as day out here.

"They want you to cry," he'd said, and now they were in the big area out front where all those footprints and handprints are, a place as big as a playground, it seemed to her back then, though now it's just the front of Grauman's Chinese. "The movies want you to cry," he'd said. "But I'm just watching them."

He'd smiled down at her, and she thought even back then, even when she was almost a baby and still wanted every time they ever went to Grauman's Chinese to put her hands and feet in those cement prints, that maybe he wasn't telling her the truth about his not crying. That maybe he wasn't crying for another reason when Bambi's momma didn't come back. On that night, the sadness in Bambi's losing his momma to that hunter, and the sound of the gunshot that made her jump in her seat, all made her just want to go home, and see her own momma, so that she didn't at all stop at those handprints, and pretend someday she'd be big enough to fill them with her own hands.

There was lots to cry about in *Song of the South:* Ginny's brothers pushing her in the mud and ruining her dress for Johnny's birthday party, a dress their poor momma made out of her own wedding dress; Johnny's momma not letting him keep that puppy, and her telling Uncle Remus to leave her son alone and stop telling him his stories. And there was Johnny getting hurt by that bull.

But none of that was what made her cry. Even when Johnny was nearly about to die there in the bed, she wasn't crying.

No. She'd cried early in the movie, even before Brer Rabbit and Brer Fox and Brer Bear ever showed up, even before Uncle Remus started on telling his stories for Johnny and Ginny and little Toby.

She'd felt it start up in her heart, this kind of crying. What started it was when Johnny knew why he was being taken to the plantation: his momma and daddy were going to live away from each other. She knew what that meant: the word *divorce.*

That word: a secret: *divorce.*

She'd cried, she knew, because this was what she thought would happen one day, what she'd thought was going to happen to her since she can remember: that her daddy and momma would get a *divorce.*

When Johnny figured out they'd come all the way to the plantation from Atlanta, and that his daddy was going back to Atlanta and leaving Johnny and his momma here, he'd gone straight to the kitchen, put some food in a red-and-white-checked handkerchief, a handkerchief almost big as a tablecloth, then tied off the corners and hung it on the end of a stick he found outside. Then he took off, into the woods.

Woods that looked all the world like the woods she and Fern and Betty Jo sometimes walked out to down the road out of Hawkins.

He was running away, she'd seen in the theater, because his momma and daddy weren't going to be together. He was a *hobo,* and though she could hear some mommas and daddies laughing a little bit here and there, this was what made her cry: a boy, a stick over his shoulder with a handkerchief holding food, running away from home.

She'd cried, because she *wanted* to go to Texas. She cried because she loved her daddy, and she loved her momma, and didn't want a *divorce.*

She cried, because she wanted them all to be happy, and she cried, she knew, because she didn't know how that happened.

"Dammit, Earl," her momma says, and Joan quickly looks up at her, sees her eyes behind the green lenses are even tighter, her teeth even harder together. She's already finished the first cigarette, and is working on the next. "I need to go home," she says, and already Joan can feel the air change out here, can feel it like the way the music changed when that bull saw Johnny.

"Saralee," her daddy says, still with his eyes looking and looking. He's in a short-sleeve shirt, the gray silky one, and Joan looks again to see if she can tell yet what it means that the shirt makes his eyes stand out.

Joan looks at the street, to try and see like she always does what her daddy sees. As far as she can tell, he never sees anything because nothing ever happens when he looks. They only stand here on Hollywood Boulevard in front of Grauman's Chinese, across the street to the right the Hotel Roosevelt shooting up like a big white castle only square, way up high on the roof a sign with the words *Hotel Roosevelt* that at night are in bright white lights, but that in the daytime are just a bunch of metal pieces, it looks like to her, like the square metal frame of wires her momma and daddy's mattress sits on.

Down the street to her right is the Egyptian, which isn't as good a place to go to the movies, her daddy's said, because the people there wouldn't give him a job when he was a young man. She's been in there once, with her momma just after Daddy went to the war, before they moved to Texas, and though all the Egyptian things were nice—there were huge pillars in there, and paintings on the wall of people laying flat and sideways—the place also scared her when it got dark, with those catmen looking down at her from the walls. And the one time they tried to get in the Pig 'n Whistle Restaurant next door, the place where Shirley Temple always liked to go when she was little, they couldn't get in, the place was so crowded.

There are cars everywhere out here, she can see, and those Yellow Cars and the bells and the electric pop when they pass under where two wires meet. And there are people. People everywhere.

But like every time she doesn't see anything, like every time her daddy makes them stop and stand here, whether he has on his gray short-sleeve shirt or the baby blue one that he says makes his hair look best, or the red and white checked one he wears only on days when the sky is cloudy—like every time they come out of Grauman's Chinese, instead of seeing anything or anything happening, there is only the way her momma and daddy start up, just like right now, with the way her daddy said her momma's name: "Sara-lee."

There is only this same beginning of things. This change in the air around her, and in this brilliant light starting to be not so bright, just like it does every time.

But then here are words, a song, come to her without her even thinking, same as the directions to their apartment, and she closes her eyes, still holding only her daddy's hand while her momma still smokes her cigarette.

Mister Bluebird's on my shoulder, she sings in her head without even wanting to, the words already in her, and it seems like some kind of sudden magic that she's watched this movie only once, and already she can remember the words: *It's the truth, it's "actch'll"—Everything is "satisfactch'll"! Zip-a-dee-doo-dah, zip-a-dee-ay, wonderful feeling, wonderful day!*

This is the best movie she has ever seen, and she sings without singing at all, just quiet, there on the street and waiting.

Brad

5

When I wake up, my grandma is already playing solitaire in the kitchen, the slap of the cards as she lays them on the tabletop bringing me from sleep. Then she begins to sing, her voice soft and dark as I piece together the words to "Somewhere My Love."

And I remember: today is The Day.

She is nearly blind, and the cards she plays with have huge numbers, the symbols just as huge, and there seems to me something sad about the loss of the one-eyed jack or the queen of hearts to just a huge *J* or *Q* with a giant spade next to it. But, I know, the value is in the game itself. She plays solitaire and sings each morning to pass time until my grandpa gets back from wherever he is. Saturdays, Sundays, and Wednesdays it's the swap meets at the old drive-in in Reseda, two or three mornings a week the empty lot next to the Dale's Market on Van Nuys Boulevard, where he parks his Econoline, opens wide the back doors, and hangs out for sale the caftans he makes in the garage.

I was discharged from the Navy two weeks ago—June 10, 1980—and I've been camped here ever since. Although I was born in Hawthorne, I live—or did live—with my mom out in Phoenix, my father transferred there only a month after I was born.

At least that's what I've been told: transferred.

But that is a fact from a history I know nothing about, that story of a young couple getting married and having a baby and moving away from California for matters of work. It's a history I know nothing about, nor care to explore, as it has, finally, the ring of the dull about it: They divorced when I was two, or so my mother has informed me on the half dozen times I can remember asking about having a father, inquiries that dried up around the time I was six or seven when I realized I was a Child of Divorce, and that my father, who lived in a mysterious place called El Paso, was long gone, and wouldn't be back.

So that I was raised by my mother, me the only child of the only child of my grandma and grandpa. The cardplaying blind woman, the ex-janitor swap meeter.

My mother: a woman of few words, one might want to say, though *remote* would be, from my vantage point as her son, the better term.

I ran away the first time when I was fifteen because of the emptiness of our house. I'd spent enough nights lying awake and watching out my window the black silhouette of Squaw Peak rising up into stars, while the house lay silent, starving from the inside out, it seemed to me, for something alive.

The second time I ran away was my eighteenth birthday, the day I joined the Navy to See the World, because I figured there had to be one out there somewhere.

Now I've been in the Navy for a little over six years.

And now here I am, some kind of refugee living on my grandparents' couch.

In the Navy I was a machinist's mate, and I figure I'll stay down here in Los Angeles for a while, see what turns up in San Pedro. There's been nothing so far, but I'm not going back to Phoenix. The problem, though, is where to go now.

I hear Grandma slap down the cards again, and I sit up on the couch, my legs tangled in the sleeping bag. Like every morning so far, I have to blink three or four times, look around the living room, take stock of where I am.

It only takes a moment. There is the wood-grain television console against the far wall, big as a coffin; to my right is a pair of velvet recliners, burgundy; above them is a pair of swag lamps, turquoise shades with gold pull tassels.

But what makes me *know* where I am every morning is the evidence of my grandpa's past moneymaking projects: on the TV console is a gold-painted plaster statue of a naked cherub, a bowl of grapes on its shoulder; on the small end table between the recliners sits a blue and turquoise and violet feather flower arrangement.

I'm at Grandma and Grandpa's house in Pacoima. I'm here in the San Fernando Valley, in a suburb city nestled next to a suburb city beside a suburb city no different from any of the thousand of them—Arleta, Mission Hills, North Hills, Sun Valley, Panorama City, the city of San Fernando.

I'm in Los Angeles, California, and not on the USS *Denver* anymore. And I have the whole day in front of me.

I stand, fish from my seabag at the foot of the couch a pair of shorts, fold up the sleeping bag, stow it next to the seabag.

Grandma sits at the kitchen table wearing one of the caftans, this one giant white lilies on a purple background. Cards are spread all over the table, three of them held up to her face, her eyes squinted nearly shut. This is my mother's mother, a woman who lost one eye to glaucoma twenty-five years ago, the other eye left with only 5 percent vision. She's told me stories of trying to raise my mother with headaches lasting months, weeks spent in bed, while somewhere a doctor continued to diagnose her pain as a problem with her glasses. Now, when she walks through the house, it's along walls, one hand touching all the way through.

Her arms are pale and thick, her face wrinkled and white, her mouth too red. Sometimes she seems *too* pale, but I imagine that's because of the caftan material and the blond-gone-gray of her hair. And, too, the fact she leaves her home only twice a week, each time for a walk to the liquor store at the corner. Grandpa on one arm, her white-and-red-tipped cane in the other hand, she buys three cartons of Benson & Hedges Gold.

But she sees things, in her way. Yesterday morning I stood in the kitchen, the cupboards open, and pulled down a box of Special K. She said, "That's for your grandfather. There's not enough of that left for the two of you," and I looked at her, a good fifteen feet away. She was hunched over the cards in her hand, eyes squinted hard as always.

She brought the cards even closer to her face, held them flat to catch light from the chandelier over the table. "What the hell you make of this card, Brad?" she said. "Is this a seven or a nine?"

This morning is no different from the last thirteen: I move past her at the table, a cigarette at her lips; to her left, next to the spread of cards, is her leather cigarette case and lighter and beanbag ashtray all placed exactly where she wants them. I pause a moment, take up the cigarette case and shake one out, say, "Mind?" She smiles, the cigarette bobbing up as she lays down a black three on a red nine.

"Just know that when you strike it rich," she says, and lays down the two cards left in her hand, takes up three more from the stack in her other, "you can buy me a whole boxful for my birthday. A whole case of Benson & Hedges. That would be nice."

By this time I'm already staring up at the open cupboards, my cigarette already lit: I'd borrowed her lighter as well. There on the shelf sits the box of Special K. I turn to her.

She shrugs, says, "So he didn't have time for breakfast. He said he had to meet Rosa early, then set up at Dale's. He'll be back around one. So you go ahead and finish that off." She slaps down one card on the rows before her, then the second one in her hand, then the third, and she stops. "And don't you worry about today being today. Just don't you worry." Then, with her eyes still squinted, she leans back in her chair, scans the cards, takes one long pull on the cigarette. I can see the cigarette burning down as she draws in deeper than any sailor I can remember. She can ash a cigarette in two easy pulls.

She brings the stub from her mouth, without looking at it tips three inches into the tray next to the lighter. There's not a trace of smoke as she gives a little laugh, says, "I won."

The business about today being The Day refers to my personal goals for life after the Navy. When the *Denver* put in in San Diego, I was not surprised to see, as I stood on deck in my dress blues scanning the crowd on the wharf, a caftan of yellow orchids on a sea of fuchsia, Grandma wearing dark glasses. In one hand she had that cane, next to her the tan face and white hair of my impossibly handsome grandpa.

I couldn't help but smile, wave back to them amid the dozens of other people down there, because my grandparents were the ones I ran *to* when I was fifteen, three days of walking and riding from Paradise Valley to Pacoima. The first night I only made it as far as Quartzsite, where I spent the night beneath an overpass, hail the size of lemons pounding down on either side of me, the next night beneath an overpass outside Indio, the heat off the desert too heavy for sleep.

When I showed up at their door here in Pacoima, they didn't seem surprised. "You have arrived!" Grandpa said as he swung open the front door, and he laughed, one hand on his hip. Grandma slowly moved toward the door, one hand to the wall of the foyer. "What child is this?" she sang. Then she laughed, too.

I'd cried, me hungry and broken, these two laughing at me. On the ride home from San Diego I'd told them of my goals: to get at least a lead on a job within the next two weeks, to let my hair grow out, to see at least three new movies a week, to shower alone. The latter ones, of course, were attainable, but if I didn't get a lead on a job in two weeks, I told them as we headed through the grass wasteland of Camp Pendleton, then I didn't know what I'd do.

I sat up front with Grandpa, Grandma behind us and in the middle of the seat—we were in Grandpa's latest acquisition, a pale yellow '76 Cadillac DeVille, Grandpa's car of choice for as long as I can remember, him buying a new used one every two years or so, though he only drove it, as far as I knew, to get groceries a couple times a week, the Econoline and its caftan mission the important vehicle.

While we drove I told them too some of what I'd done on this last cruise, another WESTPAC, my third one since enlisting: how once again I'd read my brains out, this trip everything from *Moby-Dick* to the *Iliad* to *The Sacred and the Profane* to *The Machinist's Guide to Valve-Bore Maintenance;* told them of the narrow cans of beer sold in Yokohama and Pusan; told them of the small fire in the engine room when I'd been on duty, and the broken nose I'd gotten when I'd been kicked in the face by the man on the ladder up before me.

"Just look at this," I'd said, leaning toward Grandpa and pointing to the new bump at the bridge of my nose. "Can you see that?" I said, and he had only laughed, his eyes never leaving the road. From behind me Grandma said, "That looks horrible," and I'd turned to face her, saw her with her glasses still on, her mouth and forehead and the lines beside her eyes screwed up into her perpetual squint. "But it's hardly noticeable," she'd said.

Grandpa laughed even harder, but then he stopped, and the inside of the car was silent for the first time since leaving San Diego.

"Your mother called," he said, breaking the quiet, and Grandma leaned forward in the backseat, said, "Earl," his name meant to carry some significant weight.

But my grandpa sensed nothing, or, if he did, acted right through the moment. He said, "She told me to inform you she just couldn't get the time off from work, that her bank wouldn't allow it, that this was mortgage season and she just couldn't get the time off. She sends her love."

"Earl," she said again, and he looked into the rearview mirror, said her name: "Saralee."

"Thanks for the info," I'd said, and let it drop there.

And, like whatever it was they knew but weren't

70

telling, there were things of my own I wasn't going to give away. Like the story of a girl named Mali in Subic Bay, and the things she did to me on more than one occasion for which I was more than happy to pay; and the fact that when I'd been kicked in the face I'd been too stoned to know it, the fire starting while three of us were all toked up on duty, most everyone I knew smoking the stuff like it was cheap tobacco, on duty and off.

And there was the story I don't tell anyone, a part that's been burrowed up in me since my first cruise, all the way back in '75, the *Denver* parked, along with what seemed every other vessel in the whole United States Navy, just off Vung Tau in the South China Sea, while helicopters came in and came in and came in, every one dripping with refugees.

There's a piece of me won't haul out and brag on this story, not because of any of this post-Vietnam syndrome shit you hear about everywhere now, and not because of any of that Bruce Dern and Jane Fonda *Coming Home* psychosis rot. I was a machinist's mate in the Navy, for crying out loud.

But I've got my reasons not to hang out this piece of me like it was a caftan for sale out the back of a van.

So the three of us, hot on our way home from San Diego and my discharge from Seeing the World, kept quiet about those things we knew and didn't want to tell. Because, I figured, they had their reasons too, and one day or another, sooner or later, I'd know what "She sends her love" really meant. If anything at all.

71

Near ten o'clock Grandma stops the solitaire, satisfied at winning her quota of nine games. She wins at solitaire more often than anyone else I know.

I have gone over the *L.A. Times* four times by now, turning up the same nothing I've seen for two weeks, when the front door bangs open. My grandpa enters, shouts, "Sons of bitches all!" in what I know is his most practiced best; he is still and ever an actor. "Sons of bitches all!" he shouts again, and though he hasn't startled me in the least—the few times I spent here when I was a child got me used to his practical jokes: the blast of the radio on after you'd just nodded off in the car; the pinch of a fingernail on the forearm, his cigarette between his fingers so that for a moment you thought he'd burned you with the tip, and then the roar of laughter, his mouth open wide, his eyes right on you—still I oblige him, let the newspaper in my hands drop, give the cigarette at my lips a quick shiver.

But my grandma only shouts, "Knock it off, Earl!" He pauses in the middle of the living room, seems to draw himself up, his eyes fixed on the woman in the burgundy recliner before him. A game show plays on the television, for a moment the room filled with only the sound of bells ringing, a woman's mad scream at having won a roomful of furniture, and I wonder just how long my grandparents have fought this way.

Earl and Saralee's only wedding picture hangs in the hall between the bedroom and bathroom. In it he wears a white dinner jacket, my grandma a gray dress. They are smiling, but in my grandma's face there is something forced, her teeth maybe clenched too tight, and every time I pass the picture I wonder if even then she weren't already feeling the small crack of pain, glaucoma setting in even before her honeymoon night.

Earl's smile is better rehearsed than Saralee's, chiefly due to the life he's lived: always in rehearsal for a part he'll never get. Though he retired five or six years ago from a place called Consolidated Film Industries over in Hollywood, where he was a "maintenance engineer"—a janitor—legend has it he's been in a couple dozen movies since back before there was sound. He's told me a million times of how he's worked with everyone from Joan Crawford to Elvis, Andy Griffith to John Wayne to Lucille Ball. I've heard a million times too about a whole reel of him doing his famous Foremost milk commercial, one long roll of Earl Drinking Milk that somehow got lost or stolen years ago.

But I've never seen any proof of him knowing any of these people. The only performance of his I've ever seen was in fact that milk commercial, a thirty-second spot I saw when I was a kid maybe fifteen years ago. In it he played a carpenter nailing shingles on a roof, pausing to down a quart of milk. A few moments later a refrigerator opens up in a kitchen somewhere, and he reaches in for yet another quart. You can see him clearly: he's right there, reaching between a jar of mayonnaise and a carton of eggs for the milk. But there's no smile on his face, only the determination of a man set on getting milk.

I remember the night I saw him there on our TV in Phoenix, the startling surprise of my grandpa entering our home through the television, his back bent at nailing, his Adam's apple bouncing as he drank straight from the carton, me just a kid in a living room in Arizona, watching, like everyone else.

My mother was there too, perched on the edge of the brown tweed couch and watching the screen intently, me in the green Naugahyde easy chair, as always no words from her about any of it, and when I think of that night I can recall dimly our sitting there and watching the set turned to this channel on purpose and at this point in time, and though I don't know the particulars, and have never thought to ask, it seems perhaps she had been told this was coming, that somehow my mother had been informed by mail or phone that there would be a night arriving soon when we would want to be propped before our TV set, and watching, waiting for this magnificent moment in time.

Then here it had come: my grandpa, on TV, drinking milk.

Then it was over, and even in that moment of him disappearing, and even though I must have been only ten years old, it occurred to me that my grandpa was already lost to the blank faces of everyone everywhere watching television, my mom and me included.

Then my mother stood from the couch, and left for the kitchen to finish with the dinner dishes.

The few times I asked my mother when I was a kid if any of this stuff was true about Grandpa and the movies, if the stories he told me really happened, she seemed to draw herself shut.

"He believes it," was all she ever said, the only thing she ever said, and then went on about her business, whether it was ironing a blouse for work or browning meat for Sloppy Joes for dinner or turning off the light switch at my bedroom door once I'd climbed into bed.

Then she would close the door behind her, and here would be the silence of an empty house; here would be those stars above Squaw Peak, and me watching them, wondering when my life might really begin. Me, counting the days until I might run away, and start.

And today is The Day.

But for now I am a captive audience to my grandpa here in his own living room, and he shouts with that practiced bravado, "Rosa will never again have my business, nor the business of any of my colleagues!"

The game show credits roll on the screen too fast to see, and Grandma has no smile, only squints.

"What now?" she says, her head weaving a little, looking for him, I imagine.

"What now?" I say.

"Oh," he says, and the actor lets out his breath. "Caftan material that fat old woman promised me. She sold it off to Clara Tipton. That means I'm going to be short for the next couple of weeks. Means, too, any caftans I make will have to be out of that rose-on-white left from last month."

"And what the hell's wrong with that material?" Grandma says. "I've got three made out of it. What's wrong with it?"

"The reason you have three," he says, and now he sits on the couch next to me, throws his arms back and onto the top of the sofa, exhausted and irritated at having to deal with idiots, "is because we can't *give* that hideous pattern away. Makes anyone who wears it look like a white whale tattooed with dead flowers." He pauses, glances at me and smiles. "Of course," he says, and clears his throat, "present company excluded."

Grandma turns to the set, still squints, holds her head as though the commercial playing there were more important than we could ever know. "Just go straight to hell, would you, Earl?" she says.

Then she turns to me, searches for me these ten feet away from her, and without her gaze ever landing on me gives a quick smile. "Pardon my French," she says to wherever she thinks I may be, and turns back to the TV.

6

I spent one month here the first time I ran away. Grandpa was full swing into the plaster statue phase; feather flowers came once I was on my way to Subic Bay. The inside of the garage was filled with rubber molds and sacks of plaster, and the first five days I was here I sat and watched him mix water and plaster in a plastic five-gallon bucket, pour it into molds for cherubs, Grecian women in tunics fallen to reveal round, full breasts, even an occasional unicorn or Head of Nefertiti. He wore his coveralls whenever we were out here, pale blue or light brown short-sleeved with the elastic belt built right in.

Up on a shelf at the back of the garage was an old projector, a 16-millimeter one like we had in high school for the films in science class. Covering it was one of those opaque plastic sleeves, gone yellow for however old the thing was, the projector just always there, never touched, as far as I ever knew. Plenty of times I thought to ask him what he had that for, and if he had any movies he was in that he could show me to prove he'd done any or all of what he was always talking about. But I never asked him, because I knew he'd launch into his story of the Foremost milk footage, and how he'd had a whole reel of film he'd gotten from CFI after everything was over, and how some son of a bitch had to have stolen it or, God forbid, he'd lost it or thrown it out at one time or another, and he'd be off on that tear for a half hour. So I never asked, only now and again glanced at that projector in its yellowed cover, like it was some sort of icon up there, a remote god to be prayed to if you worshipped all this movie stuff.

He had an old record player out there, too, this down on a low old coffee table in the far corner, off to the left when you walked in through the garage door. It was the granite-looking suitcase kind we had in grade school, and while he worked he'd play old albums— thick syrupy stuff, *Mantovani's Golden Hits* and *Ray Conniff's World of Hits* were a couple of them, the records all stacked in a pile next to the record player and veiled in the thinnest blush of plaster dust; another one was *Percy Faith's Greatest Hits,* another a Doris Day album, *Love Me or Leave Me,* the soundtrack to some 1950s movie about a singer named Ruth Etting, a young and beautiful Doris Day on the cover in a turquoise outfit with legs so long I couldn't put her together with the goofy woman in *The Doris Day Show* on TV.

With the volume way down, that music lying low and full beneath us, Grandpa'd tell stories of being an actor, and stories about actors.

Someone named Clifton Webb, he told me, never knew enough to sit on three of a kind no matter how many times Grandpa'd bluff him with a pair; and once he'd had a contest with an actress named Claudette Colbert at the RKO commissary over who could eat the most pieces of bacon: she won with thirty-two, though she couldn't have weighed more than ninety pounds soaking wet.

And one afternoon, while he dumped into the bucket a bag of plaster, then filled it with water from the garden hose snaked in under the closed garage door, he told me of how he'd been there for Walter Brennan's first role, the conductor in a Three Stooges short called *Woman Haters,* and how hard my grandpa'd fought for that role and only ended up one of the passengers on the train, though he'd met Moe Howard years before; and he told me of how he'd almost had the role John Wayne started with too, a radioman up in the boat in *Men Without Women* talking to men down at a submarine wreck, clearing a tube of the torpedo, but it all had to do with those USC tickets John Wayne kept getting for whoever it was wanted them that he'd gotten the role. He told me how even though John Wayne hadn't gotten his name in the credits of *Men Without Women,* same as Walter Brennan hadn't gotten his name in *Woman Haters,* still that wasn't what mattered: it was the being seen that mattered, he said.

"I knew those Stooges boys would be big soon as I laid eyes on them," he said while he stirred a wooden spoon in the water and plaster mix, dust rising up around his hand and into the air of the darkened garage as he worked. "Best thing they ever did was lose that straight man Ted Healy." He paused, his hand on the spoon, his other hand on a knee, him looking in at the plaster like it was a puzzle he might be able to solve if he looked long enough. But then he stirred it again, this time harder, faster, pulled out the spoon, slapped it hard on the edge of the bucket. "But the fact I didn't get that role of the conductor and Walter did nor the role Duke got too was something we all worked out once we were on the set for *Red River,* Walter and Duke and me." He picked up the bucket, that spoon still in his hand, and tipped it toward a rubber mold of a cherub, the empty mold like all the rest upside down in a wooden rack against the back wall of the garage. "No hard feelings for either of them," he said, his eyes to the filling mold, the plaster working up to the edge of the mold like milk poured to the brim of a glass. "We all used to go out after work to the Chevron Bar right there in Culver City, but Mr. Hawks never came with us, no matter how hard I tried." He set the bucket on the ground, with the back of the spoon smoothed over the plaster. "No hard feelings at all, because we all three were working in the end, and working for Howard Hawks. Not a bad place to be." He wiped the edge of the spoon with his finger, wiped that finger on the pants leg of his coveralls, then looked up at me, him smiling. "Lunch?" he said.

He let the filled molds dry in the afternoon heat of the garage. Later that evening the plaster, once the rubber mold was peeled away like a thick layer of dead skin, was warm, and Grandpa would execute the finer touches: with a small piece of chamois he would dab at the seam in the plaster where the two halves of the mold had met, then fill in any small holes or irregularities in the statue. He knew what he was doing, the seam disappearing with the smallest touch of the chamois, the pockmarked breast of a Greek woman made smooth, unblemished, with the touch of a penknife and a bit of wet plaster.

There were things I wanted to ask him even then, me

only fifteen and fresh off the desert between here and what I'd already started to think of as being where I *used* to live.

I wanted to ask him about his life, about acting. Or about not acting. I wanted to ask him what my mother had meant when she'd told me those times she did that he believed his life as an actor was true, and if that made it true, to believe it.

I wanted to ask if he really knew Walter Brennan and John Wayne.

I wanted to ask him, *What will happen to me?*

But I didn't, only watched him work, there in his cluttered and warm garage.

The next morning we'd go back into that garage, dark and cool now. Grandpa would break out the spray paint, put the statue on a potter's wheel, and lacquer it over with metallic gold or silver. Then he'd stand back from it, his hands on his hips, on his face the actor's scowl no matter the only work he'd ever done might be a milk commercial, and no matter how perfect the cherub seemed to me. Satisfied, he'd place it among the other statues on the shelves against the back wall of the garage, waiting for the next swap meet.

All that time, Grandma played solitaire inside the house. On occasion we might hear her singing all alone in there, hear her move through "Stardust" or "That Old Black Magic," tunes I'd heard her sing as many times as I'd heard the stories from Grandpa about John Wayne and Lucille Ball. Or we'd hear her shout at the television, "Take the car! Take the car, you idiot!"

After six days of me watching him work, Grandpa let me try spraypainting a cherub whose arm had broken off while the mold was being removed. Halfway through, the head and one arm and torso covered in gold, I heard the phone ring inside. We both glanced up at each other, looked back to the work at hand.

A few minutes later the door at the back of the garage opened, the dark room flooded with midmorning light. I stopped spraying and turned. Grandma stood in the doorway in an old housedress, one hand just touching the doorjamb.

"Brad?" she called out.

"Right here," I said. Grandpa hadn't turned to her. From the corner of my eye, I could see he was staring at the statue, his head moving one way and the other, assessing how well I'd done so far.

"Brad, it's your mother."

I put the can down on the potter's wheel, wiped my hands on my pants legs, started toward her. "She's on the phone right now?" I said, and I thought I might have felt on my face the beginning of a smile.

Grandma put a hand up to stop me. Her hand hovered before her, moved back and forth as if she were touching the air. From the record player came the soft scratched voices, almost too quiet to hear, of Ray Conniff's women singing, "I fall in love too easily, I fall in love too fast . . ."

"No, she just left a message," Grandma said above the song, and I stopped, her pale fingers inches from my chest. She said, "She said she just wanted to make sure you were all right." She reached toward me, and I felt her fingers just touch my chest.

I closed my eyes. "That's all?" I said, and waited for an answer.

From behind me I heard the sound of the metal ball inside the paint can as my grandpa started shaking it.

"Come on," he said, "I see a few runs in the job here. You got to make your sweeps smooth and easy. Just smooth and easy," and I heard the hiss of metallic gold out of a can. "Eve Arden has one of these in her living room, you know. Made by me."

Though I had no idea who Eve Arden was, I said nothing, only swallowed down my questions and turned to him, and the work left of painting a broken statue.

"I fall in love too terribly hard for love to ever last . . ." those sad women sang from the corner of the garage, their words surrounded by leaden strings and a piano plunking out its own sad map.

Grandma blinks off the TV now, moves the recliner to upright. "Let's go for cigarettes," she says.

"Get those godforsaken coffin nails yourself!" Grandpa shouts with the same predictable bluster he always does, and suddenly I am standing up from the couch, heading toward the front door. "I'll take her," I say, though I've never taken her before. It's just that today is The Day, and there is nothing in the newspaper for me.

Grandma is at the door a few moments later, her red-tipped cane at the ready, dark glasses on, and Grandpa yells, "And I'm glad to see you up and moving, Popeye! Atrophy kills!"

"It's the caftan material," she says to me once we are on the driveway. "He'll grab any opportunity he can to go ranting around the house." She holds the cane perpendicular to the ground, the bottom tip never touching earth. Her posture is impeccable, her neck straight and sure, and as we make our way between the van and the Caddy on the driveway and out onto the sidewalk, I see too clearly I am still a boy who's run from home, away to his grandparents' house.

We make it to the corner, her left arm looped in mine, before us the midday traffic of Laurel Canyon Boulevard. Though I've passed here any number of times, have known that Hanshaw's Liquor Mart II is where she buys her cigarettes, I see only now that the place is directly across Laurel Canyon. There is no crosswalk before us, only four lanes of fast cars and a double yellow line.

With my arm I begin to steer her to the right and the traffic light at the intersection a hundred yards or so away, but she draws to a dead stop.

She says, "Where the hell are you going?" She wrestles her arm free from mine, grasps the cane with both hands, the tip still inches above the ground.

"Down to the light," I say. "And then across, right?"

"Hell no," she says, and she smiles, the wrinkles nearly gone, and I can see the young woman in the wedding picture in the hall.

"Watch," she says, and turns to the curb, inches up to it. She stands there a moment, then extends the cane out before her, angled down to meet the pavement. She taps it hard in a perfect rhythm, the tip making an arc from left to right and back again, and she steps off.

I reach for her, but she says over her shoulder, "Back in a minute."

Cars everywhere roar to a stop, and I watch my grandma in a purple caftan covered with huge white lilies cross Laurel Canyon Boulevard without hesitating a moment.

She makes it to the sidewalk across the street, and she moves slowly again, the cane no longer touching ground but hovering above it, just as before. The door into the place is only a few feet away from her, but still it takes a minute for her to make it, one hand out in front of her until a woman with blue-black hair and thick glasses appears in the doorway, smiles, and calls out "Saralee!" so loudly I can hear it over the traffic between us, all cars back to well above speed limit. Grandma disappears inside.

When she comes back out, she's carrying a paper sack, inside of which, I know, are three cartons. She moves just as slowly as before, until she reaches the curb. She touches the cane to the street again, and the world seems to halt around her, cars freezing as she taps out the ground before her. Then she is next to me, her arm looped in mine again, and she is pulling me back down their street, me too stunned to say a thing.

"Not bad for a loudmouth blind grandma," she says,

and I can only nod in agreement. "I won't let Earl take me across that street. It's the only thing I have left, I think," and she goes quiet for a moment. "You should hear us bitch and moan at each other, all the way down here," she starts up again, "and every time it's over whether or not he'll let me cross alone. Him and his frustrated actor business, flailing his arms everywhere, but I just go right across, and he hasn't stopped me a single day yet. By the time I get back, he's still steamed up, and we march on off into the sunset bitching and moaning away."

I haven't yet said a word, and we are quiet for a while until she says, "It's not that she doesn't love you." Then, a few moments later, a few feet farther away from the sounds of traffic behind us, she says, "But then how do I know that's true?" and she stops walking.

She looks for me, reaches her fingers up to my face and touches me. "I love you," she says. "You know that, don't you?"

I nod, her fingers still at my cheek, and I say, "I love you, too," surprised at how the words sound out here on the street, the silence that follows them. And because of how much I fear that silence, the dead sound around us, I say, "Sing for me."

"What?" she says.

"Sing for me," I say and give her hand a small squeeze.

She stops squinting a moment, the wrinkles gone somehow. The street is quiet, no cars anywhere. She smiles, and with no more hesitation than that she begins to sing: "Evening summer breeze, warbling of a meadowlark, moonlight in Vermont . . ."

By the time we make it to the driveway she's gone twice through "Moonlight in Vermont," once through "Blue Skies," and is in the middle of a song I don't recognize, a song about being lonely and about how she's always thinking of you, and I can't help but think it's me she's singing about, that it's me she's missing, and suddenly, even though the song says the opposite thing—that the singer is lonesome—I don't feel so alone. I believe, for a moment anyways, that blue skies are smiling at me, and that with my grandma thinking of me, maybe this will all work out fine, and I look at her beside me as she leads me back between the van and the Caddy on the driveway and to the house.

The things she's lost since the wedding picture in the hall—the blond hair, the girlish figure—don't matter. What matters is that the woman next to me, posture still perfect, gives to the hot summer air around us a voice clear and simple.

And I want to ask her: *How is it I could have the mother I do, when I have the grandmother I do?*

It's a stupid question, stupid as the one I'd wanted to ask my grandfather all those years ago, when I ran away to here: *Does believing you're an actor make you one?*

And yet again, I wanted to ask him and my grandmother both, *What will happen to me?*

But when we are halfway up the drive, and the words seem possible, seem almost lined up in me and ready to go, I look up, see Grandpa standing at the open door. One hand is on the knob, in the other a fistful of mail. On his face is no expression, and I realize the look he gives might actually be who he is, the real Earl behind the failed actor.

We make it to the three concrete steps up to the door, and I say to him, "What now?"

Grandma turns to me, unaware, I believe, that Grandpa stands before us. She says, "Why not 'Someone to Watch over Me'?"

"Mail call," Grandpa says, his voice flat and dead. "You got a letter."

Grandma looks up at him. "From?" she asks, but there is no suspense in her voice, only dread somehow.

He says nothing, pulls from the wad of bills and flyers in his hand a small thank-you note of a letter.

But I only hold the envelope in my hand, stare at handwriting familiar yet foreign on the front of it, and at the small return address sticker. The name and numbers there mean something, I am certain, but as I stare at them they become only bits of ink on a self-adhesive strip. I don't know anyone there, don't even know where the hell Phoenix is, and I look first to Grandpa, then to Grandma, then to the envelope again.

I fold it in half, and half again, a small square of white paper in my hand. I shove it deep into my back pocket, hoping I might not remember where I put it later on.

A moment of silence again passes before us, the quiet so great I hear the rush of blood through me, and Grandpa's hand is on my shoulder. He looks at me a long few seconds, his chin down so that I can see the whites of his eyes beneath his green irises, and then he lets go my shoulder, leads me up the steps, my feet moving on their own. I turn to Grandma still on the driveway.

"Don't worry about me," she says, and again I am amazed, wondering what she can see and what she cannot. "I'm fine."

"Today is the day," Grandpa says as he leads me through the kitchen, through the laundry room, and out onto the small porch in the backyard, down three more steps and to the back door into the garage.

Then we are inside, the air enormously cooler, and he clicks on the light to reveal three industrial sewing machines, rolls and rolls of rose-on-white material stacked around the room. Hanging from rungs wired to rafters are caftans, dozens of them, some beige with yellow carnations, others crimson with blue dahlias, but most of them in that rose-on-white pattern.

His hand is on my shoulder again, and he weaves me through piles of cardboard boxes and past two of the sewing machines to the third one. He sits me down on the stool before it.

"The other two are temperamental," he says, "maybe just a little too much so. This one here is reliable, won't skip a beat and sew your finger right into the hem of the dress some old woman will slip over her head. You sure as hell don't want that," he says, and he laughs, slaps my back in a gesture, I suddenly realize, might be real.

I turn to him, see he is already kneeling at one of the boxes behind me. He pulls out a huge piece of material, his face all concentration, lips drawn tight and closed. What we are about to do matters to him.

He lays the material over one arm, with his free hand reaches beneath the machine top and flicks a switch, and a small light on the machine flashes on, a soft whir begins.

"We'll just practice right now," he says, and folds one edge of the material onto itself, leans over me to drop the material in my lap, the colors brighter now because of the light from the machine.

He puts his arms around me from behind, places his hands on the platform beneath the needle and machinery, and says, "Feel around with your foot. There's a pedal down there."

The back door opens up. We both turn to the light, and again I see only her silhouette. But once she's inside I see that she's changed from the purple-and-lily caftan into one made from the same rose-on-white I hold now.

"I don't give a damn if I *do* look like a tattooed whale," she says. "I like this pattern." She moves toward us, her hands to either side of her, slowly maneuvering through the obstacles around her. Before she reaches us, Grandpa turns back to the machine, his arms around me once again, his hands on the material.

"Good for you," he says loud enough for her to hear. Then, quieter, he says, "Find the pedal?"

"Yes," I say, my foot on something square beneath the table.

"Okay," he says, and slides the edge of the material beneath the needle. "Now press down slowly on it, not too hard. Slowly."

I press down with the tip of my shoe, the touch tentative, near nothing. The needle moves almost imperceptibly down toward the material, and I press harder.

The needle goes wild, shoots the material through, the whir of the machine gone to a mad whine, and before I can let up my foot, Grandpa yells, "Easy! Easy!"

Grandma is next to us now, and I feel a blush come over me, close my eyes a moment.

"Easy," she whispers, and I open my eyes to the machine, my foot on the pedal. I ease it down, let the material feed itself through, perhaps too slowly right now, the needle hesitating each time before slipping into the material. But the line leading out is as straight as I can make it, and there seems some direction in this movement, though what I am beginning I cannot say.

"Billie Dove has three of my caftans," Grandpa says, quiet as a prayer. "She saw me at the Rose Bowl Flea Market, and she recognized me. But I wouldn't let her pay me." He pauses. "The peach dahlia on black is her favorite."

"Who?" I say just as quiet, my eyes still to that hem, this start.

91

"Earl," Grandma says beside me. "Don't start," she says, but there is on her voice no fury, not even a breath of annoyance.

"I love you, Saralee," Grandpa says, his voice the same quiet prayer, meant only for the three of us on the face of this earth to hear, and I wonder at that, marvel at this profession of love, because I don't remember ever hearing him say it before.

It is a remarkable thing, and for a moment I don't know what to do with this news, this world-shift whispered right here beside me: My grandpa told my grandma he loves her for the first time I've ever heard.

But then Grandpa moves right on. "The Rose Bowl Flea Market," he says. "That's coming up. We'll have to prepare." Then he lets out a sigh, says, "Billie Dove," his voice near a whisper. "We were in a movie together. Long time ago."

"Oh," I say, and we have been ushered through something with just these next new words.

And I go with him into that world, and go there with my grandma, too, a new world in which I am sewing a caftan, and I hold my foot on that pedal steady as I can, the line out from beneath that needle maybe even straighter now.

Joan

7

It's like a secret, but not really, her daddy being in the movies. It's like a secret because her momma doesn't talk about it, and her daddy does, so actually it's like a half secret.

But the real secret is her momma and her singing when she's sitting on the bed and Joan is pretending to be asleep all the way. And there is a really *real* secret about her momma that Joan thinks she knows but can't be certain it is true. About her momma's singing, about her being a singer.

There are other secrets in the apartment, secrets that she has put into *categories*. Two of them: first, there are secrets that are words; and second, there are secrets that are things.

Her momma and daddy say words late at night that they yell out, so that isn't what the secret words are—even the neighbors who yell back at them to be quiet sometimes know what they are saying.

Sometimes, sometimes she wakes up out on the divan when everything is quiet and dark and she can see by the light from the streetlight outside those three chairs and maybe even the little square of the hot plate on the counter there across the room, beside it the stack of movie magazines her daddy is always bringing home, and she will hear them whispering to each other on the other side of the wall, if they didn't yell at each other before. Those words are a kind of secret, but not really the kind of secret she put into the two *categories*. Everybody whispered things to each other, just like she did to Betty Jo and Fern in Texas and like they whispered back. She whispers things to her friends at Alvarado Street School all the time, to Harriet and Babs and even sometimes to Lincoln, who is a boy. Everybody does that, and when her momma and daddy whisper when they go to bed if they didn't yell before, that is good, because it means they are happier. Sometimes after the whispering she can hear her momma and daddy on the other side of the wall wrestling or playing tag, it sounds like, and even sometimes one of them or both of them will laugh. So that kind of whispering isn't any kind of secret.

No, the first kind of secret is the quiet words they say to each other when they aren't yelling and when they aren't whispering. The words she will lie awake at night on their bed and listen to and try to stay awake to hear. These aren't the words *screen tests* and *glossies* and *shoots* either, those words her daddy always has ready to hand out once she is in bed, because when the talk has those words in it, it's her daddy doing the talking, her momma like always just quiet.

But then the talk will go down, and then the secrets start. It isn't easy to hear these words, because they are *calm* and have on them a kind of serious sound that doesn't jump up high or lay down low. Still, they are words she can hear through the door and the wall, words that always make her think of a map, words like a drawing of roads on a piece of paper, roads going one way and another, lying flat and hard to understand, because they aren't real. Their words out in the other room, the two of them at the table and smoking, flicking now and again the ashes into the beanbag ashtray, are flat, like the lines on a map, and they are going somewhere all the time, and they are always going away. That's what she pictures in her head when she lies there at night listening, trying to understand what they are talking about: a map, with lots of roads going away from her.

What is it they talk about? she wants to know. Her momma and daddy are adults, and the way they talk when she's not there to hear them makes what they say a secret. Sometimes, sometimes she falls asleep thinking of the map they are talking out there, and how the sounds are flat, like those roads, and how she wishes she knew what they were talking about. She knows what it means when she hears the yelling and the leaving of the apartment, and she knows what it means when she hears that whispering in the dark sometimes and even a laugh in the dark, too. But it's the words between the whispering and the yelling that she really wants to know.

Because the secret, the really real secret of those words, is the way a road on that map of their words can lead to that yelling, and the way a road on that same map can lead to their whispering and maybe that laugh.

That is the secret she wants to know: how quiet words she can't really hear can lead you to happiness, and how the same words can make you walk down a road that goes straight to sadness, a secret she wants to know so bad sometimes her dreams go right into that map, and she is walking on a blue stripe in a field of white somewhere. This isn't a happy dream, not like Dorothy on the Yellow Brick Road, where a little girl is having an adventure all her own with friends along to help her and guide her and sometimes to protect her.

In this dream she is alone, and this is what frightens her: to be alone, and to have around you nothing, no color or flowers or anything, only a stripe at your feet that you know you have to follow, but you don't know if the stripe is going to take you to happy, or sad.

So that is the first *category:* words between yelling and whispering, and how there is a kind of path you can take with the words you say that can lead you to happiness or sadness. She just doesn't know what those words are, and so she doesn't know which ones to say and which ones not to say. If she can just learn the secret out there—if she can just learn to read the map that her momma's and daddy's words are—then she could always find a way to go to happy, and she could use that secret to get her momma and daddy to go there with her. She knows she could do that. But it is still a secret.

The second kind of secret is even more mysterious, but this kind is the one she thinks maybe she's almost going to find out any minute now. Any minute at all.

This is the *category* of secret things in the apartment, things she can't *solve* just by looking at them or holding them. But she can't ask about them, because they are hidden in places she isn't supposed to know about.

Things: three photographs, and a record.

She knows they aren't meant for her to see or to touch, because they are hidden away, and so she knows too that what they mean—whatever secret they have—isn't for her to know either. It's one thing to put something away where people wouldn't find it, like when she put her tap shoes in Granny Holmes's closet instead of her own, where she knew Betty Jo or Fern would get hold of them if they wanted and maybe wear them. But just hiding them didn't make it a secret, because anybody who found them would know exactly what they were: tap shoes, meant for dancing.

No, the deeper secret is what these things mean. Three photographs, and a record.

She found them four weeks and two days ago. She'd been in the apartment alone like she was most afternoons, when she would do her homework at the little table with the chairs. Her daddy came home every day around three thirty from Albert Sheets Restaurant, and she would watch out the window between *If Jane rides in a train going forty miles per hour and Robert rides in a train going fifty miles per hour* and *Children in China sometimes eat rice at every meal,* waiting for her daddy to come around the corner from Sunset Boulevard onto Alvarado, his *shift* over at the restaurant.

When her daddy came around the corner onto Alvarado, he always stopped, pulled out of his shirt pocket a pack of cigarettes, pulled out of his pants pocket a silver lighter, and lit up the cigarette. But it was always more than that, she could see from the window. Lighting the cigarette was something else, for the way he popped the pack hard against his palm before he shook one out, and for the way he snapped his wrist to open the lighter, then snapped it again to close it.

But he still wasn't done after he'd closed the lighter and put it back in his pocket. Once the cigarette was lit, he always turned back to Sunset and looked both ways, him standing tall as he could there on the street corner while cars went by fast, and streetcars whirred along loud. He always took two long breaths in on the cigarette, and shot them out of his mouth like a dragon, and she knew her momma, if she ever saw it, though her *shift* at Transparent Shade Company wouldn't be over until five o'clock, would say what she always said out front of Grauman's Chinese: *You and your street corner screen tests.*

Once he had let out those two dragon breaths, he would turn from the big street and start walking slowly along Alvarado, and she knew she had a couple minutes more to find something happy to say to him about the day, or to find something for him to help her with on her homework, though he always wanted to talk about who he had seen at Albert Sheets Restaurant. Then she would sit and listen, though she didn't know who they were. But she would listen.

That afternoon four weeks and two days ago, Joan dropped her pencil when she was moving her books around on the little table, and the pencil rolled away from her toward the divan. She'd gotten down from the chair and reached for the pencil, but her shoe hit the pencil first and kicked it, and she'd thought that was funny, almost like something she saw in an Our Gang movie, when a man walking along a street tries to grab a dollar bill from the ground but the dollar bill is tied to a fishing line that Spanky and Alfalfa keep pulling just when the man is about to grab it.

She laughed at the spinning pencil rolling quick away from her toward the divan, and so when she bent to pick it up again, she kicked it on purpose, and she laughed again, but this time the pencil went under the divan all the way, and she had to get down on all fours and reach for it. Still she couldn't quite touch it, and she lay flat on the floor, put her arm all the way under for it. Then she had the pencil, and started to pull her arm out.

But then she saw something under there: a little edge of paper hanging down from the wooden frame of the divan, the barest small brown corner of paper. She thought it was maybe a tag from when they made the divan, but she looked as hard as she could into the dark under there.

The little edge of paper was the corner of a big square of brown paper wedged flat against the frame, back in the corner where the back of the frame met the side of the frame. Above the brown square she could see the springs of the divan, and now she could see a cutout circle in the middle of the square paper—a record!

She let go the pencil and reached up to where the record was wedged flat against the frame, put her fingertips to it, tried to pull it out of place. It was a record, yes, and she pulled again, careful not to tear the paper or scratch anything. The record was in there tight, a record hidden in a strange place, like buried treasure, and she pulled a little harder one more time.

Here it came, fell out of its place and flat onto the floor, and she pulled it out, sat up and held it in her hands. The brown paper was smudged here and there where dirty fingers had held it, the edges of it a little worn. One of the corners had been torn off, but just the littlest bit of it.

Who had put it there? she wondered, and thought of somebody building the divan and accidentally leaving it when they were finished. But that was silly, she knew as soon as she thought of it, and she thought again of buried treasure, of somebody putting it there to keep it hidden away from everybody. They didn't own a phonograph, didn't even have a radio like everybody else she knew.

The middle of the record, what she could see for the cutout circle in the middle of the brown paper, didn't have a label on it, didn't have the curly writing or even the boring square letters like she'd seen on records at Granny Holmes's house, and at Lincoln's house when they sometimes went over there to listen to him play the piano and then to listen to the records on his phonograph. There was nothing, just the black waxy flat of the record itself, in the center of it the little hole where you put it on the phonograph.

She turned it over, careful with it because she didn't know what it meant, or who could have put it here, or why.

But when she turned it over, she saw something in the cutout circle. Not a label, but a part of a picture, a circle picture of people, pieces of shoulders and shirts and a part of a dress: a photograph inside the paper holder.

She set the record in her lap, the heavy thickness of it even more like buried treasure now that there was this new surprise—this new clue—to what she'd found, and she reached into the paper holder, pulled out not one photograph but three.

Three photographs, all of them big, nearly the size of the record itself, and she fanned them out in her hands, her heart beating harder in her for what this all was, all these *secrets*.

The first one, the one she'd seen part of through the cutout circle, was of people in a big room. There were tables filled with people all around, men and ladies laughing and smiling and drinking from glasses, not a one of them looking at whoever was taking the picture. Past the tables were people pushed together and dancing, all of them so close she couldn't tell who was dancing with who, and at the far end of the room, a room bigger than the gym at Alvarado Street School, was a big band up on a stage.

This had to be a nightclub, just like she'd seen in *Shall We Dance* with Fred Astaire and Ginger Rogers and a hundred people, a thousand all in one bright room with music and dancing and smoking and drinking. She looked closer at the picture, saw the walls behind the stage were draped with silvery looking curtains thick and pillowy, just like in the nightclubs she'd seen in the movies. Some of the people in the picture had on clothes like she'd seen in that movie, too, some of the men in those black suits—they were *tuxedos,* she knew, though she'd heard her daddy call them *monkey suits*—and some of the ladies in pretty dresses that let you see shoulders and that her aunts and Granny Holmes would have shouted *I swan!* at even louder than they would at the idea of a woman wearing pants.

The photograph beneath that one was closer to the stage where the band was playing, a man standing in front of them with his arms up. She could see he had a *baton* in his hand and knew he was the *conductor,* but not like a *conductor* on the railroad, which was what one of her uncles did back in Texas. This man wore a black jacket and pants, and had on glasses. He was smiling at the band, all set up in three rows in front of him, with the drums in the center at the back, behind them all the same pillowy silver curtains as in the first photograph. The men in the band were all playing, too, the trumpets in the back row, the trombones in front of them, and the men playing the saxophones in front of them, and now she noticed along the bottom of the photograph the heads of people dancing in front of the stage, men and ladies all dancing.

And to the far left of the photograph, off to the side, stood a lady at a microphone. She had one hand up in front of her like she was pointing to somebody at the back of the gym, but her eyes were closed, her face tilted up just a little bit. The microphone was as big as a saucer, so Joan couldn't see any more of the lady's face than her closed eyes, but she thought she was beautiful anyway, in a dark dress that showed off her shoulders.

The last photograph was of the band again, but this was a different time and somewhere else—in the center sat all the men, every one of them in those *monkey suits,* including the *conductor,* who stood off to the right side of the band. He was smiling, and was half-turned to the camera so you could see he had his hands behind his back, the *baton* in them and pointing down behind him like the skinniest tail. He had those glasses on still, his hair slicked back, and she could see he was younger than she'd thought, the glasses making him look older.

To the left of the band were three ladies side by side and half-turned to the camera too. They were all young and beautiful, though their hair looked flatter than how the ladies she saw out front of Grauman's Chinese wore theirs—one of the ladies even had a *bob,* with a curlicue of hair pasted onto her cheek. Their dresses— one white, one gray, one black (that was the lady with the *bob*)—had almost no shape to them, sort of came from the shoulders straight down to just below their knees. The way the men wore their hair was different too, she noticed now, lots of them with their hair parted in the middle and slicked down flat as flat could be on their heads, and now she knew these were old pho- tographs, maybe from before she was even born. The edges of the photographs were worn, Joan noticed now, and she could make out the thinnest smudges where somebody had touched the pictures.

What was this about? Why was this hidden beneath the divan, and who had put it here?

What was the *secret?*

She looked at the ladies again to try and figure out which one had been the one singing in the other pho- tograph, but none of them had on the dress that singer had on. She didn't think it could be the one with the *bob,* though it was hard to tell for the way the lady singing had her face tilted up.

Maybe it was one of the other two, she thought, and looked at them both, looked at them, smiling and smiling, both of them with what she thought might be blond or maybe light red hair—maybe they were even sisters.

Then she heard steps on the stairs outside the apartment, the sound something she knew by heart: her daddy. Home from Albert Sheets Restaurant.

This was when her heart jumped in her like she had never felt it jump, not even like it did when she and Fern and Betty Jo stood in the studio in Mineola for the *recital,* all three of them tap-dancing to "American Patrol" with all those people watching from folding chairs in rows that filled the whole place. Her heart jumped more even than when her daddy and momma both yelled and the neighbors yelled too. Her heart jumped even more than that.

She quick put the photographs back together and slipped them in the brown paper holder with the record, and started to move onto her back so she could wedge the record back into place, but then she stopped: Which side was up when she'd pulled it out? Was the side with the photograph peeking out facing the springs, or was the side with the record, that black waxy circle, facing up?

She flipped the record over in her lap, looked again at the black circle there, and heard too the footsteps on the stairs out there getting closer, a little louder.

The side that didn't have the photographs was up, and she scooted around to the divan, made to move onto her back again, and just then, just then, in the way the afternoon light shone in through the window and onto her and onto the record in her lap—why was the sun so low already?—she saw something in the black wax of the record, saw something that looked like writing.

She stopped, even though the footsteps out on the stairs were almost to the top, almost here. Her daddy's footsteps, she thought, but now she thought maybe not, maybe somebody else's—they seemed slower even than her daddy's, whose steps were so slow that sometimes she thought he didn't want to come home at all.

And why, she wondered again, was the sun so low already, already right there in the small stripe of sky between the top of the window and the top of the apartment building across the street?

But the writing on the record, the writing—this was a secret, a really real secret, and she lifted the record up close to her face, held it to catch that light from the window, and here it was again: writing, scratched right into the black wax.

Above the little hole where you put it on the phonograph were the letters *KKO* and then a space and then *TOY;* beneath the hole was scratched *SK* and then a space and then the numbers *2634.*

It was someone's handwriting, someone scratching right into a record with a straight pin, it looked like.

The footsteps stopped at the top of the stairs, and Joan held her breath, listened to see if it was her daddy, listened, and then the footsteps started again, right for their door, and she knew she had only eight steps left before he would be home, and she was on her back and did the best she could to wedge the record back up there in the frame of the divan, the black waxy circle with the writing on it facing up, and she pushed at it, pushed, and it held.

She pulled her arm out from under the divan, sat up just as the door opened across the room.

There stood her momma.

Not Daddy, but Momma, and Joan looked to the window once again, saw it wasn't yet a five o'clock sky out there, but it was long past three thirty. That was why the sun was so low.

Her daddy had never come home. She had been looking at the photographs all this time, maybe an hour or so. Just looking.

Her momma was squinting hard, looking into the room and the divan and the little table with the three chairs, squinting so hard at all of it that Joan always thought she was looking for a needle on the floor or the divan or on that table.

She had a headache again.

"Momma," Joan said. She got up from the floor, and her momma turned to her, saw her there like it was the first time she'd ever seen her, like it was a surprise Joan was even here. The same way her momma always looked at Joan when she had her headaches.

She held out her hand like she always did, and Joan took it, led her to the bedroom without another word. Inside the room, she let go her momma's hand and pulled the quilt back, and her momma came to the bed and sat down slowly, like she always did, and slowly lifted her legs and turned, lay back on the bed, her eyes closed already but still squinting so hard she couldn't close her mouth.

Where's Daddy? Joan wanted to ask, but she knew

she shouldn't speak, and she reached to her momma's feet and slipped off the brown leather shoes she wore, set them under the bed—Were there any secrets under the bed? she wondered—then lifted the quilt over her mother, lay it down on her careful as she could.

She'd almost been found with a secret, she thought. But she didn't know what it could be, and in a way she was glad for her momma's headache, for the way it made her momma not want to speak, not want even to ask the question *What were you doing on the floor in front of the divan?* and now Joan leaned over on the bed, and touched like she always did at her momma's forehead, trying to push away gently as she could the wrinkles her momma had up there.

She thought of the woman at the *microphone,* her eyes closed, face tilted up just a little bit, one hand pointing to somebody at the back of the gym. The lady whose face she couldn't really see for the *microphone* big as a saucer. Only those closed eyes, her eyebrows, and her forehead, no wrinkles at all.

Joan touched harder at the wrinkles, tried to push them away just the smallest bit faster, the smallest bit deeper. She pushed at them with the first two fingers of both hands now, one hand above each eyebrow, and pushing.

"Honey," her momma whispered, then, "Honey," her whisper more a moan with no voice on it, and quick Joan took her hands away. She could feel already her face gone hot, caught now at everything she had done: finding her momma's secret things, wanting to make sure it was her momma in that picture, and wanting already too to get the photographs out again and figure out which one of those three ladies was her momma. She'd been caught at it all.

Her momma let one eye open, and Joan could see the work of it just to do that little: the wrinkles went even tighter, her momma took in a breath, the sharp grin on her face for how hard she squinted even sharper for a second, and her eye opened, finally.

Her momma looked first at the ceiling, then found Joan there beside her. She tried at a smile, Joan could see, but there was nothing to it for that squinting.

"Honey," she whispered, "I didn't mean—"

The door to the apartment banged open in the other room, and Daddy shouted, "O daughter of mine, don't panic! I've got a sack of hamburgers and some fries, so nobody panic for me being late! And ol' Hank Worden came in today! He told me they're going to release *The River Is Red* now that Howard Hughes has quit his bellyachin', but it's going to be called *Red River* for some reason I—"

He said all this before he'd even made it to the bedroom door, and now here he stood, his words just as suddenly gone, him in a blue and white striped shirt— a shirt Joan had never seen before—and gray slacks. He had a brown paper bag in one hand, the bottom of it wet through for the grease off the fries, the other hand on his hip, rolled up in that hand a magazine.

"Saralee," he said, "you're home a tad early," and shook his head, turned from the door. From where she stood, Joan could see him go to the table, pull out a chair, and drop the magazine on it. He pushed aside her books, set the bag down, opened it. "I tell you what," he said, and peeled wax paper from a hamburger, took a bite. "I tell you what," he said again, now with his mouth full and chewing, "we had fun making that one, Walter and Duke and me." He swallowed, looked up from the hamburger and saw Joan watching him. He smiled, winked at her. "Going over to the Patio to see *Cuban Pete* tonight, see this new kid everybody's talking about, Desi Arnaz." He bit into the hamburger, chewed a second, then said with his mouth full, "It's a musical, and if it's any good maybe we'll go see it together." He winked again, opened the magazine, him still chewing. "I already set up a shoot for new glossies tomorrow, seeing as how the movie is coming out and I'm sure I'll be needing them."

She smiled at him for the wink he'd given her, even though he wasn't looking, and just then, just then, with the way he'd looked down at the table and his new movie magazine, she remembered: the pencil, still under the divan.

Could he see it from where he sat?

All of this in a few seconds, just like in a movie when everything happens all at once, just like when Dorothy looks out her window in the middle of the tornado and sees a cow and a chicken on top of a coop, then men in a rowboat and then the old lady on her bicycle who turns into the wicked witch on her broomstick, all of them swirling right in front of her and so close she can almost touch them all, but so dangerous she wouldn't dare.

That was what it had been like that afternoon four weeks and two days ago, when she found the secret things, a *category* more mysterious than the secret of words, and the map you could follow with them to *happy* or *sad:* this was just like *The Wizard of Oz,* and she thought of the way color came into everything right after that storm, and how the real adventure began then, but only after she had gone through that tornado.

But that afternoon, she'd turned from her daddy eating hamburgers and back to her momma, saw her eyes were closed, any idea of a smile gone for the slam and bang and loud words her daddy had made. Her momma had pulled the quilt up tight to her chin, her fingers on either side holding on hard to the edge, her wrinkles sharper and deeper than ever.

Joan reached one hand, just like she always did, and touched at her momma's forehead, tried to smooth away the wrinkles one more time, just one more time, like every time.

But this time was different. Maybe this time, once she'd pushed away the pain on her momma's face, she would find the woman in the photograph.

Her daddy, even if he saw the pencil, which she knew he wouldn't for the magazine in front of him, wouldn't think anything of it. Because, Joan knew, the secret things she had found weren't his. He didn't

111

even know they were there, wedged tight into the frame of the divan.

"Blue skies," Joan began to sing, though the words were quiet and a secret and all for herself, almost a whisper-hum, she made them so quiet, "smiling at me, nothing but blue skies do I see."

In a few minutes she would leave her momma and go in, sit at the table with her daddy, and she would talk to him about who ol' Hank Worden was, and Howard Hughes bellyachin', so that she could keep him happy and away from saying anything more about Momma being home early from work. She would ask him, too, about being in this movie, *The River Is Red* or whatever it was called, and hope he wouldn't see somehow her pencil under the divan.

Later, much later, after he got back from the movies, and after her momma and daddy both were asleep all the way, she would get the pencil in the dark, the only light that coming in through the window from the streetlight outside. Though she wouldn't get out the record, she might touch it, just touch it there under the divan, and make sure it was safe back in its place. But nothing more than that: just touch it.

She touched at her momma's forehead, still looking for that lady, and still whisper-singing, now a different song, only loud enough for herself to hear: "I get so lonely," she sang, "thinking of you."

8

A slapstick two-reeler, and he couldn't get the part.

He stood at the chain-link fence at this farthest corner inside Columbia lot, his broom leaned up beside him against the fence, and looked out at the hills to his left, hovering like they did above the low-lying buildings that hashed up Hollywood. The hills were brown, like all the hills around here, the only green you could find the green folks planted on purpose, or dressed a set with. For a moment he missed it, the green of Hawkins all summer through, and the wet of it, the smell of it on the air when you got up of a morning out on the sleeping porch.

But that was all it lasted, a moment, and he let it go. Because he was here. Where he wanted to be, no matter he didn't get the part.

Something was coming. He knew it. He hadn't been tossed out a boxcar and then picked lettuce for a month in the godforsaken town of Buckeye, Arizona, just to turn up in Hollywood with nine dollars in his pocket so's he could spend the next seven years sweeping lots, first at DeMille even before it turned into Pathé, then over at Paramount, and now here to Columbia, where he'd been for almost a year. He hadn't hoboed to California only to sleep every night in a run-down boardinghouse on Wilcox with a front lawn scuffed down to dirt.

But that was the way it'd all turned out so far. He was going on twenty-two, and still wondering why he was only pushing a broom while the mucky-mucks pulled up in their Stutzes and Pierce-Arrows and spit on the concrete he'd just swept.

He could see a few houses inched up the slopes of those hills, little shards here and there of white stucco and red-tile roofs, and wondered like he did every time he ever looked up to there what falderal was going on in those houses: who was lounging poolside already hooched to the gills, what vipers were reefing it up in broad daylight, who was playing tag in the sack with who right now. But mostly he wondered how those houses got to be owned and who owned them, and why couldn't he get a part, any part. Even in a two-reeler.

He turned, leaned his back against the fence, and looked to where the work was being done, to the center of the world that allowed, in its own small way this bright April morning in Hollywood, USA, all that hooch and weed and skirt and those red-tile roofs even to exist: there was the swing gang, and the gaffer and the electric and their crowds, and the cameraman too, a good twenty people busy as ants setting up lights and tarps and electric lines and a camera, all of it out at a Pullman car.

This deepest and cheapest back corner of the Columbia lot was an old rail spur they'd parked a Pullman on for a cheap set in cheap movies with bit actors who would never amount to anything. The spur dead-ended at this corner of the lot, and gave way to the sea of concrete, and to real pictures being made, and to the job he had: sweeping that gray sea, him in his old slouch cap, the coveralls he always wore, that broom beside him like it was a lost dog wouldn't leave him alone.

The Pullman sat up on the rails like any other car, the gravel on either side of it spilling away like any other railbed. A gravel railbed like one a punk kid had been pushed onto from a boxcar full of laughing tramps, that barefoot kid left only to pick the grit out of his hands and his knees before he figured a way to the New World on the coast of California to become a star.

A punk kid. A snot-nosed know-nothing kid, couldn't get a part in a stupid two-reeler. Here to watch the damned thing be shot, same as any snot-nosed kid would pull off a scab only to watch blood well right up in its place.

But something was coming. Something. It was all he had left to hope: that something was coming.

He picked up the broom, edged out from the fence toward the hubbub, and started at the sweeping, hoping someone might see him. Because the only way you got a part was if you were seen. There wasn't any-thing coming, Earl knew better than anything else, if you weren't seen.

Every night at the table in the house on Wilcox, while the fight over a chicken thigh or dumpling or forkful of green beans went on for the couple minutes it did, all any of the eleven men lived there talked about were the parts they were going to get, or the parts they had lost, the parts they had deserved, the parts the parts the parts. Every sentence Earl heard once he came in the door was about parts, including those from the owner of the place, a deaf old widower who held a tin horn to his ear whenever you talked to him, but who also cooked up the best food Earl'd ever eaten, including his momma's back home. But when the old man set the plates to table and the men dug in, he was talking about the parts he'd had too, how he'd been one of the Klansmen in *Birth of a Nation,* the judge in *Thirty Days* with Wallace Reid, and a sailor who gets thrown overboard in five different reels of the Captain Kidd serial, among the four thousand other parts he'd had.

But Earl was acting in his own part, he always thought, pushing his broom, and wearing his coveralls and slouch cap, the tweed one he'd paid a dollar for before the crash. Back when a slouch cap looked snappy, had a kind of kipped up shine of hope to it, even Harold Lloyd wearing one now and again. Then here had come the crash, and now the cap was only what a sweeper wore every day to work.

And the crash? One thing he liked about work on the lot was the fact there'd never come a crash to this place. Walking onto the lot, past the iron gates at the Paramount entrance and at DeMille and here at Columbia—at any lot, really—was like strolling into a foreign country where Roosevelt's alphabet soup might as well have been a sad movie they were watching from here inside. Sure, the actors cried in the *Reporter* and *Variety* about the cuts they'd taken in pay. But the money'd never stopped here, seemed even to roll in all the harder the worse things got outside the golden city.

He'd seen stars and directors and producers all dressed to the nines and gabbing so much you couldn't hope to chunk in a word even when you were there and holding open the door of that Stutz or the now-and-again Silver Ghost. He'd seen whole parades of people with too much money to know what to do with: Richard Arlen in his beaver coat, and Fay Wray in those pearls she always wore, Mervyn LeRoy and his alligator shoes that cost more than Earl had seen in seven years of work, and Mary Astor and Clara Bow and Betty Bronson all honeyed up in mink and chinchilla and sable too, all of them talking to each other and over each other and around each other so that nobody, nobody was listening at all.

The directors were different, though he couldn't figure out how you were supposed to treat them if you were a star. Sometimes the actors trailed them like dogs yapping, trying to make their master happy. King Vidor made people do that, and that Kraut Fritz Lang did too. And of course there was Mr. DeMille and the way he walked, head down low and watching the ground like it might tell him something, while around him people, no matter you were a script girl or Claudette Colbert, walked in awe and silence and waited for whatever word came for them to jump and how high they ought to do it.

Earl'd watched Mr. DeMille shoot part of that one with Colbert, *The Sign of the Cross*. He'd gotten into the soundstage with his broom in his hand to see the famous scene with Colbert as Nero's wife bathing naked in asses' milk, her all the while trying to seduce Fredric March, Nero's first in command, who's trying not to look at her because he's in love with one of the Christians he's supposed to feed to the lions.

Here had sat Mr. DeMille in his director's chair, with what little hair he had left slicked back on his head and those round owl-eye glasses on, the megaphone tight in his hand like it was a bag of money. However saucy Colbert ended up when she was on the screen wasn't anywhere near the fearful thing she was on the set: Every time DeMille shouted "Cut!" she'd drop the hard frolic of Nero's wife, and here was a naked and shivering girl in whited-up water, her standing up and wrapped in a towel by a stagehand quick as could be. Then she'd squint to try and find Mr. DeMille past the lights bright on her, looking to see what she'd done wrong, while Fredric March would turn from it all to light up a cigarette and puff away in his toga, a crown of gold laurel leaves on his head.

They were all scared of Mr. DeMille, Earl could see, Colbert chief among them for whatever it was he was about to say. But the day Earl'd watched them shoot this part of *The Sign of the Cross,* Mr. DeMille had only popped out the single word "Again!" sharp through the megaphone. In answer, the world shut down and moved backward in time a minute or so to let Colbert get all sizzled up and naked again, and Fredric March get all nervous and fidgety again. Earl, broom in hand, couldn't see the difference from one take to the next, nine of them in a row, before Mr. DeMille seemed happy enough not to shout "Again!"

He'd seen them shoot that one, and'd had that much to croon about over dinner at the boardinghouse. But it was news, like always, that was lost and one-upped and shouted down for everybody else's talk about parts, and what was the word on parts out of *Variety*, and who'd been seen betting on which horse at Agua Caliente down in Tijuana, and what has-been silent star had dosed and been found dead, and parts and parts and parts.

Of course it was at the table a week ago he'd heard about this shoot, and the casting call. Cal Garney, his bunkmate, a cool cucumber from Sacramento who spent ten minutes every morning grooming his Adolphe Menjou mustache, had crowed about how he had the inside dope on the call the next morning for some two-reeler over at Columbia, and how he was going to be in it, even get a line this time. Cal was a couple years older than Earl, and'd been in eleven pictures so far—he kept count by notching the bedrail closest to the wall so the old man wouldn't see it, convinced, he'd told Earl, that the bed would end up in a museum one day—but hadn't yet landed a line.

That next morning Earl'd gotten up before Cal, quiet out of the room and into the bathroom at the end of the hall. He had the beat-up manila folder he kept his glossies in under his arm, in his hands his clothes, him intent on beating Cal to the punch this time. Like he did for every call, he put on his one good shirt, the white McDonald with blue pinstripes, and the only tie he had, a red rayon Olds and King hand-painted with what looked like palm tree leaves. He Brylcreemed flat his hair, then parted it down the middle, made the one little curl above his left ear. The same getup he had on in his glossies.

Like always, he took the Yellow Car to Central Casting out in Burbank, and like every time, the call was nothing more than a casting girl behind a foldout table in a hallway. Though he'd made it to the call at eight on the dot, Cal still asleep for all Earl knew, the line was already fifty people long.

Not fifteen minutes later, it was his turn. The casting girl had Carole Lombard hair and eyebrows plucked to single rows of hairs, in one hand a cigarette in a bright red holder. To her right on the table sat a thick pile of glossies facedown, to her left a thin pile faceup. Between them lay a clipboard and a series of typed out lines: the roles she was looking for.

She said nothing, didn't even look up from the clipboard. But this silence was his cue, Earl knew from as many times as he'd been through this, to hand her his glossy, one of the seven he had left of the latest batch of fifty.

Then he gave her his line: "Hiya, doll." He leaned toward her over the table, smiled the same smile he'd given in the glossy, the left corner of his mouth up, his lips open the smallest bit, his eyebrows just so. He'd been going for Buddy Rogers in *Working Girls,* and knew this damned smile better than the calluses on his hands.

"Never heard that one before," she said. She took a drag off the cigarette, the holder the same gash-red as her lips. With her other hand she took the glossy, all without looking up at him.

She made to pass it off to the facedown pile, but then she paused, looked at it a moment longer, another moment. Earl felt his face go instantly hot, the blood rush for this extra second of his face in her hand.

She squinted up at him. "Say," she said and drew the word out too long. "Haven't I seen you pushing a broom over at the Columbia lot?"

She shot the smoke out and, without looking away from Earl, set his glossy on the facedown pile, one slow and smooth movement that spelled all he needed to know.

He looked to his left, down to the end of the hall and the frosted glass door there, a door he'd never made it through yet for the end of the trip these calls always were. There was an agent in there, a man who'd see him for what he was. A man who would see he was an actor.

He turned back to the girl, who took in another hard drag on the cigarette.

Aren't you the ten-cent trick I saw working the alley off Highland? he'd wanted to say, right then, right there, the words lined up and ready just that fast.

But he couldn't, and wouldn't. She was the casting girl, the front line that kept the rabble out of the office at the end of the hall, and word would get out, and that would be that. He'd only held on to that Buddy Rogers smile, nodded, said, "Ma'am, I'd sure like a part in this fine picture."

"Next?" she'd said too loud, and looked down to the clipboard.

Like every time he didn't get the part, he told himself it didn't matter he didn't get it. That was what he knew, the one single thing he'd gathered about him to keep himself strong after all he'd been through out here: a part didn't matter. Because there was another part in a minute, another one just around the corner, just down the street, right outside your window, just turn over that rock right there in front of you. And there it'd be: another part.

"Thank you, ma'am," he'd said, and left.

Last night, once lights were out and he and Cal were lying in the dark and smoking the last butt of the night, Cal was all goosey about the shoot and how he'd gotten a part in it. "I'm a sophisticate in this one," he said there in the dark, "which of course is what I'm after. Warner Baxter, John Boles. That's me. The agent saw it."

Earl was silent, only watched smoke off his cigarette swirl up in the dark above him, and thought of that casting girl, those eyebrows of hers, and the bottle blond of her. Cal had shown up near nine, gotten past the girl and in to see the casting agent proper. He was as broke as Earl, worked as a dishwasher at the Pig'n Whistle, the closest Cal'd ever gotten to any stars the rinsing off of their dirty plates, and Earl wondered like he did every time Cal got a part what it was Cal had that he didn't.

He heard Cal moving, turned and saw in the dark him pull out the Barlow knife he kept in a shoe beneath his bed, then face the wall and lean over to carve the next notch in the bedrail over there. When he'd finished, he leaned over toward Earl's bunk, snapped shut the knife, and half-whispered, "Magic Number Twelve is the one in which the world will hear me speak!"

Earl wanted to ask him, like he wanted every time, what Cal knew, what it was *like* and how could he get hold of that to get himself *his* own part. But even before he set the knife back in the shoe, Earl said, "Every one you ever been in you predicted the same thing."

Cal drew in on his cigarette, the tip a bright orange that faded soon as it found itself, and Earl thought of his brother Curtis smoking out on the sleeping porch the night before Frank died, his momma in her room and crying already for what she knew was coming. Then Cal shot out the smoke, took a deep breath. Earl could see out the corner of his eye Cal ease back onto his pillow, both hands behind his head now, the fading orange tip some kind of dagger and blessing in Earl at the same time: It didn't happen to me; but if it happened to Cal, it will happen to me.

"Back at the Pullman," Cal'd said in the dark, "is where we're shooting, if you deign to grace us."

Still the crew worked at the railcar, fed cable this way and that, tilted the lights every which way, slipped in front of those lights first this gel and then another. Two men were up on ladders leaned against the Pullman itself, in their hands a bucket of green paint each, slathering the thing one end to the other to make it shine, while under the car three more men quick pulled weeds that'd grown in since the last time anybody'd been back here.

The camera, up on its tripod, stood in a steel cart with small rail wheels, the eyeline of the camera, Earl could see, even with the windows of the Pullman. Just past the cart five more men were nearly done laying wood and rail the length of the Pullman itself: a dolly track on the concrete for the shot they were going to line up. The camera was splayed open, and a man up in the cart wearing a beret and with his sleeves rolled back swished at the insides with a soft brush to clean things up before they loaded in the film.

Inside the Pullman, more of the crew worked more lights, these down on the floorboards, five or six men all bent to the work of moving them around. The lights were pointed up so that, even in this morning light, the car seemed to spill out light from its own sun, and now tarps were being lifted into place on the back side, where the sun came in all of its own. Only here to Hollywood would they block the sun for need of light.

To the right and twenty yards off was the gray metal siding of the last stage on the lot, an old dead one with holes in the roof that was sometimes used to pen cattle for other sets on the lot. Against that gray wall, like a testimony to the cold fact of what a cheap shoot this was, stood two khaki tents, what looked like leftovers from the Great War: dressing rooms. No trailers here, nor cars parked and ready to go pick up the stars from their bungalows. Just Army tents.

A cheap two-reeler nobody'd even sneeze at when it came out in the month or so it would take to slap together.

Now here came out of the old stage a small clutch of people. Earl stopped with the broom, leaned on it, and watched the players—seven of them, he counted—move out in a posse. They were all in costume, dressed like people you might see on a train, Cal in with them, him in a gray suit with a celluloid collar and a straw boater, his Adolphe Menjou mustache doing its sophisticate work, Earl could see even from here.

Earl had never ridden a train save for in a boxcar, so though he knew these people were dressed for travel, he knew that the only people he'd seen dressed for riding on a train were people he'd seen in pictures dressed for riding on a train. There was so much he'd seen since moving here, and so much of it the big awful lie: a soundstage dance floor crowded with a hundred people in evening gowns and tuxedos, but that dance floor kept waxed so sharp you'd swear no one ever stepped foot on it; gangsters who got shot with fifty rounds off a tommy gun and whose clothes got nary a hole, no blood to be found anywheres at all; a naked woman bathing in asses' milk who was, after it all, nothing but a scared girl.

But it seemed what these folks wore was the real thing. Three of them were dolled up glamour girls in long dresses, almost evening gowns but not quite as showy. In with the posse was a heavyweight matron in a black skirt and jacket and small black hat with flowers around the thin brim, and a professor type with those glasses that pinched on at the bridge of his nose and a shoestring hanging off one end.

At the head of them all and talking to the script girl—she was a cute thing, Earl saw, with bright red hair and a gray skirt and green sweater, a pencil tucked behind her ear and a clipboard in her arm— was the conductor of the train, and Earl thought for a second he might recognize him. But it was always like that here. You saw someone on the street, or at the five-and-dime or at the diner or just anywhere doing anything, and you thought for a second *That's Warner Oland,* or *Isn't that Ruby Keeler?* or *That sure looks like Wallace Beery.* You knew it was somebody, then thought maybe it wasn't, or that it really was. But you had to keep walking or looking at the Brylcreem on the aisle at the five-and-dime or ask for another cup of coffee at the diner, because you couldn't stop and ogle and be thought of as nothing but a fan if that person—if it was Warner Oland or Ruby Keeler—saw you watching.

That's what it was like with this conductor, in his dark blue trousers and jacket with gold buttons, the jacket opened to show he had on a matching vest with a gold chain that led into the watch pocket, and the conductor's hat with the shiny black bill. That was somebody who'd been around. But Earl couldn't say who he was.

The script girl looked at the clipboard and talked while the conductor stood tall, his eyes to the set, the rest of the actors trailing behind. The painters were just this minute done and climbing down the ladders, and the weeds were gone, the lights both inside and out turned off now that they were set, that tarp in place on the far side so that from here the Pullman was dark inside.

Then every one of the crew, the all of them, stopped of a sudden and looked in one direction away from the car, and now the posse of actors turned their heads the same way, and stopped dead.

The tent flaps were open, and here came the stars from inside. All three of them, stepping out onto the concrete sea, and to everyone set up just for them.

9

Earl had seen them in a few shorts, but not without
Ted Healy, their straight man in that crumpled hat
he always wore, a hat not a whole lot different than the
man he'd seen killed had worn. The three of them
looked lost out here on the lot, somehow too alone for
the fact that Healy, who stood head and shoulders
taller than all three, wasn't in the lead.

These Stooges boys were a flash in the pan, Earl
knew already, no matter how big they might have been
in vaudeville and on Broadway or in that handful of
shorts. Everybody on earth knew they lost the contract
at MGM once Healy'd gone, this shoot their first for
Columbia. It was the end of them, sure, Earl thought
as he pushed the broom closer to the hubbub of it all.
Better that he hadn't landed a part in this wreck of a
picture.

To the right stood the fat one with the shaved head—
Curly, Earl knew, only for the joke of a bald man being
called that. He had on a yellow wool suit with brown
stripes, that suit three sizes too small, the sleeves
halfway up his forearms, and wore red leather shoes so
big he might as well have been in the circus. On the left
was the one with steelwool hair nearly to his slumped
shoulders, his suit an old black one three sizes too big,
the sleeves hiding his hands. And in the middle stood
the one with the bangs and pinched-up mouth, his suit
closest to fitting best, but too long in the back so that

he looked almost like a maestro. His shoes were just as big as Curly's, but were white patent leather with heels so thick it was a wonder he could keep his balance.

They stood there out front of the tent a moment, the all of everybody on the set looking at them, and then like it was all planned out—like it was a part of the picture and the cameras were already rolling—the one with bangs turned to the fat one and slapped him with a long stalk of limp celery he'd pulled from nowhere. The fat one fell down flat, kicked and wiggled his feet up in the air like he was a mule rolling in sand, and then the one with the steel-wool hair yelled "Hey!" and the one with the bangs quick turned to him, gave him a two-fingered eye poke. The steel-wool hair one bent in half over the pain of it, which got him in too close to Curly's feet up in the air, giving him a kick in the chin, which made him stand up too fast and knock his head into the chin of the one with the bangs. Then they two collapsed to the ground, all three of them suddenly flat and still and on their backs.

All of it in two seconds.

Everyone laughed, from the script girl and the tall conductor to the men who'd pulled weeds to the painters to the cameraman in the beret. The whole set laughed, loud and long and sharp in this bright morning air.

Earl stood outside this all, though he was close enough to touch the camera and dolly cart. But he wasn't inside the circle, however invisible it was, that meant he was *here*.

Because he wasn't. He was the lot man, the sweeper. The janitor with a glossy facedown in a pile, the only thing left him, like every time he was on a set, the sick delight of watching them all do what he wanted to do.

But there was something in what he'd just seen that he didn't think was funny, and he wasn't sure why.

Sure, he was leaning on a broom handle, watching a picture about to be shot, one he didn't even want to be in, but one he wanted to be in with everything he had. His life a scab, him come here to pick at it, while still everybody—Cal's head was tipped back for his laughing so loud, that boater about to fall off—carried on and on and on.

Earl looked at the Stooges again, looked at them, flat on their backs and still. Then Curly gave a shiver head to toe, a quick bolt of lightning through him that lifted him off the ground and made his arms and legs all quiver at once, a shot that was over soon as it'd begun. One last hammy gag.

But in that moment of movement and laughter all Earl could see was Ben Turpin before a scrap-wood fire outside Albuquerque, his skull crushed in by Montagu Love. He only saw the quick shiver that man with the battered hat and the donkey-tail mustache had given, the same bolt through him, to show Earl, a punk kid hot on his way to Hollywood who'd thought it all no more than a flicker show, what it was to die.

He'd seen a man killed.

Now everything seemed to fall in on him, seemed for this laughter out of the whole world and himself silent in it to crush him somehow with a thought that'd never entered his mind, through all the escapes he'd made into the Rose back in Tyler, and through the feel of those velvet chairs, and through the mournful sound of the old lady with long hair down past her shoulders making love through her piano to the flicker stars up there on the screen.

Stars he'd seen—*people* he'd seen—up close and ugly, from the pimples on Clara Bow's forehead as she climbed out of her Duesenberg to the murky, ginned-up eyes of John Barrymore as he staggered out of his bungalow, two gate guards propping him up to haul him to a set, to Billy Haines strolling around the MGM lot between scenes for *Just a Gigolo,* his pansy boyfriend Jimmie Shields on his arm for all the world to see.

A thought came to him, unbidden and unwelcome at once, a thought in the face of slapstick and death right here in front of him, with all the world laughing for it, all save him: Were they all laughing, he wanted to know, because they believed it was funny, or were they laughing because the stars of this two-bit picture *expected* them all to laugh?

Was a picture nothing more than making you watching it do what you didn't have a mind to do?

Was a picture shot only to make you *think* you knew what it was to laugh, or to cry, or to get all stiff watching a naked come-on vamp bathe in asses' milk, when all the while she was just a scared girl shivering between takes?

He knew the old trick of everything Hollywood really was: a series of pictures flickered in front of your face to make you think what you saw was real. The same old trick as sitting inside the black beyond black of a boxcar, while out the wedge of open door stars seemed to move past, and moonlit desert, far-off mountains, all of it moving and moving. But not moving at all. He knew that old trick, knew it as close as he did these damned calluses, and the angle of his own lips in a glossy, and the shapeless smoke-ghost off a cigarette as he lay in bed and listened to his friend grinning at the good fortune of a bit part in a Stooges picture.

But those stars out the boxcar door were fixed in the sky, he knew. They weren't ever going to change, and it'd been him who was moving, himself the one quick on his way to the shit end of a broom, and to calluses with no point, and to six glossies left before he'd have to scrape up enough dough from God knew where to buy another set. Earl, quick to the dead end of a rail spur in a sea of concrete, himself left only to sweep it all clean.

He looked at the three of them, these Stooges, still in a heap on the ground, clown shoes on and in suits out of a trash bin, haircuts like they'd done them themselves in a broken mirror.

He took in a breath, felt his neck go cold, his hands go tight on the broom handle.

Was the all of this, he wanted to know, your whole life, what you'd done with twenty-one years of it, only a worthless somersault on a bedroom floor for a brother you already knew was going to die?

Still they all laughed. The conductor took off that shiny-billed hat of his and put one hand to a hip; the cameraman shook his head and leaned back, his shoulders heaving; the painters and carpenters and weeders and posse of actors all still laughed, and now the tent flaps on the other tent opened, and here stood two men in suits—the director and writer, Earl figured—laughing too, though they hadn't seen a thing.

The Stooges finally looked up, just lifted their heads from where they lay flat on the ground. It was the steel-wool hair one to smile first, then Curly.

But the one with the bangs and that pinched-in mouth wasn't smiling, his eyes quick to the crowd before he was even on his elbows. The three of them got up off the concrete, dusted off those costumes, and here came a round of applause from everyone, and the two smiling ones shrugged, smiled bigger, gave little waves.

Still the one with the bangs and that maestro's coat hadn't smiled, his eyes moving and moving, scanning the crowd, for what Earl couldn't say.

Then his eyes met Earl's. His mouth seemed to pinch up even tighter, and he stopped dusting off his hands, the man frozen a moment inside the laughter and smiles.

He was looking at Earl.

Earl blinked, swallowed. He stood from leaning on the broom, took the handle in both hands, this lost dog wouldn't leave him alone suddenly his best friend as he bent to that concrete, took a clean and serious swipe across it, and another.

But here came the one with the bangs toward him, Earl could hear, those huge white patent-leather shoes heavy and purposeful on the concrete, and Earl heard now too the laughter seem to die off, felt a silence coming up, cold and obvious, inside that silence the sharp slap of footsteps across the concrete, all twenty yards between the two of them.

"You," he heard, the word a black stab meant only for him, and Earl glanced up a footstep later, as though unaware it was himself this man was after.

What he saw made the cold of his neck turn white hot, and his face too, and his hands wrapped tight on that broom handle: the entire crew and all the actors and even the other two Stooges were all turned to him, and watching him. Earl, the brightest bright center of the world.

Gone, just like that, was any thought on the meaning of his life, or on a dead man by a scrap-wood fire, or a somersault for the only person ever cared a whit about him. All of it gone, just like that.

"Yeah, you," the man with the bangs said, and Earl stopped with the broom, held it an inch or so above the ground in mid-sweep.

Now here he was beside Earl, the man a good six inches shorter. His mouth was pinched in so tight his lips were gone, and Earl could see in the pocket of his maestro coat the top end of that limp celery stalk.

"Look at me, wise guy," the man said, his jaw clenched. "Drop the sweeper gag, too," he said.

Earl blinked, made his eyes finally meet this man's, the move just to bring his eyes to meet his hard work, solid work. His eyes were black, and seemed ratcheted down to pinpoints of cold stone.

"I said drop it," he said, and instantly Earl let go the broom, heard it clatter to the concrete.

He heard a small wave of sound from behind the man, a sound from the set and all those gathered to watch whatever was happening.

It was laughter they'd given out, he only now heard. They'd laughed. This was the end of it, himself fired even from pretending to sweep lots.

Finally, he'd been seen.

"Wise guy, eh?" the man said, and put his hands on his hips. Earl felt his own hands at his sides, useless stripped of that costume prop of the broom. "Not funny, eh?" the man said, and crossed his arms.

"Sir?" Earl said, and let his eyes drop to the man's clenched jaw again.

"Look at me, wise guy!" the man said. He leaned in close, and Earl's eyes shot to his again.

"Moe," the one with steel-wool hair called out, "leave the sap alone."

"I'll leave him alone. I'll leave him alone," he whispered, words meant only for Earl again, his eyes even smaller, sharper. "So, Mr. Broom, what's not to laugh at?" he whispered. He crossed his arms again, put them back on his hips again, just that quick.

135

"Why weren't you laughing, Mr. Wise Guy, eh?"

"Hey, Moe," Curly said, "like he said. Leave the boy alone."

"Moe," Earl heard now, from farther off, and let his eyes for a moment leave the ice-pick stare Moe gave to see it was one of the two men in suits at the tent who'd called out.

"Moe," one of them said, and slowly shook his head. "He's off the set. He's gone, Moe, so let's get back to—"

"Come with me," Moe said, and grabbed hold hard to Earl's arm through his coveralls, yanked him away from that broom, and the chain-link fence, and any chance he ever had of finding what was coming.

He pulled Earl through the thin ring of the crew, past the cameraman and the weeders and set men, their jaws dropped open like they were singing the lowest notes to the song everybody out here was singing, all of them with their mouths open, stunned into silence.

They were headed for the other two Stooges, and Earl saw Curly with his hands at his sides look up and away, his eyes squinted for the morning light, and saw the steel-wool-hair one look at the ground, slowly shake his head. The two men in suits were walking toward them, too, and both of them reached into their jackets at the same time and pulled out sunglasses, slipped them on like it was a routine of their own, some sad gag in which they fired the lot man in front of the whole wide world.

"Moe—" the one who'd called out began.

"Look at him, Archie!" Moe shot out before the man—the director, Earl knew—could say another word, and now they were together, the three Stooges and the writer and director and Earl himself in a knot out front of an entire set and crew for a confab in which the sweeper gets the boot.

A scene right out of a flicker. An old Chaplin one, maybe. Or maybe a Mack Sennett, himself in the next shot getting run over by a bus or a streetcar or dropped from a plane.

But this time he shut down the notion of his life being a flicker. What, he wondered, even through the hot wash of blood to his face, and through the thick cloud of eyes on him, and through those talons on his arm digging in and digging in, had seeing his life as a flicker ever gotten him? Where had it led? Only, of course, to here, and to getting fired for not laughing at a hammy gag.

He let himself think again on that green out to Hawkins, the sweetness of the air of a morning, the sun just breaking above the tree line, and his longing for it all.

What he'd seen wasn't funny. These Stooges and their celery stalk and Curly's death quiver just weren't funny, and he'd seen that.

"What do you mean, 'Look at him'?" the director said, and pulled from his jacket pocket a pipe, put it to his mouth. He glanced at Earl, back to Moe. "I told you he's off the set. He's fired. You won't have to—"

"Look at him," Moe said, and let go Earl's arm, took a small step back.

The steel-wool-hair one let out a deep breath, shook his head. "Moe, we can't—"

"Oh yes we can," Moe said. He was smiling now, though his eyes hadn't lost the sharp stab, and though his lips were still pinched in. But somehow there was a smile inside there, Earl could see.

That was when Moe shot out a hand toward Earl's face. Earl flinched, but all Moe did was tap the bill of Earl's slouch cap, then put his hand back to his hip.

"He's already in costume," Moe said. "I can see it already. He'll be in the middle of the car, his back to the window, and he'll have a newspaper out and reading it. When we pass, he'll shake the paper a bit." He paused. "Won't even see these coveralls. Just this cap, and the top edge of a newspaper shaking when we pass." He paused again, seemed to size Earl up as though he'd never seen him before, head to toe, and the director pulled the pipe from his mouth, crossed his arms. "College boy," Moe said, "riding home to see his momma. That's what it'll look like."

What were they talking about? College boy? A newspaper?

"Moe, we already blocked it out," the steel-wool-hair one said, a kind of whine on his voice. He shook his head again. "We already got the gag all set."

"Larry," Moe said. His eyes were still on Earl, still sizing him up. "What you lack is the desire to meet a challenge." He took another small step back, and the steel-wool-hair one—Larry—let out a low whistle of air, still shook his head. *"Mea culpa!"* Moe said. "Seize the day!" and pointed to Earl's chest.

What was he talking about? Earl still wondered, and blinked. A costume?

"Or is it *Veni, vidi, vici*?" Moe said, suddenly right up in Earl's face, his finger sharp on Earl's chest now, digging in.

Earl swallowed, swallowed again, then managed out with everything he had, "If you'll let me, sir, I'll just get my broom and clear on out of here."

They all laughed, this clutch of people who knew everything in the world just this moment, and not a sliver of it available for Earl. What were they talking about? Why were they laughing, including Moe, who took a step away again and shook his head at Earl? Both the director and writer were looking at each other and laughing, Larry laughing too, and even Curly, who'd only squinted up at the sky all this while.

Why wouldn't they let him go? Why were they laughing?

And what was this talk about costumes?

"Let's do it, Moe," the director said, and the other one, the writer, put his hands in his pockets, shrugged once. They both turned, headed back to the tent. "Five minutes," the director called out loud to the air, and for a moment Earl wondered what that was about too, what calling out a couple of words to this bright and evil morning could mean.

But in the next second he heard movement all around,

and it came to him, something he knew from all the shots he'd seen, all the sets he'd been on: this was the last heads-up before things got started, and the shoot, and the making of a picture. Of course he knew that.

Earl started to turn away, hoped to salvage a quick exit in the midst of all this activity—it didn't seem anybody'd *fired* him, and maybe he could still just get hold of that broom and slip out of here. But before he'd even turned all the way around, here were those talons on his arm again, and the hard tug of Moe back to face him. Here were those eyes again, any smile he might have had long gone.

"Son," Moe said, his voice back to that whisper, "are you retarded or something?"

Earl looked at him, blinked yet again.

What was this about? What was he after in this? What did the man *want* of him?

"I'm scared is all," Earl heard himself say, the words a surprise soon as they came out. But, he knew in the same instant, the truest words he'd ever said.

Moe pinched his lips tight together again, his lips disappearing for it, and Earl suddenly knew the smile he thought he'd seen had never been there at all.

"Son," the man whispered, "we all are. So get used to it."

He nodded hard once, then looked past Earl's shoulder, jutted his jaw in that direction. "She'll take care of you," he said.

Earl quick looked over his shoulder, saw the script girl with her bright red hair and that green sweater

140

right behind him. Her eyes darted from Earl to Moe and to Earl again.

"Find him a newspaper," Moe said, and the girl shot out, "Yessir."

Moe slapped hard Earl's shoulder. Earl turned back to him, and here were his eyes again, ground down to pinpricks of black so sharp they could draw blood.

"I'll show you funny," he whispered. "Wise guy."

"Tough way to get a part," the script girl said.

They were walking fast back to the posse of bit players, Earl breathing in for the first time since he'd let go the broom. He was looking at the ground, and had to think about the next step, and the next, this concrete sea suddenly quicksand beneath him.

"What part?" Earl said.

"Oh, you kid," she said. "Stop with the gag already," and here they were to the actors, and the conductor, still with his hat off, and here was Cal too, his boater still on.

He hadn't been fired. At least he hadn't been fired. But for some reason he'd walked here with the script girl, and not to his broom.

He looked away, back to the fence, saw the broom lying there, waiting.

But he saw too the cameraman looking at him as he and another man loaded on a can of film, and saw the set men glance at him as they busied themselves with a last touch of paint, a last adjustment to the dolly track.

They were all working—five minutes, he remembered, five minutes—but all of them stealing a look at him, and another.

"Here," he heard a man's voice say beside him, and he turned, saw the conductor holding out a folded-up newspaper. "Haven't read it yet this morning, so I want it back."

The man smiled at him, but it was a kind of smile that didn't know what to make of itself: could be a glad-to-meet-you, Earl thought, or a smile you give to next of kin.

"Your first bit?" the man said.

Earl looked at the newspaper. It was folded in thirds, and he let it fall open in his hands, held it out in front of him.

A newspaper.

He saw words there, saw a photo of something. But suddenly they were words in another language, the photo something with angles and light and dark that made no sense, and seemed in the same instant held in the hands of someone else. Here was a newspaper, a mile away and in a foreign tongue. And he was the one holding it.

A part. He'd gotten a part.

Had he gotten a part?

He looked up from the paper to the conductor. His smile was different now: *Glad to meet you,* Earl could see loud and clear.

"Your first bit," the man said, and winked. "Just make sure I get that back," he said, and put the hat with the shiny bill back on.

Earl felt himself smile, felt himself nod. He said, "Thank you, sir." He glanced down at the newspaper, saw letters he might recognize now, saw the picture was of a person, maybe.

"Places!" the script girl called, and looked around at the actors. "Let's go," she said, and nodded toward the Pullman, then looked at her clipboard. The actors were all movement of a sudden: the dolled-up girls touched at each other's shoulders and tugged at the seams there, the conductor hitched up his pants a bit, the matron touched at her flower-brimmed hat. Then they were gone, headed for the Pullman.

But here was Cal suddenly beside him, smiling and smiling, reaching to Earl's shoulder and holding on and shaking him and smiling. "You cheesed him off pretty bad," Cal said, "so don't think I'm going to act like I'm your best pal from here on out." He shrugged, shook his head, still with that smile. "But Earl, boy," he said, "you got a part. You got a part!"

Then he too was gone, straightening his celluloid collar as he hustled away toward the Pullman.

"And you," the script girl said beside him. "Mr. Moxie," she said, and Earl looked at her. "I never seen anybody get the sweatbox like that just for a part," she said. "You must have balls of granite. But you got it. And you got your newspaper, Mr. Strong-arm. But I don't have a clue where you're supposed to go."

Her mouth was in a kind of smirk, the clipboard cradled in both arms, and now Earl noticed wrinkles beside her eyes he hadn't seen before, and a thin

143

wattle at her neck, the bright red of her hair, he could tell, just a shell over gray roots. The pencil she'd had tucked behind her ear was in her hand now, and Earl could see it was all bit to pieces.

She was near old as his momma, he figured. No cutie pie at all, and it seemed as if he'd only now, for the first moment in his life, put on a pair of glasses that gave him a way to see what he'd never seen before: Himself, an actor.

This was what it was like.

He looked at the newspaper, read the banner at the top, a banner only a lamebrain lot sweeper would think was in a foreign tongue: *Los Angeles Examiner,* he read, beneath it *April 3, 1934.*

He shook his head. He'd gotten a part.

"Best day of my life," he said to the woman, and winked at her, same as that conductor had to him. "I'm in the middle of the car, back to the window," he said. "I'm the college boy going home to see his momma."

He leaned in to her, pecked a kiss on her forehead, and pulled back, winked again. He turned from her to the everything inside this circle, and to the best day of his life.

"Just nail your cue, Mr. Hoo-ha," he heard her say.

Best day of my life, he whispered, and started for the Pullman, parked at this dead-end spur of the start of his life.

Then, as if it were a pebble of gold he'd suddenly found in his mouth, he whispered a word, the taste of it sweeter than he'd ever imagined it could be, after all the shit he'd eaten all his years here, from the casting calls to the doors he'd held open to the scabs he'd had no choice but to pick until they bled.

He whispered the word, savored it, let it flourish and thrive in his mouth a long moment.

Hurrah, he whispered.

What was wrong with a somersault? he wanted to know as he took hold of the bright brass handhold on the side of the green and gleaming Pullman, a railcar about to bustle with glamour and comedy and sound and *life.*

What was wrong with a somersault on the bedroom floor of a brother you knew was going to die, he wanted to know, especially if it made your brother *smile?*

He saw Frank's smile, slow and bewildered and uncertain of itself, and saw too his hand move out from beneath the quilts, reaching out to Earl.

He pulled himself up, and into the car.

10

He missed his cue the first three takes.

He couldn't get the newspaper in his hands to shake on time the Stooges tussled past him there inside the Pullman. Each time he heard that word *Cut!* shouted from behind him outside the window, he felt the eyes of the others—especially Moe—stabbing into him.

He'd thought it would be easier.

145

It was a gag that ran the full length of the car, Moe, Larry, and Curly tearing each other apart in a kind of acrobatic tumble head over heels, eye pokes galore, now and again that celery stalk making an appearance. The joke of it, of course, was that the camera outside just caught the highlights: One or the other or all three of them popped up in one window, and then the next, and the next, while people inside the car reacted to the fracas. The three glamour girls, closest to where the Stooges started at the far end of the car, all gave out squeals when the roll started, and the professor-type, just past the girls and on the other side of the car from Earl, let the pinched-on glasses on his nose fall off, his mouth open wide and eyebrows high on his forehead for the scuffle before him; next to him sat the matron, who let out a high-pitched "My *word*!" as it all churned past.

Then came Earl in his slouch cap, and the shake of that paper. The conductor was next in line, his bit to stand with arms crossed and watch the whole thing, the Stooges at that point pausing in the middle of it all, Moe with fist cocked at Larry, who had his hands in front of his face ready for the blow to fall, while Curly stood with his eyes screwed up in confusion, that celery stalk draped over his head.

They were to stop a moment, and look quick to the conductor, who'd caught them at the scrap, then a beat later continue brawling last past Cal, whose sophisticate reaction was to speak the line "Say!" and stand up, hands hard on his hips.

They'd run through it once before rolling, and Earl had gotten it right. But when the Stooges had walked back through the car and past Earl to set up again where they'd started, Moe had paused a moment—no more than an instant, if that—and looked at Earl, his eyes still those pinpricks of black.

"I'll show you funny," he'd whispered, the words again only for Earl, and Earl felt himself shiver, a cold gust through him.

Then Moe and the other two were back in place, and Earl wondered if Moe had even said anything to him.

But he had, and the look was enough of a cold gust through him to make him lose his place three times in a row, shake this paper in his hands too late. "Cut!" came through the window behind him, the word like a gunshot, the Stooges frozen in front of the conductor, Curly with that celery on his head, Larry braced for Moe's fist.

Like the two times before, here had been their eyes hard on him, especially Moe's, and those pinpricks of black.

"Try reading a line in the paper," he heard, and Earl turned in his seat, looked up at the conductor. "Try acting like you're reading the paper," the man said, "instead of watching out the corner of your eye what's coming your way." He wasn't smiling at Earl, but at least his words weren't tough on him.

Earl moved in his seat, only plywood and two-by-fours, the interior of the car stripped otherwise for the lights in here. The floorboards were littered with them, all pointed up, so that the conductor looked pale, older than he might really be; it seemed, too, the man might could have a set of false teeth on, for the way his upper and lower lips pooched out a bit. He had blue eyes, Earl only now noticed, and seemed somehow trying to help him.

"Read it?" Earl said.

"What else do you do with a paper?" the man answered, and glanced behind Earl, then to the Stooges. He looked back down to Earl, said, "Trust me, kid," and nodded.

"Yessir," Earl said, and opened the paper again, leaned back against the wall of the Pullman.

He heard the clap boy behind him call, "*Woman Haters,* scene nine, take four," and the snap of the clapper. "Action!" the director shouted once more.

Here they came.

But Earl's eyes were on the newspaper. He could see there were words, certainly, and he focused, read *the world and its,* and felt himself sweat in the instant the words came to him, words each perched alone and hollow against the gray newsprint, and before he'd even blinked there came a ruckus at his feet, and he shook the paper, shook it hard, then let it drop to see the Stooges a beat later standing in front of the conductor, his jaw clenched at these boobs fighting in a Pullman car, that ridiculous stalk of celery perched on Curly's head.

He hadn't heard any of the girls squeal, hadn't heard *My word!* out of the matron. He'd only heard a ruckus at his feet, felt that sweat, seen those words floating before his face. This was almost, he thought, magic.

Then the gag rolled on, and here, finally, came his bunkmate Cal's grand entry into talking pictures: "Say!" he said.

All of it, right on cue.

"And print!" came the director's voice from the megaphone.

"Let's do it again," Moe called out, before anyone could even move.

"Moe, it's fine," the director said, though not with the megaphone. But Moe was already walking back to the front of the car, all the bit players still in place, even if the word *print* meant that was the take the director wanted to use. Every time Earl'd heard it before, the actors, from bits to stars, knew to fold up shop and move on to whatever was next.

But here was Moe, already back into place at the far end of the car, Larry and Curly still down in their finish positions at the opposite end, there in front of Cal.

Moe glanced at Earl, nodded once. "Let's do it again," he said, the words this time more a growl than anything else.

"Moe, we got three days to make this picture," the director said, "and we don't need—"

"Archie!" Moe cut in.

"Let's go!" Earl heard the director say, quieter now, beaten, and heard too the grips push the camera back into place, while all the actors settled themselves again. Earl looked up at the conductor, who was rub-bing his chin, his eyes to what was going on outside.

"It worked," Earl whispered up at him, and held the paper out as if it were proof of some kind.

"Told you," the man said, still looking out the window. He glanced back to where the Stooges were settled, then down to Earl.

"Just keep it up. Read that paper," the man said, and paused. "But I don't get why we're rolling again," he whispered. He ducked his head one way and another, looking out at the crew outside, behind Earl.

"Yessir!" he said, and suddenly felt a smile come up on him. He'd hit his cue, and he was an *actor,* and this was the beginning of everything.

This, he saw, was what he'd known was coming. He'd known it all along, even up to this morning, when he'd stood at that fence and seen the wonder and beauty of Hollywood and its hills and buildings, and the industry of that swing gang and the rest of the crew, and the crazy play of these Stooges, and he saw in this instant as well the genius of them, of giving Ted Healy the ax because, he realized, Why did slapstick need a straight man? Whoever said anybody needed a straight man?

He opened the newspaper to a different page, settled himself in the hard seat, all set and ready, because he was an *actor,* and he'd have news for them at the table tonight in the house on Wilcox. He'd come banging into the house tonight and shout into the old man's tin horn loud as he could, *I got my part!* and count on an extra thigh or drumstick in it for him.

Then the thought came to him, one even sweeter than the crowing of his news at the dinner table, even more rewarding than carving a notch into his own bedrail: he'd send a telegram home.

He'd show them all what he was made of. The only word he'd ever sent from here had been the now and again picture postcards, written on them no return address or news of a job sweeping lots, only the scribbled line that he was doing fine. He'd sent one of the La Monica Ballroom on Santa Monica Pier to Pearl, the sister closest to his own age; another, this one of a set in the middle of filming some picture he couldn't name, he'd sent to his closest brother, Chilton, whose quick breaths in and out as they lay on the sleeping porch the night before Frank died had always seemed to Earl some sort of pact between them. He'd even sent one to his daddy of the coastline down near Laguna Beach, a place he hadn't gotten to yet, but that he thought his daddy might like to see for how strange the view, all those black rocks, swept up into them the cool blue sea.

But he hadn't sent a thing to his momma. No way in hell would he have allowed her the pleasure of climbing into bed of an evening, her spectacles off and tucked into her handkerchief and set on the dresser, her hair down in those twin braids, to hold a picture postcard close and savor some sunny California view. And maybe, just maybe, savoring word from her boy too.

No way in hell would he have granted her that

blessing, and that joy, of knowing her kid, the one she'd damned with a slap, was even thinking on her. Then again, she'd probably burn the thing in the stove the minute it came in the post.

But a telegram. A telegram! That was the ticket, to let her know he was on his way, to slap her in the face on his own with the good news of his career as an actor begun this day, and himself—

"Action!" he heard, the world and his plans for it wrapped and gone in that one word. But still he smiled: he knew what he was doing, knew how to be an *actor.*

Tonight! he read, his eyes as comfortable with words on a sheet of paper as ever, *The Cocoanut Grove Presents the New Swing Sensation! Kay Kyser and his—*

He saw a celebration in these words, saw an evening dressed in his best and not these coveralls and costume slouch cap. He'd have some dough at the end of the day, and felt himself smile even bigger at the picture in his head of him and Cal marching over to the paymaster's office and turning in his pay slip and getting the money right on the spot, like every bit and extra got paid. There'd be money in his pocket, money nearly to burn, and he and Cal could go to the Cocoanut Grove after dinner and the news *I got a part!* he'd deliver to the table—he'd have to borrow a jacket from Cal or somebody else in the house—and they could head out after dinner and then—

Here was something at his feet, a struggle rough and loud, and the paper shook in his hands at the surprise of it. He quick brought it down, looked to see a fight at his feet roiling past, then this wad of three men stand of a sudden before a conductor with his arms crossed, his jaw clenched.

One of them, with bangs, was about to punch in the nose a slope-shouldered man with steel-wool hair. Next to him stood a fat bald man in a yellow wool suit too small on him, the trousers split at the fly and tied together with a shoelace.

Draped on his head, the pale green leaves down between his eyes, was a limp stalk of celery.

The smile on Earl exploded into a laugh, a single burst of sound out of him that led to another, and another, his shoulders heaving, his mouth open for how funny this all was: three grown men caught fighting in a Pullman car, the conductor about to give them the heave-ho right out onto the gravel railbed, and didn't they deserve it, these stooges! And that celery stalk, that celery stalk!

"Cut!" he heard.

He felt the laugh in him tail off dead at that gunshot word, felt his chest collapse, his throat seal off forever.

He'd laughed in the take.

"Next scene!" Moe shouted.

He was smiling at Earl, his eyes easy now, those pinpricks only a man's eyes. Here he was, coming straight at him, and Earl wondered a moment at the strangeness of everything, of a Pullman car on a dead-end spur housing the humor and mystery and ever-evolving tale of Earl's own life, this place on earth where he'd been let in on the secret and age-old sorcery of *story*.

Himself too stupid, Earl knew already, not to laugh in the take.

"Told you I'd show it to you," Moe said to him now. He held out a hand to Earl.

Earl blinked, swallowed, still smiling. He folded the newspaper in on itself, tucked it under his arm. He took Moe's hand, stood as he shook it.

"It was funny," Earl said, and let go Moe's hand. "All y'all were funny," he said, and quick nodded behind Moe to where Larry and Curly stood, beside them the conductor, his arms still crossed, his eyes to the floor. "Guess I couldn't help myself," Earl said. He shrugged, smiled, the words out of him a grab at something he couldn't see, a reach for some solid place he wasn't even certain was out there.

Slowly Curly reached a hand to his head and, his eyes on Earl, found the celery stalk, put it in the pocket of his yellow wool suit. Larry cleared his throat, and moved off and away.

"Everyone, let's go!" Earl heard from outside, not the director but the voice of that script girl with the thin wattle at her neck, that impossible red shell of hair. "Back inside for shot seventeen."

Now the bit players around him were up and moving out of the Pullman, while still Moe stood before him, his eyes easy, and friendly, and just the least bit, Earl thought he could see, cold.

He felt the familiar race of blood to his face again,

heard the commotion dim to a dull buzz in his ears as the swing gang kicked in like lightning, breaking everything down. "All y'all were funny," he tried again, but the words merely trickled out of him, seemed to puddle up in a pool of black blood on the ground around him, himself dead by a broken bottle he'd smashed on his very own head.

"Don't I know it, kid," Moe said. He reached up to Earl's shoulders, put both hands there: those talons again. "I know what's funny," he said, "and when you don't laugh, all I know is it's my job to teach you." He looked at Earl's left shoulder, pinched off it an invisible piece of nothing, flicked it away. "I know funny," he said, "and now you do too."

Moe took in a slow breath, while outside men tore down lights and dolly tracks, and actors moved to the next set for the next shot, and a director and writer eased off into an old Army tent, and the rest of the whole ugly world moved right along without Earl.

"I catch you anywhere near one of my sets again," Moe said, and leaned in so close his chin nearly touched Earl's chest, "and you'll be on the next train to Hayseed so fast you'll forget to bring your name." He let his hands drop, put them into his maestro coat's pockets. "You understand?" he said, and eased back. He was still smiling, happy, Earl could see, while still his own face burned, his hands hot at his sides.

He looked down at the floorboard of the car, at his coveralls, and at the white patent-leather shoes this man who believed he knew everything wore. Clown shoes, for a clown whose job was to clown in front of a camera for people who'd know he was a clown the second they laid eyes on him in whatever stupid picture this was. *Woman Haters,* the clap boy had announced each time he slapped the clapper. What a name for this wreck of a picture.

But he'd been in the picture. He'd been in it, even if it was only the back of his slouch cap and a newspaper he shivered in his hands.

Earl swallowed, felt air in his lungs of a sudden, and felt the calluses on his hands, as though they might have been coins he'd been holding in his fists all along. He felt light burn into his eyes, and glanced to his left, saw the tarps come tumbling down in that instant. Here was the sun itself, the morning still new, that sun not yet even above the Pullman window.

He looked back at this stupid man with bangs, swallowed again.

"Thank you," he said.

"Thank you is right," the man said. "You're lucky I don't can your ass right here and now. You're lucky I don't get Harry Cohn out here and—"

"Moe, just get off it!" Larry called, and they both turned to see him outside on the concrete, his hands on his hips, shaking that head of steel wool in the midst of the crew breaking down and breaking down. "We got work to do!" he said.

"Lucky," Moe said, and turned, headed off to the end of the Pullman. "You're lucky," he said one more time without looking back. "If I see you again," he said, and he was down off the Pullman, and gone.

Men came onboard not a second later, started in on the lights inside here while they stole the same glances at Earl as he'd gotten when this whole thing had begun, and as he made his way toward the door and the platform and that great brass handle he'd pulled himself up with, he thought he heard a snicker here and there, low whistles, thin words—all of them about him—passed between the six or seven men already down on their hands and knees and working.

He held tight that gleaming brass handle on his way down the step—Frank would have laughed at those Stooges too, he tried to convince himself, Frank would have laughed—then, finally, he put a foot to the gravel railbed, and another, and here it was before him once more: that great gray sea of concrete. He looked to his right, off and away and outside the circle disintegrating before his eyes, the dolly tracks being torn apart and the cable being coiled and the camera rolling in its cart away and toward the old stage, to see his broom on the ground. That same lost dog, just waiting for him.

"Son," he heard from his left, and he turned.

It was the conductor, smiling at him. That hat with the shiny bill was pushed back a little on his head, his hands in his pockets. He nodded, said, "Can I get my paper back now?"

"Oh," Earl said, then, "Yes." He reached up to where he held it under his arm, handed it to the man. "Much obliged," he said.

"Forget it," the man said. He glanced down at the paper, then to Earl. He snapped the paper back into thirds, tucked it into the pocket of his jacket.

He breathed in, crossed his arms. "He treated you pretty badly," he said. "But it goes with the territory. You handled him best as anyone could, tell you the truth." He paused, seemed to look Earl up and down, same as everyone in the universe had today. He rocked back the smallest bit on his heels, then rocked forward. "Make you a deal," the man said. He leaned his head one way, then the other. "I like you. I think you're an okay Joe. Green as horseshit, but okay."

As with everything so far this day, Earl wanted to know what was going on, and why this bit player was even talking to him. He quick looked to the gray metal siding of the stage and those old tents, afraid Moe might be on his way back out here to fire him proper.

"Here's the deal," the man went on, and Earl looked at him. "Next time you see me on the lot somewhere, you come up to me and ask for my autograph, and you tell me how good I was in the last picture you saw me in."

"What?" Earl said, and leaned back an inch or so.

Who was this man? Sure, Earl might have seen him a time or two somewhere, he'd thought when he caught him coming out of the stage with that script girl. But he was nobody here.

"Look," the man said, and let out a breath. "You want to make it in this business, you got to quit being so damned starstruck. You have to look at this as a business." He paused, screwed up his mouth, seemed for a moment to think better of having said anything at all. But then he smiled again.

"The business here is getting someone to look at you. This here bit is the ninety-second picture I've done. It's number ninety-two, and I've been at it nine years." He looked down, shook his head, himself amazed, Earl saw, at his own life. He looked up at Earl again. "I'm turning forty years old this year, and even for all I've seen in this business I couldn't tell you one way or the other if these Stooges'll percolate on their own. But somebody upstairs thinks they can make the mash with this silly stuff." He shook his head again. "And that's their business. But my own business is being on for the long haul. I mean to make a mark. So *my* business is to get people to be starstruck at *me*. Not the other way around."

Earl put his hands in his pockets, looked at the ground, then to his broom, still waiting. "Sir," he said, "I don't even know who you are. I don't even know for certain if I even seen you in a picture before." He looked up at the man, sort of squinted at him, not for any sun in his eyes but for fear of what the man might say to this truth.

"You're missing the point," the man said. He was still smiling. "Who in this glorified cabin camp *knows* anybody? I can count on one hand the number of folks I truly know here. There's a couple hundred I've *worked* with, and who I know enough to get along with. You don't get work in as many pictures as I have and not know who to snuggle up to and who to stay clear of. But the people I count as friends—the folks I *know* here—got nothing to do with anything. What matters in all this claptrap is who sees you." He paused, looked to his left, and Earl could see his eyes were on the broom. The man nodded toward it, said, "And I don't mean being seen pushing a broom. I mean being *seen.*" He looked at Earl again, put a hand to the back of his neck, rubbed at it. Still he was smiling.

Earl shrugged. "At least I got a part."

"And blew up the bridge while you were at it." He shook his head the smallest bit. "My advice to you is to laugh at any gag you ever see anyone do who's had more parts than you have. And cry when that some-body wants you to. Wet your pants, and blow your nose, and eat their shit, and wipe their butts while you're at it, too. That's what they want you to do, and in the business, you do what they want you to so's you'll still be on deck when the next part comes along." He stopped, smiled again. "Just don't laugh in the take is all, son. Unless that's part of the gag."

Earl looked at him. "And you figure it's me can help you?"

"You're on the lot," the man said. "You work here. I want people around here to think I'm being seen. I want people on the lot to think folks out in the world are taking notice of me. It's ninety-two parts I've had so far, and not yet one of them have I gotten my name on the screen. And there's nothing like giving an auto-graph while you're standing on the lot to make somebody stop a second, think things over, whether it's a script girl like Ada here or Harry Cohn himself."

Earl looked at the ground again, swallowed. It made sense. But there was something else he wanted to ask, needed to ask. He still wasn't sure there was anything a lot man could do to help a bit player, but he still needed to ask him one thing, and needed too the courage to ask it.

He took in a small breath, looked at the man. Earl let go the coy squint he'd had and didn't even smile. To hell with Buddy Rogers, and trying to act your way through the sort of audition this was turning out to be. This was a business, he saw. The man was right.

"What's in it for me?" Earl said.

"Now you're talking." He let out a small crank of a laugh, a sound like a shard off the hard cackle the old hobo who'd stolen Earl's shoes off his feet had given, a cackle that'd cut through the rumble of the train as it left him there in rows of lettuce outside Buckeye, Arizona.

"Now you're talking," the man said again, and put both hands in his back pockets. "Now you're getting the idea."

"Walter!" Earl heard, and he and the man both turned to the voice: The script girl, this Ada, stood outside the stage, the clipboard cradled in one arm, a cigarette in her other hand. "We need to block this out in here!" she called, and took a hard drag, shot out the smoke. She nodded at Earl, took another drag. "And I need to give you your pay slip."

"We're on the way!" the man called back, gave a kind of wave.

The woman took another drag, let the smoke out her nose. Slowly she shook her head, disappeared inside the stage.

The man turned back to Earl. "What's in it for you," he went on, "is that I've got four more pictures lined up in just the next month. A word from me now and again to a casting girl or to a swing gang chief or a set man or anybody else will go a little farther than anything you've been rustling up on your own." He tilted his head one way, smiled. "I saw you in there, too. Not bad. You could do this job, I'm thinking. Once you stop thinking about thinking about thinking on it."

"You figure?" Earl said too fast, and felt his hands in his pockets ball up, his palms go sweaty.

"Don't go getting a big head," the man said. "I'm just a bit player, trying to figure out how to keep getting more of it. That's all." He stopped a moment, nodded. "But I think you can be in front of a camera. Just you make sure and have a pencil and piece of paper with you next time you see me. We'll see what turns up."

"I mean now, Walter!" Ada shouted, this time a solid edge to her voice, and they both turned to her. She stood with a hip out hard, the clipboard held up like the man could read from here the important news of this scene and the dire need for blocking it out.

"Cheese it, kid!" the man hollered out to her, on his voice a perfect smile, and he started for the stage and those twenty yards to another world, one Earl knew enough not to enter for fear of Moe seeing him and ruining any chance at all he had left around here.

But now that chance somehow seemed bigger for this man he didn't even know being willing to give him a hand. Somebody was helping him.

The man looked over his shoulder as he made for the stage. "Well, you going to get your pay slip," he said, "or are you just another Jiggs with pocketfuls of dough?"

Earl gave a laugh, the feeling in his chest something he didn't recognize for a moment. A laugh out of him, after he'd nearly killed himself by laughing in that last take. Who would have thought? And himself Jiggs in the funny papers, with Maggie throwing a rolling pin at him for eating corned beef and cabbage, Earl's slouch cap traded in for that shiny top hat and red vest Jiggs always wore, in his pockets money to burn.

He glanced a moment to that broom, still waiting, still waiting, and shook his head. He'd be back soon enough to pick it up, once he'd gotten paid for his first part.

He'd gotten a part.

He ran then to catch up to this man, in him a kind of bravery: Let Moe find him. He'd done the part, he'd nailed his cue. He was an actor.

"Sir," Earl said. He was beside the man now, Ada ahead of them and still with that hip out hard enough to knock down the whole stage. "Sir," he said again, this time louder, though he was right there beside him.

The man looked at him, his newspaper held out in front of him as he walked, and now here they were to Ada, her mouth in a grimace, the clipboard cradled back in her arm again.

Earl smiled at her, and reached to the shell of red hair hovering above her gray roots, pulled from above her right ear that gnawed yellow pencil tucked there.

Her eyebrows shot up at the surprise of a nobody lot man being so bold, but Earl only held on to that smile, nodded at her. "May I?" he said, and turned to this man in a conductor's suit, a man he thought maybe he'd seen in a picture or two, but couldn't be sure. But a man who'd helped.

"Sir," Earl said, and the man seemed puzzled, his eyebrows together, the smile back to that fence-sitting one: *Glad to meet you,* it said, or *My condolences.*

"Maybe," Earl said, and smiled, "if it's not too much trouble, sir." He dipped his chin at the newspaper, held the pencil out to the man. "Maybe," he went on, "you might could tear off a corner of that paper."

"Son?" the man said, and glanced at Ada, then back to Earl, that smile even more puzzled.

Earl took in a breath, felt his own smile grow even bigger, felt it almost explode into a laugh. But you didn't laugh in the take. Anybody knew that. Everyone knew that. He wouldn't make that mistake again.

"I'm a big fan, sir," he said, "and it'd be an honor to get your autograph."

Right on cue.

A somersault, he thought, is a good thing. A mighty thing, necessary and true.

"Why, it'd be my pleasure, son!" the man said. He stood taller now, winked at Ada, and took the pencil from Earl's hand.

11

Never heard of him!" Cal shouted over the noise in the place. People gabbed and girls laughed and glasses sparkled and dresses swished and above it all, thick as fog, hung cigarette smoke and more laughter and the deep buzz of life going on and going on and going on. All this sound, and the band hadn't even taken the stage yet.

"That's not the point," Earl said, then, louder, "You don't understand the first thing about this business!" and carefully, slowly, he smoothed flat the torn-off piece of newspaper lying before him on the white tablecloth.

Cal had his elbow on the table, a cigarette pinched between his thumb and first finger: Adolphe Menjou at his best. His eyes were to the crowd, scanning and, like always, like everyone, waiting to see and be seen.

Earl touched at the highball glass on the tablecloth like he meant to take another gulp, but thought better of it, the drinks seventy-five cents each here. He'd have to make it last—he'd only made three dollars for the shot he'd been in, and that had been generous, Ada in pity writing him up for a whole day—and reached instead to his cigarette perched on the edge of the ash-tray between them. The tray was big as a hubcap, black glass with the words *The Ambassador, Los Angeles, California* printed in gold around the rim. In the center of the tray, nearly hidden for the ashes they'd already piled up, was a drawing of a woman carrying what looked like a torch, *Cocoanut Grove* next to it, all of it in that same gold.

The table was only big enough for the two of them, though in plenty of places four and five and six people had jammed themselves in to tables the same size, everyone laughing and knocking back drinks like they were free. Their own table was backed up to the wall, the dance floor four rows of tables away; past that, against the wall to their left, sat the stage, all set for the band. Fake coconut trees about eight feet tall rimmed the dance floor, so that to get out there you had to pass under them, the ceiling twenty feet high, painted green with white wood crossbeams up there and a skylight in the center of it.

The dresses the girls wore seemed every one of them made of silk, and shimmered in every color he knew, some sleeveless, some with little jackets, some strapless so that when the girls leaned forward to laugh or grab a drink off the table, almost everything popped out for all the world to see. They all looked like somebody, too: here was Norma Shearer, over there Katharine Hepburn, Barbara Stanwyck leaning her head back and giving out a deep laugh to his right, two rows over Joan Crawford in a swizzle stick swordfight with Jeanette MacDonald. Men in white dinner jackets and black tuxedos and plaid sports coats and blue blazers sat around them all and watched and made jokes and elbowed each other, every one of them a George Brent or a Clark Gable or a Herbert Marshall or an Errol Flynn.

Cigarette girls roamed the place, called out the same song every few seconds—"Cigars, cigarettes?"—the question for all the world a come-on, Earl could hear; camera girls made the rounds, too, stopping at tables here and there to flash off shots, everyone at the tables huddled up a moment and holding still for the bulb to pop, then easing back into that laughter, those drinks. The cigarette and camera girls wore short skirts that poofed out for the petticoats beneath them, the dresses jet black, those petticoats bright pink, the heels the girls wore taller than any Earl had seen save for in the pictures, the all of everything here at the Cocoanut Grove aces-up elegant.

"I got to get me one of those monkey suits," Cal said, and turned to Earl. He leaned forward, tapped his cigarette into the tray, and nodded at the piece of newspaper in front of Earl. "And put that thing away," he said, "before some Jane in here thinks we're reading the classifieds, looking for a job."

"What's a monkey suit?" Earl said, and looked at him.

"A tuxedo, kid." He shook his head, reached inside his jacket for a pack of cigarettes. He said, "Moe was right. You are retarded," and lit up the next smoke.

But Earl only smiled, smoothed his hand over the piece of newspaper one more time, moved the high-ball glass one more time, touched at his cigarette one more time.

There it was, the top right corner of the front page the conductor had torn off once he'd signed it, *Examiner* the only word left from the banner at the top for its having been torn off. Under it was the whole date, same as he'd read this morning: *April 3, 1934.* Beneath that was part of a story about a new racetrack somebody was building out in Arcadia.

But above all of this, floating in a scrawl on the blank gray of the top right corner, was what the man had written: *Walter Brennan, with all best wishes.*

"I never heard of him either," Earl said, and slowly shook his head. "But you got to admit, it's a pretty good idea. And if he can help me, then it's the best idea to come along in a good long while."

"Sounds like he thinks he's the Big It," Cal said, and took a drag, still with his cigarette in that pinched way. "Maybe I ought to hire somebody out to come ask me for my own John Hancock. Then maybe I could assure myself I'd be in ninety-two bits over the next nine years without my name anywhere to be seen. Really make it big!" He leaned his head back, shot the smoke out as dramatic as he could, then took his own glass from the table, slammed back the last of his whiskey sour, and set the empty glass down hard on the table. "And the best idea to come along in a good long while," he said, "is for the two of us to lay hands on a couple of these choice bits of calico and grow some carpet burns." He reached across the table, grabbed the piece of newspaper, and folded it up, stuffed it into his pocket.

"Cal—" Earl began, but Cal cut a look at him, put both hands on the table, leaned toward him. "Earl," he said. "Start paying attention. You got a part, we're here to have a good time. You keep pining away at a piece of paper with a no-name nobody on it, and our chances of having any fun at all are taking a dive in the first round."

He eased back in his chair, turned to the noise again. "You were the one wanted to come here, brother!" he shouted. "Now let's at least try to show up!"

Earl leaned back, too, and reached to his cigarette, pulled it out of that ashtray. Cal was right. They were here—both of them *actors*—and the beauty and noise and hoopla were all they needed. Part of the job.

He grinned, took up the highball glass, heavier than he'd imagined any glass could ever be, and finished it off.

At dinner Earl had had to rely on Cal to give the news, Earl somehow suddenly without any of the words he'd planned to holler out when he'd been in the Pullman. Everyone banged out a hard applause, especially the old man, who dropped his tin horn and stood and made a toast to him with his coffee cup—"Here's to a long life in the pictures!" he yelled, convinced as always that everyone else was as deaf as he was—and

169

they all stood and cheered, touched glasses. Earl had blushed, still no words out of him, and the old man had given him an extra slice of Salisbury steak.

Later, Earl and Cal walked the three blocks over to Vine and climbed on the streetcar, rode it down to Wilshire, and changed cars for the couple-mile ride out to the Ambassador, then walked up the drive like they owned the place, Cal in his good navy blazer, Earl in Cal's beige three-button jacket, the one he wore when he went to the casting calls for comedies. Earl wasn't sure the red tie with the palm tree leaves matched, but that and the McDonald with the blue pinstripes were all he had, and Cal'd whispered to him he looked like Bing himself just before they got to the awning above the entrance. The doormen had held the doors open wide for them, smiled and nodded, and so it all seemed to have worked, this pretending to be somebody.

Of course he'd never been here before. The Cocoanut Grove was only a place he'd think about when he'd read reports on who'd been spotted there the night before in the papers they passed around at the dinner table. He'd never made it into a speakeasy before the Prohibition was over, and since then had only been into a bar or three, some of them with a singer and a piano or a small gang of players pushed into a corner and doing their best to give the joint a ride.

Maybe a half dozen times or so, back when he first got here and the whole city seemed some sort of romp never going to stop, the crash as far away as the farthest star, he'd gone all the way down to Santa Monica and walked out on the pier after he'd gotten off work, and looked into the windows of the La Monica Ballroom. The place was a real live palace, lights on it as bright as any premiere at the Chinese or the Orpheum, with turrets and flags and a dance floor big enough, far as he could tell, to hold everyone in Mineola and Gladewater both.

But he'd only looked in those windows and watched the folks in there move around with the music, a giant swarm of people wobbling more or less in time, and everyone laughing. Then he'd walked to the edge of the pier, leaned on the railing and looked out at the black water down there and listened to waves crashing, a sound relentless and calming and cold and mysterious all at once. The closest sound he knew to these waves was the cold and steady promise of a night train coming closer, him in his room in Hawkins and looking out his window at those stars, until suddenly it was here, the Texas & Pacific line a slow meteor that nearly hit the earth right out the back door of his daddy's shack a half mile away, the sound changing of a sudden to a different pitch as it picked up speed once it was through town, and hurtled away.

That was what those waves reminded him of, and why, finally, he'd stopped going out to that pier, and those lights, and the glory of all those folks dancing to that beautiful music. The sound of those waves, he knew, was too much like home.

No. He didn't go out to party after he got off work, or to drink or to dance. Instead, he did what he knew he had to do: go to the pictures, and sink into a seat while the lights went down, and here would be the same moment of quiet and dark and certainty that he was about to go someplace he'd never been before as that first time at the Rose.

He'd go four or five nights a week to the Chinese, or the Orpheum, or the State or the Cameo or the Tower or the El Capitan or sometimes, if he felt like it and the picture was supposed to be good, the Egyptian, though it turned his stomach to enter that place, the fools there too dumb to hire him when he'd applied to be an usher. Look at him now: busting out in a Stooges picture he'd see in a month or so at one or another of those theaters—maybe even the Egyptian itself. That would show them.

Here he was, at the Cocoanut Grove. He'd read the ad in the paper he'd held just this morning on the set of a picture he'd been in on the Columbia lot, the news of some new band a kind of prophecy of this moment, and of this noise, and of this beige coat he had on and this ashtray big as a hubcap, and of all this life going on and on and on.

He *was* somebody. He'd been in a picture. He had the money in his pocket, an empty highball glass before him, and the press of pretty girls everywhere, everywhere.

He was having a drink at the Cocoanut Grove.

He was an *actor.*

Now here was the band moving out from behind the stage, a passel of men dressed in *monkey suits* emerging out of nowhere, it seemed, and smiling and joking with each other, and now here was a woman with them, too, in a dark blue dress with the sleeves off the shoulder, the dress almost short enough to show her knees.

She was blond, her hair pulled back at her neck, and even from here, all the way against the wall, the stage a good fifty feet away and with the room jammed as full as it was and with all this noise all around, he saw the milk white of her shoulders like it was a dream and not a movie and not a set and not a glossy.

Her skin, her shoulders, her neck were all like a dream, the softness and the white of her skin and the blond of her hair and the wispy curl that fell just behind her ear—he saw all this from across the room! he saw all this as though he were a foot away!—all of it was a dream he was having right here, right now, and he stopped thinking everything and anything in this moment, only felt himself breathing in and breathing out, only felt his own life inside himself.

He watched her as she and the others took their seats, hers out in front of them all, and he watched her while a man's voice boomed out of the speakers hung from the ceiling above the stage—*Ladies and gentlemen, for the first of three nights here at the Cocoanut Grove, please welcome, direct from San Francisco's famed Hotel St. Francis, the next sensation in swing, the Kay Kyser Orchestra!*—and Earl watched her while a man in glasses and with a baton in his hand leaned in to the microphone in the center of the stage and drawled out, "Evenin', folks, how y'all?"

It was a genuine drawl, not like those fake ones he'd heard in a hundred pictures, no put-on southern charm, and around Earl people clapped and a few people laughed. Already the bandleader, smiling big and genuine and charming as his drawl, was tapping out the first two beats, and the band was on, really *on,* just like that, and Earl watched as the woman in that dark dress with the sleeves that fell off her shoulders just for Earl, he knew, just for *him,* slowly stood.

A hand to either side of her dress, holding on to the blue silk of that dress and swishing it one way and the other as soft and smooth as a breeze, the woman made her way to the microphone, where the leader still stood. He turned from the band, smiled at the woman, and now the two of them stood side by side. The woman, this dream of a girl, smiled out at the crowd like she knew them all, every one of them a friend, and then leaned to the microphone, sang out "Did you ever see a dream walking?" right in time with the music—as right on cue as anything he'd ever heard— then leaned away, still smiling, even though there was more to the song. Then the bandleader, taller than the woman Earl loved already—yes, he loved her already, just like that—leaned in and drawled, "And now, heah's the lovely and gifted Saralee Kennedy, with a favorite we know y'all are gonna love! C'mon, children, let's dance!"

Cal turned to Earl, said, "Get a load of that!" but Earl was still watching the woman up there—Saralee Kennedy, what a name!—as she took over the microphone altogether, the bandleader easing back toward the band. The tables emptied out in a moment, the dance floor filled just that quick.

"Did you ever see a dream walking?" she sang. "Well! I did. Did you ever hear a dream talking? Well! I did!" she sang, her hands palms up and out to her sides in the gentlest surprise, as if what she'd seen were a kind of gift she couldn't turn down.

Her voice was a dream, too, a perfect dream, and Earl was sorry the microphone was so big he couldn't see the whole of her face, and the lovely and gifted beauty of it, couldn't see her mouth shape the words she sang about a dream she'd seen, just exactly like the dream he himself was witnessing this very second. But he could see even from here the sharp and cool blue of her eyes above the mike, and the way she squinted them closed the smallest bit with the phrasing she gave out, the song as effortless and true as the sun just topping the trees of a spring morning when he was a kid.

"Did you ever find heaven right in your arms, saying I love you, I do?" she sang, and now she had a hand on her hip, the other arm out and pointing to the crowd, a kind of lilting movement to her arm, her whole self a part of the music, the band romping behind her and sharp and calm and *on,* and her out front and in charge of it all.

She was a *singer,* and she was *famous,* though he'd never heard of her or this band. But here she was out front at the Cocoanut Grove, and he was in love.

"Well, the dream that was walking," she sang, "and the dream that was talking, and the heaven in my arms was *you!*" and she closed her eyes, squinted in that perfect way, and pointed her arm out in front of her.

In that same instant a bulb popped, the stage and the woman lit up in a harmless strike of lightning, and Earl saw a camera girl in her short black skirt and pink petticoats a few feet from the stage bring her camera down, look at it, then pop out the bulb.

"I'm buying that one," Earl said, and Cal said, "What?" but Earl was already standing, moving through the tables for the camera girl all the way over there at the stage to let her know the photo she'd just shot was the one he'd be bringing home.

"Old boy!" Cal shouted after him. "Bring me back another whiskey sour!"

Here were these fake coconut trees, and people and more people, and he brushed past them and into this new circle just like he'd moved into the circle of *fame* and *pictures* and *acting* by Moe and by some would-be It named Walter Brennan earlier today. Here he was, an actor in love—he was in love!—inside the toddle and rub of the dance floor, making for the camera girl, who'd turned from the band and was moving off into the rows of tables on the other side of the room.

It was then he glanced up from his rough passage

through all these happy children to the stage, himself only a few feet from the woman now, to see she was looking down at him, and suddenly he felt undone somehow, discovered for who he was: a kid not from around here, a kid whose prettiest picture he could muster to compare with this woman's voice and skin and blue eyes and blond hair was a sun coming up over treetops.

But then, then: She smiled at him, at *him,* and she winked, her hands holding on to the material of her dress and swishing it back and forth just like a breeze, just like a breeze, while the band set in to its glory job of kicking out this tune.

She smiled at him, and winked.

Still everyone danced, and people knocked back drinks like they were free, and the fact of fame itself— this woman who'd smiled and winked at him was a *singer,* he himself was an *actor*—hung above them thick as the cigarette smoke and laughter and buzz of life going on and on and on.

He stopped, stood still in the middle of the dance floor at the Cocoanut Grove, here in the middle of everything in the world, around him the struggle and tug of all these dancing children.

He stopped, the sun just breaking over the tree line of a morning, sunrise on the best day of his life for certain now, April 3, 1934, when he'd become somebody, and found somebody, too.

He was in love, and now, standing still at the brightest bright center of the world, he looked up at this dream singing who'd smiled and winked, and he showed her his love the only way he knew how: He winked back, and smiled his Buddy Rogers smile.

Joan

12

Daddy always sits at the window on the Yellow Car, next to him Momma, Joan always in the seat behind them. This is the part of the direction song she's *memorized* that goes *you must pass Highland, you must pass Vine and North Western.* They're riding along on Hollywood Boulevard, her daddy's face turned to the window so that she can see his *profile,* him looking at everything—the big white half-round building at the corner of Cahuenga, all glass on the front, above it in neon letters what seems twenty feet high *Drs. GREEN & CHASE,* down the side of the building the word *Dentist;* the ugly brown Equitable building on the corner of Vine, across the street from it the beautiful and perfect *cursive* handwriting of *The Owl Drug Co.* sign all in bright red neon letters wrapping around the corner of the building; the White King soap billboard on top of one of the shorter buildings between Vine and Argyle; and now here is the Pantages Theatre at Argyle, the strange shape of the letters, round and square at the same time, in an orange neon line down the building.

Between the big corners the buildings are smaller,

only two or three stories, and as they ride by she can see down side streets places like the one they live in, buildings that don't have decorations like they all have here on Hollywood Boulevard. Everything out here has green or blue or black awnings above the store windows, those windows filled with signs about sales, some of them with their own neon signs inside or on the roof. There are shoe stores, and cafés, and music stores, and signs for car parks, and every now and then a palm tree standing right on the street. And there are streetlights, each light post with two lights at the top that always make her think of the *candelabra* at Granny Holmes's house, the one she had on the piano in the front room, though that *candelabra* had three candles on it, and the streetlights here on Hollywood Boulevard have only two.

The sun in on her daddy looking at all this makes him more handsome than ever, she thinks, and she smiles because they haven't headed off for *sad* yet, even with Daddy standing and standing out front of Grauman's Chinese for as long as he did.

She can see only the back of her momma's head. She's looking straight ahead, puts to her mouth now and again a cigarette, Joan can tell by the way she moves and the smoke that shoots out above her head. Her eyes are closed because of the headache coming up on her, and Joan tries to imagine like she has a thousand times since the day she found the record and those photographs what her momma looked like on a stage in front of a big band.

She's looked at the pictures five times in the last four weeks and two days, though she still doesn't know which one of the ladies is her momma. She thinks it can't be the lady with the bob, it just can't be, for how black her hair is, and how skinny her face is too. So it has to be one of the other two, one in a white dress, the other in a gray one. She just can't tell, because of those clothes, and their hair, and how old the picture is, and the way they have their hands behind their backs and are half-turned to the camera. But she also can't tell which of the two ladies is her momma, she has figured out, because the ladies in the picture are smiling bigger than Joan has ever seen her momma smile.

And she's found another clue: on the other side of the record is more scratching, just like on the front side. But instead of *KKO* and *TOY,* it says *KKO* and then *BS;* beneath the hole is still the same *SK* and a space and the same numbers, *2634.*

But she still can't tell what it all means, and she can't ask. The only thing she can do is look at it all when she has enough *nerve* to pull the record out in the afternoons, afraid every second she has the photographs spread out in front of her that time will pass as quickly as it did that first afternoon.

She thinks of Johnny's momma in *Song of the South,* and about when his daddy comes into Johnny's room after that bull almost got him. The look on his momma's face started out afraid and then went straight to gladness that Johnny's daddy was there.

How quickly her face turned from the wrinkles of fear on her forehead and into the wide, soft, and beautiful smile! And there was the lady's hair, so perfect and full, and her dress too, the big green skirt with layers and layers of *petticoats* underneath it, all of it—the dress, the quilt on Johnny's bed, even the gray suit his daddy wore when he came into the room—all of it in a kind of color that only happened in Texas.

"Your gramma's piano is an upright," Lincoln had told her one day while they were in line to go inside before school started. Joan had told him about Granny Holmes's piano in Texas, and how none of her relatives in Texas knew how to play it. She'd told him about how tall it was, and how the top opened up like the lid on a hamper, and that she and Fern and Betty Jo took turns looking in there at all the pieces moving while one or the other of them played on the keys.

She'd told him because she knew he played piano himself, though he never bragged about it or talked about it much. She only knew he left school two times a week right in the middle of the morning for lessons somewhere, lessons he couldn't take after school.

"We have a grand piano," he'd gone on, but not in any way that made Joan feel bad, or that made him look good. He'd said it the same way he'd spell a word correctly in class or recite a part of the multiplication tables. He shrugged, looked at the ground, then back up at Joan. "My birthday is next week," he said, "and I'm going to have everybody come to my house." He shrugged again. "My momma wants me to play for everybody."

"I'll come," Joan said quickly, and then the whistle blew, and they turned to face front, and the line started into the building.

That was how it started, going to Lincoln's house and listening to him play, and listening too to the records his family had over there.

Now there is a whole gang of them that sometimes goes over to his apartment: Joan and Harriet and Babs and sometimes Dot and Shirley, and even Robert and sometimes Ronald and Donald, the twins in their class. Joan likes when they all go there after school, though they aren't over there very often, just *once in a blue moon.*

But at Lincoln's birthday party, the first time any of them had been to his apartment, none of them knew what would happen. There weren't any paper hats like Babs had given out at her party, and no paper horns, or Pin the Tail on the Donkey. Instead, his momma had made punch and cookies, and they had all listened to Lincoln play.

The piano was huge, black and shiny, the bench Lincoln sat on just as shiny and sleek, and now Joan understood about the *upright* that her granny's piano was. Lincoln's piano was as beautiful and big as every one she'd seen in a hundred Fred Astaire and Ginger Rogers movies. The piano and that bench, with its black leather cushion, felt to Joan like a brand-new car was parked right there in the small front room of Lincoln's apartment on Park Avenue, right across the street from Echo Park and the swans.

It was a bigger apartment than Joan's, and had a kitchen and its own bathroom, something she couldn't even imagine for how nice that must be, and a Victrola that stood in one corner just like the one Granny Holmes had, tall as a pie safe. And there was the park right across the street.

And here was a *grand* piano in the middle of the room, sleek and shiny and black, big as a car, Lincoln sitting in front of it like the driver.

Once they'd all come in and set their presents on the tiny table by the front door—Joan had bought a Hopa-long Cassidy notebook at the Woolworth's, on the cover a picture of Hoppy sitting on Topper, and wrapped it in the Sunday funny papers—Lincoln's momma had everybody sit on the floor of the front room and be quiet before Lincoln could start to play. Joan could tell already Lincoln and his playing the piano were the most important things in the world to his momma. She'd seen it with the way his momma directed all the kids to sit down, and in how shiny and perfect that piano was, centered in the middle of a room with wooden floors as worn and old as they were at her own place.

She'd seen too how important the piano and Lincoln playing it was with the way his momma gave out the cookies: they were on a paper doily on a large plate, the edges of the plate painted with flowers, each cookie—they were small as silver dollars and covered with powdered sugar—set by itself and not touching another. His momma held that plate with one hand, in the other small white napkins no bigger than the ones that came out of the shiny metal *dispenser* next to the salt and pepper shakers on the tables in Albert Sheets Restaurant. But these napkins were thicker, nicer ones, Joan could see, and when she took her own cookie and napkin from Lincoln's momma, she saw the edges of the napkin had rows of flowers pressed into the paper itself, and she hesitated a moment at the idea of putting this cookie on that napkin, the napkin was so nice.

The cookie was covered in powdered sugar as white as snow, whiter even than the napkin, and it seemed that they matched, the cookie and the napkin, and she set it on the paper, held them there in both hands for a few moments just looking at the delicate beauty of them both, and she wondered if she might even eat the cookie at all, or ever wipe her mouth with that row of flowers.

"These are Danish wedding cookies," Lincoln's momma said, and Joan looked up at her, standing there and smiling down at Joan, her words spoken in an *accent,* the sharp cut of the words still a kind of surprise though Joan had heard it every day after school, when Lincoln's momma called out to him there at the chain-link fence at the end of the walkway out from the front door of the school.

His momma had gray hair pulled back in a bun, and wore a blue dress with big flowers on it that Joan couldn't quite name, though they looked maybe like roses, and she had silver earrings that were like tiny chains that hung down almost to her shoulders and ended with beautiful blue jewels. She was thin, and pale, and seemed as strange and odd as the sound of her *accent*. Still smiling, she nodded at Joan, then went on passing out the Danish wedding cookies.

All the kids were looking at each other while she passed them out, their eyes open wide—*cookies for a birthday party?*—and then Ronald said, "When's your wedding, Lincoln?" and Donald said, "It's Harriet Radloff, I bet," and they laughed and Harriet only held her cookie and *scowled,* though Babs and Shirley and Dot and even Joan laughed a little.

Lincoln's momma stopped passing out the cookies, and smiled a smile at Ronald and Donald that let them both know they were stupid as dirt. Ronald and Donald sat up straighter there on the floor, minding her quicker than they ever did Miss LaValley at school, something in that smile she gave them that made them obey. For a moment Joan wondered what it must be like to have a momma like that, who thought her child and what he did were the most important things in the world, important enough to make his friends be quiet and at the same time pass out cookies for them to enjoy.

Lincoln's momma held the fancy plate and the napkins out now to Dot, then to Robert, no more words from anyone, not even a giggle. When she was done, she stood tall, the plate still in her hands, and said,

"Children, enjoy your cookies!" and at that they all picked their cookies up from the napkins, and all took a bite together, Joan saw, as though this were a test, Lincoln's momma their teacher.

It was sweet, and light, crumbled in her mouth to melt away save for the smallest pieces of nuts, which she chewed, the sweetness of it all filling her. She'd never had anything as sweet and light and perfect before, and she took another bite, and another, and the cookie was gone.

"Now, children, let us listen to Lincoln," his momma said, and everyone turned to Lincoln, there in the driver's seat of that piano, him and the piano and what he was about to do the most important things in the world.

For a second Lincoln didn't say anything, only looked at the keys, closed his eyes, opened them. Then he brought his hands from his lap, and set them to playing.

It was beautiful. It was perfect.

This was *music,* and was filled with colors and light. Sometimes it sounded like what she heard in the movies, sometimes like something she heard in church when she was in Texas with Granny Holmes and everybody else, and sometimes like nothing she had ever heard at all.

No one said anything, all the children even quieter than at story time in kindergarten, but then Lincoln's momma said, "He is descended from Beethoven!" and they all quickly turned to her. She nodded hard once, still smiling and standing there with the plate of cookies in her hands.

But it was a different smile now, not one about getting kids to be quiet. Her eyes were on Lincoln, and the smile seemed more than a momma smiling at her kid doing something good. It seemed more even than *happiness,* and even more.

She was *proud,* Joan saw.

Joan turned back to Lincoln, watched his hands move, and listened to the music coming out from the piano, music that poured and flew and bloomed and danced, like the dancing flowers in *Fantasia,* and then she knew where she had heard some of this music before: in that movie, back when she was almost a baby, before her daddy went to the war and Joan and her momma moved to Texas. But she remembered it, remembered the music, and the colors, and the little dancing half-horses, half-people in the forest, and those flowers that looked like beautiful ladies but were flowers all the same.

Still Lincoln played, but now he looked up from his hands at the piano to his momma, and now he got a smile on his face, a smile with no teeth showing, a smile she'd seen before in class whenever he was *up to no good.* She'd seen him smile this same smile at them all when the teacher called on him the week before to spell *pagoda,* a word she knew he could spell because they had practiced on each other waiting in line to go into the classroom before school. Now here he was, with that smile, looking at his momma.

And the music suddenly changed, his hands quickly moving big and high back and forth on the keys, the music not the blossoming but still beautiful, moving all over back and forth and jumping. It was a song she'd heard before, loud and silly and far away from the dancing flowers. But it had to do with dancing too, and she remembered it was a song an older girl had tap-danced to at the *recital* in Mineola, after she and Fern and Betty Jo had danced to "American Patrol." A fast song with fast dancing that made everyone clap even harder and louder than they had for anyone once that older girl was finished.

"Lincoln!" his momma boomed out like a cannon, that single word above the jump and bounce and brightest color and light Joan had ever heard.

Lincoln still only smiled at her, no teeth showing, and now the song got even jumpier and funnier, and he closed his eyes a second, then smiled at all of the kids sitting around him, smiling at them, Joan saw, because he wanted them all in on it, this trouble.

"Lincoln, this minute!" his momma said, even louder, but Lincoln didn't even look at her now, just kept with his hands moving sharp up and down over the piano, the music crisp and spiky and funny still, even with his momma getting mad like this, and Joan looked at Harriet and Babs and Shirley and Dot, who were all looking at each other, the boys looking at each other too, all of them in on this trouble, and all of them starting to smile for it, too.

"Name it, Momma," Lincoln said, and glanced at his

momma, then back to the piano, his hands moving even a little faster, but the sounds still just as crisp and sharp and outlined with the trouble of this all no matter how funny the song.

"Return to the Beethoven!" she shot out, and she set the plate on top of the packages on the little table, then turned and put both hands to her hips, her mouth a sharp line.

But there was something else in her, too, Joan could tell. Something familiar, same as a few minutes before, when she'd seen in his momma's smile the pride she had for him.

Joan saw it in her eyes, the corners of them. There was still a smile there, at the corners of her eyes, in the wrinkles there.

"Not until you name it, Momma!" Lincoln said, the music going even faster now, still jumping and jumping and still funny and still trouble for it, all at once.

The children all sat up even straighter, Ronald's and Donald's mouths open like fish, Robert with his hands together in his lap like he was saying a prayer, his eyes open wide as Shirley's and Babs's and Harriet's and Dot's, all of them, all of them, afraid and delighted at once.

This was a *game.*

"You impetuous boy!" his momma nearly shouted and brought a hand from her hip, pointed at him, shook her finger. "You will be my death!" she said, those earrings shivering all the way down to the blue jewels at the ends of the chains.

"Name it, Momma," Lincoln said again, the song faster and faster, his hands bouncing back and forth high above everything and back to the keys, and now Robert let out a laugh, short and solid, and Joan quickly looked to him, saw the surprise on his face at the fact of what he'd done, as though he'd tipped over a vase in this house instead of just laughed at this game—and now Babs let out a laugh too, and Ronald and Donald shook their heads at the same time and giggled, everyone letting up from inside them laughter at this whole birthday party game, a game better than any Pin the Tail on the Donkey game could have ever been.

"It is the Gershwin again," his momma said finally, and now she bowed her head, slowly shook it, both hands to her hips again. "Always with the Gershwin," she said, her voice just loud enough not to be lost on the joy and sharp fun of the music. "And his 'Fascinating Rhythm.'"

"You win!" Lincoln let out loud and laughed, and Ronald and Donald rolled over onto their sides there on the floor, overdoing it like always, and Babs and Shirley both pulled their knees up under their chins and held on tight and laughed, and Harriet smiled big as anybody, her eyes on Lincoln and with her napkin in both hands like a fancy painted plate of cookies all her own, and Joan thought maybe, maybe, someday they really would get married, those two.

His momma turned from them all, this trouble and

fun, and went to the empty chair beside the Victrola in the corner, and she sat down, put her hands together in her lap, and slowly shook her head.

"I am raising the next Kay Kyser," she said, and let out a heavy breath. "He will be my death," she said, and smiled.

"He's a regular Kay Kyser and his Kollege of Musical Knowledge," Ronald said, and Donald shouted out, "Evenin', folks, how y'all?" just like Kay Kyser called out at the beginning of every show, and Babs, the quietest girl of all her friends, shouted out above them all, "That's right, you're wrong!" and all the kids laughed, even Joan. She'd heard Kay Kyser on the radio every week when they lived in Texas, the show one of Granny's favorites, though Momma always left the front room when it came on, wouldn't listen to it for the headaches she said she had or for how tired she was at the end of a day, though she wasn't working back then, only helped Granny around the house.

"Play 'Three Little Fishes,'" Shirley nearly shouted out, and Dot said, "No, play 'Don't Sit Under the Apple Tree,'" and Robert said, "'Jingle, Jangle, Jingle'!"

Kay Kyser's Kollege of Musical Knowledge, the show was named, *College* spelled with a *K* for the funny way it matched the man's name, she figured, when she'd seen it spelled out on a sign for his records in the music store in Mineola. Kay Kyser would ask questions about music, and people in the audience would answer, and people would laugh, and the songs his band would play were funny and sometimes sad, and sometimes crazy, the audience always always laughing.

"Play 'Huggin' and Chalkin'' for Harriet Radloff," Ronald said, and everybody let out a whoop because that song was about a boy hugging a girl, but it was about a girl so fat the boy had to mark on her with a piece of chalk where he started hugging so he'd know he was done when he got back to the mark, and they all laughed, even Harriet, who wasn't fat at all, her so skinny she could circle her wrist with her thumb and pinkie finger.

Then Lincoln changed the music again, made it climb up a cliff, it sounded like, and then fall right off that same cliff and smash at the bottom, where in a second it turned into a different song, but not the one Ronald said about the fat girl, but "Jingle, Jangle, Jingle," and they all still laughed, and still his momma sat next to the phonograph, shaking her head and smiling at this all, and Joan wished she had a radio and a phonograph both, like Lincoln had, and maybe even a piano so that she could bring some of this fun to her own home. But for now, she laughed, and made herself not think about what she didn't have, because here, right now, she was *happy*.

"My death," his momma said again, but Joan knew what she really meant, with that smile of hers and all this crazy commotion going on: *I am proud of my child.*

The streetcar pulls to a sudden stop, and the doors at the middle squeeze open as slow as they ever do, and they are already here at Hillhurst and Sunset, where they will change cars and head on down Sunset to Alvarado. They are all standing, everyone in the car on this Saturday afternoon, the sky outside still as bright blue and clean as when she'd had to squint into it all coming out of Grauman's Chinese.

Her momma's finished the cigarette and takes hold Joan's hand as she steps onto the street, Joan the last of their family on the streetcar, and she can see her momma's eyes still squinted behind her green glasses, sees her daddy scanning the sidewalks for anything that might happen, and here she is stepping down onto the street with all its cars and buildings and people and those palm trees and car park signs and awnings and shops and cafés. Everything she has known for over a year, since she moved from Texas, where the real colors of the sky are, and the real colors of the trees and streams and clouds.

She has her friends here, she thinks, and there are those afternoons *once in a blue moon* when they all go to Lincoln's and listen to him play and then play records on his phonograph, which all makes it easier to live so far from her real home in Texas. But there are Betty Jo and Fern, those two cousins who are like sisters more than anything else, though she doesn't have any sisters or brothers and so she wouldn't know what it really meant to have one.

She looks again at her daddy, who is smiling like he always does when he looks around for his street corner screen tests.

"The next car's going to be here in a minute," Joan's momma says out loud, and Joan looks up at her, sees her against the blue sky, sees her mouth open for her squint, and the dotted-swiss dress and that thin thin white belt.

Is this the lady in the photograph? Joan thinks, and thinks again of the music she's just heard at the movies, and the words already living in her: *My, oh, my, what a wonderful day!*

As though her momma is reading her mind, she looks down at Joan, and the wrinkles leave her for just the smallest moment, the squint gone for just an instant, and she smiles.

"That was a good song, wasn't it?" her momma says, still smiling, her forehead without a care, Joan can see, smooth and full and soft. But here are her sunglasses, and Joan can't really see, *really* see enough to tell if it *is* her, but it has to be, it has to be.

"Which song?" Joan says, and puts a hand up to her own forehead to block the sun so she can see, really see.

"The one you were singing just now," she says. "Zip-a-dee-doo-dah," she says, and she sings it, right there on the street corner at Sunset and Hillhurst: "Zip-a-dee-doo-dah, zip-a-dee-ay!"

The words are full and rich but quiet, sung only for Joan out here on the sidewalk, sung just like she sings to Joan late at night after Daddy has gone wherever he goes when they fight, those songs about blue skies and sitting under the apple tree, and the song, her favorite, about being so lonely without her.

And now, as though a special magic dust has been spilled over her, Joan knows exactly what she will do, knows how she can find the secret to the secret things hidden beneath the divan. How had she not figured this out before? she wonders, and thinks perhaps it is the movie, *Song of the South,* and the magic from it, the best movie there has ever been, and the *happiness* from that song she has sung without even knowing she has sung it, that has given her the key to her momma's secret.

She will sneak the record out of the apartment, and take it to Lincoln's next time they all go there. It will be a snap!

She will listen to the record, and if there is a woman singing on it, she will know what her momma's voice sounds like, and she will know if that is her on the record. She will know, same as right now, right now, when she is going to see in her momma's smooth smile a woman smiling from back before Joan was born, a woman with her eyes closed at a microphone in a *nightclub,* one hand up in front of her like she's pointing to somebody at the back of the room.

She will ask her, now, because Joan is awake and not pretending to be asleep and her momma is singing to her, and because her momma's voice is so beautiful, so beautiful, and her forehead is so smooth, and because she is smiling.

"Momma," she says, bold and afraid at the same time, though she doesn't know what she is afraid of, "were you ever a—"

"That's it," her daddy says, loud and sharp, and he snaps his finger hard, and Joan looks at him, the last word she'd wanted to speak gone for how sharp that snap and his words.

He is looking down at her, his shadow over her and blocking out the sun so that he is lit from above and behind, and for a moment she can't see his face, only that shadow of him blocking out the sun.

But now here comes his face, her father and his pipe-cleaner mustache and his black hair slicked back. He is smiling at her, and suddenly, suddenly, she sees in the color of that gray silky shirt he has on and sees in the color of his eyes—they are a kind of gray-green—what it means that the shirt makes his eyes stand out.

He is handsome, and he is smiling, and it is like the magic spell has been broken between her momma and Joan with that smile, and his words.

"What is it now, Earl?" her momma says, and lets go Joan's hand, fishes for a cigarette in her purse, and Joan quickly looks to her.

Her eyes are nearly squinted shut behind her sunglasses, and she finds the cigarette, pulls it out, lights it.

"You're going to be a star," her daddy says to Joan, and now he puts his hands to his knees, leans close to Joan, smiling and smiling. "You and me," he says.

"Together." He nods to something behind her and to her left, and Joan turns, looks behind her.

It is a row of shops out here on Sunset, three of them, and then an alleyway with a car park sign pointing down it. Three shops, all with bright blue awning over the fronts: a tailor, a music store, and a dance studio.

"Earl, what are you talking about?" her momma says, and she is looking at the shops too now, moving her head one way and another, as though she can't see there are even any buildings there, and the spell has been smashed to pieces.

"Came to me just now, like a shot. Maybe because of Uncle Remus and those kids doing that little dance on the road." He stops a second, his eyes still on the shops behind Joan. "Dancing," her daddy says. "You and me, a dance team. Father and daughter," and he looks at Joan again, and he winks, and she can feel her face going hot right now, right now, and feels her breath go small in her, and she looks back at the dance studio, sees in the window in neon lights the words *Adults* and *Children*. "We'll be the ticket," he says, "you and me. Like Bill Bojangles and Shirley Temple, but better, because it's a father and daughter team."

"Dammit, Earl," her momma says, and lets out a shot of smoke, "you're not going to do that to her. You're not going to make her—"

"Let's go!" her daddy says, and he takes Joan's hand, stands up tall, still smiling. "You still have those tap shoes, right?" he says, though he isn't looking at her, his eyes on the window beneath the bright blue awning, and she can see him smiling. "There's never been anything like it, far as I know," he says, his voice going away now, on a kind of dream, or a magic carpet. Or in his own magic spell, magic dust sprinkled over himself by himself.

Joan's face is red, she knows, for how hot her skin feels, and how her breaths are small and hollow, and she knows the word for this: it's a *blush.*

"Earl," her momma says from behind them now, "don't you dare put that girl through this. Don't drag her into your sorry little schemes."

But the words don't do anything, and she looks down at the sidewalk, the gray of it and the cracks of it as he leads her toward that studio, and those neon words, and that bright blue awning above it all.

She doesn't want to dance with her daddy, doesn't want to be in any *recital* with him, because he is her daddy and she is his daughter, and there is only one reason that her daddy would dance with her.

Because he is an *actor.*

"Hope you still have those tap shoes your granny bought you," he says without looking at her, his voice the kind of happy it is when he is talking about *screen tests* and *glossies* and *shoots.* And she wonders, though it is a mean thing to wonder, a mean thing to think at all, if her daddy could ever find a smile like the one Lincoln's momma had for Lincoln, that smile that said she was proud of her boy, a smile Joan had seen even when Lincoln was banging away at a song his momma didn't want him to play, a smile she had even when she wasn't smiling at him.

It would be up to her, Joan knew right then, on the sidewalk with its cracks and lines. To get a smile like that out of him would be up to her. It would be her *work.*

But maybe she could do this *work,* so that she could see her daddy smile that way. Maybe her momma would smile again, too, if she saw Joan and her daddy dancing together, even if it was about her daddy and his being an *actor,* though she's never seen him in a movie yet.

They are almost to the door now, and still Joan looks at the sidewalk, those lines in the cement, and the cracks, and suddenly she sees that here, here is the map she sometimes dreams about, the secret map of words going somewhere all the time, and always going away. And still they are a secret, the way words out on the corner of Sunset and Hillhurst can be a map that leads to her daddy's happiness, and to her momma's anger, and to her very own *blush* and sadness.

She will bring the record to Lincoln's, and play it, and she will watch more than ever for a moment when her momma's face, just like a moment ago, is soft and smooth and she is smiling, and maybe, maybe she will finally solve the secret of who her momma is.

She will try to dance with her daddy.

But for now there is still this secret map of words, these cracks and lines, and her walking it, headed somewhere away.

13

The story I want to tell here is about a young man and what could have been a family. I want to tell a story about how they lived and were happy somehow, despite each other and maybe because of each other both. It would be a story about growing up and living and sharing meals and breaking bread and all that, and about vacations to see the grandparents during summers, and about happiness and about happiness and about happiness.

But that's not a story I know at all, and even saying that will sound like a whine, like the crybaby shit of some twisted sorry stupid fool because nobody, nobody lives like that, and to blame the idea of it on television and *Leave It to Beaver* and *Father Knows Best* and *The Andy Griffith Show* and all the rest of that rot is to cop a kind of plea, to ignore the fact that family and happiness aren't the same thing.

But even though I know I'm a crybaby for saying this in the first place, and even though I know that to blame things on others—on television and the movies and, mainly, your mother and the way, while you were growing up, she seemed as far from you as the moon—even though I know that to blame the *un*happiness of a life elsewhere is a cop-out that reveals me to be as spineless as the huge jellyfish we'd sometimes spot deep at sea, jellyfish that looked more like oil spills than anything alive but that would kill you soon as you touched them; and even though I know that to blame this life on something else is as stupid as a kid lying awake at night and watching out his window the black silhouette of Squaw Peak rising up into stars, hoping his mother might burst into the room holding the hand of his long lost father, the two of them dancing in the moonlight and laughing for it— even though and even though and even though I know all of this, there is still, I also know, hope, though it is a kind of scuffed up and scarred hope, a kind of hope that's had an eye gouged out and lost an arm and has only the clothes on its back and no hope for anything other than the hope of itself, because no one out there wants anything to do with it.

I have hope, because I've seen it. I've seen that intersection between family and happiness. I have.

This:

Evacuees are camped out on the flight deck of the ship, while in the night sky to the west lies a line of clouds lit up orange, the whole of Saigon burning down. We are just off the coast of Vung Tau, the two small mountains at the southern tip of the island vague silhouettes to my right, on one of them a lighthouse that flashes its calm and predictable routine, the light a kind of breathing that helps me breathe myself, after all I have seen.

The helicopters have stopped, the processing of evacuees out to other ships from ours finished too. But here are the people who'll stay onboard our ship, camped until we put in at Subic Bay, where they'll begin the next part of whatever it is their lives hold for them. There is about them all an animal chaos and order, a layer of people in knots and fists that must somehow be families or neighbors, all aware of each other but acting as though they cannot and will not see each other, like zebras and hippos and gazelles and water buffalo gathered at the smallest watering hole on the continent, all of them in blankets and sheets and clutching what look like carpetbags and pillowcases and themselves, women and children and men. There are even fires here and there in small hibachis some of them have gotten onboard, and some of them are speaking, their words like songs, wide and flat and diced to pieces all at the same time. Some of them are crying, and some of them are still and silent, and some of them are only rocking back and forth, quiet, nowhere near the USS *Denver,* but somewhere very far away.

It's quiet, finally.

And I am a kid who's only been onboard three days. I am only a kid fresh out of Great Lakes Naval Training Center, where I've done pushups and marched around and studied how to work on an engine, and where mostly I've stood guard duty while frozen wind off Lake Michigan chewed bitterly right through me, me the butt of a stupid joke that involved quitting high school just because I'd turned eighteen and wanted free from that house in Phoenix and that mother. The upshot of that wise decision was, of course, a frozen wind that chewed right through me while I shivered holding an old Springfield rifle, wondering what I'd done, wondering where I'd end up, wondering what my life would *be,* and what might happen were I to pop off a few shots from that old rifle in order to try to kill a wind that wouldn't stop, a wind that seemed to chew like a starved ghost right through me.

Then I'd graduated—Mom made it out for that, stayed only long enough to watch my unit parade by, then give me an awkward hug after the whole thing was over, her eyes never meeting mine, before she was on a shuttle back to O'Hare, and home, and suddenly—suddenly—here I was onboard the USS *Denver,* LPD 9, an amphibious transport dock. The trip began in Chicago with a flight to LAX, then one to Hawaii and on to Manila, next a bus ride to Subic Bay, followed by a two-day ride on a destroyer to the coast of Vietnam, and then a helicopter ride from the destroyer and across water so choked with Navy ships and with sampans and trawlers and more Navy ships that it seemed this was D-Day and not just an early afternoon on my first day of duty, and then that helicopter settled on the deck of the ship, my five-day excursion ending with me stepping off alone in dungarees and work shirt and brown chukka boots—my seabag with my work boots had been lost at the airport in Manila—only to be chewed through yet again by a CPO who'd run up to me like I'd stolen his mama's purse because, as he put it, his nose touching mine now and again with the importance of his message, *This is a flagship, you little shit, this is the flagship for the fucking evacuation of Saigon, and there's admirals up on the bridge looking down at you right this very fucking second, you little nothing piece of shit E-2 machinist's mate, and they're wondering what in the fuck are you doing wearing these pansy-ass queer-bait little ankle boots like some fucking San Francisco queer reporting for duty on the flagship of the whole fucking evacuation.*

Suddenly—suddenly—I was here.

Then the helicopters started coming in not a half hour later, only time enough for me to meet the duty chief and hand him a wad of papers. Before I'd even stepped foot in the engine room, I was helping evacuees off these Hueys not because I'd had any training being near a helicopter but because there were so many of them, and because more and more Hueys, a swarm of them, hovered like hummingbirds at a feeder off the stern and to port and starboard while we lifted children and women and held the hands of men, all of them with faces shocked with joy and terror at once, because they were *here,* they were *here,* and everything they'd ever known was long long gone, and some pansy-ass seaman in chukka boots was helping them run out from under the heavy chop of air, air that banged down like a hammer and drowned out even the notion of trying to hear, so that children screaming seemed like something on TV with the sound turned off, and women looking at you and shouting loud as they could and pointing at whatever the hell they were pointing at felt like the same program, and men climbing out with no shoes on or with spit-shined leather shoes or in straw sandals all seemed like part of a program, some fucked-up episode of *McHale's Navy* with no sound but for the hammer of air in your ears.

Helicopters were landing on any ship that could take them, and when I'd have a minute I'd look up from the mayhem here and see those helicopters everywhere coming in and coming in, and now they weren't Marines flying them in anymore, but South Vietnamese army, and our flight deck lay littered with our own helicopters, no room to land anyone else anymore, and still the helicopters—two of them, now three and then four—hovered about us, until one of them came in close and tried to land, tried to land, his skids dipping to the deck and rising, dipping and rising, each time our deck men waving him off. Then the pilot eased off to port, floated above the water, then settled his aircraft into the South China Sea itself, and I saw the helicopter pitch to the left, the blades thrash a moment in bright blue water before forced to stop by the weight of the sea and the angle of the blades and the sinking helicopter.

In the instant all this happened there arose from the evacuees and sailors and Marines and anyone else, everyone watching this all from the deck, a sudden cry and moan, a deep and dark and confused utterance I had never heard before and hope I never will again, and there came in the exact moment after it the crack of the shipboard siren, the sharp wail accompanied by shouts of *Holy shit!* and *Sonofabitch!* and *Fucking crazy-ass gooks!* and lines were thrown down all the way to the water where people in the bright blue down there screamed and swam and made for those lines, and here came out of the stern a rescue boat that motored right up to them and fished out every one.

A minute later the boxy red crash truck and its crew pulled out of its slot at the base of the bridge, lights flashing, and eased forward, a way made for it as it weaved around helicopters on deck until the crash truck came to the last helicopter in a row of three on the starboard side, and I watched as the truck moved right up beside the helicopter, men out and standing around and watching, one man waving the driver in, waving him in, until the grille of the truck touched the side of the helicopter. Men shook their heads, hands on their hips, and the one who'd waved the driver in waved him in yet again, and now the truck pushed at the helicopter, slid it sideways across the deck until, with a kind of slow and perfect and peaceful resignation, the Huey tipped overboard, fell to the water, and I and everyone else ran to the deck edge, made it in time to see its belly, like the carcass of some giant dead insect, the skids its stiff and useless legs, wash over with that blue, and disappear.

They pitched seven helicopters overboard before it was done, a hole made for another helicopter hovering off the stern each time one disappeared into that blue, more and more and more evacuees spilling out onto our ship, until word came down that we were full, that we had too many evacuees onboard and we'd have to move them out to other ships, so that next I pulled my first duty as a machinist: riding aboard an LCM-8, the landing craft supposed to be used to carry troops or cargo from ship to ship or from ship to shore, six of them down in the amphibious dock inside the stern. The whole stern of the ship opened up like an oven door so that the transports could be spit out into open sea, and here I was, a CPO strapping a helmet on my head and pushing into my hands an M16, his words to me an explanation and order at once: *Policy is no vessel leaves without it's machinist onboard to fix anything goes wrong, and policy is you fire this sonofabitch at anything weird, don't wait to see what it is, just fire at anything weird.* Then he paused a moment, looked at me, tilted his head a little, said, *Who the fuck are you, boy? Ain't never seen you before, peachfuzz!*

But before I even answered he'd shoved me inside the transport, around me crammed a hundred Vietnamese, and it seemed even more a kind of D-Day for the all of us jammed here, but a D-Day with no purpose, no goal, just to hustle these people off our ship and onto another. Down inside the stern, jammed onboard the transport with all these evacuees, all I could smell was the stink of people and fish and the heavy caul of diesel exhaust over us all, and I made my way up to the front of the pen to the podium where, like a preacher with his back turned to the congregation, there stood another sailor in a helmet, his hands on the wheel. He looked down at me, said, *We break down, you know how to fix one of these things?* to which I only shook my head, swallowed. *Welcome to the U.S. Navy,* he said in answer, his eyes to the sea in front of us as we motored out into bright sunlight from the dark inside the stern, and here to my right came *Fuck that Navy shit!* shouted loud and tough. I turned, saw a Marine at the corner of the pen, between us six or eight huddled Vietnamese, all of them shorter than any of us, the Marine geared up in his green and smiling at me. Then he glanced behind him and started singing loud as he could, *From the halls of Montezuma,* a song picked up by the three other Marines, one posted inside each corner of the pen, *to the shores of Tripoli. We fight our country's battles on the land as on the sea!*

The sailor at the wheel slowly shook his head, said *Fucking jarheads,* and suddenly—suddenly—I was back on guard duty, this time with an M16, something I'd fired at the range at Great Lakes, but in this moment, the here and now of an order to fix a transport I had no idea how to fix and an order to shoot at anything weird when every single thing around me was more weird than anything I'd ever seen in my life, the best thing I knew to do was to put my finger on the safety, and keep it there.

Now, finally, this third day I am onboard—I have slept a total of nine hours and have met some of the other machinist's mates, though I have as yet to pull duty in the engine room, or to have been issued a locker or a bunk—there is quiet while I stand out here on the deck, the clouds to the west lit up orange. There is quiet, though those voices flat and wide and diced all to pieces still sing out here, and there is quiet even inside the crying I can hear, too, and there is quiet inside the all of this animal order and chaos, because I am breathing, the light at Vung Tau and its predictable flash my calm.

Here is where I find hope, where I find the unexpected joy of family and happiness: I am leaning against the gray steel bulkhead of the bridge out here, the ship's lights on so that the deck is lit up like a Friday night football field, that field filled with these people, and I am smoking a cigarette, the smoke in my lungs a kind of easy friend who will never betray me, and when my eyes leave the calm that lighthouse gives me, and when my eyes leave those orange clouds, and when I let go the smoke in my lungs and bid good-bye to that friend I know will be back soon as I breathe in the next drag, my eyes fall to a knot of people two rows of people—maybe fifteen feet—away.

A small fist of them, like any of the small fists out here: a man, a woman, a little boy and a little girl, a grandma.

A family.

There are dozens and dozens of these out here, but this is the family I see, where my eyes have fallen once they let go the calm of the lighthouse. In the light out here on deck, I can see they are all seated in a circle on a gray-green wool blanket the U.S. Navy has given them, to one side of the mother a stack of five empty beige plastic bowls from the galley. Earlier tonight cooks had hauled up here garbage cans filled with cooked rice and had ladled out helpings to everyone, served up in these bowls. I can smell out here cooked fish from off the hibachis, somehow wood or charcoal and fish the items some of these people have thought to pack with them. But this family has nothing with them, only, it seems, the clothes on their backs. No pillowcases or satchels or carpetbags beside them or clutched close. There are only the five of them in a circle on a U.S. Navy wool blanket.

The boy, seated at four o'clock in the circle—the mother is at eight, sister at nine and snuggled in to her mother, the father at twelve, Grandma at two, all of them in shadow and light so that I can't see their faces clearly but only in angles of light and shadow—leans forward to the middle of the circle, and with his hand moves something there. He is seated on his haunches, as are the grandma and mother, the daughter and father with their legs crossed beneath them, and the boy, now that he is finished with whatever he has done, eases back, and nods hard once.

This is when the girl reaches to the middle of the circle, moves something there too, her hand quick at it, and just as quickly she snuggles back in to her mother, and the boy's hand slaps hard the deck in frustration at what she has just done.

The father gives a small laugh, and I push myself off the bulkhead, take a step toward them slow and easy. There is something I can see and can't quite name in their actions, this movement.

I take another step, take a drag from the cigarette too, and now, from this angle, I can see there is a ring of small rocks on the gray-green wool blanket, maybe a dozen of them, each only a little bigger than a pebble. The grandma reaches to the ring now and moves one of them, snatches up another, and the boy slaps his hand down even harder, and though from here I can see only half his face, I can see this kid drama for the act it is: there is in his grimace a kind of smile trying to get out.

Now the mother chuckles, and the daughter—she's maybe six or seven, the boy maybe ten—looks up at her and says something quiet, her first finger between her teeth as she speaks, and the mother leans in closer to her and says something back.

The boy moves a rock to a different place in the circle—this is some kind of game, it comes to me, my mind so dulled with the lack of sleep and the plain bliss of this cigarette and the quiet that what they are doing has taken me this long to understand—and finishes his move with snatching up two other rocks. He does this all with one hand, his left, his moves so precise and certain I can tell he's played this game a million times, and when he has the rocks in hand, he nods hard twice, says a single-syllable word, something hard and decisive, and brings the hand with the rocks to his side, sets them on the blanket.

The mother chuckles again, and the daughter, still snuggled in and still with her finger between her teeth, glances up at her. The mother nods, and the girl sits up, leans in, and quickly moves one rock three times. When she is done she picks up five of the rocks, leaving in the circle only six or seven.

The family erupts in laughter, all of them save for the boy, who explodes in a boy way at losing a game he knew he had in hand. He slaps hard the deck three times in a row and rolls over and away from the circle of family and toward me, and it is only now, as he rolls away from them and as they laugh in these angles of shadow and light that I see it, I see it: this boy has only one arm, his left, the right sleeve of his shirt empty and loose. This boy has lost an arm, and I take a sudden step back while still they laugh at him, and while he sits back up and slaps the deck with his only hand, and I see now the mother rock forward with laughter, and the daughter pointing that finger she'd just had between her teeth at her brother, and she's laughing too, and the grandma is smiling, and she is slowly shaking her head at the folly of believing you were going to win, though in the low chuckle she gives I can see this boy has been like this every day of his life: a handful and a handful and a handful.

The father leans his head back for his laughter, and I see the next piece of this hopeful puzzle, one more avenue into this intersection of happiness and family: with his leaning back I can see his face full now in the deck lights, and I see he has only one eye, the place where his right eye should have been a hollow depression, and he has no eyebrow above it, the skin there rough and puckered.

They laugh, and laugh, and I take a step back, and another, and my back is against the bulkhead again with a sudden bump that makes me drop my cigarette.

And I have seen it: hope.

It is scuffed up and scarred. It's had an eye gouged out, and lost an arm. It has only the clothes on its back, and has no hope for anything other than the hope of itself, because no one out there wants anything to do with it.

It is a family that has found, in this moment, at the intersection of happiness and family, itself.

The father sees me against the bulkhead, and he nods, lets the laugh draw down to a good and solid smile, I can see, and then the mother turns to me, and the grandma looks at me, and the daughter, and, last, the boy, who turns on his haunches to face me, and he is smiling, like all of them.

The father says words to me I can't understand, and with them he lowers his head the smallest way, his eye never leaving mine, and still he smiles. The mother says the words too, and then the boy; the daughter draws even tighter in to her mother, and the grandma nods, stays silent.

Quickly the boy reaches his one hand to the stack of

bowls beside his mother, lifts one of them, holds the beige plastic galley bowl up and says the words again, and the father repeats them: *Kom um now,* it sounds like, and now I know the sounds for what they mean, the gesture and their smiles and these words all meant for me, though I am nothing but a kid wearing chukka boots who kept the safety on the whole five trips between this ship and the others while the weird of his world swallowed him whole.

Thank you, they are saying to me, and I smile as best I can without breaking into the million pieces I will break into for the gift they have given me: hope in family and in happiness. Because, I see in their tattered lives, in their scars and poverty, that I am from a family, too. A mother, and a grandma, and a grandpa.

Kom um now, I say as best I can, and their eyes open wide at this, even the father, whose eyebrow over his good eye arches high, and they all nod, and they smile.

The boy says, *Thank you.*

It seems a five-day trip from America to here before I hear his words, before I understand in my heart and head that, yes, he has said this in my own language, because the world I have seen in this family is a foreign one, a place I've never been before, and now the boy smiles even broader, even more deeply, and I nod, and nod again.

I have hope. I do.

The envelope Grandpa gave me when he met us on the porch after Grandma and I got back from buying her three cartons of Benson & Hedges Gold—the small thank-you note of a letter with the familiar yet foreign handwriting on the front, the return address naming a place called Phoenix; the envelope I folded in half and half again, then shoved deep into my back pocket, hoping I might not remember where I put it later on—I still have that envelope, three weeks later.

It's still in my back pocket, the edges of those folds frayed now with how long it's been there. Each night I get it out, hold it in my hand, touch at those frayed edges, because there is a mystery here, me in the middle of it and at the outer edge too, my life and my mother's and my grandma and grandpa's a circle of stones being snatched up one by one with what won't be said.

But there is an envelope, here in my back pocket.

I have hope. I've seen it.

Somehow it seems the next move is mine.

14

I am about to nod off, the van filled with the smell of hot coffee, in me the first few hits off the Styrofoam cup and the maple bar we got at the Winchell's on Roscoe Boulevard. The radio is down low, tuned to some easy-listening station that won't play anything anyone under fifty will listen to—right now it's a woman singing "It must be him!" like it's a fistfight to get the words out—and the heater at my feet and the fact it's 5:15 A.M. and the slow movement of all those caftans behind me as we tear down the freeway, the gentle whisper of all that fabric against all that fabric, makes me lean my head forward the smallest bit, makes my eyelids heavy as stone.

We're on the Golden State Freeway South in Grandpa's Econoline, the back of the van jammed with caftans hanging from the five rods he's installed widthwise in here, on our way to the Mecca of all swap meets, the Rose Bowl Flea Market. It's a trip I am supposed to feel excited about, jazzed up for all the talk Grandpa's made about it the last three weeks, ever since I sat down at a sewing machine in the garage and decided to give that a try.

But it's 5:15 in the morning, and I am about to nod off.

Of course this is when Grandpa pulls the old trick, the one I fall for every time, though I see it coming out the corner of my eye.

He pushes in the lighter on the dash, fishes a cigarette out of the front pocket of his flowered shirt and puts it to his lips, and the lighter pops. I can see even with these eyelids easing down the bright orange of the coils as he brings it to his face, carefully finds the tip of the cigarette, and here is yet another soothing layer to the coffee and the donut and the heater: the perfume of a flame touched to tobacco.

He pops the lighter back into place, the cigarette he's just lit in that same hand, and here it comes, with the perfect timing of years and years of this slapstick routine of his. Just as my eyes are slipping closed but the instant before, when I am still awake and still aware, he moves that hand with the cigarette to the radio dial, and twists the volume up high.

Instantly the van fills with that fistfighting woman's shout, "BUT IT'S NOT HIM!"

Of course I startle at it.

Coffee sloshes out of the plastic lid on the cup between my legs, and before I can say or do anything Grandpa has turned the volume back down, both hands to the wheel as though he hadn't touched a thing, that newly lit cigarette just smoking away.

He's done this since I was a kid, and the next thing that always happens is that he roars with laughter, his cigarette in one hand, the other on the steering wheel, his mouth open for that laugh, teeth shining bright, his eyebrows high and eyes wide open too. He's laughing at *you* like you've just done the funniest thing in the world. But the truth, I have known just as long as he's been doing this, is that he's acting. He's laughing at himself and what *he's* done, which is always the role of the practical joker: *Look at me,* the practical joker says, *and how clever I am at your expense.*

I snatch up the napkins from the dashboard and blot coffee from my Levi's, shake my head and look at him, ready to shout with as much actor as I have in me *Cut that out!*

But there's something missing in this moment, and here it is, as clear for its absence as the heat through my jeans: he's not laughing, only smiling. He's got both hands on the wheel, and I can see in the light from the dash his white hair, but I can't see those white white teeth of his the way I can when he's laughing.

He looks at me, slowly shakes his head, and I can't tell if he's acting now or not.

"What?" I say.

He's quiet a moment, turns back to the freeway traffic. He's still smiling, takes a drag off the cigarette. "Guess maybe that joke's getting a little old."

"For real," I say, and wad up the napkins. There wasn't much, finally, that spilled. But I don't want him to know that, and so wadding up the napkins and dropping them to the floorboard with a flourish—I hold my arm straight out in front of me, open my fingers all at once, a claw letting go its cargo—seems like some act of defiance.

Though I feel stupid for just such a sentiment, for being suddenly the pouty child who believes that in his insolence he'll show them all, I begin to hear the true import of his words: maybe the joke of me being here and living with my grandparents is what's getting old.

"And then I die. That's when I die!" the woman on the radio is singing now, her voice gone from those bare knuckles to a certain shame and sorrow.

Every second Sunday of the month there's this flea market at the Rose Bowl, and calling it a kind of Mecca isn't a joke, judging from the reverent way he's talked about it while we've worked. My grandpa's regard for this event is no act at all.

I'd heard it in the way his voice went quiet and steady as he'd pinned up a hem Friday afternoon and told me how he wasn't an "occasional"—his word—seller but had his own California resale number, the permit "procured"—his word—precisely for this event eleven years ago. I'd seen as well the steady way his eyes met mine to tell me, after I'd finished running that hem, that we'd need one hundred forty-five caftans, not one more or one less, for this endeavor.

There'd been a kind of solemnity, too, in how we'd loaded the van after dinner last night, the van backed up to the open garage door. The only light had been that from inside the garage, those two fluorescent light sets Grandpa'd hung from the rafters, so that he was a silhouette to me inside the van while he handed in sets of caftans. "Fifteen red camellia on royal blue," he'd said, and handed them in to me, watched as I placed them on the rod so that, as he'd instructed me, the open ends of the hangers faced the front of the van. "Twenty-two peach dahlia on black," he'd said next, handed this batch into me, and said quietly, "Space them out on the rod, two fingers between each hanger." I turned to him once I'd gotten them on the rung, had ready a smile for him at the joke of that, spacing out the hangers.

There was his silhouette, his hand held out to the side so that I could see his first two fingers held together. "Two fingers," he said.

"Yes sir," I'd said, and I'd spaced them.

Then last night at nine, he'd stood from his burgundy velvet recliner just as the theme song to *The Love Boat* started, and said, "Time for bed."

I looked up from the sofa, smiled, nodded. "Good night," I said. I had plans to go see a movie a little later on, take the Caddy out to what I'd read in the paper was some crazy thing called *Roadie* that starred Meat Loaf and had a scene where Deborah Harry wrestles with dwarves.

But Grandma, seated in the other recliner, reached to the end table between them, found the remote beside the blue and turquoise and violet feather flower arrangement there. She squinted, pointed the remote at the TV as though the straighter and stiffer her arm the better the electronic signal, and blinked it off.

She turned, squinted at me, weaved her head a little one way and another, trying to find me.

"Tomorrow," she said, just as seriously as Grandpa'd told me how to space hangers, "is the Flea Market." She paused, without looking settled the remote back beneath the feather flowers, and said, "Time for bed."

We were out of the house at 4:45.

But here's the strange thing: I like it, all this sewing and pinning and cutting. There's something about pressing slight as you can on the pedal hidden away beneath the machine and the material. There's something about easing the material in, finding the line, working the pedal at just the right speed that gives me a way around everything—what I am supposed to do with my life—with making a straight line.

I can do this.

I've been out to the parking lot at Dale's with him twice now, helped him set up the van and the caftans, hang them on the portable racks he's built that fold down and break apart so that they lie flat in the back of the van when we're done. We've got two lawn chairs, and once we've got the racks up and hung, we sit down, and we talk, and we sell, and we smoke, and we joke.

And people really do pull off Van Nuys Boulevard and into the lot, and they climb out of their cars, and they actually *buy* this stuff.

But even more amazing than the fact people buy these things is when I see Grandpa turn into the actor I am beginning to believe he may very well have been, though there is still no proof of anything, only his Tall Tales of Walter Brennan and Claudette Colbert, this guy Clifton Webb and Lucille Ball, and John Wayne and Elvis—Elvis!—and somebody named Buddy Rogers, and of course this Billie Dove.

When someone pulls up, he becomes somebody else, which is why I have to look at his eyes, listen hard to his voice, take in his gestures, to try to divine when he's putting on no act at all, and why such a small thing as no laugh, or the gesture of two fingers silhouetted against lights from inside the garage, is something remarkable, worth answering with "Yes sir" instead of the joke or the smile.

He has his roles: With an old lady, he becomes a kind of doddering old man himself, seems to shrink in on himself and shuffles his feet the smallest bit, his voice feeble and thin, and he never fails to introduce me as a grandson whose name he seems unable to remember. Around a younger woman he stands tall, becomes the caring father, ushers her to his wares and tells her how comfortable the caftans will be while she's working around the house or simply relaxing at the end of a long and busy day. With Samoan women—and there a lot of Samoans here, Arleta, the next town over, some kind of Samoan capital—he puts on a thick southern drawl, puts his hands in his back pockets and rocks back and forth on his heels, the caftans no longer called caftans. Now they're muumuus. If anyone has any kids, he gives them each a quarter from his pocket.

And for Mexicans he speaks Spanish, a surprise to me the first time I heard him launch into it. As best I can tell, he works them with the beauty of the flowers in the material, because I can hear the words *daLEE-a* and *RO-sa,* and see him hold the fabric in a way to show off the patterns there. Around the Mexicans he treats me like a nothing, sometimes ordering me in English with a heavy Spanish accent to pull from inside the van another pattern the woman might like. I know enough to be silent, my role not to let my eyes meet his in this play, and every time I retrieve what he calls for he turns to the woman, shakes his head and nods over his shoulder at me, then spurts out something in Spanish I figure is an assessment of how hard it is to get good help these days.

It's an act, all of it. But he is good at it. Very good.

And we make money, enough to keep me in cigarettes and movies—just this week it's been *The Shining, Brubaker,* and *The Blues Brothers*—with a little left over for some weed from the butcher at Dale's.

Scoring that was easy. When Grandpa dispatched me into the store to get a couple of cold Cokes the first day we were out there, I simply walked the aisles until I saw the one I knew would help: a stock clerk, down on his knees and putting up cans of Campbell's soup on the shelf. He was my age, had pasty white skin and hair down past his ears, and I walked up to him, asked point-blank, "Where can I buy?"

He stopped with the cans, looked up at me a long moment, his eyes on my hair and how short it was, I knew, and I said, "I just got out of the Navy, man. Just tell me where I can buy," and I nodded.

He smiled, said, "I don't suppose you mean where's the checkstand, right, man?"

"Nope," I said.

"You want Ned," he said, and nodded behind me, to the back of the store. "Back in the meat department. Tell him Dougie sent you."

I smiled, nodded. "Thanks," I said.

Now at night, once I am convinced Grandma and Grandpa are asleep, I can get up, move through the dark of the living room and kitchen, through the laundry room and out to the back porch, where I can smoke, and think.

But you can't see stars out there. Not like from my bedroom growing up. There are too many lights around, too much city, to let any stars even show up.

Yet this isn't what worries me. That's not what I think about, those missing stars.

What worries me, what puzzles me too, is the fact I have begun to *like* sewing caftans.

I open my eyes, and here we are, stopped in traffic on a surface street, before us a line of cars and trucks and trailers, all with their red taillights flared up. We're in some kind of residential area, houses with no lights on to our left and right, but far back and spaced far apart, like big square ghosts hiding in the woods, watching us, and I blink, pick up the coffee from between my legs, and stretch.

"Surprise, surprise," I say, trying to be funny, to make amends somehow, "the old man let me sleep."

But he's not buying. He rolls down his window, puts his hand out, flicks the ash off his cigarette. "You'll need it," he says. "I want you *on* today," he says, and taps the air out his window with his cigarette for that word *on*. He takes another drag, lets the smoke hang around in him a few seconds before he breathes it out through his nose.

I look at my watch, see it's not quite five thirty; I was only asleep maybe ten minutes, and I take a deep pull at the coffee, just at the very edge of too hot, and for that reason it's perfect.

We inch forward, and forward, and Grandpa's got both hands to the wheel again, and I notice the radio is off now.

"I'll be on," I say, and take another swig at the coffee. "Don't worry about me."

He grips the steering wheel, lets it go, grips it again. The cigarette in his mouth is burned down almost to the filter, the ash an inch long.

"You want to flick that baby, or you want to burn a hole in your brand-new shirt?" I say, one more attempt in this new atmosphere to show him how very on I will be, and I move in my seat, sit up a bit taller. The flowered shirt he's wearing is a new twist in the business: it's made out of that red camellia on royal blue, colors he says make his eyes stand out. He's going to see, he told me while he was cutting it out on Tuesday, if anyone says anything, gives him any compliments. If he does, he told me, he'll start making these too, for the husbands. He'd wanted me to wear one—yellow hibiscus on forest green—but I'd passed.

He turns to me, the move too quick, and the ash breaks off anyway, and now he's brushing at it fast. "Son of a bitch," he says, and again there is nowhere any acting in this. Neither is there any malice, nor any surprise. Just an empty curse. Just my grandpa, ticked at ash down the front of his shirt.

Traffic moves a little bit faster now, though it's still a crawl. I can see a few cars ahead, the road curving to the left, up there a cluster of more lights and a gate, the houses on either side of us disappearing, those ghosts giving way to a chain-link fence.

Beyond it is a parking lot, and suddenly off to my right, out my window, I can see now the huge and hulking shape of the Rose Bowl itself, maybe a quarter mile off. Lining its top is a row of lights like streetlamps spaced every twenty yards or so; down here at ground level are more streetlamps spaced evenly throughout the parking lot.

A thick and trembling moment shoots through me right now, right now, because this is no parking lot.

The shape of that stadium from here, its shoulders and mass and heavy presence, is a ship berthed at the docks at Subic, me in the back of a cab and stoned on vodka and hash both, fresh off a stint with Mali in her stall upstairs above the Jump Off bar, trying to make it back to the *Denver* for my 0400 duty.

I am in the back of a cab and leaned against the door, my face to the glass and looking at the world out there, and all I can see are these lights at the Subic yard, above them and beyond them a ship at berth.

Just like that.

Mali's stall—maybe four feet by four feet with only three sides, the floor a thin mattress wall to wall, the fourth wall open to a hallway where men walked on their way to whatever stall we were being led to—had been draped with a thin tapestry and lit with a black light so that the whites of her eyes and her teeth and the bikini top she had on before she unhooked its clasp between her breasts all shone with the predictable bright purple. The air pounded with Black Sabbath, the cliché soundtrack of every sailor bar I'd been in, the sound up loud enough to preclude any talk between us—the price had been settled downstairs by a toothless woman four times Mali's age—and when here were her breasts and her smile and her legs spread wide, in one hand the hash pipe and its acrid promise of an even deeper buzz than the vodka thus far, in the other hand the washrag she'd use to wipe me clean before she even opened the rubber, I'd thought this was it, what the world was about: fucking and drugs.

For what else was there? What other joy was there to be had?

But even in that moment, and in every opportunity after that one and every one before it, when a woman's open legs and the burning out of brain cells with every toke and shot knocked back seemed like some easy path to fulfillment, I knew the truth: there would be a journey away from this passing appeasement, a journey on which in one manner or another I would be in the back of a cab with my face against the glass and heading for duty, in me ringing hollow as my heart a game of stones picked up one after the other.

Here beside me just like that loomed the hull of a ship berthed in Subic Bay, a structure as huge and awesome as some kind of stone-cold and towering god.

Now we are at the gate, Grandpa easing the van to a stop, and I turn from nothing other than a predawn football stadium and a parking lot to see Grandpa working his wallet out of his back pocket, past the open window a man even older than him wearing a ball cap and a blaze orange road crew vest, a clipboard in his hand.

"Merchandise?" the man says.

"All new," Grandpa says, "and we're going to sell it all," and I can hear on his voice the actor back among us: some kind of Humphrey Bogart.

"Occasional or permanent?" the man says.

"Permanent as the Hollywood Hills," Grandpa says, and hands out to the man the slip of paper he's found in his wallet.

The man takes it, writes down on the clipboard the numbers—his resale permit, I figure, procured for precisely this event—and the man says, "But one good earthquake—"

"And the Hollywood sign gets set up out in Blythe," Grandpa cuts in, and the old man gives a laugh, looks up from the clipboard, holds out the permit.

"You know the drill," the man says. "Pull on up to first available, Blue B or G."

Then the man looks past Grandpa to me. "Who's this?" he says, and nods at me. "He with you, or selling his own?"

"Oh," Grandpa says, and turns to me, looks me up and down as though surprised I am even here. "That's my grandson," he says, Humphrey Bogart gone, the actor vanished with the reminder of my presence.

Grandpa turns back to the man, takes from him the piece of paper. "Loyal sidekick," Grandpa says. "Don't worry about him."

"Have a good one," the old man says, and touches the bill of his cap. Though I should smile at him or at least nod, I only turn back to the stadium, this ship stuck fast.

We follow some predetermined course it seems only Grandpa knows across the parking lot for what seems a half hour for the silence in the van, no radio on, no words between us. He steers the van this way and that around traffic sawhorses set up, taped to different ones paper signs with the words *New Pink* or *New Blue, Antique Orange* or *Miscellaneous Green* or *Antique White,* each with its own arrow pointing left or right or right or left depending on where we are in the lot. Cars peel this way and that to follow their own signs, and though it's still dark out here, the place is filling up like it's New Year's Day, the Rose Bowl about to start.

We turn past one more *New Blue* sign, this one with the block letter *B* beneath the words, and move down one more row of parking slots to close in on the edge of it all, before us cars and vans and pickups, around them people out and working. In the sweep of our headlights I can see people at tables heaped with cardboard boxes, see people setting up racks not unlike our own, see people unloading out of trunks and pickup beds and from inside vans boxes and more boxes, all of it growing closer, all of it ready for us to pull in and start up on our own work.

Then we are here, Grandpa easing the van in beside an old green station wagon with, strangely, no one behind it and working, just a station wagon parked and still. "Irving," he says, and gives a sharp *tsk,* and I say "Who?"

But before he can answer, before he even puts the van in park, here is a man and a woman waving at us in our headlights, the man with a shaggy beard graying at either side of his mouth, the woman with salt-and-pepper hair in pigtails. They're both in shorts and T-shirts and holding big ceramic coffee mugs.

Grandpa parks, pops open his door, and climbs out. "Kids!" he calls, and here they are at his side between that station wagon and the van. The man slaps him on the back, says "Dig that shirt!" and the woman leans in and gives Grandpa a peck on the cheek. "How's Saralee?" she says as soon as she's pulled away, her words quiet, both hands on her coffee mug, and I see the man leave his hand on Grandpa's shoulder.

I open my door, climb out, and here behind the van is the stadium even closer now, even bigger, and for the position of the van—we'll be opening the back doors and setting the racks up in the slot directly behind us—I know I'll be looking at it all day long. The silhouette of it is even sharper now, but the sky above it is maybe—maybe—the least bit lighter. Maybe dawn really will come, and this hulk will leave me, set out of Subic on its own WESTPAC cruise away from me.

"Let me introduce the heir apparent," Grandpa says, and I turn, look across the short hood of the van to the three of them in the odd dark and light out here of car headlights pulling in and pulling in.

We all meet at the front of the van, and Grandpa says, "This is my grandson, Brad, late of the U.S. Navy. A virgin Rose Bowl flea marketer. Riding shotgun the last few weeks since he got out."

"I'm Eva Germain," the woman says, and takes a hand from the mug, puts it out to me, and I take it. "Brad," I say. "His grandson. Guilty as charged." Though the woman's hand is a little rough, a little dry, it's warm in mine, and she holds my hand tight a long moment, then lets go, and in a passing headlight I can see wisps of steam off the coffee in her mug.

"Johnny Rayford," the man says, and here's his hand out to me too, but the handshake he gives is what we called the Bro in the Navy, our thumbs interlocking, fingers wrapping up and around like we're about to armwrestle, and I recover quickly enough, I hope, to where my part in this handshake comes off smooth. Just then another set of headlights rakes across us all, and I can see the faded remnants of the words *Just Passin' Through* printed across his gray T-shirt, and I wonder at Grandpa and how he's hooked up with these people: old hippies.

Johnny holds my hand in his what feels a moment too long, just as this Eva had, and I can feel the warmth of his hand too. He says, "You give your grammy our love. You tell her we miss her," and I can hear on his voice that he means it.

"Will do," I say, and tighten my grip a little on his, resisting in the same moment tacking on at the end of my response the single word *bro,* like we always did when we shook hands like this in the Navy. Nobody I knew shook hands this way unless they were giving you shit.

Still this Johnny holds on, and here is another set of

headlights, and now I can see his eyes, and in this momentary light I glance at Eva and see her eyes on me as well, and it comes to me that they are earnest in this, and that they are, indeed, friends. They want me to give this news of their regard to my grandma.

"Will do," I say again, and let go Johnny's hand.

"You come on down to our setup," Eva says, "and pick yourself out a mug. On the house." She taps the side of hers, holds it up. "We're three spots down. The Hearty Pot. Ceramics. We've got fresh coffee too."

"Sounds great," I say, and Johnny slaps me on the shoulder, lets his hand hang there a moment, just like he'd done with Grandpa. "We'll be looking for you," he says, then, "You're in for a righteous time today, bro," and he nods, his eyes and hers gone for no headlights, the three of us back in shadow.

Bro. Righteous. It is all I can do not to laugh.

"Let's go, Popeye," I hear from behind me, Grandpa already at the back of the van. "Thanks," I say to the couple, "I'll come over in a little while," and nod, then head down my side of the van to where the back doors are already open.

Grandpa's already assembling the first set of portable racks in the middle of the slot behind the van, and I lean in the van and pull out another set of bars and the rung.

"Never figured you for one to hang out with hippies," I say just loud enough for him to hear as I set the collapsible contraption beside his and start in, fold out one side, and the other.

"Who?" he says, and stops a moment, looks at me. He's got the rack done, ready to pick it up and move it where he wants it to go on this tiny piece of real estate we've got for the day, one car slot in a parking lot.

"Joni Mitchell and Neil Young," I say, though as soon as I've said it, I know the joke is mine alone.

"Never met them," he says, and picks up the rack, sets it out at the farthest edge of the slot, parallel to the white stripe between our slot and the one behind the station wagon, a stripe it seems is suddenly brighter in the dark going gray all around.

I glance a moment up at the stadium. There's more light behind it, though the sun itself is a long, long way away.

"Earl?" I hear from behind us, the word somehow muffled. I turn, see the back gate of the green station wagon slowly lift open, and a man in there sits up. He's in a sleeping bag, I can see in this gray, and the bottom end of the bag swings around, settles on the pavement. The man brings a hand out from inside the bag, scratches his head hard and fast.

"Irving," Grandpa says, "time to get up." He moves the rack one last time, right up to that white line, then steps over to the station wagon, both hands on his hips, and stands before this Irving.

"I was getting up," he says. "I'm up," he says, and scratches under his chin, and slowly, slowly I can begin to make out that this station wagon is full with whatever is in there—the space where he'd been curled up in a sleeping bag is the only open space in the entire vehicle. I can't see through the car windows to the other side of the car, the inside solid with boxes.

"For a fisherman, you sure don't get up easy," Grandpa says, and now he puts a hand out to Irving, who takes it, shakes.

"You know I'm no fisherman," he says. He lets go Grandpa's hand, and now he stretches, yawns, says inside the yawn, "I just sell this shit."

"Time to get up" is all Grandpa says, and he turns back to the van, pulls out another set of rack parts, but I can see as I finish up with my own set that Grandpa is smiling, shaking his head.

"How's Saralee doing?" Irving says, and eases out from inside the station wagon and from under the gate. He lets the sleeping bag drop, and even in this gray I can see he's dressed in some kind of khaki getup: a shirt with the sleeves rolled up, a vest with zippers and pockets, shorts with more pockets.

Grandpa doesn't lose a beat as he works, says, "She's terrific. Couldn't be better."

"Horseshit," the man says, and steps out of the sleeping bag. He's got heavy socks on, sits down on the rear bumper, pulls from inside the back of the station wagon a pair of some kind of boots. "Your better half—"

"Irving," Grandpa says, "meet my grandson, Brad," and slaps on the rung at the top of the rack.

"The sailorman?" Irving says, and finishes with the laces on one boot.

I've been watching this all, my first rack not even put together. There is something strange to this play between them, the banter, or at least these beginnings of it, and before I can think anything further of it, here is Irving coming at me with just one boot on, a hand out to me to shake.

"Heard a lot about you. Maybe too much," he says, smiling, and we shake. He's got a thick mustache, sharp jaw, and curly hair, and I can see as he gets closer that this khaki vest of his has little feathery things all over it, small as bugs. Fishing flies, I can see, hooked in all around.

"You ever get rid of the drips you picked up over there?" he says.

"What?" I say, and let go his hand.

"The drips," he says. "Clap. Gonorrhea. What happens when you play Ping-Pong with the ladies over there. Earl told us all about how you—"

"What?" I say again, and turn to Grandpa, shoot out "What are you telling him—"

"Nailed you!" Irving says, and lets out a laugh, and Grandpa says, "It's an old tradition in the history of our military forces, Popeye," his voice—here's the actor again—some kind of evening newsman.

"Just giving you shit," Irving says, and laughs, hands on his hips. "Nothing but good is all they ever say about you. Nothing but good. Especially Saralee. She loves you, man."

"Oh," I say, and try at a smile, turn to the rack and act like I'm interested in putting it together.

"Grandma's great," I finally say, and try not to sound like too much of a jerk. "She's taking care of me," I say. "Good care. Better than I deserve."

"Truer words," Grandpa says, and here's another rack already done, him settling it on the edge of the white stripe on the other side of our slot just as an ancient black pickup pulls in beside us.

The driver's window is down, and I see a thick arm rise up and wave, hear from inside the cab a deep and raspy voice call out "Earl!"

Then, from across the open lane out front of our slot, I hear a woman's voice call out, "Is that you, Earl? How's Saralee?" and I turn, see across from us in this gathering gray light a woman behind a table stacked with plates and bowls. She's waving, her hair poofed up high on her head.

She's got on a caftan: our rose-on-white.

"This the sailor we heard tell so much about?" I hear from beside me, and turn to a huge man with red suspenders and a flannel shirt, a Dodgers cap pushed back on his head, sleeves rolled up. The door to the pickup is still open, and I see past him a woman inside the cab lit with the dome light, Grandpa leaned in and holding her hand, some small words passing between them.

"That's him," Irving says from over at his station wagon. "CPO Sharkey. Ask him about the ladies in Subic," he says, and laughs, him bent to the work of unloading boxes out of the station wagon.

I swallow hard at that word—*Subic*—and the

looming hull of the stadium just here, close enough to touch, and I want to know what this Irving knows, what it is Grandpa has told him, and I want to know what, if anything, I have told Grandpa without even knowing it.

I want to know if I've given away a family on the deck of the *Denver* in telling of them to him.

Because I'm holding tight to that story. Because I'm keeping that one close. As close as this envelope folded down to nothing in my back pocket, whatever dispatch it is I've been sent from the burning city of my mother's life.

I'm holding it tight, because I am afraid that once I tell a story about hope, scuffed up and scarred, it will disappear, like the carcass of a helicopter washing over with the blue of the South China Sea.

"Chuck Van Hoof," the huge man says, and puts his hand out to shake. He's smiling, in that smile the same sort of strange closeness I'd seen in Eva's and Johnny's eyes, the same sort of intimacy as I'd heard in the banter between Grandpa and Irving.

"Just ignore Irving," this Chuck says. "Mind like a turd won't flush." He nods at me, says, "I want to hear how this boy's grandmama's doing." He's still smiling, still with his hand out to me.

"Hey, Earl!" someone calls out from somewhere behind me, and then there is another call from somewhere else nearby—"Earl? How's she doing?"—and another—"Hey, Earl! Is this him?"—before I can even think to take this man's hand, tell him my name.

15

Before we had half the caftans out of the van there'd been at least a dozen people come over, stop Grandpa and chat, every one of them asking after Grandma and wanting to meet me, all of them telling me their names and where they were located on the lot and why I had to come check out their wares—rugs and sandals and hubcaps and jewelry and ball caps and candles and carburetors.

Now it's daylight, the sun broken behind the stadium, I can tell, for the halo around it. I'm parked in my lawn chair, the racks up and caftans out. Grandpa's gone, out making the rounds, shaking hands and giving hugs and slaps on the back and laughing and joking with everyone before the show gets going any minute now.

And so, because Grandpa's gone, and because I want to make sure, I ask Irving for the third time: "You're sure he didn't say I told him anything?"

"You think you're the first kid ever to join the Navy?" Irving shoots back. "Of course I know Subic. I was in and out of there—pardon the pun—from 'sixty-four to 'sixty-seven, onboard the *Tolovana*. Boatswain's mate first class, round about time our ol' XO LBJ got the ball rolling over there."

From where I sit between these racks of caftans, I can see him in his khaki getup perched on a short stool behind a table at the bottom of a U of tables stacked with fishing paraphernalia. He's got out eight or ten clear plastic bins filled with Day-Glo red and orange and green lures, three or four others stuffed with dull gray weights all sizes, from BBs to chunks as big as tennis balls, still a couple more bins packed with spools of fishing line. Fishing poles stand at attention out front of the whole thing, crammed into two white five-gallon buckets, one each on the ground at the heads of the tables.

He's bent to a wooden toolbox on the tabletop in front of him, on his head like an orthopedic visor a set of those industrial magnifying eyeglasses. Off one end of the toolbox is a small vise, off the other a desk lamp with a bendable steel neck, the light pulled over and shining down on the vise. Spread across the top of the box is a set of delicate and purposeful tools: he's tying flies out here, in one hand what looks like a set of tweezers, in the other a pair of scissors, his face so close to the vise his nose almost touches.

"So he hasn't told you anything," I say, just to make sure.

"Give it a rest, Mr. Roberts. He hasn't said a word about any of your naval explorations," Irving says. "But he *has* told me he used to play poker with Howard Hughes once a month for three years, and he never got any work out of it. But who around here *hasn't* he told that to?" He whips his hand once, twice, three times around a pinch of feathers and a hook clamped in the vise, then quickly reaches to a pair of needle-nose pliers from the top of the box, just as quickly twists at the fly and twists again. "He's been telling that one for years, since way before that nut died."

"Me," I say. "He hasn't told me." I would have remembered his playing cards with that crazy dude with the fingernails and hair and too much money.

"Can't explain that one," Irving says. He turns, looks over at me, his eyes huge cartoons for those magnifying eyeglasses. "I'm ready for my close-up now, Mr. DeMille," he says, and smiles, blinks three times in a row.

"I'm telling you, just ignore him" comes from my right, and I turn, see Chuck sitting on the tailgate of his old pickup, in his hands a ceramic coffee mug just like Eva and Johnny'd had when we pulled up. "And I don't want any more of this talk about women and bars when Serena wakes up, you hear, Irving?" He leans forward, looks past me to Irving.

Chuck's wife—Serena—is asleep in the cab of the old pickup, and I can see through the back window of the truck a pillow up against the passenger window, see too just the top of her head, her red hair.

She's beautiful, pale skin with a quiet spray of freckles, brown eyes clear and true, and that red hair down to her shoulders, though it struck me when I met her that that hair was a little too perfect, a little too robust somehow for how fragile this woman seemed. For whatever reason, it'd taken her a little while to get out of the cab when they first got here, and when Chuck introduced me—she stood a full foot shorter than him, a tiny woman next to this Bluto of a man, a knitted green afghan over her shoulders, a white blouse and blue jeans—her hand in mine as I'd shaken it had felt like a small and trembling bird, soft and breakable and warm all at once, and I'd let go maybe too quickly, a shot of fear through me that somehow I'd hurt her with just this touch.

But she'd only smiled, nodded. "I'm glad to meet you," she'd said, then nodded again. "Tell Saralee we miss her sunshine."

"Yes ma'am," I'd said, and nodded myself, did a little bow, quick and shallow. I'd known it was an odd thing to do even as I'd done it, a move more reaction than anything else to this brittle dream of a woman.

"Sorry," Irving says now, quiet, and turns back to the vise, wheels loose the fly. "No more bad-boy talk. But Ensign Parker here started it, asking me what Earl said about Subic to me. The kid's the one you ought to keelhaul. Not me."

"Scurvy dog," Chuck says, and he smiles at me, takes a sip of his tea.

He and Serena make and sell leather Bible covers and Christian whatnots, everything from key chains to belts to hair bands to purses, those oddball items all intricately tooled and printed with *Maranatha* and *IXΘΥΣ* and *Praise the Lord* and the fish symbol. They've got spinning racks out front hung with those purses and the belts, and on two tables—theirs are in a U as well—are trays of those hair bands and checkbook covers and wallets and the key chains.

But at the bottom of the U, right out front of Chuck sitting on the tailgate, are the Bible covers, each one around its own Bible, and they are exquisite. I'd looked at them once Grandpa and I'd finished with our setup, Grandpa shooting the breeze with Irving just before taking off to see his groupies. Serena was already back in the cab and settling in while Chuck unloaded the Bibles in those covers from the truck, set them out like the pieces of art they are, one at a time and each lying flat on the table, not in piles or trays. About thirty of them, all out on display.

Some of the covers had, of course, the fish sign and the same phrases as on the wallets and checkbook covers, things you see on bumper stickers everywhere. But most had pictures on them, fully composed scenes of trees in a woods, or seascapes with rocky shores and waves just cresting, or a road in the country some-where, easing off and away. They were all predictable, sure. But it was in their execution that the quality shone.

The last one he'd put out was the best of them all. Carefully he lifted this one from the box in the bed, then placed it in a book stand on the table and stepped back, arms crossed, and we two looked at it.

It was a portrait of a woman sitting beneath a tree in a meadow, her back to the viewer, beside her a road that led off into the distance where jagged mountains rose beyond the horizon. Though maybe the composi-tion of it was still a little predictable—a road, a horizon, a person alone—there was to this one an even deeper sense of grace, and of artistry: You could see the wind in this one, its trace in the leaves of the tree above the woman, and in the pattern of it across the grass in the meadow. You could see it too in the thinnest strands of the woman's hair being lifted from her shoulders, the wind blowing toward that horizon, and then I saw that the way the woman was sitting was strange somehow. She sat with her knees to her chest, but had a hand to the ground beside her and was leaning the slightest way onto that hand, and I realized she was about to get up, that she was just inside the moment before she would leave on that road. A decision had been made, I could see, and she was this instant acting on it.

"That's my Serena," he'd said quietly, his arms crossed.

Of course it was her. It was her, the woman whose hand I'd held just a few minutes before.

"It's beautiful," I'd said, and knew the work of that word wasn't enough. "It's alive," I'd said, then tacked on for no better reason than that I wanted to impress him with my own sophistication, with the fact of all those books I'd read in the Navy, "It's like the shield of Achilles, it's so real."

He looked at me, grinned a moment, shook his head. "Maybe if Bezaleel had made that thing instead of Hephaestus," he said, "then Achilles wouldn't have taken that hit in the heel."

"Who?" I said, and blinked. *Bezaleel.* I couldn't recall any Bezaleel in the *Iliad,* though it was tough trying to keep all those names straight in the first place. I'd even forgotten it was Hephaestus who'd made the thing. Maybe Bezaleel was one of those minor gods playing cards up on Olympus while everyone down at Troy eviscerated themselves.

Chuck smiled at me, shrugged, then eased back onto the tailgate. "Exodus thirty-one," he said. "The Bible. When Moses gets told to build the ark and the tabernacle. God tells him to put a fellow name of Bezaleel on the job because he's a true craftsman." He stopped, tilted his head a little, his eyes on me. Then he looked past me, as though there were something of interest in those racks of caftans behind me. "God says about this Bezaleel," he began, " 'And I have filled him with the spirit of God, in wisdom, and in understanding, and in knowledge, and in all manner of workmanship, to devise cunning works, to work in gold, and in silver, and in brass, and in cutting of stones, to set them, and in carving of timber, to work in all manner of workmanship.' "

"Oh," I said. "Yes," I said.

I'd known Christians in the Navy, Jesus freaks who had prayer sessions onboard ship and who quoted Bible verses all day long. They were guys I'd stayed away from, like everybody else, for fear of that crazy glee they all had. They were, in fact, the only people onboard who'd give the Bro when they shook hands, and mean it.

Now here was another one, I figured, and so I looked down at the table, away from him, not certain if his next move would be to give me a Four Spiritual

Laws tract, or one of those cartoon pamphlets with gaudy drawings of druggies with needles in their arms going straight to hell, devils meeting them with pitchforks and all. The kinds of things we'd find on our bunks sometimes before we went on leave, or once we got back.

But he'd read the *Iliad,* even knew who'd made the shield.

"Nothing in that list of God jobs about tooled leather key chains," Irving called out from beyond the caftans, and I looked over there, saw him working at unloading the station wagon, all those bins and boxes.

Grandpa was gone, no word to me about when he'd be back or what to do until then. He was gone.

I turned back to Chuck, who looked at Irving a long second, then got this grin, shook his head. "You get the idea," he said to me. "The craftsmanship is a gift from God, one I'm going to use. And who knows what would've happened to Paris's arrow if Bezaleel had made that shield." He pushed off the tailgate, reached into the bed for another cardboard box, pulled out of it a battered thermos and a wadded T-shirt. "It's a good book," he said. "But I got to say I liked the Lattimore translation better than the Fitzgerald. Don't care what anyone says."

"Me too," I said too quickly, though I had no idea what version I'd read. I'd only been down in my bunk, reading and thinking, and watching Achilles and Patroclus and Hector and everyone else like it was some gruesome movie.

"And don't you worry," Chuck said, and picked apart the wadded shirt to reveal that ceramic mug, inside it a tea bag. "I'm not going to beat you over the head with the Bible like it was a two-by-four." He worked the screw top off the thermos, leaned back against the tailgate again, poured hot water into the mug. "Just know that we're praying," he said, "and when Serena's on the case you can bet—"

"Chuck," Irving cut in, "would you come down off the cross a minute and give me a hand with these poles?"

I'd turned to him, saw him past the caftans standing with his hands on his hips there at the back of his station wagon, two empty white buckets in front of him, that khaki vest of his sprayed with flies. "You're evangelizing the boy to death."

Chuck had looked at him, then at me. He'd grinned again, shook his head, set the coffee mug down. "Why do the heathen rage?" he'd said, and went to help.

"You know," Irving says from beside me, "there are whole theories about your gramps and the film industry." He's eased up from stooping to the flies, sits straight on that stool of his.

"Raging controversies," Chuck says, and lets out a small laugh.

"Really?" I say, not sure who to look to and ask, Chuck to my right, Irving to my left, all three of us waiting for whatever it is they know will happen next, me without a clue.

"He ever talk about that stuff to you?" Irving says, and I turn to him, see he's looking off at the stadium, and I look back to Chuck. He's refilling his mug with hot water out of the thermos, facing forward on the tailgate, and I figure it doesn't matter who I look at.

"Nonstop," I say, that halo behind the stadium sharper, brighter. "I can't tell you how many times he tells me about Walter Brennan and about Claudette Colbert and Lucille Ball, and some guy named Clifton Webb."

"Clifton Webb!" Irving says. *"Mr. Belvedere Goes to College!"*

"Three Coins in the Fountain," Chuck says, and I can hear him screwing that lid back on the thermos.

They are quiet a moment before Irving says, *"Titanic,"* and Chuck says almost too quiet to hear, *"Laura."*

"I guess you guys know who he is," I say, and they both let out laughs, but neither with anything behind it. Just a reaction to me.

"Eve Arden, too," I say. "Something about Moe of the Three Stooges. And John Wayne and working on a movie called *Red River* and how he worked some problem out with him and Walter Brennan at—"

"The Chevron Bar," Chuck and Irving say together, and laugh, though this time with a little more life inside it.

"We've heard that one," Irving says. "And about Claudette Colbert naked in that old Cecil B. DeMille picture—"

"The Sign of the Cross," Chuck says, and Irving says, "Of course it would be you to remember that title."

"But the theories go," Chuck says, "that he really was somebody at some point, or that it's all made up. People believe one or the other."

"Kind of like that Jesus of yours," Irving says.

"My boss is a Jewish carpenter," Chuck says. "One of the chosen people, like yourself, Irving."

"Don't start," Irving says, and I can hear him move a little, the stool creak, and I turn, see him bent over the vise again and settling what looks like the smallest hook in the world into the jaws, then wheeling that vise down.

Chuck is quiet, and I can see people across the open lane before us sitting in their own chairs, or standing and leaning against their cars, or primping the merchandise as though this thing will never get under way: that lady in the rose-on-white caftan who'd called out when we first got here an hour ago lifts one of the plates from her table, wipes it with a dish towel; next to her a man and woman at a dried flowers setup move vases full of flowers back and forth, trying to find the right spot for each, but settle them exactly as they were; next to them a man in a panama hat sits asleep in a director's chair at a slot filled with wooden wind chimes, tons of them hanging on racks not much different from our own, but the morning air out here so still they don't make a sound.

It's quiet.

So I say something, anything, because it is too quiet, and nothing yet has happened here, and Grandpa is who knows where, enjoying his fame.

"I saw him in a Foremost milk commercial one time when I was a kid," I say. I say it without any charge to the words, no sense of pride or shame or amusement or gloom. I just say it, because it is quiet out here, and because it is fact.

"What?" Chuck says, and Irving says in the same moment, "You what?"

I look at Chuck, who holds the dripping tea bag out of the mug, his eyes open wide, eyebrows up in what is nothing less than amazement.

I turn to Irving, who's already gotten those magnifying eyeglasses flipped on his visor. He's standing from the stool, on his way to me, his eyes open just as wide as Chuck's.

"Say that again," he says.

I shrug, move in my chair, too suddenly something all the way different in the air, and I turn back to Chuck, who's standing now too, that mug set on the tailgate. He's got both hands on his hips, his eyebrows still high, his mouth open a little too wide.

"He was in a commercial when I was a kid," I say, and try at a smile, these two men looking down at me. "Foremost milk. I saw it in Phoenix. When I was a kid." I shrug again, and now Irving turns from me, looks out to the open lane before us.

"Janet!" he calls out, "come on over. The kid says he saw Earl on television!"

"What?" I hear, and turn, see the woman with the plates stop polishing, drop the dish towel on the table, and set the plate quickly back on its stack, and she's already on her way over. But before she's even halfway across she turns, calls out to the dried flower people, "Bill, Juanita! It's true, about Earl!"

The two, once more in the middle of moving vases here and there, stop, look at her over their shoulders, and then at me, and set down the vases, start toward us too.

Now the wind chime man in the panama hat snaps awake, and he sits up, looks at the commotion going on, and he's starting toward us, and then someone peeks her head around the caftans on Irving's side at me, and someone else beside her, all of them people I've already met. I can't remember any names, none of them save for Irving and Chuck, all these people descending on me for the thin news of a commercial I once saw my grandpa in.

I look at Irving, see his eyebrows drawn up in some kind of preinquiry mode, gathering together a question from the nothing I've given him, and I turn to Chuck.

He's gone, the mug still there on the tailgate, but then I see some movement on the far side of the bed, up near the cab, and here's Chuck ushering Serena out of the truck, the two of them on their way around the bed toward me. She glances at me, her arm looped in Chuck's, her shoulders covered by that green afghan, Chuck whispering words to her as they make their way.

"I never doubted it," the woman in the caftan says, right up in front of me now, poofed-up hair stiff, her arms crossed and her eyes on me. She shakes her head, says, "I knew I'd seen him before. All these years I've been telling him that, that I've seen him. I knew it."

"Dammit, Janet," the dried flowers guy says, "you've been saying he was a liar from day one. You know it, too," and the woman he's with says, "Bill swears he saw him on *The Andy Griffith Show.* On Channel Eleven about a year ago."

"I knew that was him in *Friendly Persuasion,*" the guy in the panama hat says. He's got the hat off, holds it over his heart like he's saying the Pledge of Allegiance. "I knew it, I could see it in that goofy stride of his—"

"Man!" I hear, and now Johnny Rayford is on the scene, right behind the caftan woman, and he's smiling through that graying beard of his. "I don't believe it," he says, "I don't believe it, man!" and he reaches in past the woman and grabs my hand in another Bro. "I didn't believe a word of it, but Eva always did. She's going to flip, man. This is just far out."

Then everyone, everyone pauses a moment, and I see them move their eyes to my right, all of them with smiles on their faces, but all of them seeming to draw in the tiniest breath at once, and holding it.

I turn, still in this lawn chair, and here is Serena, kneeling beside me. She sets her hand on my arm, and she is smiling, her eyes a little thick for the sleep she's just been roused from, but the brown of them as sure and true as when I'd held her hand. Chuck stands just behind her, his hands at his sides and his eyes on her, his mouth in a careful smile at whatever this news of a milk commercial may mean to her.

She says, "So it's true?"

I work up a smile, glance from her to Chuck and back to her. "I don't know," I say. "But he was in a commercial. And my mom says—"

"His mother!" someone whispers so loud everyone can hear, and someone says, "She'd have the goods on him," and another whispers, "Wonder what that would be like, growing up with Earl and Saralee for parents."

"Let the man talk!" Johnny says, then, to me, "Go on, man. Tell us."

I swallow, turn from Johnny and this crowd to Serena again. "My mom says," I start, "that he believes it. That my grandpa believes it. That's all I know." I pause, swallow again. "And that commercial. I saw it."

Her smile hasn't changed at all. I feel her hand on my arm, the fragile comfort of this touch, and I hope I have given her what she needs to hear.

"So then it may be true about Saralee, too," she says, and gives the smallest nod.

Before I can even open my mouth to ask what she means, the woman in the caftan says softly, "Serena, honey, of course it's true. She told me herself last month the tests came back positive."

Serena's eyes go straight to Janet. "Janet," Chuck says then, and though his mouth is nearly closed, he lets out the words, "She's not talking about that. She means about Saralee's singing," the words a gently seethed rebuke, and Irving looks at Janet too, shakes his head, and I see Juanita of the dried flowers cut her eyes to Janet, whisper, "Be quiet," and shake her head.

"What tests?" I say. "Who?" I say to no one, to everyone.

"It's me," Serena says, and I can feel her hand on my arm a little firmer now, heavier, and I look at her, see her eyes back on me. She's not smiling now, but serious. "It's me," she says again. "Janet's thinking of me, and about me when I finished chemo a while ago. My tests came back that I'm in remission." She smiles again.

"But I thought Saralee was—" the panama hat man says, and a kind of commotion rises up around me, a patter and fumble of words everywhere around me while people look at people and speak in hushed tones each other's names, say shards of sentences: *She told me* and *But* and *Last month.* It is a covert argument these people are having, me they're trying to hide it from.

"Everyone!" Johnny says, and his single word cuts through this tribe of people, this family that can have an argument all of them at once, everyone with a stake in it, and no one going to leave anyone out.

Except me.

"Quiet, people!" Johnny says, and he closes his

eyes, shakes his head slowly, deeply. "Everyone just has to cool it," he says.

I look at Serena again, and there is trouble in her eyes on mine. She's *in remission,* I hear only now, words coming into me slowly for this clamor and chaos, for this circus of hidden knowledge and piece-meal revelation.

She's had cancer, and now I understand why it took her so long to get out of the cab when we first arrived, know why this red hair of hers is so perfect and strong. It's a wig she's wearing, and now I know why there is a brittle strength to her, and why that hand in mine had felt as though I might break it.

Now I know why Grandpa'd leaned into the cab to talk to her: he wanted to know how *she* was.

Because Saralee's tests came back positive.

Maybe he wanted to tell her what he seems to have told most everybody here, save for this Janet and the man with the panama hat: Don't tell my grandson.

"Tell us about Earl and the movies, man," Johnny says then, but there isn't anything to it. His words are a sad stab at stepping back in time somehow, at removing us from here and this revealed knowledge that my grandma is somehow sick; his words are a try at returning us all to a moment ago, when the every-thing of the world had as its center my grandpa and some dumb idea of fame and glory and film.

But there is no going back.

I look at Serena beside me, this trouble in her eyes I feel I am responsible for somehow, and I see Chuck hovering just behind her, both hands up and almost touching her shoulders to comfort her.

"Tell me what's going on," I say to her. I know she will tell me, because I have seen her beneath a peaceful tree in a wind-blessed meadow, strands of her hair lifting on the fact of sun and wind and a road leading to mountains.

She opens her mouth the smallest way, and her eyes well up, and a tear breaks, slips down her cheek and its quiet spray of freckles.

"Have you heard her sing?" she asks, the words almost too quiet to hear.

"Yes," I say. "Yes," and now I am on the sidewalk with Grandma on our way back from buying her cigarettes, listening to her ease through "Moonlight in Vermont" in a way that makes no job and no prospects of one seem nothing but a troublesome dream I might have had the night before.

"Then if Earl was an actor," Serena says, and pieces together a smile despite the next tear that falls in the exact same path as the first, "then maybe Saralee was the singer Earl says she was, too." Here is her smile, finished, and full.

"She's never told me she—" I begin, but Serena's hand on my arm is even firmer now, and she leans a little closer in, whispers, "She's never told anyone. And Earl will only talk about it when she's not here. Which," she says, and here is one more tear, "makes it a mystery."

She smiles, nods once, and everyone around us

seems suddenly gone. Even Chuck hovering behind her disappears for this moment of Serena's face, and her words.

"Tell me what's going on," I say again.

"She sang to me every time she ever came out here. Through all my chemo." Her smile seems to quicken at this, a good memory spoken through careful tears. "We sat in the cab of the truck, and I had on my surgical mask, and I slept and I was awake, but I was always listening. And she gave me that gift. She gave me that sunshine."

I swallow, and swallow again. "But what tests? What does she—"

"I can't answer that," she whispers, "because Earl asked me not to tell you." She lets go my arm now, and brings her hand, that warm and tenuous bird, to my chin, and holds it. "But she loves you. It really doesn't matter if she was a famous singer or not, because of the way she gave me her voice when I needed it."

She lets go my chin, and puts her arms together beneath the afghan. Slowly she stands up straight, and here again is Chuck, who has finally let both hands touch her shoulders, him holding on as though she were the one to keep him standing tall.

"He loves you," she says. "Earl. So try to understand when it comes to why he might not want to tell you."

I open my mouth, then close it. I swallow again, and breathe in.

I think of Grandpa, and the joke gone stale of the radio

blasted loud; I think of his losing Humphrey Bogart when he remembers me beside him when we checked in at the gate, my empty calling named by him and him alone: *loyal sidekick.* Then his warning to the old man in the orange highway vest: *Don't worry about him.*

I think of his remarkable words to Grandma there in the garage, when I'd begun to ease a line through an ugly flowered material for the very first time.

I love you, Saralee, he'd said.

"What have we here?" comes from behind the crowd—W. C. Fields—and I turn, see everyone looking behind them and making way, and as though this were a movie—of course as though this were a movie—here stands Grandpa in that red camellia on royal blue shirt, hands hard on his hips. He's right on cue and right on his mark, his head haloed by the sun finally broken above the top of the stadium.

But I still stand from the chair. I don't look to Serena for anything, or to Chuck or Irving or anyone else. There is only my grandpa before me, and I make my own way between these racks of caftans and through these people, this tribe of his, and stop right in front of him, so close I see for the first time the depth of the smallest lines beside his eyes, and see beneath that white hair the age spots in his hairline, and I see in the deep green of his eyes a kind of shine that betrays him: he knows what we have here.

But I tell him anyway.

"The truth," I say.

And I walk past him, away from here.

This is when the sun finally appears, blinds me a moment as I move out from his silhouette and onto this continent of hawkers and merchandise, and now the ship docked at Subic is gone for that blindness, that hulk finally unmoored and allowed to set sail.

It takes me a moment to blink back my sight, and I wipe at my eyes, the wet in them as I take off down this open lane before me, and I look up, astonished to see only the gray shell of a football stadium. Only that.

"Brad!" Grandpa calls, but I do not turn to him, only keep walking.

Because first I have to reach into my back pocket, and I do. I reach down deep into it until I feel with the tips of my fingers the soft edge of paper frayed with too much touching and too much avoidance. Then I've got it, tweezed between my first and second fingers, and I pull it out.

Here is my next move, I know, and unfold the thank-you note of a letter, and unfold it again, and I am looking at my mother's handwriting, no longer alien, but real. Hers.

It's addressed to me, my name written in her hand, held right here in my own.

There is no work to opening the envelope, the top edge nearly worn through, and as I walk inside this parking lot, pass slot after slot of detritus new and old for sale, I pull from inside this folded shred of evidence that I have a family a single piece of paper folded in half, and I unfold it.

And now I have no choice but to stop, because here

is hope, one-armed and scarred and scuffed, but strong for it, as strong as the words there, right there, beneath the soft yellow flowers that decorate the top of this single page of my mother's stationery.

Forgive me, she has written. Nothing more.

I hear something then, a quiet hustle of sound coming toward me, a ripple and shimmer of sound, like a tide might make at sea when it finally decides it has no choice but to turn, and I look up, see people in the slots around me standing, moving, touching their things, and I see them glancing ahead of me, and I look down the open lane before me.

Here are people, a kind of wall of them, a wave, easing into this lane.

"Here they come," someone says from a slot to my left, and to my right someone says quietly, "And they're off!" and somebody else says, "The grunion are running!"

They're maybe a hundred yards away, and from here I can see them touch at the tables, pick things up, and move and move and move, with them and ahead of them a sound like life.

So many people. More even than carpeted the deck of an amphibious transport dock one night a long time ago, a night when clouds to the west burned orange, and a lighthouse flashed to help me breathe.

I look back at the paper, these two words and the hand in which they are written. This is my mother, and I look up one more time, watch as the world moves at me, ready to swallow me whole.

I turn, head back toward racks of caftans, and Day-Glo lures and *Maranatha* key chains, and a road carved in leather that leads into mountains.

I see the poofed-hair woman back at her post, her eyes glancing from me to the crowd behind me to me again, and here's the panama hat man standing at those wind chimes. He's got his hands behind him, the hat back on, and Bill and Juanita, I see, have finally decided upon the perfect place for each vase. They're all watching me and that wave behind me both.

Irving stands out front of all those bins of fishing stuff, his arms crossed, a kind of smile on his face as he watches me, that visor still in place, the lenses flipped up. Chuck is sitting back on the tailgate, an arm around Serena beside him, that green afghan doing its good work of keeping her warm, before them on a table books wrapped in leather tooled to look like life. They're both smiling, and watching.

Here, too, is Grandpa in that horrid flowered shirt. He's out front of all those racks of caftans, his arms crossed, his mouth closed, and his chin is trembling.

Those wind chimes start up now, slips of furtive notes, momentary shards of color and light, the quiet and openhearted play of wood touched to wood touched to wood, the air around us all beginning to move.

16

Everything she wants is disappearing as they finally, finally make their way home.

Even with the best movie she has ever seen, the song of *Zip-a-dee-doo-dah* already in her so deep she can sing it without even knowing she is singing it, and even with the question she wants to ask her momma about her own singing and the secret record and those photos right on the *tip of her tongue*—even with all this surprise and mystery and joy of music, everything she wants is disappearing.

They have said nothing on the whole streetcar ride from Hillhurst to here. No words at all, from the time Joan and her daddy walked out of the dance studio, her momma outside with a cigarette at her lips, her arms crossed so that she was holding both her elbows, all the way through to here at the corner of Sunset and Alvarado, the bright yellow streetcar already gone, the clear blue sky above them still clear blue.

But because the sun up in that sky is so bright, hard afternoon shadows cut across the wide street before them, shadows as sharp as knives, she thinks, shadows *angry* for how hard they are.

Her momma walks away, toward the apartment building. The sidewalk on that side of the street is in the sun, their apartment building on the left, and the shadows cut down from the top of the building on the right, slice Alvarado in half. Though her momma's back is to them as she walks, Joan knows her eyes are squinted down even harder than before. She can see even in the few steps her momma has taken the way her legs move inside her dotted-swiss dress, soft as she can make them but fast, because the headache is full on her again, and she wants to get home.

Her daddy's hand lets go of hers, and Joan turns, the release a surprise, and she looks up.

They are on the shadow side so that he's not lit from above and behind, like he'd been when they were on the street out front of the dance studio. Back when she hadn't been able to see his face, her daddy only a shadow himself for a moment, blocking out the sun.

Back when the magic of the question she'd been about to ask her momma—*Were you ever a singer in a big band?*—disappeared with the snap of his fingers, and his two words: *That's it.*

He pulls from the pocket of his gray silky shirt his pack of cigarettes, pulls out of his pants pocket his silver lighter. Quick as that, he pops the pack hard against his palm, shakes one out and puts it to his lips, snaps his wrist to open the lighter, snaps it again to close it. He takes two long breaths in on the cigarette, shoots them out like a dragon, and looks one way and the other out onto Sunset.

Just like every time he stands at the corner of Sunset and Alvarado, him tall as he can make himself there on the street corner while cars go by fast, and streetcars whir along loud: her daddy and his street corner screen tests.

He drops the cigarette pack into his shirt pocket, the lighter into his pants pocket. Without looking away from the street, he puts out his hand for hers, and she takes it, and they stand there at the corner a little longer, a little longer. Her daddy's fingers are too tight around her own as he looks once more up and down Sunset, lets out two more dragon breaths.

Don't you dare put that girl through this, her momma had said to him. *Don't drag her into your sorry little schemes,* she'd told him, the last words Joan has heard from her today.

Once inside the studio, here had been her daddy the *actor,* smiling at an old lady behind a counter who was all smiling herself. She was fat, her hair piled in a knot at the tip-top of her head, and wore makeup so thick Joan could see the cracks of it beside her eyes and around her mouth, her eyebrows hard black tipped-over C's drawn high above her eyes.

The old lady had a wattle at her throat like the chickens Joan and Fern and Betty Jo chased before Sunday supper back at Granny's house in Texas. It was a game, trying to catch one of them in the bare dirt in the pen around the coop, three girls laughing and chasing a crazy chicken with its wattle jiggling like this old lady's throat. A game that always ended the same: One or another of them got hold of a chicken and brought it to Granny, who stood on the steps up to the *sleeping porch,* her arms out for whichever girl was bringing it to her. Then came the quick and terrible move, the thoughtless twist of her hands around the chicken's neck so quick it was a surprise every time Joan ever saw her do it.

Her daddy talked to the old lady, words Joan didn't listen to because she was thinking on Texas, and then the old lady smiled down at her, nodded. Joan smiled and nodded back because it was what she was supposed to do, and she saw her daddy bring from his back pocket his *billfold* and pull out two five-dollar bills, and the old lady wrote something in a book she had on the counter in front of her.

Joan looked past the woman as she wrote, saw the studio was the same as the one in Mineola: a big room with mirrors on one wall, a rail. A record player played somewhere back there, though no one was *rehearsing,* the music sad and slow, a big band playing a song she knew she would have to be an adult to understand.

The place was the same as in Mineola. But different all the way because she was here with her daddy. He'd never been with her to the studio in Mineola, and hadn't been to the *recital* either.

"Next Tuesday at four," the old lady said, and handed a piece of paper to her daddy. She looked down at Joan, nodded, said, "What a treat! A father and daughter together. This is an act I'm certain will find the stage!" The old lady smiled, and Joan saw the cracks in the makeup beside her eyes and around her mouth grow even wider.

"Let's hope it's not the next stage out of town!" her daddy said too loud, and they both laughed.

She didn't want to do this, to dance with her daddy.

Her momma wouldn't even look at her once they were back outside. She only held her elbows, puffed at the cigarette, and turned, headed back to the corner of Hillhurst and Sunset, where they'd waited for the next Yellow Car and its doors to wheeze open, suck them in for the silent ride home.

Her daddy leads her down Alvarado, but they stay on the shadow side, and of course the song comes to her, the one everyone knows and that she sometimes sings when she is walking afternoons home from school in these same shadows.

She almost hums it, that tune, almost says the words—*Grab your coat and get your hat, leave your worry at the doorstep, just direct your feet to the sunny side of the street!*—but she doesn't, because she knows what is going to happen. She looks down from the sunny side over there to the sidewalk in front of her as they take slow steps toward home, steps going slower, because her daddy knows too what will happen once they make it home.

Here they are: the cracks in the concrete she walks, cracks like the lines on maps in her dreams, lines she wishes she knew how to walk so that they would all arrive at *happy,* but that are leading straight to *sad* right now, with each slow step her daddy takes beside her.

• • •

Her momma is at the table when they make it into the apartment. She's already got her dress off—she's tossed it on the divan, an empty ghost settled across the cushions, her white high heels lying sideways on the floor in front of it—and sits in her beige slip and stockings, her elbows on the table, her head in her hands. Right next to the beanbag ashtray at the center of the table is a brown glass pill bottle, the black lid off and set right beside it.

"Saralee," her daddy says, and closes the door. Joan steps only a little farther into the room, a room with so very very little in it when she thinks of *Song of the South,* and the furniture they had in their *plantation.* Joan and her momma and daddy have only this room to live their lives in. Just this room, Joan thinks, and the sink in the corner, the hot plate on the counter, the stacks of movie magazines next to it. Their three chairs and the little table her momma sits at right now. And the divan, where the secret of her momma hides.

But then she remembers that they have the bedroom to live in, too. Joan is the one who lives in only this room, she sees. Only her.

"Earl, don't—" her momma says. She doesn't move, her head in her hands perfectly still. "I can't even—" she says, her voice clear and far away at the same time.

"You can't deny me this opportunity," her daddy says, and lets go Joan's hand, takes two steps into the room, the cigarette nearly burned down to nothing in his mouth. He pulls what is left of it from his lips, holds it pinched between his thumb and first finger, cupped in his hand the way the bad men, usually Germans, hold their cigarettes in the movies. "This is a stroke of genius," he says, and waves that hand with the cigarette through the air in a big circle. "Have you ever seen something like this?"

Suddenly he is at the table, and pulls out the chair next to her momma, scrapes it across the floor so loud that her momma jolts: her shoulders shoot up, her head snaps up and out of her hands, all of her shivering in just that instant, and now her hands before her are empty, her fingers the claws of an old lady for how curled they are, and empty.

"A father and daughter. Just imagine that!" he says, and sits in the chair, drops the butt into the ashtray. He takes her empty hands in his, leans in close to her.

She doesn't move, her body seized up and stiff with her headache. Just like her body will do after Joan has led her to bed when she comes home from work with a headache like this, her whole body as tight as those wrinkles on her forehead Joan tries to push away gently as she can.

But her daddy doesn't know any of this, Joan thinks, because he still holds tight her hands, says too loud, "The woman at the dance studio said this will work. We start on Tuesday, and I can swap shifts with Poncie at work. You said yourself how good she was at the recital. You said it yourself."

He turns and looks at Joan, still just inside the room.

But she doesn't want to move any farther in, because she knows where this all is already heading. It's all halfway there right now, she thinks, and lets that word, the secret one, surprise her and scare her at the same time. That word, the secret one: *divorce.*

Her daddy stands and takes two big steps across the floor, and suddenly he is holding Joan's hands in his, and now he pulls her in a circle with him, looks down at her and smiles, his eyes shining and bright, his hair combed back and his pipe-cleaner mustache and the silky gray shirt all making him handsome, and she has no choice but to move in a circle with him and pretend to dance, and now he is singing himself—"Don't sit under the apple tree with anyone else but me!" he sings, then sings the same words again, and Joan knows he doesn't know any of the words, and she can tell too by how he moves in this circle and how his feet do nothing but shuffle right to left, right to left, and nowhere near the rhythm of the words he sings, that this will not work, no matter how hard she tries, and no matter how hard he tries too.

He can't dance, and she feels her face going hot, feels another *blush* already on her, and now she imagines the *recital* she will have to do with her daddy, who can't remember words to a song or move his feet to music. She feels already the embarrassment of it, sees in the rows of fold-up chairs in that studio on Sunset her friends: Here are Harriet and Babs and Dot and Shirley, and even Robert and Ronald and Donald. And here is Lincoln, who plays the piano so well his momma is proud of him even when he's playing a song she tells him not to play, a crazy song that makes his momma say *You will be my death* and smile at him at the same time.

Still her daddy moves her in a circle, and she can see he's gritting his teeth now inside the smile he gives her, and he shouts over his shoulder to her momma, "Bigger than Bill Bojangles and Shirley Temple. It's my chance." All the while his eyes are on Joan, and now he sings again the same words, moves his feet the same all this while, him singing without singing, her daddy dancing without dancing at all. Still they move in this circle, and still Joan blushes, embarrassed and embarrassed and embarrassed.

"Stop it!" her momma chokes out.

Her daddy lets go just that quick, turns away from this circle and to her momma, and Joan turns too.

Her momma has her forehead to the table, her hands in her lap, her all curled into herself in her beige slip and stockings.

For a moment Joan thinks her daddy will go to her and hold her and try to walk her to the bedroom because of her headache, and because of this noise and commotion and *hubbub, bub* he is making. She hopes this is what he will do.

But as soon as she thinks this, she knows he won't.

Instead, he puts his hands to his hips, shouts, "Don't you think we deserve this? Don't you think this is something people will want to see?" He lets out a quick breath, runs a hand back through his hair, as though any of it were out of place. "Don't you think we—"

" *'We' has nothing to do with it!* " her momma screams, and the words are a piercing, the words are a sword, they are a knife, and her momma jolts again, shoots up straight, her eyes to the ceiling, and she slams both fists on the tabletop, and the pill bottle beside the ashtray jumps for it, tips over, and Joan jolts, too, as though there were some wire between them, electric shock to electric shock. " *'We'* has never meant any—"

"Damn you to hell!" her daddy shouts, and cocks his jaw at her, *sneers*—that is the word, the only word that ever existed—and crosses his arms. "Damn you to hell," he shouts, "for all the work you've never done to try and help me make my—"

Here it all is, Joan sees: just what she has known all along. She takes a step back from everything disappearing right in front of her eyes.

"Who do you think you are?" her momma cuts in just then, her words a growl Joan has never heard before.

Joan takes in a breath at this sound, a thoughtless and quick breath, the sudden pinch of it in her chest a surprise. This is a sound she has never heard before. This is a sound that could never sing a song on a record, or hum late at night when her daddy has left after yelling. This is a sound she has never heard before, a whisper soaked in black, and old.

Slowly her momma looks up to the ceiling, her eyes

squinted tight but open, as though there is something ugly miles away up there. "Just who do you think you are," her momma whispers, "that the all of everything that ever breathed is centered on you?" Her hands are still in fists on the table, and Joan lets herself look away from her a moment, like a dare, to the spray of pills on the tabletop, a dozen or so of them spilled out from the tipped-over bottle.

There was a house in Texas, she thinks. There was a place where Joan was happy, and where sometimes her momma was, too, and where Joan could climb into bed with her momma and push away the wrinkles in her forehead. It's on a map. It's a real place.

But who, she wants to know, is her momma? Where does this whisper come from?

"Here we go again," her daddy says, "with the same old gag, the same old hammy act." He looks at the floor, his arms still crossed. He shakes his head, lets out a low whistle, and Joan can see on his face now a *smirk*. "Predictable as a Tom Mix serial," he says. "Predictable as—"

"A failed actor in Hollywood," her momma whispers, and she looks from the ceiling to him, finally. Her eyes are still the same squinted shut, her momma still looking at something ugly and miles away.

"Sixteen movies," her daddy shoots out, and uncrosses his arms, points hard at her momma, who flinches for it, and Joan flinches, too, though he's across the room from her. "I'm on for the long haul," he shouts, and leans in closer to her momma.

"I mean to make a mark. *My* business is to get people to look at *me*." He points a thumb at his chest, taps it hard once, and it seems the perfect way he moves, so much like people she's seen in the movies whenever they have arguments—the cigarette waved in the air, the hand through the hair, the crossed arms and shaking head and now the finger pointed—that her daddy isn't her daddy, but the actor he's supposed to be. A real live actor. But not her daddy.

He takes in a breath, crosses his arms again, looks at the floor again, then the ceiling. He shakes his head again. "And if it takes dragging my darling daughter here—"

"Earl, don't make her—" her momma says, and now she turns to Joan, her eyes open the smallest sliver, her teeth clenched in the rigid smile she holds when she feels this much pain. Her momma moves her head back and forth in the smallest arc, as though she's looking for Joan and can't see her, as though Joan herself is miles away.

"If dragging her into my success is what it takes," her daddy goes on, "then my mark will be made, and no one will call it 'dragging her in' because she'll be a star too. And this family will be glad for it when it comes, because then everyone here will know I'm on for the long haul for all of us. Then they'll all know I didn't take a dive in the first round." He pauses a moment, takes in another breath.

"They'll all know," he says, and the words have

gone suddenly quiet, "that I didn't take a dive in the first round. Like someone around here we all know and love," the words and the quiet of them meant to cut her momma. She's seen that in the movies before, the whisper that tells all and destroys the one listening. "At least I didn't quit when I was almost there," he whispers.

Her momma's head stops moving in its search for Joan only right here, right here across the room from her. But she closes her eyes, gives up, Joan can see, and the wrinkles on her forehead grow even deeper.

She turns to the tabletop, slowly takes a hand from her lap and sets it there. Joan can see her momma's shoulders move up and down with each breath in and out, breaths going harder and quicker for these words that have just passed from her daddy to her momma. But then she speaks, and the words, no matter how hard she is breathing, no matter how hard the wrinkles on her forehead and how tight her eyes are closed and how clenched her teeth are for the pain she is in—no matter all this, her words come out flat, and smooth, and quiet.

"At least," her momma says, "I had the talent. At least I could sing." She pauses, takes in two more quick breaths. "Which means," she lets out, "that at least I had a chance."

Her daddy reaches quick as that to the chair in front of him, grabs hard the back of it and lifts it in both hands, lifts it up as Joan watches and as her momma breathes hard in and out, in and out, her eyes closed so she can't see him lifting the chair, and for a moment Joan wonders what he is doing, what the chair has to do with anything at all.

He has the chair above his head now, swings it behind him like an ax about to be brought down, the legs as they swing back almost touching the ceiling, and her daddy looks to the floor, all of this in an instant, and he makes a face that is more than *sneer* or *smirk* for how he clenches his own teeth, his face a frown but more than that, and more than pain or anger, more and more and more, she can see.

His face is a face she has never seen before, because it is real.

Everything is different, Joan knows in this moment. This is not a secret talk, like late nights when she dreams of maps that lead to happy or sad. This is her momma's voice, and her daddy's face.

He swings the chair down.

He means to smash it, like in the movies, when the bad man in the saloon smashes one over the head of a cowboy, the chair splintering into pieces, the man it has broken over sometimes crumpling to the ground, other times turning around and taking a swing or a shot at the one who has broken it.

But nothing happens. There is only the hard and hollow sound of a chair banged against the floor of this apartment, and her momma jolts again, her shoulders and head and arms and hands and hair all shivering an instant, again. And there is only the stunned surprise on her daddy's face, his mouth open, his eyebrows high, his hair finally fallen down in his eyes for all this work of swinging a chair. For nothing.

"Wrong again," her momma says, her words that same flat, that same quiet. "It's not a breakaway chair," she says.

"We will not move back there," her daddy says right away, like it's an answer to a question her momma has asked, a question he's known all along and has only been waiting for the chance to answer, and now he leans on the chair back, both hands still on it. He takes in hard breaths, closes his eyes, bows his head as if, Joan thinks, he is about to pray.

"I don't care how much she gets for those leases. I don't care how long they pump oil out of there. I don't give a damn if she has a castle set up for us to welcome us back," her daddy says, "or if there's a banner strung up across Blackbourn Street that says—that says—"

He stops, takes in a breath. Joan can't see his face for his bowed head, and for that hair down over his eyes. But she can see he is trembling now, his hands on the chair back and his arms and even his legs, it seems. He is trembling, and suddenly she can feel her own arms tight to her sides, her legs stiff and heavy, her feet stuck to the ground, growing down through the floor like roots on a tree. She can feel her own breath going short, and shallow, her chest pressed down on and heavy, stones stacked there.

All because with each heavy second bearing down

on her, she is seeing something now, something big and right here, in this empty room.

Her daddy's mouth is moving, his lips working up secret words small and frightening.

"She's waiting for us," her momma says, the words difficult work through her clenched teeth and the hard squint of her eyes. But the words are still flat, still quiet. "We won't have to take her money. There's another job with the railroad she says Chilton's holding open for you again. But she says this is the last time. This is the last time she'll—"

"We won't go back to Texas," her daddy says, his head still bowed, his arms and legs and head trembling, "even if she has a banner strung up that reads *Hurrah*."

Joan can see it, the huge and awful and ugly thing between them—the secret—she has wanted to know forever and ever.

Texas. Her granny.

Money. A job.

Texas.

"Then damn *you* to hell, Earl," her momma says. But the words aren't the flat and quiet. They are in that black whisper again, old and dead.

Nothing is disappearing, Joan sees. Nothing. This is everything, she sees, right here before her. Everything is right here, like it has always been. She has been wrong about everything disappearing. She knows, in this moment of her daddy's prayer and her momma's curse, that everything has been *right before her very eyes* all along.

There is a place in Texas waiting for them, and her daddy won't take them.

Slowly, carefully, her momma opens a hand, reaches to the tabletop, and sweeps the spilled pills to the edge and into her other hand, cupped beneath the edge of the table. She holds them like a handful of candy, and lifts that hand out to her daddy. Her momma's eyes are open the smallest bit, and here is the sharp grin she always wears when she has her headaches.

She finds him with her eyes, finally, and holds the pills up even higher to him, as though she might mean to share this candy with him.

Her daddy lifts his eyes from the chair, looks, Joan can see, first to her momma's hand, then to her face.

Her momma brings her hand to her mouth, slips all the pills in, empties them in just like that, and Joan watches now as her momma chews on them, just like candy, like Good & Plentys or a mouthful of candy corn. Even from here Joan can hear the crack of the pills, the hard jumble of sound from inside her momma's mouth as she chews, and chews.

For a moment Joan thinks about the pain this must mean for her momma, the shock of breaking up these pills in her mouth piled on top of the headache.

But then she sees what has happened: these are pills, a whole handful of them.

Her daddy has to save her. He will save her. He has to. He will.

But her daddy stops trembling, lets go the back of the chair with one hand, runs that hand through his hair, gathering up the strands down in his eyes, and smoothes them all back into place.

He says, "I used to walk down to the end of Santa Monica Pier when I first moved here. I'd look in at the La Monica Ballroom and watch people in there dancing, and then I'd walk to the end of the pier, and I'd look out, and all I'd think about was how much—"

He stops, lets go the chair with the other hand, puts both hands in his pockets. He takes a small step back, and another.

He says, "I thought you would believe me."

"I thought you would tell the truth," her momma says, the pills already swallowed down. "But I guess I knew going into this deal that that was never going to happen."

Joan's chest goes even heavier, her arms even tighter against her sides, the roots through her feet pulling her down, through the floor, away from here, and away, the weight of her own self crushing her, pushing her all the way to China, right through the center of the earth.

"I'm going to jump off the end of the pier," he says. "I'm going to kill myself."

"Ever the dramatist," her momma whispers.

Her daddy turns, steps to the door, opens it and pulls it shut behind him. He doesn't slam it, like he does when they fight and people downstairs yell. He only pulls it closed, and leaves.

He hadn't seen Joan here in the middle of the room. He hadn't even let his eyes fall on her as he'd passed her.

Now her momma begins to stand from the table, both hands to the tabletop and pressing down hard to help her. Once she is up, she takes from the table the pill bottle, shakes out the pills left in there, and puts her hand to her mouth, begins to chew again. Joan watches as she staggers toward her bedroom, a hand first to the table, then to the second chair, and the third, the one her daddy tried to break that sits in the middle of the room now, right there in her momma's path to the bedroom, like a stone in the middle of a creek she'll need to make it across.

"Momma?" Joan lets out, though she doesn't know she has said it until it comes out, a single small word, small as a pill.

But her momma doesn't stop, only keeps moving across this creek, and she lets go the last chair in here, takes three steps toward the bedroom door, her arms out to either side to help keep her balance, as though she might fall any second into this water.

Just before she reaches the doorway she pauses, lets her hand touch the arm of the divan right there against the wall.

"Momma?" Joan tries again, though the word is even smaller out of her now, a grain of rice, a puff of air, a smudge on a photograph. Nothing.

Because her momma doesn't do anything but pause for that moment, lean against the divan, where the ghost of herself, that dotted-swiss dress, lies empty. Joan's word is nothing, because her momma only leans against the divan, where the secret of her own life is hidden away and is no secret at all, and moves through the doorway, into her bedroom.

Her momma is going to die, and her daddy is going to die too. They will kill themselves, and she will be left in here, with this world pressing down on her, shoving her down through the center of the earth. Her daddy hadn't seen her when he left. Her momma doesn't hear her when Joan calls out to her.

She was wrong about everything disappearing. Everything is here, everything is as big as the world, and bigger, filling up this room and pushing her down and crushing her.

Now she knows, she knows, she knows: the only thing disappearing is herself, crushed through the earth and down and balled up and smashed and hidden and hidden and hidden.

Her momma softly closes the door behind her, pushes it until it clicks, the tiny sound loud as the gunshot in *Bambi,* loud as a grain of rice dropped to the ground, loud as the single word *Momma?*

Light shifts, the shadow from the building across the street edging up toward the window, Joan knows for how many times she has sat here to do her homework. There is no sound from her momma in her room, no sound of her daddy's steps on the stairs up.

She waits, and waits, and now here is the shadow, broken over the windowsill and spreading like black paint spilled, and the day is getting ready to end.

She hasn't moved from where she stands in the

room, the chairs still in their places, her arms still at her sides, her feet still through the floor and away from here, away and away.

There is the shadow, proof you can't stay on the sunny side of the street, because there will always be a shadow to chase you, because the sun is always on its way down, even when it is starting up in the sky in the morning.

And so, when the shadow has spilled to her feet, when it has crept to her shoes and touched her the way hate and death have touched her this day, she steps away from herself, lifts her feet right through the world and into the shadow of this room she has disappeared from, and she steps lightly, surely, to the divan and a dotted-swiss dress, and she kneels, pushes aside two white high-heeled shoes lying on their sides, and she pulls out the news everyone in the world knows: the record, and those photographs.

She has disappeared, and no one will know anything. Because no one will care, because they will be dead.

She holds them in her hand, things she'd thought were treasure once but today have become something like trash for how everyone knows what they are, and what they mean, and no one cares.

It will only take a few minutes to get there, she thinks, where she can play the record. It will be easy, she thinks, because she is invisible, and because no one cares, and she wonders a moment if when she knocks on their door over on Park they will even hear her, because she has disappeared. Will her hand be able to knock on an apartment door, and what if Lincoln is practicing, and the sound of her invisible hand knocking at the door is hidden away by the music he makes?

It will only take a few minutes, no matter if Lincoln or his momma will hear her. It will only take a few minutes to get there, so that she can play this record on their Victrola, and she can know, she can *know* what it is that has been lost, the sound of her momma singing the only thing left to know.

She tucks the record with its photographs inside its sleeve under her arm, and opens the apartment door, pulls it to even quieter than her daddy had, and she imagines him at the Santa Monica Pier, and she can feel herself crying of a sudden, tears up in her and out and hot and cold on her face, all of it come to her without her thinking anything. Here are tears, ones she doesn't even want. She is invisible. She has gone, and her momma and daddy are dead.

The street is all in shadow, and she turns to the left, heads away from Sunset, where they got off the streetcar a million years ago.

Alvarado meets Montrose a little ways up, across from the school where she and her friends play four-square at recess, and spell words out to each other before tests, and where they talk, and talk. Then just a little ways to the end of Montrose and left onto Lake Shore Avenue, then right onto Park. Just a few minutes from here. Just a few minutes.

But the sidewalks are covered all over now, covered all the way with shadows. This is the start of night, these shadows all over everywhere. This is the start, the beginning of what is left to her: her momma and daddy dead, and herself invisible in the world.

She is alone.

So she begins to sing, to keep these shadows away, and the life she has in front of her, and to protect somehow the record and those photographs she has tucked under her arm. She has to protect them.

"Zip-a-dee-doo-dah, zip-a-dee-ay," she begins, but there is nothing after these sounds.

Where are the words? she wants to know. She'd sung them today, when her momma was alive and they were out on the street waiting for the streetcar.

That was a good song, wasn't it? her momma'd said, and Joan can see her smiling down at her, see her forehead without a care, smooth and full and soft.

"Zip-a-dee-doo-dah, zip-a-dee-ay," Joan tries again, and then sings the sounds again, searching for the words that come after, while she moves down the street toward the record player, and toward a friend who can make music that will be the death of his momma, she is so proud of her child.

She tries to sing the words she *knows* she knows, but the shadows are coming up, they are coming, and she has no words from the best movie she has ever seen, she has nothing, that emptiness a piercing, a sword, and she can feel tears still coming, and coming, and she walks faster and faster, trying to make it to somewhere else before all these shadows carry her away, because even though she is invisible, the shadows will still swallow her, they will take her, and it will never matter what side of the street she stays on, because the shadows will have taken her away, and no song she can ever sing can protect her, and her arm holding the record and photographs will mean the nothing they have meant her whole life: her momma and daddy don't care. They are dead, and she is alone.

She walks faster, and now she lets herself run, she is running, and she is invisible to everyone in the whole wide world.

But then she hears inside herself and on this street in shadow and through her breaths trying to catch up, trying to catch up, a song.

It's a song, and she is the one singing, and it means nothing because she isn't even thinking of it while she sings it, it is simply here inside her and on this street.

It is what she knows, this song. She knows this song by heart.

Oh, you must take Hollywood, she hears herself sing, *you must pass Highland, you must pass Vine and North Western, then change at Sunset right there at Hillhurst, Alvarado is your home.*

This is how to get home. These are the words that will take her there from Grauman's Chinese, and the *pagoda,* and the movies, all the movies, all the movies.

This is a song that will bring her home, though she will never go there again.

But now there is a word worse than the secret one, that word: *divorce*. There is a word even more secret, and terrifying, and blacker than any whisper, any shadow that can chase her.

It is her, this word. It is who she is. Not her name. Not even that, because a name is nothing, a name is meaningless, just what someone calls you because you had a screen test with a movie star who had the same name.

No. There is this word, who she is: *alone*.

A word she has known forever, but only now means what it has meant all along, no secret at all, big as the world and crushing.

Still the song comes, and still she runs, an apartment with a record player and a momma who loves her child only a few minutes away, even in the dark of these shadows all around.

Oh, you must take Hollywood, she sings, *you must pass Highland . . .*

Earl

17

He counted his real life as an actor as starting that day he'd been in *Woman Haters,* and that night when he'd met Saralee Kennedy. Everything before that—everything, from his brother Frank's death and his momma's slap to him seeing a man murdered before his eyes to picking lettuce to sweeping lots—

all of it didn't matter. That was all someone else's life.

He'd asked Saralee Kennedy out that very night at the Cocoanut Grove, the two of them standing at the oak and brass bar against the far wall of the hall, Saralee's first set finished, the next one about to begin.

"Yes," she'd said, and she'd reached for his hand, took hold of it and squeezed, the move so forward and her blue eyes so light and her voice so sure and beautiful he'd gone on to tell her the only thing he knew to impress her: "I'm an actor." He'd tried at that Buddy Rogers smile one more time, but this time, with him standing next to her, it had faltered, he could feel even as he worked at it.

"You *are*?" she'd said, and smiled, squeezed his hand once more before letting it go. "Imagine that," she said, and tipped her head a little away from him, looked at him out the corner of her eyes, as though she might already be onto him even through the swirl and tug and noise of all creation around them in this jumping club, this Saralee Kennedy setting it to spin the way it did right that moment with her voice and smile and beauty.

She was a star, already out and shining. She was a singer with a big band, and he knew already she'd outshine that skinny Carolina clown with his glasses and drawl, the bandleader with the German name a hasbeen before the get-go. She'd be her own success, no need one day for her to be dragged about by a band, because she could stay here to Hollywood, and be in the pictures herself. Like that Ruth Etting in *Knee*

Deep in Music singing "Love Me or Leave Me," or Jeanette MacDonald in *One Hour with You* singing "We Will Always Be Sweethearts." Maybe, Earl thought, he could be Maurice Chevalier to her Jeanette MacDonald now that his career was up and running, him an actor already. Who knew?

They would be a team. They would break into the biz big time, what with his acting and her voice. Just what this town needed.

They went out to the pictures that Friday night, her gig finished at the Cocoanut Grove and the band with two days off before heading to San Diego and the Del Coronado. He picked her up at the fleabag hotel she and the band were camped out at over on Olympic and Vermont, and she came out into the cool April night in a gray wool coat with wide lavender lapels, a flowered silk scarf over her head and knotted at her chin. They rode the Yellow Car the three minutes down Olympic it took to get to the Orpheum, the two of them smiling and looking at each other and away and back again, same as any kids in any of a million pictures he'd seen. *The Big Race* was the first one, a racehorse picture with Boots Mallory and John Darrow he forgot soon as "The End" showed on the screen; then there'd been *Fashions of 1934* with Bette Davis and William Powell, some drag of a story about people stealing clothes, when all he could think about was this doll beside him who he knew would be even more famous than Davis once she got up there on the screen.

Afterward, they went to Jimmy's across the street from the theater, and he had just enough money to get them each a malted, and they talked. The whole thing felt corny, like some picture once again, this girl Saralee nursing her straw and only sipping now and again at the malted, him never touching his own. He kept his hands folded on the tabletop before him while his malted glass sweated and he talked about being an actor, and about Moe Howard and the way Earl had suggested to him a gag that stretched the whole length of the railroad car, and how Larry Fine with his Brillo pad hair was against it, but that Moe had stood up for Earl, convincing the director, some guy name of Archie, it could work.

It was all of it lies. Of course it was lies. But how else did you woo a girl like this? How else could you hitch yourself to a star already up there in the sky? He couldn't tell her about pushing a broom, or about the coat he wore being borrowed, or the fact the sixty cents these malteds cost and the ten cents he had in his pocket for the streetcar ride home was the last money he had until next Friday.

So he lied, because it seemed the only way through this moment now, here, and if there were any future between them, he'd have to tell her one day—she would understand, wouldn't she? They would be in love, and she would understand!—that he'd had to lie to win her, because there was nothing to him, finally. Nothing at all. In order to woo a girl, you went to a picture, watched people up there acting like they were falling in love, like they had a future together, though you knew there'd be the hardship and sadness. But you knew they would make it. You *knew it*. This was the pictures! And so he sat there with this gorgeous girl across from him, with her blond hair neatly covered in that flowered scarf knotted beneath her chin, and with her wide smile and those delicate fingers of hers touching at her straw. He watched her eyes as she spoke, the way they only now and again looked up and met his, and the way it seemed now and again too that there was a kind of pain there, a sadness maybe that showed up in a wrinkled brow and that gave him to know she wasn't some dumb dame, that there was going to be more to her than standing in front of a traveling band nobody ever heard of. This Kay Kyser's one-shot gig at the Cocoanut Grove would end up memorable only because it was where Saralee Kennedy began her life in Hollywood, and where she met Earl Holmes, and where the two of them had started their careers in the pictures.

She'd forgive him his lies because of what the future held out to them, starting right now.

They held hands on the streetcar home, and on the concrete stoop of the hotel she kissed him on the cheek, told him she would be leaving the next day and would be on the road for the next two weeks. After the Del Coronado was a stop in Phoenix, next Denver, and then the band would head back to Chicago and their regular gig at the Blackhawk there. He wrote down for her the telephone number at the boardinghouse on the back of his movie ticket stub—he found a nubby pencil in the pocket of Cal's jacket, just like this was a picture and Props had done their job, the pencil showing up right on cue!—and she wrote on the back of hers her number in St. Louis, where she lived when she wasn't with the band.

"St. Louis?" he said. "But you're with the band, right?" he said, puzzled out there in front of the hotel. She ought to have a number in Chicago, he figured. She was a singer with the *band*.

It came to him: He'd been the one talking all night long. She'd said next to nothing. He'd only jabbered about himself, and all of it lies. He hadn't even let her open her mouth, which was why she'd finished off her malted before he'd even taken three sips off his.

"Not actually," she said and shrugged, looked down. The scarf, knotted at her chin, suddenly looked a little off center, maybe too tight. "This whole road trip is a test, a kind of audition," she said. "There's three of us traveling with the band, three girls. We each get one night of the gig in each city." She shrugged again, and here was that pained look, her eyebrows together the smallest way. "Kay's looking for a front girl, a lead to sing for him. He's got big plans. Big ones." She got a small smile, one side of her mouth up in a way that stole his heart, right now, right now.

"We're all three of us traveling," she went on, the smile gone. "He's road testing us, seeing who works best with the audience, with the band. And when we get back to Chicago he's going to choose who it'll be."

She paused, let her eyes come up to his, and she tried that smile again. "I'm not even sure this road stuff is for me. The shenanigans, the grabs. The reefer and hooch. You don't want to know the kind of—"

"You don't need him," Earl said right then. He didn't know where the words had come from. Maybe that cockeyed knot at her throat, or that half smile. Maybe her fingers on the straw, or the fact a pencil had popped into his pocket like the magic he saw every time he went to the pictures. "You don't need him," he said again. "Stay out here. You can be in the pictures with me. You can sing the skirts off any girl he's got trying out for him. You're better than any gal I've ever heard. You're better than Ruth Etting. You stand out front of the Chinese and belt out 'Love Me or Leave Me,' and you'll be in the dough by the end of the week."

"Aw, go on," she said, and tilted her head, looked down.

He put his hand to her chin then, lifted it until their eyes met. He smiled, said, "I've even got your first glossy. That shot of you the photo girl took."

"What shot?" she said, and here were her eyebrows together again, though there was still this smile to her.

"At the Cocoanut Grove. The photo girl took it, and I bought it, and now it's pinned up on the wall in my room." Which it was. This was no lie, and he felt himself breathe a little easier suddenly, his lungs relieved somehow, and he took in a deep breath for it, let it out in what sounded all the world like a lovesick sigh some Joe would heave in a B movie.

"Oh," she said, and slowly he let go her chin, put his hands in his pockets. "Oh," she said again, her eyes right on his, no hint of any pain or sorrow. Only her beauty.

She said, "I don't even know if I want to sing. I don't even know if I want that life."

"It's a good life," he said. "You'll love it."

Then they kissed, her lips as soft as he'd imagined, the moment like a dream come true but a dream he never knew he'd even had, a kiss like he'd seen in a million pictures, but with the warmth and soft and wet you'd never find your entire life, he suddenly understood, sitting and watching it on a screen somewhere.

She pulled away, smiled up at him, and said, "You don't know gimp about this life." She put a finger to his cheek, just touched him there. "And if you're an actor big as you've been talking all night long," she said, "then I'm Bette Davis."

He swallowed, blinked, felt his mouth go dry just like that.

She said, "I've got your number," and here came that half smile, and he knew she'd seen through him. He knew it. She'd seen him for the nothing he was all along.

But then she held up the ticket stub from the picture, held it right there in front of his nose, though he wouldn't let his eyes leave this suddenly startling woman. "Telephone number, that is," she said.

She was no girl in a band. She was something else. Maybe, Earl thought in this moment, she was *it*.

She turned, stepped to the glass door into the hotel,

and pushed at it. But then she paused a moment, looked back at him over her shoulder, and smiled. She reached to her chin, and as deftly, as perfectly as he'd ever seen such a move, she unknotted the scarf, pulled it away to reveal her hair back in a cool blond pony-tail, and she shook it just the gentlest way.

"Good night, you liar," she said, and the words were the most beautiful he'd ever heard.

"Good night, Miss Bette Davis," he said, and smiled right back.

Two and a half weeks later he and Cal and everyone else were at the table in the house on Wilcox, the old man with the tin horn to his ear and watching all of them dig in to the chicken and dumplings he'd just laid out. Some new kid sat across the table from Earl and was holding court on the bit he was going to land in some Randolph Scott joker called *Wagon Wheels,* when the telephone rang in the hall, and half the men stood at once because it was always about a part, always about a lead to something might could make them each the next Gary Cooper or Paul Muni.

It was Cal to get the phone, him up and gone before anyone else could leave the table. "Earl!" he called out, and Earl turned, saw Cal already back from the hall and settling himself in his seat, his eyes to his plate. "For you," he said. "It's a dame."

It was her. Saralee Kennedy.

"I'm at Central Station," she said. "Now come and get me, Mr. Gable."

"Yes, Miss Davis," he said, then ran upstairs, grabbed Cal's coat, and left to get her.

She had on a yellow dress with a wide black patent leather belt, her hair in a snood, beside her a cardboard suitcase, and they hugged right there out front of the brick station, and they kissed, and she held him longer than he'd thought possible from a girl. Then she was crying into his shoulder, and apologizing for it, and crying still, and she said into his shoulder, "I quit. I told that son of a bitch to keep his hands off me, to just keep his hands off me, and I told that squid he could keep his fucking band and there wasn't a chance I'd be caught dead onstage beside him ever again."

He took in a breath at the words out of this girl's mouth, and he held her away from him, looked at her face, saw her eyes and mouth all crumpled down to loss and anger and somewhere inside it happiness too. It was like nothing he'd ever seen before, no actress on a screen filled with all this, all this, and showing it all so perfectly. Her face and what he saw there gave those words she'd used the perfect pitch and purpose. That bandleader was a son of a bitch, he knew. A squid, and the gang of players behind him was a gang of useless fuckers. She was right, and he held her to him again, let her cry, and cry, and then she pulled away, tried at a smile.

"Pardon my French," she said, and let out a broken laugh. "And thank you."

This wasn't a movie at all. Nothing like a movie. She was *it*.

He brought her back to the boardinghouse to show her around, and to ask after leads on where she might live, and to see too if there was a chance there'd be any chicken and dumplings left. Cal slapped Earl on the back when he introduced her, and all the boys reached in to shake her hand, smile at her and Earl as though he'd maybe landed the biggest part any of them could ever understand. Saralee smiled and nodded and smiled, dabbed at the corner of an eye now and again with the wadded hankie in her hand. The old man shouted out his hello as well, told them of his cousin's place four blocks over on Lexington and La Brea, a boardinghouse for ladies, and then volunteered to whip them up an omelet each. "On the house!" the old man shouted and added, "This gal's as beautiful as Wanda Hawley was back in *Thirty Days*." He nodded, winked at Saralee. "I played the judge in that flicker. You wouldn't forget me if you saw that one," he said, and led them off to the kitchen.

By seven she had a room. She paid the full five dollars for the first week, pulled the bill from a small roll she had in her purse, on her face, Earl saw, a kind of nervous smile, her eyes squinted a little for the effort of handing over this much money to the house matron, the old man's cousin a woman so big and ugly she might as well have been his brother, and by seven thirty they were in the fifth row at the Patio to see *Carolina* with Janet Gaynor and Lionel Barrymore. But even before the newsreel was over—here were the Texas Rangers on the trail of Bonnie and Clyde after they shot those two policemen last week, and here was the first time anyone had flown an airplane over Mount Everest—Saralee was leaned against his shoulder, her mouth open as she softly snored away, dead asleep.

Then here came the short before the feature: none other than Ruth Etting singing her way through a two-reeler called *A Torch Tango*.

They saw each other each night for a week solid, Earl this time careful—sometimes—to let her talk, to find out who she was, where this voice came from. He'd only let on to her that he worked at the Columbia lot "in maintenance," a steady job and one he'd had for going on three years now, and that he'd moved here in '27 from Hawkins, Texas, and was number ten of thirteen children. But that was where he'd stopped. This was his life, here, a life he'd started only a few weeks before with meeting her, and with being in that Stooges picture.

Her story was that her momma'd died when she was five, her daddy'd remarried a year later a woman ten years older than him, Saralee with no real memories of her momma other than her at church, up front at Memorial Presbyterian and playing the organ. They'd lived in a neighborhood called Kingsbury, where her daddy'd owned a clothing store, and when the place went belly-up with the crash, his wife had suddenly gotten a lot older, took to her bed and didn't get out. Saralee'd sung in church all her life, and one night the summer of '30, when she was fifteen, she'd snuck out of the house, her daddy too filled with tending to his wife even to notice, and took the trolley down to south St. Louis and the Casa Loma Ballroom, and entered a singing contest.

"The biggest room you've ever seen," Saralee said, "with a balcony around the whole place, maple wood floors. The biggest room I've ever been in. And it was me at the center of it for two minutes to sing my song." The two of them were walking along Hollywood Boulevard toward Highland, and he could see up ahead where the forecourt of the Chinese was, across the street the white shining tower that was the Roosevelt, its lighted sign on the roof shouting out the President's name like it was a paid billboard.

They'd seen *Palooka* at the Pantages an hour or so before, that mumbling, jittered up Jimmy Durante chewing the screen to pieces. Through the whole picture Earl'd thought Saralee, with her looks and that voice of hers and her attitude to boot, would've given Thelma Todd a run for her money if she'd been cast as that moll Trixie. He'd told her as much when they'd left, and now they were walking along, passing time on Hollywood before they'd have to head back to her boardinghouse, and the kiss good night that would mean there were hours before them until they would see each other again.

He'd never felt anything like this. Nothing even close, and all he could think to blame it on was that they were here, and they were in Hollywood, and their

297

lives lay before them ready and open and chomping at the bit to be lived.

He believed they were in love.

She said, "I stood up on that stage, and I sang 'Button Up Your Overcoat,' and they went crazy, all of them. Debs and mugs both, and I was standing there and thinking this was the life, this was what I wanted." She paused a moment, stopped on the sidewalk out front of Musso & Frank. People were in there at the green leather booths, and were eating, and talking, and living like Earl wanted to live. Though he'd seen through this same window Clara Bow in there one time, and Charlie Chaplin too, he'd never eaten here. It cost money, and suddenly, the two of them on the concrete sidewalk and looking in at comfortable people eating hot food that wasn't put together by an old deaf actor or a he-man woman, he knew something for certain: he wanted to take care of her.

"Is this the life?" Earl said, too loud, his line blown without his even knowing he had one, or that there was a cue to listen for, a mark on the sidewalk for him to find to deliver this line.

"Not yet," she said, and she turned to him, the bottom edge of her plaid skirt beneath that gray wool coat she wore twirling just the least bit with how quick she'd turned. She was smiling up at him. "Not yet," she said again, and she touched his chest dead square, tapped once, twice, three times. Then she turned, headed on up the sidewalk.

By that Saturday, Saralee had had a set of glossies

done, had a lead on a job too, this at a music store all the way out in Glendale. He thought about her working that far out as he rode the jammed Yellow Car home from the lot—Saturday was a workday like any workday when it came to the pictures—and how it was too far away for Saralee to be seen by anybody from the studios prowling for the next pretty face. But at least she'd gone out there, had filled out the application. And there were those glossies. She'd need to go register at Central Casting next, and there she'd be, all primed and ready. They were going to go out again tonight, maybe to the Patio, maybe the Rialto. It depended what picture was showing, though Saralee had said last night she'd like to go hear some music sometime, maybe even make it out to the La Monica Ballroom on the Santa Monica Pier, a place some guys in the band, those assholes, said was quite the romp, the bands there tops.

Maybe, Earl thought as he made his way up the steps to the front door of the boardinghouse, they could do that sometime. Maybe. But there'd been those nights so long ago now, back when he'd been new to town and he'd peered in the windows at the La Monica at the swarm of people wobbling in time to the band in there, when he'd then walked to the edge of the pier, leaned on the rail to look down at the black water, that the sound of the waves crashing had been too much the sound of a night train coming closer to him in bed in Hawkins, too much the reminder of him being a kid and watching those stars out his window and way out of his reach.

He put his hand to the doorknob, but stopped a moment. Maybe they'd go out there to listen, and to dance. But he wouldn't go on past the ballroom and out to the end of the pier without holding tight to her hand, he decided, and pushed open the front door. That would be the only way he'd visit that lonesome place again, where the sounds of those waves had been too much like home. The only way he'd go out there again would be with her.

He closed the door behind him, and turned to see Cal on the phone in the hall, leaning against the wall and trying to work up a dame for a date.

"Aw now, honey," Earl heard him saying, "it's my own picture, and you're my regular wren. I'm the sophisticate in this one. You got to go with!"

Earl stopped, his hand already to the banister, his foot to the first step up.

Sophisticate.

That was the word Cal'd used to describe his bit the night before the Stooges shoot started, him with his cigarette there in the dark and waxing thick with his own importance, the notch in his bedrail with his Barlow knife, the line he would speak to introduce him to the world.

This was about the Stooges.

Earl turned to Cal, who stood smiling at him, a hand over the phone. "Got word today," he whispered hard. "The Orpheum. Tonight. The Stooges short," and he nodded, turned his back to Earl, started working the girl again.

Earl shot straight upstairs to the bathroom at the end of the hall, shaved for the second time that day, put the tonic to his hair once more, combed it and combed it and combed it again until there came a knock on the bathroom door, Cal calling out, "I've got a world premiere too, you know!" Then Earl leaned to the toilet, and threw up, the sudden burst and relief a surprise that had him brushing his teeth one more time too.

18

And so, because once he and Saralee stepped off the streetcar at the corner of Olympic and Broadway, Earl saw that the traffic and people and all the hubbub of this city was a whole lot like the toddle and rub of all those dancing children around him as he'd stood in the middle of the dance floor at the Cocoanut Grove only a month before; and so, because as they walked up Broadway the short block to Ninth and waited along with everyone else to cross the street, he could see up ahead the bright neon candy of the Orpheum's marquee and the white words against the black lined up there the commencement of everything he'd planned to achieve in just those white letters settled into words; and so, because he was out with a dream walking, her arm looped right here in the crook of his elbow, and because she was the one, she was a dream, she was *it*—because of all this, he spoke his line.

He stopped there on the sidewalk out front of the

Orpheum Theater, a string of people snaking off from the ticket booth guaranteeing him this introduction to the world would be a success, a triumph, and turned Saralee to him, pulled her close, and looked into her blue eyes.

"Marry me," he said.

"Yes," she said without a beat, the single word a gift outright in this early evening air, same as that little word had been when she'd spoken it at the bar in the Cocoanut Grove, and his life had begun. She smiled, and here was the blue past blue of her eyes, and here was her blond hair free this time, no snood, no scarf, and he leaned to her, touched his lips to hers, and they kissed out front of the Orpheum on the night of his debut.

Then he turned her to face the marquee above them, the brocaded red and green and orange and purple neon for all the world a string of fantastic glittering jewels framing the black face and white letters all in a row up there:

ORIENT EXPRESS
HEATHER ANGEL NORMAN FOSTER
NEW STOOGES SHORT

"Here we go," he said, and nodded at the words up there, looked down at her beside him, and he saw a smile grow on her that beat every smile he'd seen from her since he'd laid eyes on her standing on that stage. She looked at him, said, "Is this it? This is it?"

and he nodded, felt himself smiling of his own, and they kissed again, and again, and somewhere behind him came a wolf whistle, then the words, "Slow down, cowpoke!" and here was Cal beside them, a girl on his arm. "Tiger, save that for later!" he said, and slapped Earl on the back, leaned to Saralee, said, "This old boy's a can of fire, so you better be careful you don't get burned."

He turned to the girl, a redhead gum-chewing beauty like any of the gum chewers Earl saw every day strutting the lot, whether they had bits or were just extra girls. She had on a low-cut purple dress so tight Earl wondered how she could breathe, let alone take a seat in a theater, draped on her shoulders a fox fur, head and all, that had seen better days. "Earl, Saralee, this is Lindy Fox," Cal said, "late of *Fashions of 1934.*"

"We saw that on our first date," Saralee said, and put out her hand, and Earl turned, looked at her. Saralee was wearing that plaid skirt from the other night, and a beige sweater with a collar that reached to her shoulders. He hadn't seen what she had on at all when he'd picked her up, so full was he with the one question he'd planned to ask, and with this picture, and with this city and this life just waiting.

Saralee was beautiful, and of a kind of beauty this sack with the dead fox on her shoulders would never know.

"I was the chorus girl," this Lindy Fox said, "next to Donna Mae Roberts next to Miss Davis in the scene where—"

"We're getting married," Earl cut in, his eyes still on Saralee, who looked at him, smiled even brighter than when she'd said yes, and she took hold of his arm with both hers, leaned hard into him.

He looked to Cal, who stood with his mouth open a moment. Then he swallowed, quick shook his head, and shouted out "Old boy!" right there in front of everyone in line for tickets. "You got a deadly case of the eagers!" he said, too loud again, and people in line turned to them, smirked or smiled or shook their heads.

But it didn't matter. He was getting married, and he was marrying a star, and she was more beautiful than any girl on any screen he'd ever seen. And her voice, her voice!

She was *it*. And maybe, just maybe, so was he. What a team they would make. Just what this town needed.

"Congratulations, sport, but we don't need to be late for our own premiere," Cal said, and tugged at Earl's sleeve. Earl turned from Saralee, saw Cal and Lindy start to the line at the box, Cal strutting, Lindy snapping her gum and somehow staying upright on those heels she wore, people looking at her, and at their watches, and talking to each other, all of them making the slow shuffle to the booth, where another gum-chewing girl would take their money, give them a ticket printed with the words *The Orpheum,* and they'd go inside where a man in a vest and bow tie would tear that ticket in half, but not before they'd parade past the glass counters beneath which lay boxed candies like jewels, and upon which stood a popcorn machine, and soda pop served in paper cups. Then the man would usher them into the near dark, where they would ease back in velvet chairs, every one of them, and wait for the story to begin, and of course he thought of the Rose, and of Billie Dove, and the way his dreams had begun with the dying down of the lights on the wall in there, and the rising of that red velvet curtain, and the music a forsaken old woman played on a piano beneath the screen.

There were people out here. They were in line. They were paying money, all waiting to see a picture, all wanting to walk into that same sort of dream. It was Heather Angel in *Orient Express* they were after seeing, of course, and those black ringlets of hers and that British accent anyone with half a brain could hear was phony a mile away. That was what they were here for.

But the theater hadn't put that Stooges news up on the marquee to drive anyone away.

All these people would see him. Earl: the college boy with the slouch cap on and a newspaper in his hands, the quick shiver of it while the gag ran the whole length of the railroad car.

Earl smiled, looked down at Saralee, who was smiling at him.

"Yes," she said again. "And if you ask me again, I'll say it again. Yes." She winked, said, "You don't want to be late for your own premiere." She pulled at his arm, turned him to where Cal and his chorus girl had already landed at the end of the line a few yards away, and he glanced again up at the marquee, and that joyful neon, and the white letters heralding his arrival.

The newsreel came up—more film of those Texas Rangers and their big talk about getting hold of Bonnie and Clyde soon; that blowhard Huey Long out of Baton Rouge screaming up in Washington, D.C., about something or other—and then the short started up, and Cal, here on his left, elbowed him hard, whispered, "Here we are, old boy!" and Saralee on his right squeezed his arm a little harder, her holding on tight.

Here was the title: *Woman Haters.*

It didn't make a whole lot of sense. The Stooges—Moe in those huge white shoes, Larry with that Brillo pad hair, and Curley in that striped suit three sizes too small—join the Woman Haters Club, a group of men in suits who have sworn off women and who tell the Stooges they have to as well in order to stay members, but then Larry with the hair falls in love and has to marry the girl—Marjorie White, that tiny blonde in *Hollywood Halfbacks* with Johnny Mack Brown—and he knows he's in trouble because he'll be betraying his Stooge pals.

It was all set to music, too, music running the whole time the thing was going on, and now Earl heard that every time anybody opened his mouth the lines rhymed, and this was a musical, he finally realized, a musical short, a novelty he knew already would be the end of these Stooges, even though there were people here and there in the audience laughing at all this, more people laughing than he would've figured. But the Stooges were a lost cause, he knew, because who would come to see them without their straight man, and who would ever remember them lousing their way through a musical, where everything they said was some dim-bulb poem?

Then here was the scene with the train, and here were Moe and Curly chasing around to get hold of Larry to thump some sense into him and get rid of the gal, though so far the shots were all on a soundstage, he could tell; they hadn't yet gotten outside to the shot he was in and the real railcar out at the back of the lot, and Earl could feel his chest press down on him because he knew it was coming, felt his lungs seem to collapse, because here it was coming, here it was coming. Now here was that conductor, the one he had the autograph of and who would never amount to anything because of how many bits he'd done and never gotten credit for, and then the conductor—what was his name? Wallace something?—lays out his one line, a line Earl couldn't even hear because of the sound of his blood in his ears, the conductor standing between Moe and Curly, and his line is over, the conductor's shoulders shooting up for whatever it was they said to him after he gave that line, and the gag was coming, here it was coming, here it would be.

Then here was some dumb love song, and the Stooges short was over.

He wasn't in it. The whole thing—the train, the gag, one long shot by a camera mounted on rails beside the car, and his own moment of magic when he'd forgotten he was on camera, when that paper had genuinely shivered in his hand because of a commotion at his feet—the all of it was gone. His part had been cut.

"Old boy," he heard Cal whisper beside him, "all they left in of me was my knee in that one shot. No one's going to—"

But Earl was already standing, and moving away down the row of seats, Saralee in the seat beside him leaning her knees away to let him through, then the people next to her and next to them, and he was out in the aisle and headed for the closed doors of the theater, and away.

He hadn't been in the picture. He'd been cut, and all that shit he'd been put through, and all these people who would have seen him and made that shit worthwhile, was gone. It was gone. A whole shot outside with the cast and crew and lights and the shit, the shit, the shit Moe had put him through just to make him laugh was all gone.

He was already through the lobby, out the double doors to the street and under the marquee before he thought to take in a breath, his chest a weight he could not bear, a weight past weight and become an ache he hadn't felt before, and he felt his hands hot with fire, and balled them into fists, jammed them deep into his pockets.

Here were all the same people as only a while

before. Here was the all of the whole heaping shitpile of the world, every bit of the stinking toddle and rub before him out in front of the Orpheum on the night of his debut, and they couldn't give a shit about him either, and he took in that breath he'd thought to take, finally, and in that breath he thought of a somersault, and the stupid emptiness of it, and he thought of a man murdered in front of his very eyes and the stupid emptiness of that too, of believing he'd seen something real happening before him when he was still just a kid, and he thought of Frank dying and the real of that, and the real of his mother's gray-green eyes behind her spectacles as she struck him in the face for his single word *Hurrah,* and the real of how she did not know him then and never would, and he thought of Texas and the slow march away from his window of that tree line, and thought of his life as a logger, the life that would have come to him had he not brought himself here, to this empty sidewalk in a city filled to the stinking brim with empty.

He thought of the emptiness of seeing any of this as being empty—this pity for himself was empty, but a kind of emptiness ringing with itself, singing and shouting to itself of the emptiness of a life lived behind a push broom for no reason at all, none whatsoever, and he jammed his hands even deeper into his pockets until it felt as though the seams at the bottom would break, his teeth clenched at the nothing of every damned thing around him.

"Earl," he heard from behind him, and then beside

him right here, right here, "Earl!" and he felt her take hold of his arm, felt this girl who'd banked on nothing at all in saying yes to him, and he pulled away from her, turned his back to her, his eyes out to the street, and all these people, and the streetcars, and there, straight across the street, Jimmy's, where you could spend the last pennies you had for a week on two malteds.

He felt her touch again at his jacket sleeve—Cal's borrowed jacket, his own life such that he still didn't have a coat, even on the night of the birth and death of his career—and she leaned into him same as before the movie, and he made to move, felt himself begin to lean away from her to take a step and perhaps another.

"Don't you dare," she said. "Don't you dare walk away from me."

He stopped.

He took in another breath. He wouldn't look at her, didn't even know how to look at her. Instead he looked out at the street, the same street in this same old world, and however much he wanted to make it an ugly place, all these people dumb as sheep stomping through their own shit, all of them shuffling one night or another into the dark of a theater to find nothing— he wanted these buildings around him to fall in on himself, wanted the marquee itself to crash down and wipe him away—however much he wanted the all of this to be as ugly as he could make it, as empty as he could feel, these people seemed just as happy now that he'd never made his face onto the screen as before, maybe even happier somehow. Here were lights even brighter for the dark he'd just come from, here was the happy brocade of the neon lights of the marquee, no matter the Stooges would disappear soon as anyone croaked a word about this miserable excuse for a two-reeler.

Here were happy people who couldn't give a shit about him.

"Ask me again," the woman beside him said, and she tugged at his sleeve.

He looked down from all this happiness, closed his eyes. He felt his hands curled tight into fists holding nothing deep as his pockets could go.

"Ask me again," she said once more, quieter now, and he looked at her. Here was that squint of hers, the blue of her eyes cloaked for how hard she was looking at him. There were only her eyes, that wrinkled brow, her hand on his arm and holding tight.

"You think I'm going to marry you because of what's inside a movie house?" she said. "You think this shit is why I'd marry you? You think it matters to me if you're famous?"

He heard that word from her—*shit*—and thought of how it seemed like a flower come from her, the way she knew the truth about what went on in there and could say it so clearly. She understood.

"Then why?" he said, and swallowed. "Why go for me?"

"Because I know you," she said, the words pitched even quieter, and she leaned even closer, close enough now to kiss. "Because I can see right through you," she said. "Because you're a liar and you know it and I know it and you'll never get away with a single thing with me, which is good for both of us. And it doesn't seem like that comes along very often at all." She paused, gave the smallest shrug. "Of course honesty would work, too, if we—"

"Honesty is vastly overrated," Earl said, another line he hadn't known was his, another cue he hadn't known was here. A line delivered right on the money.

She laughed, and he heard her voice out here on the street. It was a song, that sound.

"And even though I can see right through you, I still like what I see," she said, and now their lips were almost touching, her words almost a whisper, the world falling away just as Earl had hoped, but not in rubble and mayhem. Instead, the world began to diminish, a slow fade like in the flickers when he was a kid, when the outside edges of the screen slowly crept toward the center to encircle the stars in their last embrace. "A kid from Texas," she whispered, and there wasn't another sound in the world. "A hard worker. A dreamer. And I'll marry you because sometimes, sometimes, when the light is right and if you smile right, you look just a little like Buddy Rogers."

He loved her.

He was nothing. He'd wake up to tomorrow, he knew, and have to begin everything again.

But not everything. Here was this girl named Saralee, a girl he couldn't take his eyes off, her voice a beautiful song that cut him to the bone. It was a good feeling, that cut.

It was then he slowly let go the nothing in his fists deep in his pockets, and it was then he felt his hands rise of their own, and then he felt his arms around this woman, this dream walking, and he held her beneath the marquee at the Orpheum, held her tight, and he kissed her. Just like in the pictures.

He kissed her, the woman he would marry, and for a moment he wondered who might be watching them right here, right now. Then he let himself wonder if there were some casting agent out on the street here. What was the harm in thinking on this? A man kissing a woman in the middle of the sidewalk out front of the Orpheum. What a picture that would make!

Or maybe someone who'd been in the picture, that Norman Foster, or the black-haired beauty, Heather Angel. Maybe they were pulling in late to the show, walking up right now, one or the other spotting him here and this kiss and then tomorrow morning putting out the word there was a new talent in town.

Hell, maybe even a director was passing by in the back of a long black limousine to catch a glimpse of him right now, this thing he was doing a kind of screen test all by itself, he thought. This kiss, out here on the sidewalk, a screen test.

Even this was an audition, he thought. Of course it was.

19

*W*hat was it like. Good question.

Turn here. Thunderbird Road is quicker.

*He let you drive all the way out here in his Cadillac.
Just to get me. To pick me up.*
A yellow Cadillac. That's something.

*I want to say one more time I'm glad you came out
here to get me. Because that was what I was hoping
for. To see you, and to talk to you.*
It's why I wrote that note to you.

But you want to know what was it like.
Why do you even want to know?
I'm sorry. I'm sorry for saying that, Brad.

*Do you remember the Smith's Food King down in
Sunnyslope? Where you were a bag boy that summer.
They expanded, and there's a section in there now that
sells TVs and appliances. In a grocery store.*

*He was always like that. He always had a new car.
After he finally got the job, the one with CFI. Consolidated Film Industries. That was the first money*

he really made, even though he was a janitor.

When I was a little girl he was a busboy at a restaurant. At a place called Albert Sheets Restaurant. He always talked about when he worked as a janitor at the Columbia lot, and before that at I think Paramount. That was all before I was born. Or right when I was born. But when I was a girl he was a busboy. This was after the war, after he'd been in the Merchant Marines.

But I bet he's told you all about that, the two of you swapping stories about being in the service.

After he was a busboy, he got a job working for the Red Line. The streetcars they had all over Los Angeles back in those days. I don't know what his job was, but he quit that because they wouldn't let him take time off to go to casting calls. I remember that lasted only a couple months.

One time he tried to open a café. I don't know what he was thinking. Or where he got the money. It was nothing, really. A single room on a side street, a few blocks over from our apartment on Alvarado. He did everything, made the sandwiches himself, washed dishes, everything. I remember I would walk home from school—this was when I was eleven or twelve—and sit down at one of the three tables he had in there, and he would make me a fried egg sandwich, and he'd always put too much mayonnaise on it.

I never told him I didn't like it that way, with all that mayonnaise. By then I wasn't talking to him.

I stopped talking to him when I was nine. To both of them.

Your grandma worked at the Transparent Shade Company all this time. She had the same job—she sewed piping on the bottoms and tops of lampshades—until she couldn't see anymore. Until they finally figured out it was glaucoma.

Then eventually your grandpa got that job at CFI, and started buying a new car every two years. But that was after I married your father, so that's not really a part of what it was like. This business of him and his cars. That's not what you're asking, I guess.

And she knows, your grandma knows you came out here to get me? I know I've asked that a dozen times.

But I need to know. That she wants me out there.

Your father wanted to know what it was like, too. He used to ask me that when we started dating, and then the first few months we were married. I don't know that there was ever any good answer I could give him, either.

Because it seemed like what he wanted wasn't to know what my life was like, but who my daddy worked with. What stars he'd seen and been in movies with. Like he was starstruck, not with my daddy, but with how close he'd been to one name or another. So it seemed like I never had a good answer for him, because I didn't know what was real and what wasn't out of my daddy's life. I didn't know what my daddy said that was the truth, and what was a lie.

All your father wanted to know was a list of people, the names of movies. He didn't want to know what it was like. He wanted to feel like he was somebody, because he knew somebody who knew somebody. If your grandpa even knew any of those people he always talked about. Because I don't know if he did.

But I don't think that's why you want to know what it was like.

This is hard for me to talk about. This is hard for me to say.

Here's what it was like.

I never felt like I was from California. I never did. I always thought I was from Texas, because that was where I knew there was a home. It was on Blackbourn Street, in Hawkins. It was a nice enough house—it had indoor plumbing when a lot of houses there didn't have even that—and there was a sleeping porch I and my cousins Betty Jo and Fern used to sleep out on. This was all when I was six and seven and eight. All during the war.

When I turned ten, they started sending me there for the summer. They did that every summer until Granny Holmes died. So there were a couple of years when I didn't get out there. When I was nine and ten it was just me and your grandpa and grandma living together.

I remember I couldn't wait to be a decade old. I wanted to use that word, decade.

I haven't thought of this in years, but it seems like there's not a day goes by that I don't see any of this. Any of that time. Because when we were in Texas, there was a kind of happiness I didn't know a whole lot of otherwise.

That's one part of what it was like. And I know even telling you this much that it's not about them. About my daddy, your grandpa. Or your grandma.

But that's part of what it was like. Feeling like I wasn't from where I was from. Living with him and with my momma, growing up in Hollywood, was like knowing there was always something over there, some place over in Texas, that I couldn't get to and that I'd been to before, and that I knew was home. Because it never felt like home, there in California.

You're okay driving? I mean, you slept all right last night? You want another drink of coffee, I have the thermos right here.

We can stop for donuts before we get on the freeway, if you want to. There's a place just past the on-ramp, just on the other side of the overpass.

But it's not a Winchell's.

I remember that about you. I remember when you were little you always wanted a maple bar whenever we went for donuts. Every time you got one here you said it wasn't as good as the maple bars you got at the Winchell's by Grandma and Grandpa's.

Do you remember we sometimes used to go for donuts on Saturday morning? So maybe it wasn't as terrible a thing as you remember, growing up with me for a mother.

I'm sorry.

Here's what it was like.

In Texas, my Granny Holmes had money. Don't go thinking that's what I wanted, or why I didn't feel like I was from California. Because of her money. That's not what I mean.

This is hard to say.

But she had money. They had land they found an oil field on. The oil people. When I was a little girl and living there during the war, it was just the way it was. There was never anything lacking for want of money. I remember we had to ration gasoline, I remember that. And it seemed like butter was hard to get too for some reason. But Betty Jo, Fern, and I took tap dance lessons, and I remember being scared to death because there was a recital, and everyone would be watching. It cost money to buy tap shoes and to pay for these lessons, and Granny Holmes paid for it.

So there was the kind of comfort we had in Texas because of money. But the money isn't the point. That's not the point here.

We want to get on I-10 up here. Right lane.

But listen to me. Telling you what to do. Like you didn't grow up here.

They called it the Hawkins Field. Everyone got a piece of that money, leasing out their land to the oil companies. I remember a derrick not but thirty yards or so off the back porch of Granny Holmes's house.

You could see it when we were out on the sleeping porch at night, and you could hear it too, this thin sort of whistle, but not even a whistle. More like a child trying to whistle and blowing nothing but air. But I would watch that arm on the rig going up and down, I remember. It was dark, of course, but you could see it out there, and I was a little girl and I thought it looked like a man working, throwing a pickax up above him and bringing it down and up and down again, all night long. I remember that.

There would be stars up there above it, and we girls giggling and laughing, and that rig going up and down.

There were train tracks out back too, but farther away. The lot behind the house went way back, then came Front Street, and on the other side of that, maybe a hundred yards more, were the tracks. But that was close enough to let you know full well the train was here. Every other night one came through, slowing down for the fact it was near a town. I didn't know it at the time—I found this out when I was a teenage girl and staying one summer out there, I don't know why—I found out your grandpa ran away when he was a boy and jumped on one of those trains. He never even told me about that. My own daddy.

That was what it was like. Finding out about your daddy, and finding out things about your momma too, all on your own. Almost like their lives were secrets you couldn't get to except by accident, being in the right place at the right time.

• • •

You know she was a singer. You know that, right? For the shortest minute in history she was a singer.

You've heard her around the house. I know it.

She was beautiful, too. I've seen pictures of her. From back then. From before me.

It was Uncle Chilton told me about that, about your grandpa running away on the train. I remember. It was Chilton. Betty Jo's daddy.

We were out on their front porch over on Lynch Street, and we girls were eating ice cream, and Uncle Chilton told me that, about my daddy jumping on a train when he was fourteen to go be in the movies.

He told me it broke his momma's heart, my Granny Holmes. I must have been twelve or thirteen. Imagine that. Telling a girl her daddy broke his momma's heart while eating ice cream.

My. What you remember.

Aunt Pearl was Fern's momma.

Uncle Chilton and Aunt Enid. Aunt Pearl and Uncle Floyd. Now those are names. I can't even tell you the last time I said those names out loud.

But that's how he ended up in California. Jumping on a train.

I didn't even know about this until then. By that time I didn't want to know. I just wanted to be out there in Texas, and as far away from my parents as I could get.

I imagine you know what I mean by that.

• • •

There was one afternoon I remember.

I was out there, and maybe I was there to help with someone being sick. It was Granny Holmes, yes. She needed a hand around that old house, and I was maybe fifteen. The derrick had stopped by this time, at least the one you could see off the porch. All that money was about gone, all of them out there spending it up like it was water they could just dump on the ground and not have to worry about where they would get a drink of it. They all had three cars apiece—there were a dozen or so children Granny Holmes'd had, but by this time there were already three or four of them passed away for one reason and another. One of them was killed out in the woods, I know. Way back before the war. And there was a little one, a girl, who died of the flu, and there was another one, the oldest one.

Frank was his name. I think he died of the flu, too.

Granny Holmes was in her old cane-back chair on the porch, the same one she sat in while she waited for us girls to get hold of a chicken. That was another thing, Sunday afternoons when Betty Jo and Fern and I were little we'd chase down a chicken so that Granny could twist off its neck and fry it up for supper.

That was so long ago.

She didn't have a whole lot of years left to her. She died in '55, and this must have been 1952 or so.

But she was sitting in that chair of hers, and she had an old green and yellow sunburst quilt across her shoulders, and it was June, so it wasn't cold at all. It was a quilt I used to sleep with when I was little. There was an afternoon train coming through. I remember that too.

What I remember most is her eyes, and the way she was looking off, and she was moving her head this way and that, like there was something back there and way off she could see. Like there was somebody out there.

"Do you see him?" she said to me, and I turned to look out into the woods. I don't remember what I was doing other than just being with her out there. Fern and Betty Jo were grown by then, just like me, and were off somewhere. I saw less and less of them each summer. So it was the two of us out there, and I looked out into the woods way back there, past that stopped derrick, that man with a pickax high above his shoulder and forever just about to let it slam down into the ground.

But I couldn't see anything. There wasn't anybody there.

"It's Frank," she said, and I looked at her. She'd stopped moving her head, and her eyes were squinted down behind her glasses, like she'd spied him out. Then she got this little smile on her face. "And it's little Earl chasing after him," she said, and I turned, looked out at those woods and the empty of them again. It was just woods, and the heavy sound through the trees of a train from over past Front Street. An afternoon train, like came through any day.

But I got the chills right then. I got the goose bumps

in a flash. Frank was dead, I knew that. My daddy was out in California, and he wasn't any little boy. But I got the chills nonetheless. Just like that.

"They're walking away," she said next, and I looked back at her, and she didn't have that smile anymore. Her chin was trembling then, and she looked up at me and said, "Somebody stop them. Can you stop them?"

And because I was fifteen years old and still a dumb kid I said, "There's nothing out there."

"Can you tell the both of them I love them?" she said, and her chin was giving way for it, and I could tell she was about to give up and cry. And she said, "Can you do that for me, sugar?"

That's what she said.

I haven't remembered this in forever.

I said, "Yes ma'am, I will tell them that for you." I said it right away, like I meant it, and like she was making total sense to me right then. Maybe there was a piece of me that meant what I said, too. That if there was a ghost out there of her dead son, and if there was a ghost of the little boy of hers who ran away to Hollywood, I would tell them both to stop, and tell them their momma loved them.

I reached down to that quilt, and I pulled it a little closer around her shoulders, because she seemed to be shivering, even in that early summer afternoon heat. She was looking back to the woods, but she wasn't crying. It was just her chin quivering like she might any second. And there were her eyes behind her glasses looking hard at those woods.

So maybe that's a part of what it was like. There was a ghost of my daddy out there haunting me, though I was as far away from him as I could get. Even his momma was seeing him, though he'd jumped on a train when he was a kid and never looked back, for whatever reason he had.

Because he wanted to be in the movies. That was the reason.

Because he was thinking on himself and no one else.

I'm trying to tell the truth, Brad. I'm trying to tell it as best I can, and I know I am sounding bitter. But there isn't any way to get away from that fact about him: he lived his life for himself. He lived it top to bottom in order to get what he was looking for out of things.

He joined the Hollywood lodge of the Masons because John Wayne and Roy Rogers and Gene Autry were members, and he thought he could wangle something out of that. But nothing ever came of it. Only him making me join Job's Daughters because there was a Queen's Ball for that. Job's Daughters was a debutante kind of thing for daughters of Masons, and there was a coming out party that meant you would get pictures of yourself in the Examiner. Pictures of yourself would mean a caption on the picture, and they always listed Job's Daughters by your name, and then who your parents were.

One time—I know I've never told you this, because I'd never before even wanted to think on it.

But you want to know what it was like. You want to know.

One time when I was seventeen your grandpa fixed me up on a date with Carl Switzer.

I've never told you this.

Your grandpa set me up on a date with Carl Switzer. Alfalfa Switzer, that kid with the cowlick who couldn't sing in the Our Gang shorts. I had a date with him.

Your grandpa came home from a lodge meeting— this was when we were living in the house on Satsuma, the first house we ever lived in. I was a senior at Venice High, and we'd just had the Queen's Ball. But he came home from a meeting, and told me he'd set it up. That we had a date on that Friday night.

I don't know if I ever saw him as happy. There were times when he'd come home from work and tell us he had been on a set, or that he'd had a bit in some movie. He'd be happy then, talking loud and walking around the place big and important. But this time he seemed even happier. I remember him holding both my hands and looking at me and telling me I had a date with Carl Switzer, Alfalfa, and that he'd set it up himself, and that Alfalfa saw my picture in the Examiner and wanted to know if he could take me out.

I remember looking from him to my momma, sitting in the kitchen at the table there, and leaning over the tabletop, both her hands holding her head.

Same as always, and no part now in anything. I think I wanted her to save me somehow. To tell my

326

daddy I wouldn't be going out with this Alfalfa Switzer, whether he was a Mason or not.

Because I knew already everything he said about this Alfalfa and a picture in the newspaper being the reason he'd asked me out was a lie. I knew it was all a lie.

I hated your grandpa. By then I'd hated him for a long time.

Since I was nine. I hated the both of them since I was nine. Though with my momma it was also a kind of pity. But I hated her too.

I know that sounds ugly. I know you don't say those things about your parents. But it's true. It was when I was nine that I think I understood the both of them. And how selfish they were.

I figured that out when we still lived on Alvarado, in an apartment. A few blocks from my school. Alvarado Elementary.

We went out. Carl Switzer and me. He picked me up at our house. He had an old Willys jeep, and had the word "Alfalfa" painted on the tail end of the jeep, where a bumper would have been on a regular car.

He was arrogant. My daddy walked me down to the sidewalk, and Alfalfa didn't even get out, didn't even lean over and open my door from inside the jeep. He still had the engine running, hadn't even turned it off. He didn't have one of those canvas tops for the thing, and all he did was nod at my daddy, who was jabbering the whole time about Job's Daughters and about the lodge and about how he loved what Carl Switzer had done in Island in the Sky *as Lloyd Nolan's co-pilot.*

Carl Switzer said, "I'll have her back before break-fast," which made my daddy laugh too loud, and then Alfalfa gave it the gas, and we were gone, and I looked back at my daddy, who was standing at the curb and smiling and waving.

I don't even know if Alfalfa knew my name. We drove around in his jeep, up and down Hollywood Boule-vard, then Sunset, all the way to the beach, then back again, and just kept driving. If he said anything to me it was about himself. My hair was flying around the whole time, and I remember I wished I'd brought a scarf.

He told me Lloyd Nolan was a has-been, and that John Wayne was a pansy. He really said that. He said he was about to break in again with the next picture he'd already shot, The High and the Mighty, *and that that one would put his name on everyone's lips again.*

At a stoplight somewhere along the way he finally turned to me, and looked at me for the first time.

He said, "I'm twenty-seven years old. I'm divorced and have a kid. I'm Carl Switzer. The only reason I'm doing this is for a fellow Mason. A has-been actor who's never had enough bits even to be a has-been. So don't get any ideas about you and me."

I didn't say anything. I wasn't even going to give him the pleasure of a word out of me.

Then we were back at the house on Satsuma, and

there's my daddy out sitting on the curb. I can see him in the headlights of the jeep standing up, and waving already. Like he'd never left that spot, not for two hours.

I got out, and walked around the back of the jeep toward the house, and Daddy just stayed out there on the street, just leaned on the hood of the jeep and talked at Alfalfa, and him not saying a word back to my daddy. By the time I was to the door, I heard the gas gun a couple of times, Alfalfa ready to go. But Daddy didn't even get it. He just kept talking.

Momma was in bed. She was seized up like she always was by that time. This was maybe two years before they finally had to remove her eye. She could barely see even back then. So I knew I couldn't even poke my head in there and tell her I was back. If I'd even wanted to. Because I didn't.

Which is all of it why I married your daddy as young as I did, and why I got away as soon as I could.

This is what I'm trying to say. About what it was like. I wanted to get away from them, just get away from them because they both of them were so—

I stopped being a child when I was nine. And they stopped being my parents then too. Because I thought I understood them, and how selfish they were.

Maybe some of this is why I wasn't a good mother. Why I left you alone. Maybe all of it is why I wasn't a good mother. Because I didn't know how to do what I needed to do.

None of this is an excuse. None of it.
But look at who I am, and how selfish I have been.

Brad.
Brad, I love you.
That's why I wrote that note to you. That's why I asked you to forgive me.
Those were the only words I could think to write to you. I asked you to forgive me, because that was nothing I ever knew life was like.
I don't know what it's like to ask for forgiveness. I don't know what it is to get it. When your grandpa called and told me about your grandma—
When he called me about her cancer, then I knew. Then I knew what I had to do, what I had to ask. Because I'd been living my life in what it's like for my whole life long. I'd never known anything other than what it was like. And asking for forgiveness from my child—from you—wasn't like anything I'd ever done before. It was real.
That's why I did it. Because I needed to know what a life that was real really felt like. Asking for forgiveness was about the most real thing I figured I could ever know.
Brad, I love you.

It's not hate I have for them anymore. It's something else.
I wouldn't even know what to call it. But it's not hate anymore.

• • •

When my mother got her headaches, I used to push at those wrinkles on her forehead like they would disappear, like they would make the pain in her head go away. I thought if I just pushed at them enough, erased them with my fingers, then I was doing some good, and she would feel better.

But I couldn't have been more wrong.

Your grandpa made me take tap dance lessons with him. Because he thought that was a way for him to become a star. If he had a little girl dancing beside him. And I did it with him, even though I'd already stopped talking to him and my momma both. This was when I was nine. We took these lessons though we couldn't afford them—he was still a busboy at this point—until he realized he couldn't dance to save his life.

Carl Switzer. He ended up murdered. That's how he died. Shot over fifty dollars and some argument about a hunting dog. That was a big day in our house. That same day was the day Cecil B. DeMille died. Your grandpa came home with a copy of the Examiner in his hand and shouting about how he'd known both of them, Cecil B. DeMille and Alfalfa dying on the same day, and he'd known both of them, and how strange that was.

It was like candy to him, this sort of thing.
Hollywood.

Oh, Brad. Your grandma had the most beautiful voice. It's her that's dying. It's my momma. And all I think to tell you about what my life was like is my daddy.

But maybe that was what my life really was like: We lived in his shadow. Always in his shadow. Though it seems to me to this day that there wasn't anything to him other than that shadow. That there wasn't any real person to cast that shadow.

I don't know any stories of your grandma. There was no one left to tell me anything about her. No Uncle Chilton, no ice cream on a porch. No Granny Holmes to see a ghost of her off in the woods.

She was from St. Louis. And she was a singer. But they never talked about that. They never did. Because it didn't amount to much of anything, I don't believe.

But she had the most beautiful voice. She'd sing to me sometimes, when she thought I was asleep.

And I have a good memory of your grandpa. I don't want you to think I don't, that there isn't anything good about him as far as I'm concerned.

But this: When I was a little girl, just after we moved back from Texas and Daddy'd started living with us, he was working at a little restaurant, a place he'd been told stars would sometimes come in and eat. It was a place called Albert Sheets Restaurant, and he was just a busboy there. Imagine that, after being in the Merchant Marines in World War II and coming home to be a busboy.

But it was the job he wanted. He wanted it because he might see those stars, and maybe get a job somehow out of it. That's how his mind always worked.

But what I remember. The good memory.

Momma and I went there for lunch some days while he was working. Saturdays or Sundays, or if we were out of school and Momma was off work for whatever reason. And there was this one day I remember. This one day.

Maybe I remember it because we were all happy. Happy he was home from the war, or happy because we were going to see a movie later on. I don't know.

But we were having lunch at Albert Sheets, Momma and me, and I had a hamburger in front of me that she'd cut in half for me, and I had a vanilla malted in a little glass in front of me too. I remember there was light in through the window on us—we were sitting in a booth by the window, and looking out at all the people on Hill Street. There were just people all walking around out there, and the Red Car streetcars passing by now and again, and I remember looking out there and feeling the warmth of the light in through the window.

Then my momma touched me on the shoulder, whispered, "Look! There he is!" and I turned, and here was my daddy in his white shirt and black bow tie and white apron that went almost down to the tops of his shoes. He had on the little white hat they wore, too, the ones like the Army had where you could fold it in half and tuck into your belt. But this was a white one.

I remember this, too, because we were the only

people in the restaurant. This must have been a late lunch, or maybe we were early. I don't remember that. But I remember we were the only ones in the restaurant at just that moment. There were maybe two dozen tables in there, and just us sitting in there, and eating.

Daddy was pushing a narrow steel bus cart, shiny and empty, and he was headed right for us at the booth. He was smiling, but it was a different smile than I knew. He nodded at me, and my momma, then said, "Ladies, how are we this fine day?" and he stood from pushing the cart, put his hands on his hips.

"Why, we're just fine," Momma said, and I remember she glanced at me. She was smiling, and I smiled too, and then I laughed, because Daddy was pretending like he didn't know us, and Momma was pretending she didn't know him. He was acting is what he was doing. They both were, and it was funny, I remember. He was funny, and my momma was, too.

Then he pulled from behind him a little towel from where he'd had it tucked into his apron strings, and he started to clear our plates though we weren't any-wheres near finished, and my momma let out this kind of squeal, this funny little giggle, and said, "Sir! Sir! We're not finished yet!"

My daddy stopped right then, froze in front of us with the plates in midair, and then slowly he set them back down, said, "My apologies, ladies, my apologies," with his voice all low and sorry. He frowned, shrugged, and then he turned back to his cart, and started pushing it away.

And then Momma says, "Don't let that happen again, or I won't let you take us to the pictures tonight!"

He stopped, his back to us, and turned to us real slow. He still had that towel in his hand, and he said, "Yes ma'am, won't happen again," and he winked at her, got this big smile, and then he looked at me. He took one big step toward me, and with that towel he reached out and gave a quick little rub on my nose with it, and he winked, and he turned back to that cart, started wheeling it fast away from us and toward the swinging double doors to the kitchen.

"Earl, that thing's filthy!" my momma let out, but there wasn't any kind of anger in her, and I was giggling, I remember, and smiling, and just feeling that sun in through the window on me.

And just before he pushed the cart through those double doors I remember he stopped, then kicked his feet up, clicked his heels together in the air, him with his back to us and pushing that steel cart, and then he was gone back inside.

Then I looked at my momma, who was smiling and shaking her head, and picking up her own hamburger from her plate and taking a bite. She wasn't looking at me, and she was smiling, and then she looked out the window beside us. She shook her head just the littlest bit while she chewed. She was smiling.

I looked out the window too, saw all those people. And then I looked back at those double doors, sort of expecting him to come back out, and it was then I noticed there wasn't a single other person in the place. Not a single person at any table.

This is the thing I remember most, though I remember all of it as clear as if it happened today. But I remember most seeing no one was around, and realizing he'd done his little acting part, his little kick of the heels and his apology, only for us.

And he'd rubbed my nose and winked at me. Only for me.

There. That's the good memory.

And it's a good one.

My, I've talked.

Look at this. We're only to Buckeye, and I've told you everything I can. We've only made it as far as Buckeye, Arizona, and we have the whole trip in front of us, and I've told you all I can.

Look at the lettuce fields out here. All the way out here in the desert, rows and rows of lettuce.

Imagine having to pick all that.

Brad.

I've been talking. I've been talking like I've never talked to you before.

Now you talk.

Brad

20

When my mom and I pull into the driveway at Grandma and Grandpa's, I'm hoping I might see Grandpa sitting on the steps up to the front porch, that place where three weeks ago he'd handed me a small thank-you note of a letter, an envelope addressed in a familiar and foreign hand on its front, a return address sticker with a name and numbers I thought were someone else's, no one I knew. An envelope I'd folded in half and half again and then jammed into my back pocket only to touch at it every chance I could get, as though it were a scab I wanted to ignore but knew I couldn't.

Three weeks. What might as well have been my own lifetime ago.

I think maybe I'll see him sitting there, just like he'd been when my mother had come back from a date with Alfalfa Switzer, and he'd been out on the curb in front of a house on a street named Satsuma, a house I'd never heard of before my mother'd uttered it into being with just her words.

But that's not how it is when we pull in this mid-afternoon in July in Pacoima, California. That's not what I find—what *we* find, my mom and I—at the end of a seven-hour drive from Phoenix to here in a pale yellow Cadillac DeVille.

I pull into the driveway beside my grandpa's Econo-line van right where he left it yesterday, and see them both sitting on the bottom step of the porch.

There they are: my grandpa, in his red camellia on royal blue shirt, the same one he wore just yesterday to the Rose Bowl; Grandma has on the infamous rose-on-white caftan, the one that makes her look nothing like a tattooed white whale.

She has on her sunglasses, her mouth as ever in its clenched squint, and she has a hand up to her fore-head, blocking out as much light as she can. Grandpa is smiling, and standing now, and I can see their arms are looped one in the other, and now Grandma is standing too, inside her grimace a kind of smile trying to get out.

She is squinting as hard as she can to see what she can see, and even from inside the car out here on the driveway, even through the windshield and all this light down on us all, I can see that Grandpa's shirt, the red and the blue of it, makes his green eyes stand out.

I think of my mom tap-dancing with this man so that he can make it big, and of her trying to push back those wrinkles on her mother, my grandma, and of the little girl's belief that she could make pain disappear.

But I think, too, of her giggling at the click of her daddy's heels, and the wink he gave her that's lasted the rest of her life, no matter how deeply hidden away she may keep it.

I ease the car to a stop, and my mother reaches a hand to the dash, leans forward. In her other hand are the straps to the square leather handbag she hasn't let go of yet, her holding tight to those straps like they're reins she believes will be ripped from her any moment now.

"There they are," she whispers, and in the pitch of the words I know she's said it not for me, but for herself.

It had been only yesterday that I'd opened the letter from my mom, only yesterday that I'd walked away from Grandpa when he'd been at the edge, finally, of telling me something true about his life, namely that Grandma was sick. It'd been only yesterday that I'd seen all those people with all their histories headed our way, the grunion running from the open gates of the Rose Bowl Flea Market, nothing holding back their perusing goods that might add yet another layer of things to their lives, everything from coffee mugs thrown by the old hippies Johnny and Eva three spots down to fishing lures from Irving next door to a hand-tooled leather Bible cover made by Chuck Van Hoof, on it the extraordinary truth of his wife, Serena, beginning a journey toward mountains.

There were even caftans they could buy, with each purchase a piece of the history of Earl Holmes, whoever that was. Actor, janitor, tailor. Grandfather. Father.

It'd been only yesterday that I'd turned from that wave of people, and made my way back to Grandpa, and whatever might happen next in light of the vague specter of what was wrong with Grandma.

Cancer, I knew from what Serena, wrapped in her green afghan, would not say to me out of allegiance to and love for my grandma and grandpa both.

When I'd made it back to him standing there in that dreadful shirt of his own making, him with his arms crossed and his chin trembling, my impossibly handsome grandpa suddenly a man with deep lines beside his eyes and age spots through his thin white hair, it was me to hold him, and to let him cry for a few seconds before I'd turned him toward the racks of caftans and our two empty lawn chairs at the rear of our spot, just beyond them the back of the van.

That was when Chuck got up from beside Serena there on the tailgate of their truck, and when Irving made his way over too, but not to us. As Grandpa and I took our seats, they made their way to the front of our spot, both men straddling the painted parking lot lines that separated our slot from either of theirs, and began to stand a kind of guard over us and this jungle of caftans.

Chuck, in his flannel shirt and red suspenders and Dodgers ball cap, looked back at us over his shoulder, nodded once, and then Irving, still with those magnifying glasses clamped on his head but with the lenses flipped up, looked back at us too. He said, "You boys figure out your order of the day. We'll take care until you're ready." Then here, pushing through the caftans to my right, a bright red ceramic mug in each hand, had come Eva Germain with her salt-and-pepper braids and beautiful smile, and I could smell what I could tell already would be a good cup of coffee.

"There's more where this came from," she said, and handed Grandpa his mug, touched at his shoulder, squeezed it. Before I took mine I carefully folded up my mom's note, put it in my front shirt pocket. Eva smiled down at me, and as I took the mug from her hand I wondered yet again who all these strangers were and why I had been considered worthy enough to be blessed by them.

I took a sip at the coffee, closed my eyes, and tasted the bitter perfection of it. And then I felt somehow something I could not name, something unexplained and certain at once, and I opened my eyes, turned to Chuck and Serena's truck.

The tailgate was empty, Serena gone. I looked to the back window of the cab, saw inside just the crown of her red hair, that wig, and a pillow up against the passenger window, and I thought for a moment perhaps she was asleep in there. But then I knew, for no other reason than that I knew, she was praying.

"They found spots in her lungs," Grandpa offered up, and I looked at him beside me. He held his coffee mug with both hands, his elbows on his knees, the mug nearly to his lips. "Of course they found spots on her lungs," he said, this time nearly a whisper, his eyes to the asphalt a few feet in front of him, him lost to this news he must have been telling himself every moment he was awake.

He closed his eyes, didn't sip at the coffee, only held that mug close to his lips, like it was a kind of temptation. "Seems they're giving her six months, maybe eight."

"When were you going to tell me?" I said, and when I heard my voice there wasn't any accusation on it, no anger or resentment or anything else that a few minutes before I'd have had up my sleeve as a Child of Divorce, a Runaway gone off to and already returned from Seeing the World.

"We were going to tell you when you were ready to hear it, maybe," he said. He paused, still with his eyes closed, still with that mug at his lips. "Maybe we thought you needed to hear from your momma first. Maybe we thought you needed to know what she had to say." He stopped again, took in a breath and let it out slowly. "I don't even know what's in that letter she wrote you. But she's the one. She's the one said for me to wait and see what happened after you read what she had to say."

He opened his eyes, still looked at the ground a few feet out front of him. Then slowly he sat up, still holding that mug with both hands, and finally, carefully, he brought it to his lips. He took a sip, winced a bit, then brought it slowly down, held the mug in his lap.

He looked at me now. "Your grandma didn't want a word of this to you, or to your momma. Because she loves you both so much." He tried at a smile, and it seemed to hold a few seconds, but then it was gone. "So I obliged her, to a degree. We got the tests back four days before you put in, and I waited to tell you, and I waited to tell your momma. Of course we were going to tell you both. Of course. We just didn't know when, or how. But when Saralee wouldn't let me tell either of you, I decided I'd call your momma, and let you alone." He gave a small shrug. "You were closest to us. You'd find out or she'd tell you soon enough." He paused, took another sip of the coffee, nodded. "I thought that's what she was going to do when she took you off to buy her coffin nails. Those cartons at the Hanshaw's out on Laurel Canyon."

"Spots on her lungs, and she still buys cigarettes by the carton," I said, and moved to take a sip of my own coffee, but stopped, wondered suddenly why we were parked here drinking coffee like it was a carefree breakfast at Denny's.

I looked out to where Irving and Chuck stood in front of the racks, their backs to us. People were passing now, some slowing here and there, touching at a wind chime across the way or pausing at a vase of dried flowers. Someone stopped at the spinning rack of leather *Maranatha* key chains to Chuck's right. He nodded, said a few words, but didn't budge off his spot in front of us. The person—a woman in a blue sweatsuit and floppy straw hat—moved on.

The day had begun, and here we were, talking, while Grandma was at home.

"That's what you call dramatic irony," Grandpa said. "Her taking you to buy those cigarettes. She and I both knew what she was up to in buying those things, and you didn't." He nodded again, followed it with a shake of his head, as though he couldn't make up his

343

mind. "Of course I haven't stopped either. And I haven't stopped her. So maybe there's no irony involved at all. Only stupidity."

"When were you going to tell me?" I said again, still on my voice no charge against him.

"I told your momma," he went on, as though I'd said nothing, "because that was the easy one to tell. Your grandma doesn't even know I called her. So I guess that's another betrayal I'll have to deal with on up ahead. But to call up your momma, I figured, was the easier duty, even if I hadn't spoken to her in years. Not since just before you went into the Navy. Truly. That's how long it'd been. I figured she'd be the easy one to tell because you're here with us, and I figured to let your grandma be the one to tell you. Not me." He took in a breath. "But your momma didn't say a thing for five minutes. I only sat there with the phone in my hand, and listened to her breathing, and I knew she was crying. And then she finally said, 'Let me write him. I know what I have to write him. Just wait for that,' she says. 'Just wait and see what he does.'"

He stopped again, and it looked like he hiccuped for the quick breath in he took. He lowered his head a bit, looked into the mug of coffee, and for a second I see him out in the garage, looking into a bucket of plaster he'd just stirred that summer when I was fifteen. For a second I hear Ray Conniff's women singing quietly from that old record player on the coffee table in there, the two of us looking at the plaster as though it were a puzzle we could solve.

"I didn't know what she was talking about, your mom," he said. "Why this involved you and what you'd do. But then it set in, and I knew." He let his eyes meet mine for a second, and he nodded, his chin trembling again. "I don't know if you do. Understand why she wanted to talk with you first. But maybe one day you will, when you have your own family. Maybe then you'll understand the way things can go so wrong. God bless you if you realize soon enough how to fix them. Because God knows I sure as hell didn't." He stopped, slowly shook his head. "God knows there's a story about us. There's things I did. And your grandma too." He sniffed, rubbed at his nose, and I could tell he was doing his best to hold back tears in all this. "So most days I can't blame her for taking off, and raising you all by herself. Most days I can't blame her wanting nothing to do with either of us. And especially me."

He sat up straight, sniffed hard, rubbed at his nose again. He glanced at me, tried yet another smile, and lost it. "But your momma says on the phone for me to wait for you," he went on. " 'I'll come. I'll come,' she says. 'But just give me this, just let me see what he does,' she says. So who am I to argue, but the shittiest father ever born?" He paused again, brought the mug to his lips. He didn't sip at it this time, only held it. "I hadn't talked to her in at least six years. Your life comes and goes. It's here and it's gone, and you make the choices you do and you realize how dim you are only after you've proved yourself just that dim. So I gave her that time, to write you. Because I thought maybe, even with the fact of your grandma's cancer, that this would be the right thing to do. As her father. As her daddy. Maybe the right thing was to let her have that time."

I leaned forward in my chair. I wasn't sure what it was I felt at all this. I wasn't sure if I was supposed to be pissed off at him for waiting this long, or if there was something right in the choice he'd made to give me the time it took to open that note. I looked at my coffee as though it might give me an answer, but of course it was only coffee, only a mug. Nothing else.

"When," I said one more time, "were you going to tell me?"

He took in a breath, and looked at me. "Remember all that shit three weeks back? About you giving yourself two weeks to get a lead on a job? To get your life in order," he said, quieter than any words he'd given so far. His eyes were right on mine, and he blinked, blinked again. "That was the day you got the letter from her. If you'll remember. That was the day you'd given yourself to get to. You kept calling it The Day those two weeks before then." He stopped, and with his eyes still on mine, he brought the mug to his lips, took a sip, and swallowed. "But as it turns out," he said, and kept the mug at his lips, and I could see this time around a real smile coming up on him. "Turns out," he said, "you were wrong. Looks to me like today is the day."

It was me to blink then, and blink again, and we

looked at each other a long few seconds, him smiling all the while.

I looked away from him, and down to the coffee in my hands. I hadn't taken but the one sip off it, but right then I couldn't remember better coffee, even with just that one taste. I couldn't remember a more beautiful mug, though it was only a ceramic mug, bright red, the glaze sharp and clear all the way around.

I couldn't remember a more beautiful day, or better people around me. I couldn't remember the sun shining any more tenderly than in that moment, just then.

But I went ahead and said it, because I knew it was the thing to do, and these pleasures of the world—coffee, sunlight, good people—amounted to nothing this moment.

"Let's go," I said. "I need to drive out there. I need to go get her and bring her back here."

Grandpa stood, still smiling. "Let's go," he said, just like that, and with the mug in one hand, he took hold of the back of his lawn chair with the other, with his foot toed it closed, folded it up.

I stood, closed my own chair, with one hand popped open first one back door and then the other on the van, and we each set our mugs inside next to the right wheel well, and started in to the task of breaking it all down.

I climbed in, and Grandpa handed me both chairs. "Good call," he said. "This is a good call. You're

doing the right thing. Maybe there's hope for you yet."
He winked, and I took the chairs, leaned them against
the inside of the van, and as soon as I turned back,
here he was holding out to me five or six caftans off
the nearest rack. "Forget spacing them out, too, that
two fingers between each one falderal," he said. "Just
get them on the rod. We've got places to go, people to
see."

"Good call," I said.

And here beside Grandpa stood Serena. He hadn't
seen her yet, his back to her with grabbing more caftans off the rack beside him. She looked up at me,
nodded, and smiled.

She still had that green afghan over her shoulders,
and it seemed the wig on her head was a little crooked
somehow, the bangs across the front slanted a little to
one side. But her brown eyes were just as clear and
true as when I'd let go her hand earlier this morning,
me afraid I'd hurt her for how soft and breakable her
hand had seemed in mine.

She looked from me to Grandpa still with his back
to her, working to grab off a good dozen or so caftans
this time instead of the five or six. "Chuck, Irving,"
Grandpa called out, "we need a hand back here."

"Give your daughter and Saralee my love," Serena
said, and Grandpa quickly turned to her, surprised.
But then an easy grin came to him just as quickly, and
she touched his arm draped with the pile of caftans.

"Will do," Grandpa said, and he leaned to her,
kissed her cheek.

She looked up at me again. "I hope I meet your mother one day," she said.

"I do, too," I said, and nodded, reached out my hand, and she took it. Here was that fragile warmth. But I held her hand a long moment, held it and held it for the strength I could feel inside her touch.

"Someone here to see you, Earl," came Chuck's voice from behind them both, and I looked past Serena and Grandpa toward the front of the spot, between those racks of caftans on either side.

Grandpa and Serena turned, and here came Irving and Chuck, between them both an older lady—an *old* lady—wearing, of all things, a caftan, this one out of that peach dahlia on black material.

She had an arm looped in Chuck's, the three of them slowly making their way toward us. Chuck said, "This lovely lady says she knows you, Earl," and patted her hand on his arm, and Irving put in, "Even better, seems she wants to make a purchase."

The woman couldn't have been much over five feet, even for the perfect posture she had, and there was a bearing about her I could see in just this moment that made her seem somehow to stand taller than both men beside her. She was smiling, her eyes on Grandpa, and had silver hair, but with eyebrows black as I'd ever seen, her eyes and mouth and neck all thick with wrinkles.

She was beautiful.

"Oh," Grandpa said, then, "Oh."

"Earl!" the woman said. "So good to see you!"

"Oh," he said one more time, and an instant later gave out "And you, and you!"

I looked at him, then turned toward this woman, and Chuck and Irving. There was something wrong with him for the way he was talking to her, and something wrong for how stiff and awkward he'd suddenly become. I'd been with him when he was working customers in the parking lot out front of Dale's, seen him speak Spanish clear as a bell, pull out that southern drawl for the Samoans, act the caring father around younger women.

But it seemed somehow he'd been knocked down for this woman simply calling out his name, those uttered sounds *oh* little more than air out of him.

Without taking his eyes off her, he handed back to me there in the van the dozen or so caftans on his arm, then took a step toward her, and another, Irving and Chuck still ushering her in, the woman still smiling, still just as regal.

"I was hoping to make another purchase this morning," the woman said, and now Grandpa had made it almost to her with these strange single steps he was taking. I glanced down to Serena to see if she'd noticed how off Grandpa seemed, how strange he was being for this woman here with us. But she was watching too, and I looked to Irving and Chuck, who had their eyes on Grandpa as well.

"We didn't mean to interrupt you and Brad," Irving said, and glanced up at me in the back of the van. He nodded once, and suddenly the wiseass, the one who'd yanked my chain every moment thus far, was gone.

I nodded back, but his eyes were already on the woman again. Then, as though they'd choreographed the whole thing, Chuck let go her arm and took off his Dodgers cap, and Irving reached up, took off that visor with the magnifying glasses, and they both took a step away from the woman.

This was when, finally, Grandpa made it to her, and he bowed.

It was a stiff bow, like a butler might make in an old movie, his hands at his sides. The woman put out her hand, and before he stood straight he took that hand, and kissed it.

"Miss Dove," he said.

"My most ardent admirer after all these years," the woman said. "Perhaps the only one left, to tell the truth," and she seemed a girl suddenly, her shoulders up for Grandpa's holding her hand, that smile she held even brighter, the woman even more beautiful for it all.

"Since *Folly of Vanity*," Grandpa said, and now he seemed to gather himself, stood tall, those first few stammers of sound out of him gone. "The first flicker I ever saw," he said. "And of course *The Black Pirate*, and *Cock of the Air*, and *The Light of Western Stars*, and who could forget *The Ancient Highway*."

The woman tucked her chin down and a little away, let her eyelids flutter a moment, and she laughed. "You do go on," she said, "but of course it won't be me to stop you."

Miss Dove, I thought, and it came to me just as Grandpa, smiling, turned from her to face me. "Miss Billie Dove," he said, "I'd like to introduce my grandson, Brad."

Billie Dove. He'd been in a movie with her, he'd told me. She had three of his caftans, he'd told me too, there at the sewing machine that first time I'd tried at stitching a straight line. Back when I was beginning something.

Three weeks ago. The day I'd gotten my mom's note in the mail, and put it in my back pocket.

"Pleased to make your acquaintance," I said without even thinking on it, those words in that order never spoken by me before in my life, and in a second I lay the caftans on the floor of the van, climbed down, and was there with Grandpa and Billie Dove, and I took her hand, did my own sort of bow.

"I see good manners run in the family," she said, and smiled at me, nodded, her hand in mine, and she squeezed hard.

"You—" I said, then, "I—" and then just the sounds "Oh, oh," same as Grandpa, and for some reason I could not say I did that bow again.

Words were gone. This was one of his movie friends, someone I'd only heard of before and so hadn't believed even existed, and I wondered who I was to be so starstruck, and then I saw Serena and Chuck and Irving, Miss Dove and Grandpa too were all looking at me. They were all smiling, all of them watching, waiting for something else from me. But I had nothing.

"Miss Dove," Grandpa said, and saved me. Her name came out crisp and clear, the attention turned suddenly from me. "I'd like you to meet my friends," he said, and started in on introducing them to her, and I let out a breath I hadn't known I was holding.

As poised and certain as I'd ever seen him, he smiled and nodded at each person as he said their name, his hands behind him as he moved on to the next. It lasted only a few seconds, all of this, but in that time I saw a different man.

It wasn't Humphrey Bogart or W. C. Fields, wasn't any sort of bravado-filled caftan guru shouting about fabrics, or any old man cozying up to a young mother, no southern drawl on him or anything else. He was only Earl Holmes.

But then I remembered what it was we'd set about doing only a moment before she'd arrived here on the set of my grandpa's life. We were breaking things down and heading home, so that I could go get my mom, and so that we could begin to be a family before my grandma died.

Today was the day.

"Grandpa," I said, and he turned from where he stood beside Serena, her and Billie Dove shaking hands gentle as could be, "you take care of Miss Dove, and I'll keep breaking things down here."

For the smallest instant his eyes creased nearly closed, the move a kind of flinch, but not even that. The smile on him flickered just a moment too, seemed ready to fade.

He slowly turned back to Billie Dove, gave another bow. He took in a breath, held it a moment, and said, "Though it would be my delight to help you find a caftan to your liking, Miss Dove, I have family obligations I must attend to."

Serena and Billie Dove still held hands, and there came to Miss Dove's face as she looked at Grandpa a kind of puzzlement, her eyebrows up and her smile perhaps a little too wide.

Then, as carefully and smoothly as anything I'd ever seen, Serena took hold of Miss Dove's hand with both of hers, leaned in to her just a little, and said, "Let me show you this new material Earl brought out today. Peaches on green," and Miss Dove's eyes were back to Serena, and her slightly crooked red hair wig.

"Please remember, Miss Dove," Grandpa said, and made a backward step toward me, easing away from them both, "your money is no good here. These are on the house, in thanks for your contributions to the film industry." He nodded, though Miss Dove and Serena were already heading away toward the front of the spot, and the racks out there.

But Serena glanced back at us a moment as they moved, that afghan still on her shoulders. She was smiling, and let her eyes touch on Grandpa's, then on mine, and she winked at me. It was a kind of goodbye, I knew, and I nodded back just before she turned to Billie Dove and whispered something to her, the two of them arm in arm. Miss Dove leaned her head back and let out a laugh, regal and true, for whatever Serena had said.

Grandpa turned to the rack beside him, him all movement and purpose, and grabbed off another handful of caftans, handed them to me, still standing there.

"I meant it," I said quietly. "Go take care of her. I can do this," though as soon as I said it I could hear there wasn't anything behind it. My heart wasn't anywhere near what I'd said.

He was already pulling off another armful of caftans, but stopped, looked at me. He seemed to be searching me for something, his eyes on mine, and then on my face, as though there might be traces in my forehead or chin or cheeks of something he might recognize any second now.

His eyes were back on mine, settled there a hard second.

"Don't start lying to me this late in the game, son," he said. "Never lie to a liar."

Here came another armful of caftans to me, these from Irving to my right. Then Chuck, to my left, loaded on another armful, and already I had almost too many to carry up and into the back of the van and the rods hanging there.

But I made it.

I hadn't even gone into the house when we'd pulled in from the Rose Bowl around ten or so yesterday morning. Grandpa'd parked the van in the grass to the left of the driveway so I could make a quick escape in the Cadillac, and as soon as he'd put it in park and before I'd even popped open my door he'd tossed me the keys, then reached to his back pocket, pulled out his billfold. He'd lifted out a fifty and two twenties, handed them to me, said, "For gas and whatnot."

I'd wanted to go inside to hold my grandma, to tell her I loved her before I set out to go get my mom.

"But I need—" I started.

"Don't," he cut in. "It's me has to do this," he said. "This part's my job," he said, and he was trying once again at a smile. "I'm the one who has to tell her what we're up to. It's your job to just get on out of here. I'll give your momma a call, let her know you're on your way. Now go," he said, and nodded.

I looked out at the front porch. My grandma was inside that house, and she was dying, and I'd been wasting time flat on my butt or sitting out front of a Dale's or smoking weed out back and trying to piece out stars I couldn't see for too much city all around me. Those stars were up there whether I could see them or not. Of course they were.

I looked back at him. "Yes sir," I said, and nodded. I opened my door. But then I stopped, turned to him.

"One question," I said.

He'd opened his own door by then, but stopped, his eyes on mine. His eyebrows were up a little, surprised at this halt to everything.

"Do you know Billie Dove," I said, "because you were in a movie with her, or because she'd bought caftans from you before?"

Grandpa smiled, let out a breath, and seemed to ease back in the seat, all with his eyes still on mine.

He said, "If I'm the liar you know I am, then what good would any answer do?" He paused. "And would either answer get you to Phoenix any faster?"

I looked at him. "Good answer," I said, and nodded.

He shook his head, still with that smile. "Go," he said, and I climbed out, went straight to the Cadillac and started it up, backed it out the driveway and into the street.

But once I was out there, just before I put it in drive and pulled away, I looked one more time up to the house.

There stood Grandpa at the door, his hand to the knob, him in profile to me. He looked up, as though he might be searching for a plane up there he'd heard but couldn't yet see. Then he closed his eyes, let his head drop until his chin touched his chest, and he pushed open the door, headed into the darkness in there.

Seven hours of desert driving later, I'd gotten to our old house. The place didn't feel like a day had gone by, save for a good amount of new building going on on the outskirts as I'd headed in. But once I'd gotten off the freeway, made it out Thunderbird Road to Cactus, then right onto North Twenty-fourth, here were the same houses I'd known in my neighborhood, the same streets and places: Larkspur Elementary, where I'd gone, and Cholla Street and Yucca, Desert Cove, and Sahuaro, all these places I'd ridden my bike past and to, and later where I'd learned to drive. In me all the while back then had been a kind of escape route mapping its way into being, until I'd followed it the best way I knew how, that big route rounding me right back to here, and the left turn off Twentyfourth onto Shea Boulevard and the quick next left onto Twenty-fourth Place, and to the second house on the right, with its yellow stucco walls, its gravel yard, its barrel cactus and the lone saguaro, all of it not a day older as I'd pulled in.

There, in the living room window, stood my mom, waiting.

It was a little after five. The air outside was, like every July afternoon I'd known growing up here, still too hot to breathe, and I sat there in the car with the engine running and the air-conditioning blowing, looking at her. The front of the house faced west, so that the sun on its way down shone in on her, and I could see from here that her hair had gone a little gray. She had on a white blouse with short sleeves, her arms crossed. Her chin was down so that she was looking at me over the tops of her glasses—she had glasses!

I could see her parents in her face for the first time ever. She had her mother's mouth, the shape of her lips and the way she pursed them just now and forever while I was growing up, a look that meant nothing other than that she was sizing me up. Just a look.

She had Grandpa's eyes, the green of them, and here he was in the way she held her chin down so that I could see the whites of her eyes beneath her irises even from here. A look just like Grandpa gave when he stared me down.

She didn't move, only stood there.

This next move was still up to me.

I cut the engine, glanced down to find the handle and popped open the door, and when I looked up she was gone from the window, and the front door opened, and here she came out onto the driveway, and suddenly, suddenly, me still only climbing out of the car, the door still open, just this suddenly she was holding me, and I couldn't remember this. I couldn't remember this at all: my mother, holding me, holding me hard now, and she was crying just as suddenly and without fear, I could feel, and without qualm or reservation or shame. She was crying.

I didn't know her. But I loved her, because I had a single piece of stationery in my front shirt pocket, soft yellow flowers at the top of it, and beneath it two words written in this woman's hand.

"I'm so sorry," she said into my shoulder, and took in tough quick breaths for her crying.

I said then what I needed to say, too, because I knew this wasn't all about me, and because I had been a son who'd run away, and who'd been as remote as a son could be, six years away and with no word at all.

"I'm sorry, too," I said.

We'd let go each other after a long minute or so of her tears, and then we'd gone into the house, the place the same icebox I remembered for the heat we'd just been out in. A brown suitcase sat just inside the front door, ready to go. I'd planned to just get her and head on back, but when I bent to the suitcase, picked it up, she'd put a hand to my arm, said, "No. You need to sleep. You need to rest."

She'd smiled at me, nodded, and I'd set the bag down, then followed her into the kitchen, where I sat at the table and watched while she made dinner, what she called Sizzle Burgers, my favorite when I was a kid: hamburgers fried in a pan with Worcestershire sauce and butter; we had Tater Tots along with them, another favorite. She'd had everything laid out and ready on the counter, even had the oven preheated for the Tater Tots, and all the while I'd watched her make this meal and while we sat together and ate it, the only words to pass between us had been the now and again comment on the heat, or the building going on in Phoenix, or how bleak the drive out here had been. We were neither of us yet ready to commit to words any more than what we'd already said out on the driveway, what'd happened out there some odd event that didn't yet seem real, like a bad accident we'd both witnessed and didn't yet know how to talk about, or a pill we'd both taken and were waiting for the medicine to kick in.

And nowhere, nowhere—neither volunteered by me nor inquired of by her—was any word on Grandma.

Finally, after we'd watched almost the whole hour of *60 Minutes* in the living room, my mom perched like always on the brown tweed couch and me as ever in the green Naugahyde easy chair, an arrangement no different than any night we'd sat in silence and watched TV together—an arrangement, in fact, no different than the night we'd watched Grandpa's triumphant Foremost milk commercial—I got up to go to bed, still in me the foreign feel of my mother crying into me and holding on tight.

I told her good night, and while Andy Rooney blabbed on about himself, I bent to her there on the couch, kissed the top of her head, and saw her hair was grayer than I'd thought. She smiled up at me a moment, no more, and here were wrinkles beside her eyes that were new to me, even after I'd held her out on the driveway, and after I'd watched her make dinner.

But she was my mom. Nobody else.

"It's awfully early," she said, and I shrugged, said, "I've been up since four-thirty. Then driving here." I shrugged again.

"Then good night," she said, and smiled, turned to the program, and the close-up of that stopwatch ticking down its last few seconds.

My bedroom was just as I'd left it. Same blue corduroy bedspread, the bed right up against the same window I'd climbed out of when I was fifteen, across the window the same pale green curtains. On the shelf above the dresser was the same row of plastic models I'd built through the years and had been too proud of to throw away: the Munsters roadster; a Zero and a P-51 Mustang mounted on clear plastic bases and facing each other as though in a dogfight; the Mummy, his arms stretched out like he was after grabbing you.

Here on the dresser itself was a single brown shoelace, a piece of quartz the size of a fist I'd found in the desert one time, and a Mercury dime I'd once gotten in change. In a neat row along the back of the dresser top were the same dozen or so books as the day I'd left, in among them *The Warlord of Mars* and *Riders of the Purple Sage, The Stranger* and *Breakfast of Champions, The Hobbit* and *The Odessa File.*

I opened the top dresser drawer, saw in there the neatly folded underwear and rolled up socks of an eighteen-year-old who'd just run away to join the Navy, and I knew already that in the drawer beneath this one were that kid's T-shirts and a couple pairs of shorts, in the bottom drawer his swimming trunks, and two or three belts coiled like snakes.

Nor did I have to go to the closet and open it up to know exactly what that held: a row of pants, shirts on hangers, a few pairs of shoes. All of it that kid's.

This was the room of a child who'd died, I'd thought. Here were the clothes, the bed made just so, the memorabilia of a life passed from this world into the next, the all of it waiting for a day that would never come.

But here was the day. It had come, and here had been my mom making her son the dinner of his dreams, and him giving a kiss to her head, then exiting into a room that hadn't been touched but to be dusted, I could see, for six years.

Though I was tempted to take off these clothes I'd been wearing for what seemed the longest day of my life thus far for all that had transpired, from the jolt of Grandpa's sad joke of the radio blasted on high to the appearance of one Billie Dove to the feel of my mom's tears through my shirt—though I was tempted to take off these clothes and perhaps burn them, put on the old clothes of the old me, the dead one it seemed might have come back from the grave, I couldn't.

I wasn't him anymore. No matter if my mom had waited for me to come back and perhaps take up these clothes and this room, no matter it had taken my whole life thus far for her to ask my forgiveness, and for me to give it and ask for hers in return.

This wasn't my life anymore, and so I only closed that top drawer of the dresser, reached to the light switch by the door, turned it off, and made my way to the bed.

I didn't pull down the bedspread, only sat, then lay back onto it, quietly eased off my shoes with my toes, put my head to the pillow.

Here was the window.

I sat up, reached a hand to the curtains, pulled them back to reveal the same view as I'd ever had. There was the fence at the back of the lot, the roofs of other houses in the neighborhood, off in the distance Squaw Peak, and above it all those stars.

But though they were the same stars as ever, the same stars as had been up there before I ever showed up and would be long after I was dead and gone to anyone's memory, I knew they were different all the way around.

21

Now here we all are. My mother's parents standing in front of their own front porch and dressed in the garish flowery wares of Holmes Originals, their daughter just touching the dashboard and holding tight her purse, and me.

We get out of the Caddy, close our doors. I go to the trunk and pull out that brown suitcase I settled in at the beginning of the day, after I'd woken up on a blue corduroy bedspread, put back on my shoes, and had come out to the kitchen to my mom at the table all dressed and ready, her square leather handbag in her lap, a cup of coffee in her hands. A full and steaming cup sat on the table waiting for me, a full thermos on the counter next to the coffeemaker, and we'd only taken long enough for me to drink that one cup before we'd left.

I watch from the back of the car as my mom walks toward them both, and though her back is to me I can see by the way she holds her shoulders she has that handbag tight to her chest, and I'm wondering what it is in there she thinks she's got to protect from her parents.

Grandma lets go Grandpa's arm then, and Grandpa puts his hands behind his back, smiles even broader now. But I can see there's something inside it, a kind of defenseless tilt to it, something forced and counterfeit and true all at once, and of course that something is the story of their lives together, the highlights of which I have only been given on the drive here, a brand-new history that's as old as their lives together.

It's a story of Texas and California both, and of something to do with the movies. It's the story of a woman with a beautiful voice and physical pain, and a story too of something that happened when their daughter was nine and that she won't tell her son about. And it's a story about that son, too, I see, a son who can't blame her for holding close whatever story it is that happened when she was nine, because once she'd given him as much of her own story as she would and had turned to him, said, *Now you talk,* he'd only told her of his broken nose after a small engine fire onboard ship, and the narrow cans of beer he'd bought in Yokohama and Pusan, and of sewing his first caftans. He couldn't blame her for holding tight her own story, because he'd not told her the story of a night on the deck of the USS *Denver,* and what he'd seen there, that family so close to him he wouldn't dare let them go on mere spoken words, sounds out of him that were here and gone before you took another breath in.

Grandpa's is a feeble smile, a broken one, and there's a troubled look to his eyes that means he is facing his daughter, he is meeting her, he is being brought to himself and who she is because of her appearance here at their home, and now Grandma, smiling beside him, bobs her head one way and another as my mom approaches, makes her way the last few steps on the driveway to them both. Grandma can't get a bead on her very own daughter, her eyes behind the sunglasses squinted near to nothing for the wrinkles on her forehead and beside her eyes and for her mouth clenched tight.

So my grandma does what she can: She puts a hand out toward my mom, holds it out to her and moves her fingertips as though she might be just touching the softest of feathers, or the sharpest of blades. She holds her hand out, her fingers moving.

"Joan?" she says.

"I'm here," my mom says, and lets go one hand from that handbag, reaches out, reaches, and now their hands are together. This is when my grandpa lets go of that smile, lets his troubled eyes close, and I can see his shoulders give way while my mom moves right into my grandma's arms, and they hold each other, my grandpa beside them both with his chin to his chest, his shoulders moving and moving as he cries.

Suddenly it seems as I walk toward them all that, with my mother in her own mother's arms, and with her father's tears falling just like this, perhaps this will all find its happy ending.

But then Grandpa opens his eyes, looks at them both, and it is in this moment my mom suddenly stiffens, leans out of her mother's arms, and turns to her father. She lets go her mother, and with that hand, the same one with which she'd so tenderly touched her mother's searching fingertips only a few moments ago, she reaches back and slaps my grandpa as hard as she can.

Grandpa's head snaps to the side with the blow, Grandma flinches for the sound, and I shout "Hey!" loud and surprised, all of it in the same empty moment after this slap.

Before I can move she rears her hand up again to let go another blow, and I can see that the troubled look is still there in Grandpa's eyes, as though nothing has come down upon him at all save for the brute fact of the history between them; I can see in just this instant that he knows he's had this coming.

My mom raises that hand to her father again, lets it begin its course down toward him to deliver his due.

But my nearly blind grandma, who sees things in her very own way, reaches up her hand, and grabs my mom's arm at the wrist just before she lets it blast away one more time. Grandma's arm gives an inch or so with the force of Mom's swing, but she has hold of that wrist, and stops her.

"No," Grandma says, the word solid and quiet and alone out here.

My mom looks back at her, and I can see Grandma's face without squint or grimace, without clenched teeth or wrinkled brow. She's looking at her daughter, though I cannot tell at all what she sees. Maybe a child who'd tried for so long to push away those wrinkles, that pain. Maybe nothing at all. But the wrinkles on my grandma's face are gone now.

Grandma lets her free hand go to my mom's face, gently touches at it. "No," she says again, the word softer, quieter, and it seems in her touch that this time it's my grandma trying to push away the sorrow on her daughter's face for the history between them all.

"Let her go," Grandpa says, and I look at him, at the red mark growing already on his cheek. But he hasn't moved, still has his hands behind him. They stand there, all three of them.

But there are four of them, I remember. There's me, too.

"Stop it," I say, though I don't know what exactly it is I am calling for them to cease, other than being the lost and confused gang of blood kin they—we—truly are.

"Just stop," I say, and my mom turns, looks at me, and I can see in her eyes a kind of stunned surprise.

Grandma lets go her wrist, looks past my mom to me, and her eyes squint up just that quickly, a kind of spell broken by none other than me, and Grandpa looks too, his chin down a little.

I stand there, halfway between the trunk of a Caddy and the three concrete steps up onto the porch. I stand there on a driveway in Pacoima, the all of the life I have left to live in front of me. But what we will do next I do not know, until slowly, slowly, my mom brings down her arm from midair, and reaches to her purse, that square leather handbag she's held tight to since I'd first seen her this morning at her kitchen table.

She holds the bag with both hands again, seems to pull it even closer to her, even closer, and then she looks down at it, parts it open. She reaches in a hand, and slowly pulls out something brown and flat, what looks from here like an old file folder, but there's a circle cut out of the center of the folder.

It's a record sleeve, I can see, inside it a record.

Grandpa, his eyes to what his daughter holds in her hand, lets out a quiet "Oh, Saralee," and takes in a breath. He lets his hands go from behind him, then settle at his sides for only a moment before he brings them toward my mom—he can't help himself, I can tell—and to this record.

"Where did you—" Grandpa starts, then stops, takes in a breath, says, quieter, the single word "How—" but leaves that sentence unfinished as well, and I take a step toward them, and another.

"Saralee," Grandpa says again, this time almost a whisper, and my mom has the record all the way out of the handbag, and she leans to one side a bit, sets the bag on the ground beside her. "Oh, Saralee," Grandpa says, the words filled with a kind of awe, and he lets both hands just touch the edges of the sleeve, as though he knows he doesn't deserve this touch but needs it all the same.

And my mom, the one who has slapped him hard as she could only a moment before, and who would have slapped him again had her own mother not held her back, lets him touch at it, lets him move in closer to her and this record between them.

"Dammit, Earl, what?" Grandma says. "What is it?" And with her teeth clenched, her head bobbing, she touches my mom's arms, lets her hands follow them down to what my mom holds like a relic.

Grandma touches it, feels the old brown paper, lets her fingers trace over the cutout circle. I can see her fingers are moving in confusion, fluttering sharp and soft to take in as much as she can as quickly as she can.

But then she stops, both hands frozen, one to the thin edge of the sleeve, the other at the cutout.

"Oh," she says, and then "oh," the sounds out of her no different than the breath knocked from Grandpa by the appearance of Billie Dove.

"What is it?" I say, and now I am almost to them, and I set down the suitcase, and it is as though I am not even here for this record in old brown paper, some kind of treasure I don't know about but that has suddenly changed everything between them.

"Oh, Joan," Grandma finally gets out, then, "Oh, Joan, no. No."

But she doesn't move her fingers from where they have stopped, and Grandpa's hands are still touching the edges, and my mom still looks at it, looks at it, and now she lets go with one hand, slips her fingers inside the sleeve, and pulls from inside it photographs. Black-and-white eight-by-tens, three of them, and Grandpa groans for it, slowly lets his hands fall away, and he breathes in.

"Saralee," he says. "It's your record. And the photos."

"What are you talking about?" I say, and though I am with them I know I am not a part of them for this piece of their story. This has nothing to do with me. But in their reverence, their silence, their touch on

these things as though in a miracle they were heir-
looms left intact after the house has burned down, I
know it has something to do with me, too. Because
there are four of us, this family.

I reach then to the pictures, and though the move is
an intrusion for the silent agreement between them to
leave me out, I carefully, gently take them from my
mom's hand.

I look at her a moment, see her eyes are on me, and
I look at Grandpa, see him look from the photos to me,
and he nods his permission, puts his hands at his sides.
I glance at Grandma, still with her fingers to the
record, but facing me.

She nods, too.

The first one is at a club somewhere, just a room full
of people, some up near the stage dancing in front of
a big band, other people at tables laughing and
drinking. It's old, from the 1930s or so, and the second
one, I see, is just as old. This one is a posed picture of
the big band, the leader standing to one side—he's got
glasses on and is smiling—while across from him
stand three girls in a row, hands behind their backs and
smiling too.

One of them is Grandma. I know it. This is the same
woman as in the wedding picture in the hallway, the
two of them smiling, Earl in his white dinner jacket,
Grandma in the same gray dress as in this picture.

I stop, look up to see them all looking at me.

"This is you," I say to Grandma. "The one in the
middle."

She says nothing, only looks at me from behind those sunglasses of hers. She's not smiling, nor is Mom, or Grandpa. They are only watching me.

And I turn to the last one, a closer shot of the band onstage, to the left of them a woman singing with a hand out and pointing to the crowd below her, her face half-hidden by the big microphone into which she sings. Her eyes are closed, her forehead smooth and carefree and young.

"This is you too," I say, but quieter, and there is coming to me the same sense of wonder as perhaps has made them all go quiet. My grandma, a big band singer.

"This, too," my mom finally says, and she hands me the record itself in its sleeve, and I lay it on the photos in my hand, and now I am holding everything, all of it some kind of center of things.

It's thick, this record. It's a 78, and through the cutout I can see there's no label on it, only the black vinyl, and I can make out something scratched into the black of it, letters and numbers: *KKO* and *TOY*, beneath that *SK* and *2634*.

I look up from it, and see my mom looking at Grandma, Grandpa watching my mom, when my mom says to her one word: "Why?"

"I threw those away," Grandma says straight out, no hesitation. "I threw them away before you were ever born," she says. "How did you get these?" she says.

"I kept them," Grandpa answers, and they both look at him. He lets his eyes go to the ground, takes in a quick breath. "When you threw them away I got into the garbage and fished them out." He pauses, swallows, that red welt rising on his cheek, and he shakes his head the tiniest bit, the move almost a shiver. "You could sing. I wanted to keep them. Because you were the one with the talent. You were. I thought I hid them under the divan we had in the apartment on Alvarado. But then one day I couldn't find them and I—"

"Why?" my mom cuts in, this time louder, her teeth clenched. She's looking at my grandma again, and I can see her taking in quick breaths, letting them out, her cheeks their own red for what this question means to her.

"Why what?" my grandma says, and the wrinkles on her forehead are there out of confusion, and fear and sadness. They have nothing to do with what she can and cannot see. "Why did I throw them away?" Grandma goes on. "Why was I a singer? Why did I cut an audition demo with Kay Kyser and have publicity shots and then never show them to you?"

"Saralee," Grandpa says, and reaches to her arm, touches her.

"It wasn't my life," Grandma goes on, and shrugs off his touch, and Grandpa lets his hand down.

"It wasn't my life, is why. I didn't want it. I could sing, but I didn't want it. Your father wanted this kind of life, but I didn't. I'd seen enough of it to know I didn't—"

"Why wouldn't you sing *for me?*" my mom nearly shouts, though the words in her throat and mouth and on this air are crushed down to pure pain.

She breaks then, her chin crumbling into nothing, and tears are here, right here, and before either of them can do anything I move the photos and record into one hand like that file folder I'd first thought it was, and I put my other arm around her, and I take hold of her, pull her to me, and here are her tears through my shirt one more time.

And then I do what I know I can do, even if my mom's unanswered question still hangs in this air like the notes of her mother's singing to me whole songs on our way home from a trip to buy cigarettes. I do what I know I can do, because I am her son.

I turn my mom to stand beside me, my arm around her shoulder now as still she cries, and I move between Grandma and Grandpa, my mom tight beside me, and I take the first step up to the porch, whisper, "Come with me," and hold her just a little tighter a moment to coax her ahead.

She doesn't look up, only leans into my shoulder, her eyes closed tight, and she takes the step up, and the next, and now we are up on the porch, and I am pushing open the door, and now here we are in the living room, moving past the wood-grain television console big as a coffin, on it that gold-painted plaster cherub, a bowl of grapes on its shoulder, and we move past the pair of burgundy velvet recliners, above them swag lamps, turquoise shades with gold pull tassels, on the end table between them the blue and turquoise and violet feather flower arrangement.

We're home.

"Anyone wants to join us is free to come along," I say over my shoulder, the door standing open behind me, and I can hear movement, the two of them on their way up. But we are already out in the kitchen now, and now through the laundry room, my mom's tears stopped but her sniffing for it all the same, and I look down to her as we reach the back door out onto the backyard porch, and see her red eyes, her mouth still crumbled up. I let go my arm from around her, take hold her hand as I pull open the back door, and we move down three more steps and to the door into the garage, and I open it.

It's dark inside, of course, and it takes a moment for my hand to find the switch against the bare studs of the wall. But then here are the fluorescent lights crackling on in the rafters above us, and here is the row of three industrial sewing machines all set and ready, caftans hanging from rungs wired to those rafters a gauntlet of color along either wall, above them shelves stacked with bolts of fabric my grandpa makes into his wares.

In the corner to our left is the low old coffee table, on it the suitcase record player, the granite-looking one like I'd had in grade school. The one Grandpa plays low when we work in here, those old syrupy records, Percy Faith and Mantovani and the Ray Conniff Singers.

I let go my mom's hand, pull from the first sewing machine the folding chair in front of it, turn it toward the aisle that runs from the back of the garage to the front. "Sit down," I say, and smile at her, make a sweeping gesture like I am some maître d'.

She takes in a breath, tries to gather herself, to stop these tears. She looks at me, and I want to see somewhere deep inside her a smile, or the thought of one. But there's nothing doing, and now here is Grandpa's silhouette in the doorway, and as he moves in here is Grandma behind him, a hand to the doorjamb.

My eyes meet my grandpa's and he nods, and as I turn to make my way back to the record player, I hear the scrape of a folding chair out from the next machine, hear Grandpa say, "Saralee, right here."

I set the photos on the stack of albums on the coffee table, Doris Day in that turquoise outfit with the legs that won't quit right there on top. But now it's my grandma there, her with that finger pointing to the crowd, and those eyes closed inside the song she is singing.

I slip the record out of the sleeve, settle it on the player, turn the little dial on the base from 33 to 78, then lift the needle arm, watch the record start to spin.

But even though I am bent to the record player, the little tab on the arm tight between my thumb and first finger all ready to settle into place, I look back at them.

Grandma's not here.

My mom is turned in her seat to the open door, and looks at me, her mouth open and still taking in breaths, and then she looks to Grandpa, who stands at the chair he'd pulled out for Grandma from in front of that second machine.

"She was on her way in," he says, "and then she just left. I hope—"

But this is my gig now, this is all my doing, so I say, "I'll go get her," and set the needle arm back in its place, start away from the coffee table.

But here she is in the doorway again, with her the hurried words "I'm here, I'm here," and she touches the doorjamb again, steps in from her own silhouette.

Her sunglasses are gone, her squinting all the more for it, and now she's got something in her hand.

A reel of film.

"You have your secrets," she says to no one, to us all, "and I have mine," and she waves the reel in front of her like a flashlight in a dark room, says, "Earl, get that projector down from the top shelf."

Grandpa takes in a breath, says, "Is that my—that's not my—"

"Just shut the hell up, Earl. I stole it. Yes. Because I had to sit through this thing more times than I care to count, and so I took it, put it where you'd never find it and never will. But if you ever want to watch this thing again, you'll get that damned projector down right now."

Grandpa doesn't say a word, and like a brand-new man he's already to the shelf against the back wall of the garage, where sits that old 16-millimeter projector in its opaque plastic sleeve yellow with age, that remote icon I'd never dared asked him about for fear of the tear he'd go on about the lost reel my grandma has in her hands right now.

The long-lost Foremost milk commercial.

He gets the projector down, sets it on the floor, and moves just as quick to right beside me, still at the coffee table. He gives me a sharp smile, whispers, "I love her," and leans past me and over the coffee table, where a kind of small fold-up table—a projector stand, of course—and a screen in its long silver case stand between the coffee table and the wall. I'd never even noticed them before, never even seen this gear, and Grandpa pulls them out, the folded-up table in one hand, the screen in the other, lifts them over the coffee table and heads for the projector.

In his moves I can see he's done this a thousand times before, a million, setting up this all and, I have to believe, watching that film Grandma's holding.

My mom is up and out of her chair, holds Grandma's hand now, guides her to that seat Grandpa'd pulled out. Grandma touches the chair back, and sits down, holds the reel with both hands, and my mom turns from her, moves to the back of the garage. For a moment I think she'll be leaving, heading away for the insertion suddenly of my grandpa's life in film when all she'd wanted, it'd seemed to me, was to hear her mother's voice.

She's at the doorway, silhouetted now all on her own. But then she stops, turns around, and puts her hand to the light switch.

She takes in a quick breath, lets it out slow as she

can. There's still no smile on her, no hope of one, it seems to me, coming anytime soon.

But she nods at me, looks to Grandpa.

"I got the lights," she says, and takes in two quick breaths yet again, then adds, "When you're ready."

In the few moments it has taken to get Grandma to her chair, Grandpa's already gotten the stand opened up, the projector set in place on it, even has the projector plugged in, the cord snaking off to an extension cord beneath the second sewing machine. He's already down past the third machine, there in front of the closed garage door, the screen's tripod set up, the center support bar telescoped up and in place to hold the top of the screen; he's already pulling the screen from its case, unfurling it to hook at the top of that bar.

But he stops at my mom's words, their offer. He stops, holds the white screen only a foot or so out of its case on its way up to that hook.

He looks at her, swallows. It's as though he's been caught at something, him as still as he is after all this movement, all this purpose and commotion.

"Thank you," he says, his eyes right on hers. "I'll tell you when," he says, and looks at her a moment longer, then down at the screen, slowly pulls it up, sets the hook at the top.

My mom says nothing, nor does she nod. But she has her hand to the switch, ready.

"The only condition for watching this thing," my grandma says from her chair, and she lifts the reel out of her lap, waves it a few inches back and forth, "is

379

that you, Earl, have to keep your mouth shut. Just shut the hell up." She's holding the reel out to him, I can tell now, for the way she's moving her head, bobbing again, looking.

"Yes ma'am," Grandpa says, and here he is, right on cue, reaching for the reel. Then he has hold of it, a slow fish weaving in a stream, and Grandma's hand stops still.

She looks straight up at him, as though she hadn't expected him at all, and doesn't let go the reel. From here I can see her profile looking up at him, and I can't tell if it is a smile or a squint she has for him.

"Promise me, Mr. Gable," she says, "that you'll keep your trap shut. Because I'm going to sing for our daughter. Because she's right, and I didn't sing for her when I should have. You keep your trap shut, because I'm going to sing for her while this old record plays, and while your old face on the screen makes a fool of you yet again."

"I promise, Miss Davis," Grandpa says right back, and she lets go the reel, and I know it is a smile she'd had for him.

Grandpa looks at Mom once he has the reel in hand, smiles at her. "This will be a blessing," he says to her. "This will be a joy," he says, then catches himself, holds up the reel, shrugs, all of it too quickly: he's nervous for some reason, a boy about to make his screen debut.

"I don't mean the footage. Of me," he says. "I mean your momma's voice. A song from her. That will be the blessing. That's what I mean by—"

"Be quiet, Daddy," my mom says from the light switch. She shakes her head, and I catch her eye, see way down in her, see miles away, years away, a smile begin in her.

Grandpa says, "Yes, right," and turns to the projector, pops the reel on the top arm, then stoops a little to feed the film down into the machine. "On with the show," he says, and now he's smiling full-on, a real smile, and he is my impossibly handsome grandfather.

"Daddy," my mom says again, and he stops, looks over his shoulder at her, his fingers still to the spools inside the projector, this task at hand.

I look at Mom, see she has her head tilted to one side, and she lets her head drop, looks at the floor, all with her hand still to that switch. Then she looks up, seems to hold her chin a little higher.

She says, "Your momma told me to tell you she loved you." She pauses. "When I was a girl. She told me to tell you that."

He lets go the film between his fingers then, and turns to her, his back to the projector. He looks at her, looks at her, and I can tell this is news he wasn't banking on, an interruption of the imminent festivities this milk commercial will provide.

He doesn't know what to say.

He nods at her, once, and twice, and he blinks before he slowly turns to finishing with the projector, and once he is turned from her I see my mom's head drop again, her eyes to the floor.

Now Grandpa's fingers are thick, dumb: they stab at

the film, push it and pull it, and it seems it takes a day before he can get it to come out the bottom of the machine, and feed it onto the empty reel on the lower arm.

"Earl?" Grandma says.

"I'm fine," he says.

He looks up from finishing with the film, his eyebrows high, as though the fact he could even do this were itself a miracle, let alone word from his own mother this late in the game, and I know with that look we'll have no problems with him mouthing off.

Then he nods at me, looks to the record player, and finally, finally, I make my own debut: I bend to the record player, lift the needle arm, and set it down on the spinning record.

He turns, faces the screen.

"Hurrah," he says, the word apropos of nothing I know.

But my mom takes it for the cue it seems to be, and turns out the lights, then moves to the aisle, and I watch in the near-dark garage as she drags her chair from where I'd set it beside the first machine to right beside Grandma, and she sits.

In the moment before everything begins, there is a kind of quiet in here. It's a moment that lasts longer than I'd thought it would, a moment that expands for the hiss and crack of the needle in this darkness, and inside this new constellation I never thought I'd see, but one I'd hoped for all the same: Grandma, Grandpa, Mom, and me.

It is a silence filled with what we haven't said, a silence jam-packed with the fact that one day soon we will get to the end of this story. One day soon we will have to leave this room and begin to say a certain word we none of us wants to utter, and we will have to begin what we will do for Grandma.

What will happen to me? I'd wanted to know, way back when all of this started. But in the silence before this commencement I know what happens to me won't matter, because it will happen with these people around me, and because it will happen nonetheless.

And so I say the only words I can come up with to describe the silence around us, and in us, and through us, all in this moment, words as old as this music about to begin, and even older, older by far than the practice of people gathering in a darkened room to watch shadows and light play against a white screen while they listen to the music that accompanies it.

The needle whispers its approach to sound, the film projected on the screen stutters its last warnings: *5, 4, 3, 2—*

"Our story begins," I say, loud enough for only me to hear.

Center Point Publishing
600 Brooks Road ● PO Box 1
Thorndike ME 04986-0001 USA

(207) 568-3717

US & Canada:
1 800 929-9108
www.centerpointlargeprint.com